AGENTS OF TREACHERY

Spy Stories

AGENTS OF TREACHERY
Spy Stories

Edited by Otto Penzler

CORVUS

First published in the United States of America in 2010
by Vintage Crime/Black Lizard

This edition first published in Great Britain in 2010 by
Corvus, an imprint of Grove Atlantic Ltd.

9 8 7 6 5 4 3 2 1

A CIP catalogue record for this book is available from
the British Library.

ISBN: 978-1-84887-513-5 (hardback)
ISBN: 978-1-84887-514-2 (trade paperback)

Printed in Great Britain by the PG Books Group.

For Steve Ritterman
With fond memories of
the masked ball in Vladivostok
and that fearsome dark bar in Prague

Contents

INTRODUCTION

Otto Penzler

THE INTERNATIONAL THRILLER is one of the most successful literary genres in the world, its primary practitioners becoming household names, insofar as any author's level of fame can compete with an entertainer, sports figure, or world-class criminal. Ian Fleming, John le Carré, Graham Greene, Lee Child, Nelson DeMille, Frederick Forsyth, Robert Ludlum, Ken Follett, and Eric Ambler, among many others, are familiar to readers around the world. It will come as little surprise to learn that for many years, one of every four novels sold in the United States fell into the espionage or international adventure category.

What may come as a surprise, if not an outright shock, is that there never has been, until now, a collection of original stories devoted to this highly respected and challenging genre. There have been a modest number of collections by individual authors largely devoted to what used to be called cloak-and-dagger stories. Fleming's *For Your Eyes Only* contained five James Bond adventures; Peter O'Donnell's *Cobra Trap* collected Modesty Blaise stories; E. Phillips Oppenheim, the hugely popular thriller writer who wrote prolifically between the two world wars (as well as before) produced numerous collections. There are a few other volumes, mostly obscure, and quite a few mixed collections by such writers as Greene, Ambler, John

Buchan, H. C. McNeile, and Forsyth, in which a small number of spy stories are surrounded by other types of fiction.

The number of important authors in this very large genre who have never written even a single short story is legion. Ludlum never wrote one, nor did Dan Brown, Tom Clancy, Follett, Alan Furst, Robert Littell, Daniel Silva, W. E. B. Griffin, Thomas Gifford, or Trevanian.

The few anthologies devoted to spy and thriller stories are all reprint collections, jostling for the right to reprint le Carré's lone spy story and several familiar tales along with some obscure (though often very good) narratives. Alan Furst's excellent anthology, *The Book of Spies*, is devoted to excerpts from novels.

One could reasonably wonder why this scarcity of short fiction by otherwise often prolific authors persists, and the explanation is simple. Short stories set in the complex world of international espionage and adventure are very, very difficult to write. A disproportionate number of novels in that category, you will have noticed, are big, fat books. Although they are seldom leisurely, they are nonetheless longer than most novels. Establishing characters and places, creating plots within plots within plots, arranging treachery and duplicity in a credible fashion within the political alliances and betrayals of the time, all take subtlety and explanation—and a lot of pages. To attempt to contain all these disparate but necessary elements in a story of twenty or thirty pages is a challenge few can manage. What often captivates the reader of this compelling fiction is not the outcome of whatever the struggle has been. We know World War II will break out. We know de Gaulle will not be assassinated. We know Hitler will not be killed by German officers. What is terrifically engaging is watching the principal characters struggle with the moral compromises they are forced to make through fear or accommodation.

Every story you are about to read, to a greater or lesser degree, deals with these issues. Some adopt a fundamental theology of right and wrong, home country versus enemy state, while others assume the philosophical position of much contemporary espionage fiction, filled with ambiguity and relativism. One country's traitor is another's hero, a duplicitous lying swine to one organization is viewed as a stalwart figure of brilliance and courage by another. There is a broad spectrum of political and philosophical ideology represented on these pages, but it is rarely overt or obvious. The single quality that the contributors to this unique collection share is an ability to tell a complex story in a simple manner. I once asked Eric Ambler what he regarded as the most difficult element of writing the kind of novels he wrote, and he said, "to make it simple." Mr. Ambler, I believe, would have approved of the stories collected here by these distinguished authors, a veritable who's who of today's most highly regarded thriller writers, as well as the most widely read.

In a relatively brief time, Lee Child has established himself as one of the best-selling thriller writers in the world. His novels about Jack Reacher, the powerful giant of a man who fearlessly behaves heroically, consistently achieve the number-one spot on the best-seller list of *The New York Times* and are equally successful in Great Britain.

Dan Fesperman has had a distinguished career as a journalist, covering events in thirty countries, beginning with the first Gulf War in 1991. The (British) Crime Writers' Association named *Lie in the Dark* the best first novel of 1999 and *The Small Boat of Great Sorrows* the best thriller of 2003; *USA Today* named *The Prisoner of Guantánamo* the best thriller of 2006.

The first career choice of Joseph Finder was to be a spy and he was even recruited by the CIA but quickly deduced that life in the bureaucratic world was less exciting than it was portrayed in fiction. His first novel, *The Moscow Club*, was named one of the ten greatest espionage novels of all time by *Publishers Weekly*. "Neighbors" is his first short story.

One of the half dozen most famous espionage novels of all time is James Grady's *Six Days of the Condor*, successfully filmed with Robert Redford as *Three Days of the Condor*. Working as an investigative reporter for syndicated columnist Jack Anderson and for Senator Lee Metcalf helped provide the background information that makes his fiction so realistic.

As one of America's most distinguished film critics, Stephen Hunter won a Pulitzer Prize in 2003, but he is even better known for his best-selling, intricately plotted thrillers, especially those about macho Vietnam veteran sniper Bob Lee Swagger, known as "The Nailer." The first Swagger novel, *Point of Impact*, was filmed in 2007 as *Shooter*, starring Mark Wahlberg.

The controversial Andrew Klavan writes blogs and op-ed pieces at a prodigious rate, but it is crime fiction, notably such novels as *Don't Say a Word*, which was later filmed starring Michael Douglas, and *True Crime*, directed by and starring Clint Eastwood, that has put him atop the best-seller lists around the world. His first politically incorrect thriller was *Empire of Lies*.

Although John Lawton's Chief Inspector Troy works for Scotland Yard, he mainly finds himself caught up in international intrigue. His first case, *Black Out*, won the WHSmith Fresh Talent Award. *A Little White Death* was a 2007 *New York Times* Notable Book. London's *Daily Telegraph*'s "50 Crime Writers to Read Before You Die" included Lawton, one of only six living English writers on the list.

A member of the U.S. Association for Intelligence Officers, Gayle Lynds is a cofounder (with David Morrell) of the International Thriller Writers. Among her best sellers are *Masquerade*, named one of the ten best spy novels of all time by *Publishers Weekly*; *Mosaic*, picked as the thriller of the year by *Romantic Times*; and three volumes in the Covert-One series coauthored with Robert Ludlum.

After serving in deep cover with the CIA for a decade, Charles McCarry was a speechwriter for the Eisenhower administration before becoming an editor-at-large for *National Geographic*. He has often been described as the greatest American writer of espionage fiction, producing such poetic masterpieces as *The Tears of Autumn*, *The Secret Lovers*, and *The Last Supper*, all featuring his hero, Paul Christopher.

Although he has published more than thirty books, had David Morrell stopped writing after his first novel, his legacy would have been assured. *First Blood* introduced Rambo, who in books and Sylvester Stallone films has become one of the iconic American adventure heroes. Morrell also wrote *The Brotherhood of the Rose*, upon which NBC based what became the most-watched miniseries in history.

After more than three decades in all three branches of the British Secret Service (MI5)—counterespionage, countersubversion, and counterterrorism—Stella Rimington was named the first female Director-General of the agency, serving from 1992 to 1996; she was made a Dame Commander of Order of the Bath (DCB) the year she retired. Upon stepping down, she wrote a candid memoir, *Open Secret*, followed by five espionage novels.

Olen Steinhauer's first novel, *The Bridge of Sighs*, began a five-book thriller series chronicling Eastern Europe during the Cold War, a decade at a time until the fall of communism. It was nominated for five mystery awards, including an Edgar, as was his fourth book, *Liberation Movements*. The film rights to *The Tourist*, his first nonseries novel, were acquired by George Clooney, who plans to star in the motion picture.

One of the rare authors who has been on the *New York Times* best-seller list for fiction and nonfiction, John Weisman cowrote *Rogue Warrior*, the real-life story of the navy's elite counterterrorism unit of the SEALS and its commander, which was on the list for eight months, four weeks in the top spot. Five fictional sequels made the list. His books have twice been the subject of Mike Wallace episodes of *60 Minutes*.

Portugal's neutrality in World War II is the background for

Robert Wilson's *A Small Death in Lisbon*, which won the (British) Crime Writers' Association Gold Dagger as the best novel of 1999, and his spy thriller *The Company of Strangers*. He was nominated for another Gold Dagger for the first of four Javier Falcón novels set in Spain, *The Blind Man of Seville*.

The assignment given to the contributors to this unique collection was deceptively straightforward and simple: Write an international espionage or thriller story and set it anyplace in the world you like, in any era. No subject was forbidden, no word length specified, no political position denied, no philosophy advanced or hindered. The wide range of styles and focus contained herein will attest to the fact that the men and women who labored over these stories and produced such masterly tales accepted the invitation in the proper spirit.

AGENTS OF TREACHERY

THE END OF THE STRING

Charles McCarry

I FIRST NOTICED the man I will call Benjamin in the bar of the Independence Hotel in Ndala. He sat alone, drinking orange soda, no ice. He was tall and burly—knotty biceps, huge hands. His short-sleeved white shirt and khaki pants were as crisp as a uniform. Instead of the usual third-world Omega or Rolex, he wore a cheap plastic Japanese watch on his right wrist. No rings, no gold, no sunglasses. I did not recognize the tribal tattoos on his cheeks. He spoke to no one, looked at no one. He himself might as well have been invisible as far as the rest of the customers were concerned. No one spoke to him or offered to buy him a drink or asked him any questions. He seemed poised to leap off his bar stool and kill something at a moment's notice.

He was the only person in the bar I did not already know by sight. In those days, more than half a century ago, when an American was a rare bird along the Guinea coast, you got to know everyone in your hotel bar pretty quickly. I was standing at the bar, my back to Benjamin, but I could see him in the mirror. He was watching me. I surmised that he was gathering information rather than sizing me up for robbery or some other dark purpose.

I called the barman, put a ten-shilling note on the bar, and asked him to mix a pink gin using actual Beefeater's. He laughed merrily as he pocketed the money and swirled the bitters in the glass. When I looked in the mirror again, Benjamin was gone. How a man his size could get up and leave without being reflected in the mirror I do not know, but somehow he managed it. I did not dismiss him from my thoughts, he was too memorable for that, but I didn't dwell on the episode either. I could not, however, shake the feeling that I had been subjected to a professional appraisal. For an operative under deep cover, that is always an uncomfortable experience, especially if you have the feeling, as I did, that the man who is giving you the once-over is a professional who is doing a job that he has done many times before.

I had come to Ndala to debrief an agent. He missed the first two meetings, but there is nothing unusual about that even if you're not in Africa. On the third try, he showed up close to the appointed hour at the appointed place: two a.m. on an unpaved street in which hundreds of people, all of them sound asleep, lay side by side. It was a moonless night. No electric light, no lantern or candle, even, burned for at least a mile in any direction. I could not see the sleepers, but I could feel their presence and hear them exhale and inhale. The agent, a member of parliament, had nothing to tell me apart from his usual bagful of pointless gossip. I gave him his money anyway, and he signed for it with a thumbprint by the light of my pocket torch. As I walked away I heard him ripping open his envelope and counting banknotes in the dark.

I had not walked far when a car turned into the street with headlights blazing. The sleepers awoke and popped up one after another as if choreographed by Busby Berkeley. The member of parliament had vanished. No doubt he had simply lain down with the others, and two of the wide-open eyes and one of the broad smiles I saw dwindling into the darkness belonged to him.

The car stopped. I kept walking toward it, and when I was

beside it, the driver, who was a police constable, leaped out and shone a flashlight in my face. He said, "Please get in, master." The British had been gone from this country for only a short time, and the locals still addressed white men by the title preferred by their former colonial rulers. The old etiquette survived in English, French, and Portuguese in most of the thirty-two African countries that had become independent in a period of two and a half years—less time than it took Stanley to find Livingstone.

I said, "Get in? What for?"

"This is not a good place for you, master."

My rescuer was impeccably turned out in British tropical kit—blue service cap, bush jacket with sergeant's chevrons on the shoulder boards, voluminous khaki shorts, blue woolen knee socks, gleaming oxfords, black Sam Browne belt. A truncheon dangling from the belt seemed to be his only weapon. I climbed into the backseat. The sergeant got behind the wheel, and using the rearview mirror rather than looking behind him, backed out of the street at breathtaking speed. I kept my eyes on the windshield, expecting him to plow into the sleepers at any moment. They themselves seemed unconcerned, and as the headlights swept over them they lay down one after the other with the same precise timing as before.

The sergeant drove at high speed through backstreets, nearly every one of them another open-air dormitory. Our destination, as it turned out, was the Equator Club, Ndala's most popular nightclub. This structure was really just a fenced-in space, open to the sky. Inside, a band played highlife, a kind of hypercalypso, so loudly that you had the illusion that the music was visible as it rose into the pitch-black night.

The music was even louder. The air was the temperature of blood. The odors of sweat and spilled beer were sharp and strong. Guttering candles created a substitute for light. Silhouettes danced on the hard dirt floor, cigarettes glowed. The sensation was something like being digested by a tyrannosaurus rex.

Benjamin, alone again, sat at another small table. He was drinking orange soda again. He, too, wore a uniform. Though made of finer cloth, it was a duplicate of the sergeant's, except that he was equipped with a swagger stick instead of a baton and the badge on his shoulder boards displayed the wreath, crossed batons, and crown of a chief constable. Benjamin, it appeared, was the head of the national police. He made a gesture of welcome. I sat down. A waiter placed a pink gin with ice before me with such efficiency, and was so neatly dressed, that I supposed he was a constable, too, but undercover. I lifted my glass to Benjamin and sipped my drink.

Benjamin said, "Are you a naval person?"

I said, "No. Why do you ask?"

"Pink gin is the traditional drink of the royal navy."

"Not rum?"

"Rum is for the crew."

I had difficulty suppressing a grin. Our exchange of words sounded so much like a recognition code used by spies that I wondered if that's what it really was. Had Benjamin got the wrong American? He did not seem the type to make such an elementary mistake. He looked down on me—even while seated he was at least a head taller than I was—and said, "Welcome to my country, Mr. Brown. I have been waiting for you to come here again, because I believe that you and I can work together."

Brown was one of the names I had used on previous visits to Ndala, but it was not the name on the passport I was using this time. He paused, studying my face. His own face showed no flicker of expression.

Without further preamble, he said, "I am contemplating a project that requires the support of the United States of America."

The dramaturgy of the situation suggested that my next line should be, "Really?" or "How so?" However, I said nothing, hoping that Benjamin would fill the silence.

Frankly, I was puzzled. Was he volunteering for something? Most agents recruited by any intelligence service are volunteers, and the average intelligence officer is a sort of latter-day Marcel Proust. He lies abed in a cork-lined room, hoping to profit by secrets that other people slip under the door. People simply walk in and for whatever motive, usually petty resentment over having been passed over for promotion or the like, offer to betray their country. It was also possible, unusual though that might be, that Benjamin hoped to recruit me.

His eyes bored into mine. His back was to the wall, mine to the dance floor. Behind me I could feel but not see the dancers, moving as a single organism. Through the soles of my shoes I felt vibration set up by scores of feet stamping in unison on the dirt floor. In the yellow candlelight I could see a little more expression on Benjamin's face.

Many seconds passed before he broke the silence. "What is your opinion of the president of this country?"

Once again I took my time answering. The problem with this conversation was that I never knew what to say next.

Finally I said, "President Ga and I have never met."

"Nevertheless you must have an opinion."

And of course I did. So did everyone who read the newspapers. Akokwu Ga, president for life of Ndala, was a man of strong appetites. He enjoyed his position and its many opportunities for pleasure with an enthusiasm that was remarkable even by the usual standards for dictators. He possessed a solid gold bathtub and bedstead. He had a private zoo. It was said that he was sometimes seized by the impulse to feed his enemies to the lions. He had deposited tens of millions of dollars from his country's treasury into personal numbered accounts in Swiss banks.

Dinner for him and his guests was flown in every day from one of the restaurants in Paris that had a three-star rating in the Guide Michelin. A French chef heated the food and arranged it on plates, an English butler served it. Both were assumed to be secret agents employed by their respective governments. Ga maintained love nests in every quarter of the capital city. Women from all over the world occupied these cribs. The ones he liked best were given luxurious houses formerly occupied by Europeans and provided with German cars, French champagne, and "houseboys" (actually undercover policemen) who kept an eye on them.

"Speak," Benjamin said.

I said, "Frankly, chief constable, this conversation is making me nervous."

"Why? No one can bug us. Listen to the noise."

How right he was. We were shouting at each other in order to be heard above the din. The music made my ears ring, and no microphone then known could penetrate it. I said, "Nevertheless, I would prefer to discuss this in private. Just the two of us."

"And how then will you know that I am not bugging you? Or that someone else is not bugging both of us?"

"I wouldn't. But would it matter?"

Benjamin examined me for a long moment. Then he said, "No, it wouldn't. Because I am the one who will be saying dangerous things."

He got to his feet, uncoiled would be the better word. Instantly the sergeant who had brought me here and three other constables in plain clothes materialized from the shadows. Everyone else was dancing, eyes closed, seemingly in another world and time. Benjamin put on his cap and picked up his swagger stick.

He said, "Tomorrow I will come for you."

With that, he disappeared, leaving me without a ride. Eventually I found a taxi back to the hotel. The driver was so wide awake, his taxi so tidy, that I assumed that he, too, must be one of Benjamin's men.

The porter who brought me my mug of tea at six a.m. also

brought me a note from Benjamin. The penmanship was beautiful. The note was short and to the point: "Nine o'clock, by the front entrance."

Through the glass in the hotel's front door, the street outside was a scene from Goya, lepers and amputees and victims of polio or smallpox or psoriasis, and among the child beggars a few examples of hamstringing by parents who needed the income that a crippled child could bring home. A tourist arrived in a taxi and scattered a handful of change in order to disperse the beggars while he made his dash for the entrance. Clearly he was a greenhorn. The seasoned traveler in Africa distributed money only after checkout. To do so on arrival guaranteed your being fondled by lepers every time you came in or went out. One particularly handsome, smiling young fellow who had lost his fingers and toes to leprosy caught coins in his mouth.

At the appointed time exactly *Was I still in Africa?* Benjamin's sergeant pulled up in his gleaming black Austin. He barked a command in one of the local languages, and once again the crowd parted. He took me by the hand in the friendly African way and led me to the car.

We headed north, out of town, horn sounding tinnily at every turn of the wheels. Otherwise, the sergeant explained, pedestrians would assume that the driver was trying to kill them. In daylight when everyone was awake and walking around instead of sleeping by the wayside, Ndala sounded like the overture of *An American in Paris*. After a hair-raising drive past the brand-new government buildings and banks of downtown, through raucous streets lined with shops and filled with the smoke of street vendors' grills, through labyrinthine neighborhoods of low shacks made from scraps of lumber and tin and cardboard, we arrived at last in Africa itself, a sun-scorched plain of rusty soil, dotted with stunted bush, stretching from horizon to horizon. After a mile or so of emptiness, we came upon a policeman seated on a parked motorcycle. The sergeant stopped the car, leaped out, and leaving the motor running and the front door open, opened the back door to let me out. He gave me a map, drew himself up to attention, and after stamping his right foot into the dust, gave me a quivering British hand salute. He then jumped onto the motorcycle behind its rider, who revved the engine, made a slithering U-turn, and headed back toward the city trailed by a corkscrew of red dust.

I got into the Austin and started driving. The road soon became a dirt trail whose billowing ocher dust stuck to the car like snow and made it necessary to run the windshield wipers. It was impossible to drive with the windows open. The temperature inside the closed vehicle (air-conditioning was a thing of the future) could not have been less than one hundred degrees Fahrenheit. Slippery with sweat, I followed the map, and after making a right turn into what seemed to be an impenetrable thicket of rubbery bushes, straddled a footpath which in time opened onto a clearing containing a small village. Another car, a dusty black Rover, was parked in front of one of the conical mud huts. This place was deserted. Grass had grown on the footpaths. There was no sign of life.

I parked beside the other car and ducked into the mud hut. Benjamin, alone as usual, sat inside. He wore national dress— the white togalike gown invented by nineteenth-century missionaries to clothe the natives for the benefit of English knitting mills. His feet were bare. He seemed to be deep in thought and did not greet me with word or sign. A .455-caliber Webley revolver lay beside him on the floor of beaten earth. The light was dim, and because I had come into the shadowy interior out of intense sunlight, it was some time before I was able to see his face well enough to be absolutely certain that the mute tribesman before me actually was the chief constable with whom I had passed a pleasant hour the night before in the Equator Club. As for the revolver, I can't explain why I trusted this glowering giant not to shoot me just yet, but I did.

Benjamin said, "Is this meeting place sufficiently private?"

"It's fine," I replied. "But where have all the people gone?"

"To Ndala, a long time ago."

All over Africa were abandoned villages like this one whose inhabitants had packed up and left for the city in search of money and excitement and the new life of opportunity that independence promised. Nearly all of them now slept in the streets.

"As I said last night," Benjamin said, "I am thinking about doing something that is necessary to the future of this country, and I would like to have the encouragement of the United States government."

"It must be something impressive if you need the encouragement of Washington."

"It is. I plan to remove the present government of this country and replace it with a freely elected new government."

"That *is* impressive. What exactly do you mean by 'encouragement'?"

"A willingness to stand aside, to make no silliness, and afterwards to be helpful."

"Afterwards? Not before?"

"Before is a local problem."

The odds were at least even that afterward might be a large problem for Benjamin. President Ga's instinct for survival was highly developed. Others, including his own brother, had tried to overthrow him. They were all dead now.

I said, "I recommend first of all that you forget this idea of yours. If you can't do that, then you should speak to somebody in the American embassy. I'm sure you already know the right person."

"I prefer to speak to you."

"Why? I'm not a member of the Ministry of Encouragement."

"But that is exactly what you are, Mr. Brown. You are famous for it. You can be trusted. This man in the American embassy you call 'the right person' is in fact a fool. He is an admirer of President for Life Ga. He plays ball with President Ga. He cannot be trusted."

I started to answer this nonsense. Benjamin showed me the palm of his hand. "Please, no protestations of innocence. I have all the evidence I would ever need about your good works in my country, should I ever need it."

That made me blink. No doubt he did have an interesting file on me. I had done a good deal of mischief in his country, even before the British departed, and for all I knew his courtship was a charade. He might very well be trying to entrap me.

I said, "I'm flattered. But I don't think I'd make a good assistant in this particular matter."

Something like a frown crossed Benjamin's brow. I had annoyed him. Since we were in the middle of nowhere and he was the one with the revolver, this was not a good sign.

"I have no need of an assistant," Benjamin said. "What I need is a witness. A trained observer whose word is trusted in high places in the U.S. Someone who can tell the right people in Washington what I have done, how I have done it, and most of all, that I have done it for the good of my country."

I could think of nothing to say that would not make this conversation even more unpleasant than it already was.

Benjamin said, "I can see that you do not trust me."

He picked up the revolver and cocked it. The Webley is something of an antique, having been designed around the time of the Boer War as the standard British officer's sidearm. It is large and ugly but also effective, powerful enough to kill an elephant. For a long moment Benjamin looked deeply into my eyes and then, holding the gun by the barrel, handed it to me.

"If you believe I am being false to you in any way," he said, "you can shoot me."

It was a wonder that he had not shot himself, handling a cocked revolver in such a carefree way. I took the weapon from his hand, lowered the hammer, swung open the cylinder, and shook out the cartridges. They were not blanks. I reloaded and handed the weapon back to Benjamin. He wiped it clean of fingerprints, my fingerprints, with the skirt of his robe and put it back on the floor.

In the jargon of espionage, the recruitment of an agent is called a seduction. As in a real seduction, assuming that things are going well, a moment comes when resistance turns into encouragement. We had arrived at the moment for a word of encouragement.

I said, "What exactly is the plan?"

"When you strike at a prince," Benjamin said, "you must strike to kill."

Absolutely true. It did not surprise me that he had read Machiavelli. At this point it would not have surprised me if he burst into fluent Sanskrit. Despite the rigmarole with the Webley, I still did not trust him and probably never would, but I was doing the work that I was paid to do, so I decided to press on with the thing.

"That's an excellent principle," I said, "but it's a principle, not a plan."

"All the right things will be done," Benjamin said. "The radio station and newspapers will be seized, the army will cooperate, the airport will be closed, curfews will be imposed."

"Don't forget to surround the presidential palace."

"That will not be necessary."

"Why?"

"Because the president will not be in the palace," Benjamin said.

All of a sudden, Benjamin was becoming cryptic. Frankly, I was just as glad, because what he was proposing in words of one syllable scared the bejesus out of me. So did the expression on his face. He was as calm as a Buddha.

He rose to his feet. In his British uniform he had looked

impressive, if slightly uncomfortable. In his gown he looked positively majestic, a black Caesar in a white toga.

"You know enough now to think this over," he said. "Do so, if you please. We will talk some more before you fly away."

He ducked through the door and drove away. I waited for a few minutes, then went outside myself. A large black mamba lay in the sun in front of my car. My blood froze. The mamba was twelve or thirteen feet long. This species is the fastest-moving snake known to zoology, capable of slithering at fifteen miles an hour, faster than most men can run. Its strike is much quicker than that. Its venom will usually kill an adult human being in about fifteen minutes. Hoping that this one was not fully awake, I got into the car and started the engine. The snake moved but did not go away. I could easily have run over it, but instead I backed up and steered around it. Locally this serpent was regarded as a sign of bad luck to come. I wasn't looking for any more misfortune than I already had on my plate.

After dinner that evening I spent an extra hour in the hotel bar. I felt the alcohol after I went upstairs and got into bed, and fell almost immediately into a deep sleep. Cognac makes for bad dreams and I was in the middle of one when I was awakened by the click of the latch. For an instant I thought the porter must be bringing my morning tea and wondered where the night had gone. But when I opened my eyes it was still dark outside. The door opened and closed. No light came in, meaning that the intruder had switched off the dim bulbs in the corridor. He was now inside the room. I could not see him but I could smell him: soap, spicy food, shoe polish. *Shoe polish?* I slid out of bed, taking the pillows and the covers with me and rolling them into a ball, as if this would help me defend myself against the intruder who I believed was about to attack me in the dark with a machete.

In the dark, the intruder drew the shade over the window. An instant later the lights came on. Benjamin said, "Sorry to disturb you."

He wore his impeccable uniform, swagger stick tucked under his left arm, cap square on his head, badges and shoes and Sam Browne belt gleaming. The clock read 4:23. It was an old-fashioned windup alarm clock with two bells on top. It ticked loudly while I waited until I was sure I could trust my voice to reply. I was stark naked. I felt a little foolish to be holding a bundle of bedclothes in my arms, but at least this preserved my modesty.

Finally I said, "I thought we'd already had our conversation for the day."

Benjamin ignored the Bogart impersonation. "There is something I want you to see," he said. "Get dressed as quick as you can, please." Benjamin never forgot a please or a thank you. Like his penmanship, Victorian good manners seemed to have been rubbed into his soul in missionary school.

As soon as I had tied my shoes, he led the way down the back stairs. He moved at a swift trot. Outside the back door, a black Rover sedan waited with the engine running. The sergeant stood at attention beside it. He opened the back door as Benjamin and I approached and, after a brief moment as Alphonse and Gaston, we got into the backseat.

When the car was in motion, Benjamin turned to me and said, "You seem to want to give President Ga the benefit of the doubt. This morning you will see some things for yourself, and then you can decide whether that is the Christian thing to do."

It was still dark. As a usual thing there is no lingering painted sunrise in equatorial regions; the sun, huge and white, just materializes on the rim of the earth, and daylight begins. In the darkness, the miserable of Ndala were still asleep in rows on either side of every street, but little groups of people on the move were caught in our headlights.

"Beggars," Benjamin said. "They are on their way to work." The beggars limped and crawled according to their afflictions. Those who could not walk at all were carried by others.

"They help each other," Benjamin said. He said something to the sergeant in a tribal language. The sergeant put a spotlight on a big man carrying a leper who had lost his feet. The leper looked over his friend's shoulder and smiled. The big man walked onward as if unaware of the spotlight. Benjamin said, "See? A blind man will carry a crippled man, and the crippled man will tell him where to go. Take a good look, Mr. Brown. It is a sight you will never see in Ndala again."

"Why not?"

"You will see."

At the end of the street an army truck was parked. A squad of soldiers armed with bayoneted rifles held at port arms formed a line across the street. Benjamin gave an order. The sergeant stopped the car and shone his spotlight on them. They had not stirred or opened their eyes as when the sergeant drove down this same street the night before. Whatever was happening, these people did not want to be witnesses. The soldiers paid no more attention to Benjamin's car than the people lying on the ground paid to the soldiers.

When the beggars arrived, the soldiers surrounded them and herded them into the truck. The blind man protested, a single syllable. Before he could say more, a soldier hit him in the small of the back with a rifle butt. The blind man dropped the crippled leper and fell down unconscious. The soldiers would not touch them, so the other beggars picked them up and loaded them into the truck, then climbed in themselves. The soldiers lowered the back curtain and got into a smaller truck of their own. All this happened in eerie silence, not an order given or a protest voiced, in a country in which the smallest human encounter sent tsunamis of shouting and laughter through crowds of hundreds.

We drove on. We witnessed the same scene over and over again. All over the city, beggars were being rounded up by troops. Our last stop was the Independence Hotel, my hotel, where I saw the beggars I knew best, including the handsome, smiling leper who caught coins in his mouth, being herded into the back of a truck. As the truck drove away, gears changing, the sun appeared on the eastern horizon, huge and entire, a miracle of timing.

Benjamin said, "You look a little sick, my friend. Let me tell you something. Those people are never coming back to Ndala. They give our country a bad image, and two weeks from now hundreds of foreigners will arrive for the Pan-African Conference. Thanks to President Ga, they will not have to look at these disgusting creatures, so maybe they will elect him president of the conference. Think about that. We will talk when you come back."

In Washington, two days later at six in the morning, I found my chief at his desk, drinking coffee from a chipped mug and reading the *Wall Street Journal*. I told him my tale. He knew at once exactly who Benjamin was. He asked how much money Benjamin wanted, what his timetable was, who his coconspirators were, whether he himself planned to replace the abominable Ga as dictator after he overthrew him, what his policy toward the United States would be—and, by the way, what were his hidden intentions? I was unable to answer most of these questions.

I said, "All he's asked for so far is encouragement."

"Encouragement?" said my chief. "That's a new one. He didn't suggest one night of love with the first lady in the Lincoln bedroom?"

A certain third world general had once made just such a demand in return for his services as a spy in a country whose annual national product was smaller than that of Cuyahoga County, Ohio. I told him that Benjamin had not struck me as being the type to long for Mrs. Eisenhower.

My chief said, "You take him seriously?"

"He's an impressive person."

"Then go back and talk to him some more."

"When?"

"Tomorrow."

"What about the encouragement?"

"It's cheap. Ga is a bad 'un. Shovel it on."

I was cheap, too—a singleton out at the end of the string. If I got into trouble, I'd get no help from the chief or anyone else in Washington. The old gentleman himself would cut the string. He owed me nothing. "Brown? *Brown?*" he would say in the unlikely event that he would be asked what had become of me. "The only Brown I know is Charlie."

The prospect of returning to Ndala on the next flight was not a very inviting one. I had just spent eight weeks traveling around Africa, in and out of countries, languages, time zones, identities. My intestines swarmed with parasites that were desperate to escape. There was something wrong with my liver: the whites of my eyes were yellow. I had had a malaria attack on the plane from London that frightened the woman seated next to me. The four aspirins I took, spilling only twenty or so while getting them out of the bottle with shaking hands, brought the fever and the sweating under control. Twelve hours later I still had a temperature of 102; I shuddered still, though only fitfully.

To the chief I said, "Right."

"This time get *all* the details," my chief said. "But no cables. Your skull only, and fly the information back to me personally. Tell the locals nothing."

"Which locals? Here or there?"

"Anywhere."

His tone was nonchalant, but I had known this man for a long time. He was interested; he saw an opportunity. He was a white-haired, tweedy, pipe-smoking old fellow with a tooth-brush mustache and twinkling blue eyes. His specialty was doing the things that American presidents wanted done without actually requiring them to give the order. He smiled with big crooked teeth; he was rich but too old for orthodontia. "Until I give the word, nobody knows anything but us two chickens. Does that suit you?"

I nodded as if my assent really was necessary. After a breath or two, I said, "How much encouragement can I offer this fellow?"

"Use your judgment. Take some money, too. You may have to tide him over till he gets hold of the national treasure. Just don't make any promises. Hear him out. Figure him out. Estimate his chances. We don't want a failure. Or an embarrassment."

I rose to leave.

"Hold on," said the chief.

He rummaged around in a desk drawer and after examining several identical objects and discarding them, handed me a large bulging brown envelope. A receipt was attached to it with Scotch tape. It said that the envelope contained one hundred thousand dollars in hundred-dollar bills. I signed it with the fictitious name my employer had assigned to me when I joined up. As I opened the door to leave, I saw that the old gentleman had gone back to his *Wall Street Journal*.

Benjamin and I had arranged no secure way of communicating with each other, so I had not notified him that I was coming back to Ndala. Nevertheless, the sergeant met me on the tarmac at the airport. I was not surprised that Benjamin knew I was coming. Like all good cops, he kept an eye on passenger manifests for flights in and out of his jurisdiction. After sending a baggage handler into the hold of the plane to find my bag, the sergeant drove me to a safe house in the European quarter of the city. It was five o'clock in the morning when we got there. Benjamin awaited me. The sergeant cooked and served a complete English breakfast—eggs, bacon, sausage, fried potatoes, grilled tomato, cold toast, Dundee orange marmalade, and sour gritty coffee. Benjamin ate with gusto but made no small talk. Air conditioners hummed in every window.

"Better that you stay in this house than the hotel," Benjamin said when he had cleaned his plate. "In that way there will never be a record that you have been in this country."

That was certainly true, and it was not the least of my worries. I was traveling on a Canadian passport as Robert Bruce Brown, who had died of meningitis in Baddeck, Nova Scotia, thirty-five years before at age two. Thanks to the sergeant, I had bypassed customs and passport control. That meant that there was no entry stamp in the passport. In theory I could not leave the country without one, but then again, I was carrying one hundred thousand American dollars in cash in an airline bag, and this was a country in which money talked. If I did disappear, I would disappear without a trace. One way or another, so would the money.

"There is something I want you to see," Benjamin said. Apparently this was his standard phrase when he had something unpleasant to show me. After wiping his lips on a white linen napkin, folding it neatly, and dropping it onto the table, he led me into the living room. The drapes were drawn. The sun was up. A sliver of white-hot sunlight shone through. Benjamin called to the sergeant, who brought his briefcase and pulled the curtains tighter. Before leaving us he started an LP on the hi-fi and turned up the volume to defeat hidden microphones. Sinatra sang "In the Still of the Night."

Benjamin took a large envelope from the briefcase and handed it to me. It contained about twenty glossy black-and-white photographs—army trucks parked in a field; soldiers with bayonets fixed; a large empty ditch with two bulldozers standing by; beggars getting down from the truck; beggars being tumbled into the ditch; beggars, hedged in by bayonets, being buried alive by the bulldozers; bulldozers rolling over the dirt to tamp it down with their treads.

"The army is very unhappy about this," Benjamin said. "President Ga did not tell the generals that soldiers would be required to do this work. They thought they were just getting these beggars out of sight until after the Pan-African Conference. Instead the soldiers were ordered to solve the problem once and for all."

My throat was dry. I cleared it and said, "How many people were buried alive?"

"Nobody counted."

"Why was this done?"

"I told you. The beggars were an eyesore."

"That was reason enough to bury them alive?"

"The soldiers were supposed to shoot them first. But they refused. This is good for us, because now the army is angry. Also afraid. Now Ga can execute any general for murder simply by discovering the crime and punishing the culprits in the name of justice and the people. The generals have not told the president that the soldiers refused to follow his orders, so now they are in danger. If he ever finds out he will bury the soldiers alive. Also a general or two. Or more."

I said, "Who would tell him?"

"Who indeed?" asked Benjamin, stone-faced. I handed the pictures back to him. He held up a palm. "Keep them."

I said, "No, thank you."

The photos were a death warrant for anyone who was arrested with them in his possession.

Benjamin ignored me. He rummaged in his briefcase and handed me a handheld radio transceiver. Technologically speaking, those were primitive days, and the device was not much smaller than a fifth of Beefeater's, minus the neck of the bottle. Nevertheless, it was a wonder for its time. It was made in the U.S.A., so I supposed it had been supplied by the local chief of station, the man who played ball with Ga, as a trinket for a native.

Benjamin said, "Your call sign is Mustard One. Mine is Mustard. This is for emergencies. This, too." He handed me a Webley and a box of hollow-point cartridges.

I was touched by his concern. But the transceiver was useless—if the situation was desperate enough to call him. I would be a dead man before he could get to me. The Webley, however, would be useful for shooting myself in case of need. Shooting anyone else in this country would be the equivalent of committing suicide.

Benjamin rose to his feet. "I will be back," he said. "We will spend the evening together."

When Benjamin returned around midnight, I was reading Sir Richard Burton's *Wanderings in West Africa*, the only book in the house. It was a first edition, published in 1863. The margins were sprinkled with pencil dots. I guessed that it had been used by some romantic Brit for a book code. Benjamin was sartorially correct as usual—crisp white shirt with paisley cravat, double-breasted naval blazer, gray slacks, gleaming oxblood oxfords. He cast a disapproving eye on my wrinkled shorts and sweaty shirt and bare feet.

"You must wash and shave and put on proper clothes," he said. "We have been invited to dinner."

Benjamin offered no further information. I asked no questions. The sergeant drove, rapidly, without headlights on narrow trails through the bush. We arrived at a guard shack. The guard, a very sharp soldier, saluted and waved us through without looking inside the car. The road widened into a sweeping driveway. Gravel crackled under the tires. We reached the top of a little rise, and I saw before me the presidential palace, lit up like a football stadium by the light towers that surrounded it. The flags of all the newborn African nations flew from a ring of flagstaffs.

The soldiers guarding the front door, white belts, white gloves, white bootlaces, white rifle slings, came to present arms. We walked past them into a vast foyer from which a double staircase swept upward before separating at a landing decorated by a huge floodlit portrait of President Ga wearing his sash of office.

A liveried servant led us up the stairs past a gallery of portraits of Ga variously uniformed as general of the army, admiral of the fleet, air chief marshal, head of the party, and other offices I could not identify.

We simply walked into the presidential office. No guards were visible. President Ga was seated behind a desk at the far end of the vast room. Two attack dogs, pit bulls, stood with ears pricked at either side of his oversize desk. The ceiling could not have been less than fifteen feet high. Ga, not a large person to begin with, was so diminished by these Brobdingnagian proportions that he looked like a puppet. He was reading what I supposed was a state paper, pen in hand in case he needed to add or cross something out. As we approached across the snow-white marble floor, our footsteps echoed. Benjamin's were especially loud because he wore leather heels, but nothing, apparently, could break the president's concentration.

About ten feet from the desk we stopped, our toes touching a bronze strip that was sunk into the marble. Ga ignored us. The pit bulls did not. Ga pressed a button. A hidden door opened behind the desk, and a young army officer in dress uniform stepped out. Behind him I could see half a dozen other soldiers, armed to the teeth and standing at attention in a closetlike space that was hardly large enough to hold them all.

Wordlessly, Ga handed the paper to the officer, who took it, made a smart about-face, and marched back into the closet. Ga stood up, still taking no notice of us, and strolled to the large window behind his desk. It looked out over the brightly lit, shadowless palace grounds. At a little distance I could see an enclosure in which several different species of gazelle were confined. In other paddocks—too many to be seen in a single glance— other wild animals paced. Ga drank in the scene for a long moment, then whirled and approached Benjamin and me at quick-march, as if he wore one of his many uniforms instead of the white bush jacket, black slacks, and sandals in which he actually was dressed. Benjamin did not introduce me. Apparently there was no need to do so, because Ga, looking me straight in the eye, shook my hand and said, "I hope you like French food, Mr. Brown."

I did. The menu was a terrine of gray sole served with a 1953 Corton Charlemagne, veal stew accompanied by a 1949 Pommard, cheese, and grapes. The president ate the food hungrily, talking all the while, but only sipped the wines.

"Alcohol gives me bad dreams," he said to me. "Do you ever have bad dreams?"

"Doesn't everyone, sir?"

"My best friend, who died too young, never had bad dreams. He was too good in mind and heart to be troubled by such things. Now he is in my dreams. He visits me almost every night. Who is in your dreams?"

"Mostly people I don't know."

"Then you are very lucky."

During the dinner Ga talked about America. He knew it well. He had earned a degree from a Negro college in Missouri. Baptist missionaries had sent him to the college on a scholarship. He graduated second in his class, behind his best friend who now called on him in dreams. When Ga spoke to his people he spoke standard Africanized English, the common tongue of his country where more than a hundred mutually incomprehensible tribal languages were in use. He spoke to me in American English, sounding like Harry S. Truman. He had had a wonderful time in college: the football games, the fraternity pranks, the music, the wonderful food, homecoming, the prom, those American coeds! His friend had been the school's star running back; Ga had been the team manager; they had won their conference championship two years in a row. "From the time we were boys together in our village, my friend was always the star, I was always the administrator," he said. "Until we got into politics and changed places. My friend stuttered. It was his only flaw.

It is the reason I am president. Had he been able to speak to the people without making them laugh, he would be living in this house."

"You were fond of this man," I said.

"Fond of him? He was my brother."

Tears formed in the president's eyes. Despite everything I knew about his crimes, I found myself liking Akokwu Ga.

Servants arrived with coffee and a silver dessert bowl. "Ah, strawberries and crème fraîche!" said Ga, breaking into his first smile of the evening.

After the strawberries, another servant offered cigars and port, discreetly showing me the labels. Ga waved these temptations away like a good Baptist. I did the same, not without regret.

"Come, my friend," said Ga, rising to his feet and suddenly speaking West African rather than Missouri English, "it is time for a walk. Do you get enough exercise?"

I said, "I wish I got more."

"Ah, but you must make time to keep up to snuff," said Ga. "I ride horseback every morning and walk in the cool of the evening. Both things are excellent exercise, and also, to start the day, you have the companionship of the horse which never says anything stupid. You must get a horse. If you are too busy for a horse, a masseur. Not a masseuse. They are too distracting. Massage is like hearty exercise if the masseur is strong and has the knowledge. Bob Hope told me that. Massage keeps him young."

By now we were at the front door. The spick-and-span young army captain who had earlier leaped out of the closet behind Ga's desk awaited us. Standing at rigid attention, he held out a paper for Ga. Benjamin immediately went into reverse, walking backward as he withdrew from eyeshot and earshot of the president, while the latter read his document and spoke to his orderly. I followed suit.

Staring straight ahead and barely moving his lips, Benjamin

muttered, "He is charming tonight. Be careful." These were the first words he had uttered all evening. Throughout dinner, Ga had ignored him entirely, as if he were a third pit bull lying at his feet.

Outside, under the stadium lights, Ga led the way across the shadowless grounds to his animal park. Three men walked in front, sweeping the ground in case of snakes. As I knew from rumor and intelligence reports, Ga had a morbid fear of snakes. Another bearer carried Ga's sporting rifle, a beautiful weapon that looked to me like a Churchill, retail in London, £10,000.

The light from the towers was so strong that everything looked like an overexposed photograph. Ga pointed out the gazelles, naming them all one by one. "Some of these specimens are quite rare," he said, "or so I am told by the people who sell them. I am preserving them for the people of this nation. Most of these beasts no longer live in this part of Africa, but before the Europeans came with their guns and killed them for sport, we knew them as brothers."

Ga was a believer in raising a mythical African past to the status of reality. The public buildings he had built during his brief reign featured murals and mosaics depicting Africans of a lost civilization inventing agriculture, mathematics, architecture, medicine, electricity, the airplane, even the postage stamp. In his mind it was only logical that the ancients had also lived in peace with the lion, the elephant, the giraffe—everything but the serpent, which Ga had exiled from his utopia.

We tramped on a bit, to an empty paddock. "Now you will see something," he said. "You will see nature in the raw."

This paddock was unlighted. Ga lifted his hand, and the lights went on. Standing alone in the middle of the open space was an animal that even I was able to recognize as a Thomson's gazelle from its diminutive size, its lovely tan and white coat, the calligraphic black stripe on its flank. This one was a buck, just over three feet tall, a work of art like so many other African animals.

"This type of gazelle is common," Ga said. "There are hundreds of thousands of them in herds in Tanganyika. They can outrun a lion. Watch."

The word *suddenly* does not convey the speed of what happened next. Out of the blinding light in which it had somehow been concealing itself as it stalked the Tommy, a cheetah materialized, moving at sixty miles an hour. A cheetah can cover a hundred meters in less than three seconds. The Tommy saw or sensed this blur of death that hurtled toward him and leaped three or four feet straight up into the air, then hit the ground running. The Tommy was slightly slower than its predator, but far more nimble. When the cheetah got close enough to attack, the little gazelle would make a quick turn and escape. This happened over and over again. The size of the paddock—or playing field, as Ga must have thought of it—was an advantage to the Tommy, who would lead the cheetah straight to the fence, then make a last-second turn. Once or twice the cheetah crashed into the wire.

"This is almost over," Ga said. "Usually it lasts only a minute or so. If the cat does not win very quickly, it runs out of strength and gives up."

A second later, the cheetah won. The gazelle turned in the wrong direction, and the cat brought it down. A cheetah is not strong enough to break the neck of its prey, so it kills by suffocation, biting the throat and crushing the windpipe. The Tommy struggled, then went limp. The cheetah's eyes glittered. So did Ga's.

Beaming, he threw an arm around my shoulders. He said, "Wonderful, eh?"

I smelled the food and wine on his breath, felt his excited heart beating against my shoulder. Then, without a good night

or even a facial expression, Ga turned on his heel, and, surrounded by his snake sweepers and his gun bearer, marched
away and disappeared into the palace. The evening was over. His
guests had ceased to exist.

We lost no time in leaving. Minutes later, as we rolled toward
the wakening city in Benjamin's Rover, I asked a question.

"Is he always so hospitable?"

"Tonight you saw one Ga," Benjamin said. "There are a
thousand of him."

I could believe it. In this one evening I had seen him in half a
dozen incarnations, Mussolini redux, gourmet, Joe College, ten-
der friend, zoologist, mythologist, and a fun-loving god who
stage-managed animal sacrifices to himself.

The Rover purred along a smoothly paved but deserted road,
bush to the left and right, the sticky night dark as macadam.
Headlights appeared behind us and approached at high speed.
The sergeant switched off the Rover's lights and pulled off the
road. The tires bit into soft dirt. Benjamin and I were slammed
together hip and shoulder. We were being overtaken by a motor-
cade. A Cadillac, the lead car, swept by at high speed, then a
Rolls-Royce, then another Cadillac as chase car.

"The president," Benjamin said calmly when the Rover
stopped bouncing. "He always has a woman or two before the
sun rises. He is quick with them, never more than fifteen minutes, then he goes back to the presidential palace. He never goes
to the same woman twice in the same month."

"He keeps thirty-one women?"

"More, in case one of them is not clean on a certain night."

"How does he choose which one?"

"Each woman has a number. Each month Ga receives from
somebody in St. Louis, Missouri, what is called a dream book. It
is used in America to play the numbers game. He uses the number in the dream book for the day."

I said, "So if you want to find him on any given night, you match the woman's number to the number for that particular day in the dream book."

"Yes, if you know the address of every woman, that is the key," Benjamin said.

He smiled and placed a hand on my shoulder, pleased as a proud father with the quickness of my mind.

FOR THE NEXT several days there was no sign of Benjamin. I was not locked up, but as a practical matter this meant that I was confined to the safe house during daylight hours. There was nowhere to go at night. Like any other prisoner I invented ways to pass the empty hours. Solitude and time-wasting did not bother me; I was used to them; both were occupational hazards. I was concerned by the lack of exercise, because I did not want to run out of breath in case I had to make a run for it. This seemed a likely outcome. How else could this situation end?

I jogged in place for an hour every morning, and in the afternoon ran the 100- and the 220-yard dashes, also in place but flat out. I did push-ups and sit-ups and side-straddle hops. I punched and karate-chopped the sofa cushions until I had beaten every last mote of dust from them. I jitterbugged in my socks to cracked 78 rpm records I found in a closet, Louis Armstrong, the Harmonica Rascals, the Andrews Sisters. Satchmo's "Muskrat Ramble" and the sisters' "Boogie Woogie Bugle Boy of Company B" provided the best workouts.

The sergeant stopped by every day to cook lunch and dinner and wash up afterward. He brought quality groceries, and he was a good cook, specializing in curries and local piripiri dishes loaded with cayenne pepper that made the heart beat in the skull. I asked him to bring me books. He refused money to pay for them or the groceries—apparently I was covered by a budget in secret funds—and came back from the African market the next day with at least one Penguin paperback by every writer I had named and a few more besides. The books were dog-eared and food- and coffee-stained, and most were missing pages.

I was in bed, reading a W. Somerset Maugham short story about adulterers in Malaya, when Benjamin finally showed up. As usual he chose the wee hours of the morning for his visit. He was as stealthy as he had been when he visited me in the hotel, and I heard no car or any other sound of his approach.

All the same I felt his presence before he materialized out of the darkness. He seemed to be alone. He carried a battered leather valise, the kind that has a hinged top that opens like a mouth when the catch is released. The valise seemed to jump in his hand, as if it contained a disembodied muscle. I rationalized this by thinking that he must be trembling for some reason. Maybe he had had a bout of fever and was not quite recovered. That would explain why I hadn't seen him for a week.

Then, at the instant when I realized that there was something alive inside the valise and it was trying to get out, Benjamin held the bag upside down over my bed and pressed the catch. The bag popped open and a huge blue-black mamba uncoiled itself from within. It landed on my legs. With blinding speed it coiled and struck. I felt the blow, a soft punch but no sting, on my chest just above the heart. I knew that I was a dead man. So apparently did the mamba. It stared into my eyes, waiting (or so I thought) for my heart to stop, for the power of thought to switch off. No more than a second had passed. Already I felt cold. An ineffable calm settled upon me. The laboring air conditioner in the window was suddenly almost silent. My hearing seemed to be going first. Next, I thought, the eyes. I felt no pain. I thought, Maybe after all there is a God, or was a God, if the last moment of life has been arranged in such a kindly and loving way.

Dreamily I watched as Benjamin's hand, black as the mamba, seized the snake behind the head. The serpent struggled, lashing its body and winding itself around Benjamin's arm. The sergeant appeared, stepping out of the darkness and into the light of my reading lamp just as Benjamin had done. It took the combined strength of these two powerful men to stuff the thing back into the valise and close it. They did so without the slightest sign of fear. In the half-light, with their faces close together, they looked more than ever like brothers. How strange it was, I thought, that this surreal scene in this misbegotten place should be the last thing I would ever see. Benjamin handed the valise to the sergeant. It jumped violently in his hand. The sergeant produced a key and, with a perfectly steady hand, locked the valise. His eyes were fixed on me. He was grinning in what I can only describe as total delight. Make that unholy delight.

To me, an unsmiling Benjamin said, "You must be wondering why you are not dead yet."

He was not grinning. The sergeant, watching me over Benjamin's shoulder, did it for him, big white teeth reflecting more light than there seemed to be in the room.

Up to this point I had not looked at my fatal wound. In fact, I had not moved at all since the snake had struck me. Something told me that any movement might quicken the action of the venom and rob me of whatever split seconds of life I might have left. Besides, I did not want to see the wound that I imagined, twin punctures made by the mamba's fangs, perhaps a drop or two of blood, and most horribly, venom oozing from the holes in my skin. Finally I found the courage to glance at my chest. It was unmarked.

I leaped out of bed, dashed into the bathroom, and examined my sweating torso. I stripped off my boxer shorts, the only garment I was wearing, and twisted and turned in the stingy light, looking for what I still feared was a mortal wound. But I saw no break in my skin, no bruise, even. The symptoms of death I had been feeling—the light-headedness, the shortness of breath, and a sense of loss so intense that it felt like the shutdown of the heart—went away.

Without bothering to put my shorts back on, I went back into the bedroom.

"Look at him!" the sergeant chortled, pointing a finger at me.

At first I thought he was making fun of my nakedness. I had spent time on a beach in South Africa, and the part of me formerly covered by my shorts was dead-white. I soon realized that he was laughing at something other than my tan line. I was the victim of the most sadistic practical joke since Harry Flashman was kicked out of Rugby College, and these two were the jokers. There is no mirth like African mirth, and both Benjamin and the sergeant were doubled over by it. They howled with laughter, their eyes were filled with tears, they gasped for breath, they hugged each other as they danced a jig of merriment, they lost their balance and staggered to regain it.

"Look at him!" they said over and over again. "Look at him!"

The locked valise had been placed on the bed. The contortions of the infuriated six-foot-long muscle that was trying to escape from it caused it to skitter across the sheets. I tried to get around the helpless men, but they kept lurching into my path, so I was not able to reach the Webley, Benjamin's gift to me, that was stashed under the mattress. My plan was to empty the revolver, if I could get my hands on it, into the pulsating valise. I was in no way certain that I could stick to this plan if I actually had the gun in my hands and this comedy team at point-blank range.

Breath by breath, I got hold of myself. So did Benjamin and the sergeant, though it took them a little longer. It was obvious what had happened. Some juju man had captured the snake and removed its fangs and venom sac. Knowing Benjamin—and by now I felt that I knew him intimately despite the brevity of our friendship—he had commissioned the capture and the veterinary surgery. Knowing also how terrified President Ga was of snakes, I could only surmise that the defanged mamba was going to be a player in the overthrow of the tyrant. Maybe, if the coup succeeded, Benjamin would make the mamba part of the flag, as an earlier group of patriots had done a couple hundred years ago with another poisonous snake in another British colony.

Benjamin offered no explanations for the prank. I was damned if I was going to ask him any questions. I was by no means certain that I could control my voice. By now the joke had cooled off. Benjamin had stopped smiling. His grave dignity had returned. He made a minimal gesture. The sergeant picked up the valise.

Benjamin said, "I will be back soon."

With a scratchy throat, I said, "Good."

The two of them let themselves out the front door. I locked it behind them, and as I tried to put the key into my pants pocket I remembered that I was stark naked. Nakedness was deeply offensive to christianized Africans like Benjamin. Maybe that was why he had stopped laughing before the joke had really worn off.

I reached under the mattress and pulled out the Webley and cocked it. It is a very heavy weapon, weighing almost three pounds when fully loaded, and when I felt its heft in my hand I began to tremble. I could not stop. I was afraid that the gun might go off, but I had so little control over my muscles that I could not safely put it down. Teeth chattering, my body chilling in a room in which the temperature was not less than ninety degrees, I understood fully and for the first time just what a brilliant son of a bitch Benjamin was.

TWO DAYS LATER, at five in the morning, he showed up at the safe house for breakfast. He said he had been up all night. There was no outward sign of this. He was fresh from the shower, his starched uniform still smelled of the iron, and he sat up straight as a cadet in his chair. But he was not his usual masked self. There was an air of excitement about him that he did not bother to conceal.

He ate the yolks of his fried eggs with a spoon, then touched the corners of his mouth with his napkin. "The president of the republic is very upset," he said.

He spoke in a low tone. It was difficult to hear him because a Benny Goodman record was playing on the phonograph—the usual precaution against eavesdroppers—and Harry James and the rest of the trumpet section were playing as if their four or five horns were a single instrument.

I said, "Upset? Why?"

"He has discovered the fangs and the poison sac of a black mamba on his desk."

"Goodness," I said. "No wonder he's upset."

"Yes. He found these things when he came back from one of his women last night. They were right in the center of the blotter, in his coffee cup. If someone had poured coffee into the cup he might well have drunk it absentmindedly. He said so himself."

I could think of nothing to say. Certainly Benjamin needed no encouragement to go on with his story.

He said, "He flew off the handle and called me immediately. He screamed into the telephone. He was surrounded by traitors, he said. How could anyone have gained access to his office in his absence, let alone smuggled in the coffee cup? How could no one have noticed this coffee cup and what was in it? There are soldiers everywhere in the presidential palace. Or were."

"They are there no longer?"

"Naturally he has dismissed them. How could he trust them after this? He also ordered the arrest of the army chief of staff. His order has of course been carried out."

"The army chief of staff is in your custody?"

"For the time being, yes. It gives us an opportunity to talk frankly to each other."

"Who is handling security if not the army?"

"The national police. This is an honor, but it is a strain on our manpower, especially with the Pan-African festival beginning the day after tomorrow. Thousands will flood into Ndala, including twenty-six heads of state and who knows how many other dignitaries and nobodies. But of course the safety of our own head of state and government is the number-one priority."

"You are investigating, of course."

"Oh, yes," Benjamin said. "Suspects, some of them of very high rank, are being interviewed, quarters are being searched, every safe in the nation is being opened, information is being gathered, fingerprints and other physical evidence have been assembled, all the usual police procedures are in place, but on a much larger and more urgent scale than usual. The presidential palace is off-limits to everyone except the president and the police."

He was in complete control of his voice and his facial muscles. But underneath his unflappable behavior, he glowed with joy. He was within reach of something that he wanted very much indeed.

"The fangs and so on are not all that we have to worry about," Benjamin went on. "The president for life has also received an anonymous letter, mysteriously placed under his pillow by an unknown hand, stating that a sample of his bodily secretions has been given to a famous juju man in the Ivory Coast."

This was momentous news. Playing the naïf, my assigned role in this charade, I said, "Bodily secretions?"

"We believe they were obtained from one of Ga's women. He is deeply concerned. This can only mean that a curse has been put upon him by an enemy. The curse can be reversed only if we can find the culprit who hired the juju man."

Imparting this news, he remained impassive. No smile, no equivalent of a wink, no expression of any kind came to the surface. Benjamin himself had, of course, engineered everything he was reporting to me: the fangs, the venom, the anonymous letter with its chilling message. But he described these things as if he had no more idea than the man in the moon who was responsible for tormenting President Ga.

*   *   *

THE JUJU CURSE was the keystone of the plot. I had known Africans, one of them an agent of mine who possessed a first-class degree from Cambridge, who had withered and died from witchcraft. The bodily secretion was the vital element in casting a juju spell. Some product of the victim's body was needed to invoke a truly effective curse, a lock of hair, an ounce of urine, a teaspoon of saliva, feces. The more intimate the product, the greater its power. Nothing could be a more effective charm than a man's semen. No wonder Ga was beside himself. And no wonder that he was now in Benjamin's power.

By now, more than thirty African heads of state had flown into Ndala for President Ga's Pan-African Conference. This was the day on which they would all ride through the city in their Rolls-Royces and Mercedes Benzes and Cadillacs, waving to the vast crowd that had been assembled to greet them. Whether any of these spectators had the faintest idea who the dignitaries were, or what they were doing in Ndala, were separate questions. Whole tribes had been bused or trucked or herded on foot into the city from the interior. Many were dancing. Chiefs had brought warriors armed with shields and spears to protect them against enemies, wives to service them, dwarves to keep them entertained. Every single one of these human beings seemed to be grunting or shouting or singing or, mostly, laughing, and the noise produced by all those voices, added to the beating of drums and the sound of musical instruments and the tootling of automobile horns, made the air tremble. Palm wine and warm beer flowed, and the spicy aroma of stews and roasting goats rose from hundreds of cook fires.

At last the sergeant found the exact spot he had been looking for, an empty space in front of the parliament building, and parked the car in the shadow of a huge baobab tree. A couple of constables were already on hand, and they cleared away the crowd so that we had an unobstructed view.

"They will come soon," the sergeant said.

It was a little before five in the afternoon. The parade was already about ninety minutes behind schedule, but there was no such concept as "on time" in Ndala or any other place in Africa. Maybe forty minutes later, we heard the faraway, warped sound of a brass band playing "The British Grenadiers." The music grew louder, and the band marched by, drum major brandishing a baton that was as tall as he was, every musician's eye seemingly fixed on the Austin as the marching men turned eyes left on the parliament and the flags of the African nations that flew from its circle of flagpoles. A battalion of infantry then marched smartly by, drenched in sweat, arms swinging, boots kicking up powdery dust. The infantry were followed by several tanks and armored cars and howitzers. Finally came a platoon of bagpipers, tartan kilts and sporrans swinging, "Scotland the Brave" splitting the sun-scorched air. If the Brits had taught these people nothing else in a century of colonialism, they had taught them how to organize a parade.

"Now come the presidents," the sergeant said. "President for Life Ga will be first, then the others." Then, even though we were alone in the car with the windows rolled up, he dropped his voice to a whisper and added, "Watch very carefully the road ahead of his car."

Ga's regal, snow-white Rolls-Royce materialized out of the dust. There were a few grunts from onlookers but no ululations or other such behavior. The masses merely watched this strange alien phenomenon, and no doubt they would have reacted in the same way if a spaceship had been landing among them. Not that the occasion was wholly lacking in ceremony. The soldiers posted along the street at ten-foot intervals came to present arms. The sergeant leaped out of the car, and he and the two constables stood to attention, saluting. I got out, too. No one paid the slightest attention to me. But then, only a few of the onlookers were paying very much attention to President Ga.

The Rolls-Royce continued its stately approach, flags flying, headlights blazing. The crowd stirred and muttered.

Then, without warning, the crowd suddenly broke and began to run in all directions, men, women, children, the decrepit old borne aloft by their sons and daughters, everyone except the dancers, who had by now fallen into a collective trance and went right on dancing, oblivious to the panic all around them. Everyone else scattered as fast as their legs would carry them. The presidential Rolls-Royce slammed on its brakes and stood on its nose. Inside it, President Ga or one of his doubles, dressed in a white uniform, was thrown about like a rag doll.

It was impossible not to see Benjamin's hand in all this. A single thought filled my mind: assassination. He was going to kill this man in full view of thirty other presidents for life.

I leaped onto the hood of the Austin, then scrambled to the roof. From that vantage point I saw what all the fright was about. A black mamba at least ten feet long was slithering with almost unbelievable swiftness across the road in the path of the white Rolls-Royce. Suddenly half a dozen brave fellows, half-naked all of them, leaped out of the crowd and attacked the serpent with pangas, cutting it into pieces that writhed violently as if trying to reconnect themselves into a living reptile. The crowd uttered a loud, collective basso grunt. This was a huge yet subdued sound, like a whisper amplified to the power of ten thousand on some enormous hi-fi speaker yet to be invented.

The Rolls-Royce, Klaxon sounding, sped away. The sergeant said, "Get into the car. We must go."

I did as he ordered. Inside the sweltering, buttoned-up Austin, I asked if the mamba crossing President Ga's path on his day of triumph would be seen as a bad omen.

"Oh, yes," the sergeant said, grinning into the mirror. "*Very* bad. No one who saw will ever forget."

Darkness fell. The sergeant did not take me home but drove

me to a different safe house on the outskirts of the city. As soon as we were inside I switched on the English-language radio. The opening ceremonies of the Pan-African Conference were now in progress at the soccer stadium. Announcers shouted to be heard above the blare of bands and choirs, the boom of fireworks, and the noise of the crowd. Needless to say, not a word was uttered over the airways about the meeting between the mamba and Ga's white Rolls-Royce. Everyone knew all about it anyway by word of mouth or talking drum or one of the many Bantu tongues that could be signed or whistled as well as spoken.

In all those minds, as in my own, the questions were: What happens next and when will it happen? I left the radio on, knowing that the first word of the coup would come from its speakers. Second only to the capture or murder of the prince, the broadcasting station was the most important objective in any coup d'état. Obviously Benjamin and his coconspirators, assuming that he had any, must strike tonight. Never again would he have such an opportunity to destroy the tyrant before the very eyes of Africa. He would want to kill Ga in the most humiliating way possible. He would want to show him as weak, impotent, and alone, without a single person willing or able to defend him.

Promptly at eight o'clock, the sergeant carried a cooler into the house, rattled pots and pans in the kitchen, and served my dinner, all five courses at once. The food was French. "This is the same food that all the presidents will be eating at the state dinner," the sergeant said. I ate only the heated-up entrée, medallions of veal in a cream sauce that had separated because the sergeant had let it boil.

Around two in the morning, the sergeant's walkie-talkie squawked. He lifted it to his ear, heard what sounded to me like a single word, and replied with what also seemed to be a single word. The conversation lasted less than a second. He said, "Come, Mr. Brown. It is time to go."

$\star$ $\star$ $\star$

WE DROVE THROUGH a maze of streets but on this night of rev-
elry saw no sleepers by the wayside. Everybody was still cele-
brating. Oil lamps and candles glowed in the blackness like red
and yellow eyes, as if the entire genus *carnivora* was drawn up in
a hungry circle on the outskirts of the party. Music blared from
loudspeakers, people danced, thousands of shouted conversations stirred the stagnant, overheated air. The city had become
one enormous, throbbing Equator Club. The sergeant maneuvered the Austin through the pandemonium with one hand on
the steering wheel and the other on the hooter, constantly beep-
ing to let people know that he wasn't trying to sneak up on them
and kill them. Not since Independence Night, I thought, could
there have been so many witnesses awake at this hour, ready to
observe whatever Benjamin was going to do next.

At last we drove out of the crowd and into the European
quarter. Through the rear window I could see the distorted,
smoky-red glow of the city. I imagined I could feel the earth
quivering in rhythm to the innumerable bare feet that were
pounding it in unison a mile or so away. The music and the
shouting were very loud even at such a distance.

The sergeant drove at his usual brisk pace, lights off as usual.
He parked the car and switched off the engine. By now my eyes
had adjusted, and I could see another police car parked a few
yards away. We were parked on a low hilltop, and the red glow
of the city caught in the mirror-shine of its metal. Soon a third
car drove up and parked close beside us. It was Benjamin's
Rover, identifiable by the baritone throb of its engine. The
driver's cap badge caught a little light. A large man who might
have been Benjamin sat in the backseat alone.

Moving swiftly, Benjamin got into the backseat with me. The
dome light blinked. He wore the dress uniform I supposed he
had worn to the state dinner—long pants, white shirt with neck-
tie, short epauletted mess jacket that the Brits call a bum freezer,

decorations. Benjamin smelled as usual of starch, brass polish, soap, his own musk.

Headlights swept up the hill, turned sharp left into the street that paralleled the one on which our own cars were parked, then stopped. Car doors slammed, men moved quick-time, a key turned in a lock, a door squeaked as it was opened, a scratchy Edith Piaf LP played five or six bars of *"Les amants de Paris."*

We were parked behind the house into which Ga had gone to keep his rendezvous for tonight. Jumpy light showed in an upstairs window, dim and yellowish, as if filtering down a hallway from another room. The back door opened. A flashlight blinked. The Rover's headlights flashed in reply.

"Come," Benjamin said. He got out of the car and strode into the darkness. I followed. The sergeant got something out of the trunk, then slammed the lid. Behind me I heard his brogans at a run. We went through the open door. Inside the house, the record changed on the hi-fi, and Piaf began to sing *"Il Pleut."* Benjamin, entirely at home, strode down a hallway, then up a stairway. At the top, in half-shadow outside a half-open bedroom door, a policeman stood at attention as if he did not quite know exactly what was expected of him or what would happen next.

In a mirror I saw a man and a woman engaged in vigorous coitus and heard the woman's moans and outcries. The sergeant marched into the room. Benjamin gave me a little push, and I marched in behind him. The room was full of burning candles. The smell of incense was strong. Smoke hung in the air. The woman shouted something in what sounded to me like Swedish. She was quite small. President Ga, lying on top of her, covered her completely. Her legs were wound around his waist, ankles crossed, feet in gilt shoes with stiletto heels. I looked into the mirror in hope of seeing the girl's face. My eyes met Ga's. The candlelight exaggerated the size of his startled, wide-open eyes. His face twisted into a mask of furious anger, and he rolled off the woman, knocking off one of her shoes. Now I saw her face, smeared lipstick and tousled hair. She was a cookie-cutter blonde, as flawless as a dummy in a store window.

I knew what was coming next, of course. The sergeant took one step forward. In his outstretched hands he held the valise that I remembered so well. Evidently that was what he had retrieved from the trunk of the Austin. The snap of brass latches sounded like the metallic *one-two* of the slide of an automatic pistol. The sergeant opened the valise and turned it upside down. The mamba flowed out of the bag with the same unbelievable swiftness, as if it were coming into being before our eyes. I tried to leap backward, but Benjamin stood immediately behind me, blocking the way. President Ga and the blonde froze as if captured in a black-and-white photograph by the flash of a strobe light.

The snake, a blur as it attacked, struck at the nearest target, President Ga. He grunted as if a bullet had entered his body. His mouth opened wide and he shouted in English, "Oh, Jesus, Sweet Jesus!" It was a prayer, not a blasphemy. In the same breath he uttered a tremendous sob. Between these two primal sounds, the woman, screaming, threw her body over the foot of the bed. Somehow she landed behind us on all fours in the hallway. Still shrieking, still wearing one gilt shoe, she sprinted down the hallway. The constable in the hall pursued her for a step or two, picked up the shoe after she kicked it off, and caught her by the hair, which was very long. Her head jerked back, but she kept going, leaving the constable with a handful of blond threads in his hand. He stared at these in puzzlement, then blew his whistle. At the head of the stairs the woman was captured by a second constable, a man almost as large as Benjamin. He carried her, squirming, kicking, screaming, back toward the bedroom. Her skin was so white that I half-expected powder to fly from it. She bit his face. He twisted her jaw until she let go, and when he saw his own blood on her teeth he slammed her twice against the wall, then let go of her, throwing his hands wide in disgust that a woman should have attacked him, should have *bitten* him. Her limp, unconscious body slid to the floor. She landed with a thump on her round bottom, her back against the wall, her head lolling inside its curtain of hair. She twitched as if dreaming, and I wondered if her spine was broken. She had shapely breasts, pretty legs, peroxided delta, and it looked as though she had lipsticked her nipples. For some reason, maybe because this touch of perversity was so unimaginative, so inno-cent, such a learner's trick, my heart went out to her, if only for a moment.

Behind me I heard a gunshot. In the confined space of the bed-room it sounded like an artillery round going off. The stink of cordite mingled with the incense. Benjamin stood over the bed with a smoking Webley in his hand. The headless snake in its death throes whipped uncontrollably over the bed, spraying blood on Ga and the sheets. With his hands protecting his genitals, Ga scooted rapidly backward over the bed to escape the serpent, even though he must have known that it was now harmless. What a seed God planted in the human mind on the day that Adam ate the apple! From the look on Ga's face it was clear that he believed that he himself was dying almost as fast as the snake had just done, but his instincts, from which he could not escape, instructed him to cover his nakedness and flee for his life.

Ga's eyes were now fixed on Benjamin. The question in them was easy to read: Had Benjamin murdered him or rescued him? Benjamin made a gesture to Ga: *Come.*

Ga, strangling on the words, said, "Doctor!"

Benjamin ignored him. Silently he pointed a finger first at the sergeant, then at Ga. Then he whirled on his heel and left the room. The sergeant picked up the writhing snake and threw it into the hallway, then grasped Ga's left arm, turned him onto his stomach, and expertly cuffed his hands behind him.

Surprised, then outraged, Ga shouted, "I order you—"

The sergeant punched him hard in the kidney. Ga shrieked in pain and subsided, gasping. The sergeant shouted an order in his own language. Two constables—the one who had been posted in the hallway all along and the one the blonde had bitten—came into the room, pulled Ga to his feet, and marched him naked down the hallway, past the headless mamba, past the crumpled blonde, and out the back door. The mamba, still twitching, would be the first thing the girl would see when she opened her eyes.

In the bedroom the hi-fi played the last words of the Piaf song that had begun as we entered the house. It had taken Benjamin three minutes and twenty seconds to carry out his coup d'état.

Outside, Ga struggled with the two constables who were trying to stuff him into the trunk of Benjamin's Rover. He kicked, squirmed, butted. One of the constables struck him on the hip bone with his baton. Ga collapsed like a marionette whose strings had been cut. The constables heaved him into the trunk and slammed it shut. One of them locked it, and then in his jubilation, knocked on it to make a little joke. The sergeant spoke an angry word to him.

Benjamin had already taken his place in the backseat of the Rover. I expected to be put into another car or to be left behind, but the sergeant opened the door for me, and I got in and sat beside Benjamin. We heard Ga in the trunk behind us—groans, childlike sobs, whisperings, appeals to Jesus, an explosive shout of Benjamin's name, so throat-scraping in its loudness that I imagined spit flying from Ga's mouth. If Benjamin derived any satisfaction from these proofs that his enemy was entirely in his power, he did not show it by sign or sound. He sat at attention in his Victorian dress uniform—silent, unmoving, eyes front.

The sergeant's Austin, driven by one of the constables, tailgated us as we rolled through the wide-awake city. It was just as noisy as before but more drunken, more out of control. What must Ga be thinking as he lay in pitch-darkness, folded like a fetus, naked and in shackles? Ten minutes ago he had been the most powerful man in Africa. Not now. He was silent. Why? Did he fear that the crowd would discover him and drag him out of the trunk and parade him naked through the howling mob? Did he imagine photographs and newsreels of this appalling humiliation being seen by the entire world?

We arrived at a darkened building I did not recognize. Somewhere above us a red light pulsed, and when I got out of the car I looked upward and realized that it was the warning beacon on the tower of the national radio transmitter. I made out the silhouettes of an armored car and maybe a dozen men in uniform.

The constables hauled Ga out of the trunk. He struggled and shouted words in a language I did not understand. A door opened and emitted a shaft of light. To my eyes, which had seen nothing brighter than a candle flame all evening, it was blindingly bright. We went through the door, a back entrance, into a cramped stairwell. A young chief inspector came to attention and saluted. He looked and behaved remarkably like the spick-and-span army captain I had met at the presidential palace. Other constables were posted on the stairway, one man on every other step. Incongruously for men who dressed like British bobbies and were trained to behave like them, each was armed with a submachine gun. I wondered what would happen if they all started shooting at once in this concrete chamber.

Ga screamed a question: "Do you know who I am?"

No one answered.

In a different, commanding tone, Ga said, "I am the president of this republic, elected by the people. I have been kidnapped by these criminals. I order you to arrest them at once."

Ga sounded like his newsreel self, voice like a church bell, and in spite of his abject state, looked like that old self, blazing eyes, imperious manner. However, the reality was that two large policemen had hold of his arms. He was naked and in chains and spattered with the blood of the mamba. A string of spittle hung from the corner of his mouth. The constables gave him a shove in the direction of the stairs. He stubbed his naked toes on the concrete step and sucked a sharp breath through his clenched teeth. This sound turned into a sob of frustration. The men to whom he was giving orders would not look at him.

I wondered if the next event in this Alice in Wonderland scenario might involve sitting Ga down at the microphone and ordering him to tell the nation that he had been removed from power. But no, he was frog-marched up the stairs and into the control room by his escorts. I remained with Benjamin and the sergeant in the studio. The control room was brightly lit. It was strange to gaze through the soundproof glass and see the wild-haired, glaring, unclothed Ga looking like one of his ancestors from the Neolithic.

The engineer switched on his mike and said, "Ready when you are, chief constable."

Into the open mike Ga shouted, "You will die, all of you! Your families will die! Your tribes, all of you will die!"

The engineer, quaking with fear, switched off the microphone, but Ga's mouth kept moving until the bigger constable put his hand over it, gagging him. Eyes rolling, chest heaving as he fought for breath, he kept on shouting. The constable pinched his nostrils shut, and the dumb-show noise behind the soundproof glass ceased.

Detecting movement near at hand, I shifted my gaze. A man in nightclothes was seated at the microphone. He was at least as nervous as the engineer. Benjamin handed him a sheet of paper. It was covered by Benjamin's perfect penmanship. Benjamin, a man who delegated nothing except, apparently, the most important announcement ever made over Radio Ndala, gave the engineer a thumbs-up signal. The engineer counted off seconds on raised fingers. He pointed to the announcer, who began reading in mellifluous broadcaster's English.

"Pay attention to this message from the high command of Ndala to all the people of our country," he said, voice steady but head twitching and hands trembling. "The tyrant Akokwu Ga is no longer the president of Ndala. He has been charged with mass murder, with treason, with corruption, and with other serious crimes and will be tried and punished according to the law. The functions of the government have been assumed for the time being by the high command of the armed services and the national police. The United Nations and the embassies of friendly nations have been informed of these developments. The people are to remain calm, obey the police, and return to their homes at once. An election to select a new head of state will be held in due course. The people are safe. The nation is safe. Investments by foreign nationals are safe. The treasure stolen by Akokwu Ga from the people is being recovered. All guests in our country are safe, and they are at liberty to remain in Ndala or leave Ndala whenever they wish. Additional communiqués will be issued from time to time by the high command. Long live Ndala. Long live independence and freedom. Long live justice. Long live democracy."

As the announcer read, Ga, listening intently, became very still, very attentive, his gaze fixed on what must have been a loudspeaker inside the control room. He might have been a child listening to a bedtime story about himself, so complete was his absorption in what was being said. His eyes were wide, his face bore a look of wonder, his mouth was slightly open. A police photographer took several pictures of him. Ga drew himself up and posed, head thrown back, one shackled foot advanced, as if he were wearing one of his resplendent uniforms.

After that, he was marched back to the Rover and again dumped into its trunk. He did not struggle or make a sound. The camera, it seemed, had given him back his dignity.

Roadblocks manned by soldiers had been erected on the road to the presidential palace. At the approach of Benjamin's Rover they opened the barricades and saluted as we passed. We were a feeble force—two ordinary sedans not even flying flags, four police constables, and an American spy with a defective passport, plus the prisoner in the trunk of the car who was the reason for the soldiers' awe.

The palace came into view, illuminated as before by the megawatts that flooded down from the light towers. A dozen stretch limousines, seals of high office painted on their doors, were parked in the circular drive of the presidential palace. The palace doors were guarded by police constables armed with Kalashnikovs. On the roof of the palace, more constables manned the machine guns and antiaircraft guns that they had taken over from the army.

Benjamin waited for the constables in charge to haul Ga from the trunk, then he got out of the car. He gave me no instructions, so I followed along as he strode into the palace with his usual lack of ceremony. We climbed the grand stairway. All busts and statues and portraits in oil of Ga in his many uniforms had been removed. Less than an hour before, he had walked down these stairs as President of the Republic for Life. Now he climbed them as a prisoner dragging chains. There was a dream-like quality to this scene, as if we did not belong in it or deserve it, as if it were a reenactment of an event from the life of some other tyrant who had lived and died in some other hour of history. Did Caesar as he felt the knife remember some assassinated Greek who had died a realer death?

A courtroom of sorts had been organized in Ga's vast and magnificent office. His desk and all his likenesses had been removed from this room, too. The Ndalan flag remained, flanked by what I took to be the flags of the armed forces and other government entities, but not by the presidential flag. The presidential conference table, vast and gleaming and smelling of wax, stood crosswise where Ga's desk had formerly been. Through the window behind it Ga's antelopes and gazelles could be seen, bathed in incandescent light as they bounded across the paddocks of his game park. Half a dozen grave men in British-style army, navy, and air force uniforms sat at the table like members of a court-martial. They were flanked by a half dozen others in black judicial robes and white wigs, clearly members of the supreme court, and a handful of other dignitaries wearing national dress or European suits.

All but the military types seemed to be confused by the entrance of the prisoner. In some cases this was obviously the last thing they had expected to see. Some if not all of them probably had not been told why they were there. Maybe some simply did not recognize Ga. Who among them had ever imagined seeing in his present miserable state the invulnerable creature the president of the republic had been?

If in fact there were any doubts about his identity, Ga removed them at once. In his unmistakable voice he shouted, "As president for life of the republic, I command you, all you generals, to arrest this man on a charge of high treason."

He attempted to point at Benjamin but of course could not do so with his wrists chained to his waist. Nevertheless, it was an impressive performance. Ga's voice was thunderous, his eyes flashed, he was the picture of command. For an instant he seemed to be fully clothed again. He gave every possible indication that he expected to be obeyed without question. But he was not obeyed, and when he continued to shout, the large constable did what he had done before, at the radio station. He clapped a hand over Ga's mouth and pinched his nostrils shut, and this time prolonged the treatment until Ga's struggle for breath produced high-pitched gasps that sounded very much like an infant crying.

The trial lasted less than an hour. Some might have called it a travesty, but everyone present knew that Ga was guilty of the crimes with which he was charged, and guilty, too, of even more heinous ones. Besides that, they knew that they must kill Ga now that they had witnessed his humiliation, or die themselves if he regained power. The trial itself followed established forms. Benjamin, as head of the national police, had prepared a bundle of evidence that was presented by a prosecutor and objected to by a lawyer appointed to defend Ga. Both men wore barrister's wigs. Witnesses were duly sworn. They testified to the massacre of the beggars. The immaculate young captain testified that Ga had embezzled not less than fifty million American dollars from the national treasury and deposited them in secret accounts in Geneva, Zurich, and Liechtenstein. The court heard tape recordings of Ga, in secret meetings with foreign ambassadors and businessmen, agreeing to make certain high appointments and award certain contracts in return for certain sums of money. Damning evidence was introduced that Ga had ordered the death of his own brother and had perhaps fed him alive to hyenas in the game park.

Without retiring to deliberate, the court returned a unanimous verdict of guilty on all counts. Benjamin, who was not a member of the court-martial, did not join the others at the table and was not called to testify. He spoke not a single word during the proceedings. When Ga, who had also been silent, was asked if he had anything to say before the sentence was pronounced, he laughed. But it was a very small laugh.

The prisoner was delivered to Benjamin for immediate execution. After this the court-martial reconvened as the Council of the High Command, and in Ga's presence—or, more accurately, as if Ga no longer existed and had been rendered invisible—elected the chief of staff of the army as acting head of state and government. Benjamin kept his old job, his old title, his old powers, and presumably, his pension.

I wish I could tell you for the sake of symmetry that Ga died the kind of barbarous death that he had decreed for others, that Benjamin fed him like a Thomson's gazelle to the cheetahs or gashed his flesh and set a pack of hyenas on him under the stadium lights. But nothing of the sort happened.

What happened was this. The generals and admirals and justices and the others got into their cars and drove away. Ga, Benjamin, the sergeant, the two constables, and I went outside. We walked across the palace grounds, Ga limping in his chains, away from the palace, over the lawns. Animals in the zoo stirred. Something growled as it caught our scent. Only the animals took an interest in what was happening. The constables guarding the palace stayed at their posts. The servants had vanished. Looking back at the palace I had the feeling that it was completely empty.

When we came to a place that was nearly out of sight of the palace—the white mansion glowed like a toy in the distance—we stopped. The constables let go of Ga and stepped away from him. Ga said something to Benjamin in what sounded to me like the same language that Benjamin and the sergeant spoke to each other. Benjamin walked over to Ga and bent his head. Ga whispered something in his ear.

Benjamin made a gesture. The sergeant vanished. So did the two constables. I made as if to go. Benjamin said, "No. Stay." The stadium lights went out. The sun was just below the horizon in the east. I could feel its mass pulling at my bones, and even before it became visible, its heat on my skin.

We walked on, until we could no longer see the presidential palace or light of any kind no matter where we looked. Only moments of darkness remained. Ga sank to his knees, with difficulty because of the chains, and stared at the place where the sun would rise. Briefly, Benjamin placed a hand on his shoulder. Neither man spoke.

The rim of the sun appeared on the horizon. And then with incredible buoyancy and radiance, as if slung from the heavens, the entire star leaped into view. Benjamin stepped back a pace, pointed his Webley at the back of Ga's head, and pulled the trigger. The sound was not loud. Ga's body was thrown forward by the impact of the bullet. Red mist from his wound remained behind, hanging in the air, and seemed to shoot from the edge of the sun, but that was a trick of light.

Benjamin did not examine the corpse or even look at it. I realized he was going to leave it for the hyenas and the jackals and the vultures and the many other creatures that would find it.

Benjamin said to me, "You have seen everything. Tell them in Washington."

"All right," I said. "But tell me why."

Benjamin said, "You know why, Mr. Brown."

He walked away. I followed him, not sure I could find my way out of this scrubby wilderness without him but not sure, either, whether he was going back to civilization or just going back.

SECTION 7(A)

(OPERATIONAL)

Lee Child

THE TEAM FIRST came together late one Tuesday evening in my apartment. There was none of the usual gradualism about the process; I had none of them, and then I had all of them. Their sudden appearance as a complete unit was certainly gratifying, but also unexpected, and therefore I was less immediately grateful than perhaps I could have been, or should have been, because I was immediately on guard for negative implications. Was I being rolled? Had they come with an established agenda? I had begun the process days before, in the normal way, which was to make tentative approaches to the key players, or at least to let it be known that I was in the market for certain *types* of key players, and normally the process would have continued over a number of weeks, in an accretional way, a commitment secured here, a second commitment there, with an accompanying daisy chain of personal recommendations and suggestions, followed by patient recruitment of specialist operators, until all was finally in place.

But they all came at once. I was reluctant to let myself believe such an event was a response to my reputation; after all, my reputation has neither increased nor decreased in value for many years, and I never met a response like that before. Nor, I felt, could it be a response to my years of experience; the truth was I had long ago transitioned to the status of an old hand, and generally I felt my appeal had been dulled by overfamiliarity. Which was why I looked the gift horse in the mouth: as I said, I was suspicious. But I observed that they seemed not to know one another, which was reassuring, and which removed my fears of a prior conspiracy against me, and they were certainly appropriately attentive to me: I got no feeling that I was to be a passenger on my own ship. But I remained suspicious nonetheless, which slowed things down; and I think I might even have offended them a little, with my slightly tepid response. But: better safe than sorry, which I felt was a sentiment I could rely on them to understand.

My living room is not small—it was two rooms before I removed a wall—but even so, it was somewhat crowded. I was on the sofa that gets the view, smoking, and they were facing me in a rough semicircle, three of them shoulder to shoulder on the sofa that faces mine, and the others on furniture brought in from other rooms, except for two men I had never met before, who stood side by side close behind the others. They were both tall and solid and dark, and they were both looking at me with poor-bloody-infantry expressions on their faces, partly resigned and stoic, and partly appealing, as if they were pleading with me not to get them killed too soon. They were clearly foot soldiers—which, obviously, I needed—but they weren't the hapless, runty, conscripted kind: indeed, how could they be? They had volunteered, like everyone else. And they were fine physical specimens, no doubt trained and deadly in all the ways I would need them to be. They wore suit coats, of excellent quality in terms of cut and cloth, but rubbed and greasy where they were tight over ledges of hard muscle.

There were two women. They had dragged the counter stools in from the kitchen, and they were perched on them, behind and to the right of the three men on the sofa—a kind of mezzanine seating arrangement. I admit I was disappointed that there were only two of them: a mix of two women and eight men was borderline unacceptable by the current standards of our trade, and I was reluctant to open myself to criticism that could have been avoided at the start. Not public criticism, of course—the public was generally almost completely unaware of what we did—but insider criticism, from the kind of professional gatekeepers who could influence future assignments. And I wasn't impressed by the way the women had positioned themselves slightly behind the men: I felt it spoke of the kind of subservience I would normally seek to avoid. They were very nice to look at, though, which delighted me at the time, but only reinforced my anticipation of later carping. Both wore skirts, neither one excessively short, but their perching on high stools showed me more thigh than I felt they intended. They were both wearing dark nylons, which I readily admit is my favorite mode of dress for shapely legs, and I was truly distracted for a moment. But then I persuaded myself—on a provisional basis only, always subject to confirmation—that they were serious professionals, and would indeed be seen as such, and so for the time being I let my worries go, and I moved on.

The man on the right of the group had brought in the Eames lounge chair from the foyer, but not the ottoman. He was sitting in the chair, leaning back in its contour with his legs crossed at the knee, and he made an elegant impression. He was wearing a gray suit. I assumed from the start that he was my government liaison man, and I was proved right. I had worked with many similar men, and I felt I could take his habits and abilities on trust. Mistakes are made that way, of course, but I was confident I wasn't making one that night. The only thing that unsettled me was that he had positioned his chair an inch further away from the main group than was strictly necessary. As I said, my living room is not small, but neither is it infinitely spacious: that extra inch had been hard won. Clearly it spoke of a need or an attitude, and I was aware from the start that I should pay attention to it.

My dining chairs are the Tulip design by the Finnish designer Eero Saarinen; both now flanked the sofa opposite me and were occupied by men I assumed were my transport coordinator and my communications expert. Initially I paid little attention to the men, because the chairs themselves had put me in a minor fugue: Saarinen had, of course, also designed the TWA Flight Center at John F. Kennedy Airport—or Idlewild, as it was called at the time—which building had quite rightly become an icon, and an absolute symbol of its era. It recalled the days when the simple word *jet* meant much more than merely a propulsive engine. Jet plane, jet set, jet travel . . . the new Boeing 707, impossibly fast and sleek, the glamour, the larger horizons, the bigger world. In my trade we all know we are competing with the legends whose best work—while not necessarily *performed* in—was indisputably *rooted* in that never-to-be-repeated age. Periodically I feel completely inadequate to the challenge, and indeed for several minutes that particular evening I felt like sending everyone away and giving up before I had even started.

But I reassured myself by reminding myself that the new world is challenging, too, and that those old-timers might well run screaming if faced with the kind of things we have to deal with now—like male-to-female ratios, for instance, and their mutual interactions. So I stopped looking at the chairs and started looking at the men, and I found nothing to worry about. Frankly, transport is an easy job—merely a matter of budget, and I had no practical constraint on what I was about to spend. Communications get more complex every year, but generally a conscientious engineer can handle what is thrown at him. The popular myth that computers can be operated only by pierced youths whose keyboards are buried under old pizza boxes and skateboards is nonsense, of course. I have always used exactly what had arrived: a serious technician with a measured and cautious manner.

On my left on the sofa opposite me was what I took to be our mole. I was both pleased with and worried by him. Pleased, in the sense that it was obvious he had been born in-country, almost certainly in Tehran or one of its closer suburbs. That was indisputable. His DNA was absolutely correct; I was sure it was absolutely authentic. It was what lay over his DNA that worried me. I was sure that when I investigated further I would find he had left Iran at a young age and come to America. Which generally makes for the best moles: unquestioned ethnic authenticity, and unquestioned loyalty to our side. But—and perhaps I am more sensitive to this issue than my colleagues—those formative years in America leave physical traces as well as mental ones. The vitamin-enriched cereals, the milk, the cheeseburgers—they make a difference. If, for instance, due to some bizarre circumstance, this young man had a twin brother who had been left behind, and I now compared them side by side, I had no doubt our mole would be at least an inch taller and five pounds heavier than his sibling. No big deal, you might say, in the vernacular, and I might agree—except that the *kind* of inch and the *kind* of pound does matter. A big, self-confident, straight-backed *American* inch matters a great deal. Five *American* pounds—in the chest and the shoulders, not the gut—matter enormously. Whether I had time to make him lose the weight and correct the posture remained to be seen. If not, in my opinion, we would be going into action with a major source of uncertainty at the very heart of our operation. But then, when in our business have we ever not?

At the other end of the sofa opposite me was our traitor. He was a little older than middle-aged, unshaven, a little fat, a little gray, dressed in a rumpled suit that was clearly the product of foreign tailoring. His shirt was creased and buttoned at the neck and worn without a tie. Like all traitors he would be motivated by either ideology, or money, or blackmail. I hoped it would prove to be money. I'm suspicious of ideology. Of course it gives me a warm feeling when a man risks everything because he thinks my country is better than his; but such a conviction car-ries with it the smack of fanaticism, and fanaticism is inherently unstable, even readily changeable: in the white heat of a fanatic's mind, even an imagined slight of the most trivial kind can pro-duce mulish results. Blackmail is inherently changeable too: what is an embarrassment one day might not always be. Think back to those jet-set days: homosexuality and honey-trap infi-delities produced riches beyond measure. Would we get a tenth of the response today? I think not. But money always works. Money is addictive. Recipients get a taste for it, and they can't quit. Our boy's inside information would clearly be absolutely crucial, so I hoped he was bought and paid for, otherwise we would be adding a second layer of uncertainty into the mix. Not, as I said, that there isn't always uncertainty at the heart of what we do: but too much is too much. It's as simple as that.

Between the mole and the traitor was the man clearly des-tined to lead the operation. He was what I think we would all want in that position. Privately I believe that a cross-referenced graph of the rise and fall of mental versus physical capabilities in men would show a clear composite peak at about the age of thirty-five. Previously—when I have had a choice, that is—I have worked with men not younger than that and not older than forty. I estimated that the man facing me fell neatly in that range. He was compact, neither light nor heavy, clearly comfortable in his mind and body, and clearly comfortable with his range of competencies. Like a Major League second baseman, perhaps. He knew what he was doing, and he could keep on doing it all day, if he had to. He was not handsome, but not ugly either; again, the athletic comparison was, I felt, apt.

He said, "I'm guessing this is my show."

I said, "You're wrong. It's mine."

I wasn't sure exactly how to characterize the way he had spo-ken: was he a humble man pretending not to be? Or was he an arrogant man pretending to be humble pretending not to be?

Obviously it was a question I needed to settle, so I didn't speak again. I just waited for his response.

It came in the form of an initial physical gesture: he patted the air in front of him, right-handed, his wrist bent and his palm toward me. It was a motion clearly intended to calm me, but it was also a gesture of submission, rooted in ancient habits: he was showing me he wasn't armed.

"Of course," he said.

I mirrored his gesture: I patted the air, wrist bent, palm open. I felt the repetition extended the meaning; I intended the gesture to say, Okay, no harm, no foul, let's replay the point. It interested me that I was again unconsciously thinking in terms of sports metaphors. But this was a team, after all.

I said out loud, "You're the leader *in the field*. You're my eyes and ears. You have to be, really. I can't know what you don't know. But let's be clear. No independent action. You might be the eyes and the ears, but I'm the brain."

I probably sounded too defensive, and unnecessarily so: casting modesty aside, as one must from time to time, I was, after all, reasonably well known among a narrow slice of interested parties for my many successful operations in charge of a notably headstrong individual. I was competent in my role, no question. I should have trusted myself a little more. But it was late, and I was tired.

The government liaison man rescued me. He said, "We need to talk about exactly what it is we're going to do."

Which surprised me for a moment: why had I assembled a team before the mission was defined? But he was right: beyond the fact that we would be going to Iran—and let's face it, today all of us go to Iran—no details had yet been settled.

The traitor said, "It has to be about nuclear capability."

One of the women said, "Of course—what else is there, really?"

I noted that she had a charming voice. Warm, and a little

intimate. In the back of my mind I wondered if I could use her in a seduction role. Or would that get me in even more trouble, with the powers that be?

The communications man said, "There's the issue of regional influence. Isn't that important? But hey, what do I know?"

The government man said, "Their regional influence depends entirely on their nuclear threat."

I let them talk like that for a spell. I was happy to listen and observe. I saw that the two bruisers at the back were getting bored. They had above-my-pay-grade looks on their faces. One of them asked me, "Can we go? You know the kind of thing we can do. You can give us the details later. Would that be okay?"

I nodded. It was fine with me. One of them looked back from the door with his earlier expression: Don't get us killed too soon.

The poor bloody infantry. Silently I promised him not to. I liked him. The others were still deep in discussion. They were twisting and turning and addressing this point and that. The way the Eames chair was so low to the ground, it put the government man's face right next to the right-hand woman's legs. I envied him. But he wasn't impressed. He was more interested in filtering everything that was said through the narrow lens of his own concerns. At one point he looked up at me and asked me directly: "How much State Department trouble do you want exactly?"

Which wasn't as dumb a question as it sounded. It was an eternal truth that very little of substance could be achieved without upsetting the State Department to some degree. And we worked with liaison men for that very reason: they quelled the storm long enough to let us conclude whatever operation was then in play. I thought his question implied an offer: he would do what it took. Which I thought was both generous and brave.

I said, "Look, all of you. Obviously I'll try to make the whole thing as smooth and trouble-free as possible. But we're all grown-ups. We know how it goes. I'll ask for the extra mile if I have to."

Whereupon the transport coordinator asked a related but more mundane question: "How long are we signing up for?"

"Eighty days," I said. "Ninety, maximum. But you know how it is. We won't be in play every day. I want you all to map out a six-month window. I think that's realistic."

Which statement quieted things down a little. But in the end they all nodded and agreed. Which, again, I thought was brave. To use another sports metaphor, they knew the rules of the game. An operation that lasted six months, overseas in hostile territory, was certain to produce casualties. I knew that, and they knew that. Some of them wouldn't be coming home. But none of them flinched.

There was another hour or so of talk, and then another. I felt I got to know them all as well as I needed to. They didn't leave until well into the morning. I called my editor as soon as they were through the door. She asked me how I was, which question from an editor really means, "What have you got for me?"

I told her I was back on track with something pretty good, and that a six-month deadline should see it through. She asked what it was, and I told her it was something that had come to me while I was high. I used the tone of voice I always use with her. It leaves her unsure whether I am kidding or not. So she asked again. I said I had the characters down, and that the plot would evolve as it went along. Iran, basically. As a private joke I couched the whole thing in the kind of language we might see in the trade reviews, if we got any: I said it wouldn't transcend the genre, but it would be a solid example of its type.

DESTINY CITY

James Grady

FOUR MEN WALKED through the December night along tracks for Washington, D.C.'s subway and Amtrak trains that rumble through America. Their shoes crunched gravel. *Musica ranchera* drifted from a nearby industrial park where Sami, who drove a taxi, remembered signs for a Latino ballroom.

"When?" Maher was a California blond born with the name Michael.

"Soon," said Ivan, their Ameer.

Zlatko said: "Ameer, I have money for my last buys tomorrow."

"Brother, I can drive you with my taxi," said Sami.

"No," said Ivan. "Work alone. Let no one see us as fingers of a fist."

"A fist is five," said Maher. "I thought there were only us four."

"Jihad is the thumb that shapes us," proclaimed their Ameer.

Sami said, "Someone's coming."

A trio of hombres swaggered toward them through the darkness.

"*Hola,* amigos," said that trio's jefe. "What you doing here, *eh?*"

"Leaving," said Sami.

"Don' thin' so." Jefe soured the night with his beer and tequila breath. "You gringos got lots of nowhere to run."

His tallest *compañero* frowned. "Not gringos. Only the blond *guero*."

"Who cares?" Jefe drew a black pistol. "Tool up, Juan."

The third Hispanic fumbled inside his coat's back collar.

Maher jumped Juan as he unsheathed a machete.

Jefe blinked—and Sami ripped the pistol from him with a move taught in al Qaeda's Afghan camps, while Zlatko and Maher wrestled the machete from Juan.

Ivan relieved Sami of the gun. "See what they have."

"Amigos!" said Jefe as Sami searched the three thugs, made them kneel on the gravel. "We all just joking, *sí*?"

Maher said, "Shut up, motherfucker!"

Sami gave confiscated cell phones, cash, and IDs to Ivan. Zlatko threw away the machete.

"Let's go," whispered Sami. "They can't tell anybody anything."

"Whach you sayin'?" called out the kneeling jefe.

Ivan whispered, "They are *kuffars*. Unbelievers."

"That is not enough." Zlatko shrugged. "But they saw we don't belong—especially with Maher."

"They can't tell police or FBI or CIA," said Sami. "They don't dare."

"You talkin' FBI? *La migra*? Don' fuck with us! We MS-13!"

Ivan said, "Loose ends. They'll tell someone. And America is full of ears."

He put the pistol in Maher's hands. The blond kid stared at it. Stared at three men kneeling before him. The night floated their clouds of breath.

Ivan told him, "You asked *when*. Allah granted you the answer."

Maher fired three flash-cracking shots. The thugs crumpled into the gravel.

Ameer Ivan led his followers away from the trackside executions. He gave Zlatko the gun. Distributed the dead men's cash to all of his soldiers. Sami saw Zlatko tuck his bills inside an envelope he returned to his jacket's outside right pocket.

The Ameer tossed the thugs' cell phones. Plastic clattered on unseen rocks.

Maher staggered away from his comrades. Vomited.

"Be proud, Maher." The Ameer wrapped an arm around the youngest man's shoulders. "Diverting the enemy with the gun let us attack." Maher mumbled, "I went wild in my mind."

"And learned a key lesson," said the Ameer. "Timing. *When* is *now*, and if all goes well with Zlatko's work . . . three days."

"*Three days?*" said Sami. "Are you sure, Ameer?"

"Yes." They neared the gap in the chain-link fence. "And only we four know."

"And Allah," said Zlatko.

"Sami," said the Ameer, "keep that *vaquera* in your control."

"She is no problem," said Sami.

They left the tracks for a street that was once a route from the capital to a rural town. Now *city* sprawled from Congress's white dome to far beyond D.C.'s Beltway.

Ivan stood alone by a roadside white pole, an ordinary, forty-ish man waiting for the bus that took him to his gold SUV stashed among a multiplex's moviegoer machines.

When the bus rolled out of sight, his three warriors walked from the shadows to a Metro subway station. Sami made Maher stand alone on the platform. Zlatko's nod approved such trade-craft for the cameras mounted on the platform's ceiling.

A silver subway train snaked to a stop. Maher carelessly drifted onto the same car as Zlatko and Sami. Words bounced in his eyes. Sami's glare welded the young man's jaws shut.

The subway slid out of the station. Zlatko sat between Sami and the window. They memorized their fellow passengers: A black guy bopping to earphone music. Two Spanish-babbling women dressed like office cleaners. A white-haired security guard.

Zlatko whispered, "Brother Maher did well, though not like our karate school teaches. But he would not last fifteen minutes in interrogation. He needs to tell. Get fame so he can be real. I worry that he'll always be a born American."

"Our Ameer must know what he's doing, choosing Maher."

"The smallest cog turns the whole assembly." His engineer past haunted Zlatko's words. "But, *brother*, that is not what troubles me most."

Brake squeals killed Sami's question. The train stopped. Zlatko and Maher stood to leave the train for wherever they would spend that night, facts the jihad brothers did not share amongst themselves.

Sami stood to let Zlatko pass. Pick-pocketed the money envelope.

Zlatko stepped onto the platform.

The train slid away.

Sami rode to a neighborhood known for vegetarians, PEACE lawn signs, and citizens who thought the 1960s meant something holy. A bus took him to twin high-rises on a smog-soaked hill.

A high-rise elevator clunked him to its ninth floor. He entered his one-room apartment and closed the door with a *thunk* for any eavesdropper. Fought for breath. *You're clear! Clear!* He eased back into the hall. Glided down the stairwell like a shadow.

In the basement, Sami dialed open the combination lock on an electric breaker box. Left the Glock pistol on the box shelf. Turned on the shelf's cell phone, texted a four-word message. Grabbed keys for a stashed car, drove toward the white dome center of town, and parked by a brick building with a peeling sign for Belfield Casket Company. The coffin factory's door flew open.

Harry Mizell—who looked like a bear—waved Sami inside.

Harry and boyish FBI agent Ted escorted Sami through the

beehive of cubicles where men and women monitored computers and whispered into phones.

They sat Sami at a conference table in a windowless room. Video cameras clung to the walls. Sami imagined the scene transmitting to the aging H-shaped CIA headquarters, to Homeland Security's new complex in a powerful congressman's district, to the FBI. Maybe even to the White House.

Sami wondered if the private contractor Argus, whose ID dangled from Harry's neck, got a direct feed.

As COOK—Case Officer/Operation Control—Harry debriefed. Ted, who wore the FBI ID Harry had forsaken, sat mute at the table.

Sami told Harry, Ted, and the cameras about the murders. About *when*. Put the pick-pocketed envelope on the table. Told Harry, Ted, and the cameras what they had to do *now, right now*.

Harry said, "When you texted 'Crash Exfilt Base Soonest,' we cocked to rock. *Now . . .* now you sit tight. Relax."

Harry left the room. Left the FBI agent in charge of their spy. The glass eye of a video camera captured Sami's slump.

Ted cleared his throat. "Do you want a soft drink?"

"A soft drink?"

The FBI agent nodded yes.

"No, Ted. I don't want a soft drink."

Hmmm. The room's CTSU—Covert Transmission Suppression Unit.

"Sami," said Ted, "I pray for you every day."

"You don't know how much that means to me."

The FBI agent nodded. "God's work."

"So they tell me."

Ted let Sami go to the bathroom alone. The fluorescent retreat smelled of ammonia and angst. Sami washed his hands, face. Stared into the sink's mirror. *Was there a camera behind that glass?*

An hour later, Harry returned. "Bottom line, our op is still running."

"*What?*" Sami whirled to the video cameras. "We've got them *right now* on triple murder charges! Scoop them up!"

"Bosses say we need to find who's behind the cell, al Qaeda or—"

"There is no mastermind link! No organizational chart like we've got. That's mirror reasoning. These guys are homegrown! Self-contained."

"So you say, and I'm inclined to agree, but . . . " Harry got up from the table, disconnected the visible cameras. "Ted, leave us alone."

"I'm the FBI liaison and thus the official presence for—"

"Ted, Homeland Security outsourced Argus Inc. to run this op. I'm Argus's archangel. Go write a cover-your-ass e-mail about how I kicked you out."

The door closed on Ted's exit.

"Realize what we've got here," said Harry.

"You were CIA special ops in JAWBREAKER hunting al Qaeda in A-stan. CIA used your real Beirut life, snuck you in with captured Taliban guys our Paki allies freed. For years, you've worked your terrorist bona fides all over the globe.

"Just like your buddy Zlatko. After Bosnia, he pops up look-ing for phony papers in Rose's outlaw gig. She's righteous enough to call her ex-FBI buddy, *moi*. My clout jerks you from CIA to Homeland Security. We put you next to Zlatko at Rose's. He brings you to Ivan, a Chechen physician who found Zlatko at the night school English class where Ivan teaches *and* fishes. Ivan had already hooked that goofy suburban kid who showed up at a mosque before they shoved Ivan out as a false Muslim.

"And presto," said Harry, "we've penetrated a terrorist cell. A cell that's going to attack in three days. And with ninety-three Islamic terrorist groups on our radar, our bosses are convinced this cell has got to be somebody's baby. Those sponsors are who we want."

"Three people got murdered *tonight*. That's enough!"

"Those thugs don't count right now."

"So we won't tell the local cops? What about those men's families? Hell, if they are MS-13, those murders could spark a street war!"

"Terrorists are America's number-one priority. Ivan compartmentalizes. He might have other soldiers. Something even the hard boys can't sweat out of him."

"They're going to hit on Christmas Eve!"

"Is it coordinated? What's their target? Their method?"

"Take them down, Harry. Get me out."

"We all want out. But we are where we are. This op—"

"No, not this op. *Everything*. I want all the way out. Now."

"Oh." Harry leaned back. "I can't make you spy. But bottom line, our gov bosses are going to let the cell run to get what they want whether it's there or not. Without you on the bricks, without me as COOK, will guys like Ted do it right?"

"Not my problem."

"My company and I get paid big bucks however this breaks. But I want to nail this job. I'm no walk-away guy. What kinda guy are you?"

That image sat at the conference table like a giant question mark.

Sami blinked. "Three days—and *before* they pull a trigger."

"Damn straight. So what are you going to do?"

Sami stood to leave, took the pick-pocketed cash. Told Harry, "I'm going to fuck with them."

The next morning Sami worked his cab between Capitol Hill and glistening downtown. Such fares made him remember his high school senior class trip to "our nation's capital," how "the Hill" had been open driveways looping past the vanilla ice-cream Capitol. White-shirted congressional cops looked like marshmallow men.

That post–9/11 *routine* December morning, concrete barricades blocked all vehicle approaches to the white marble heart of Congress. Steel barriers funneled pedestrians past barbell-muscled, black jumpsuited, mirror-sunglassed sentinels with M4 assault rifles or shotguns strapped across their armored chests.

But it's not Beirut, he thought. *Not yet. I can stop that clock.*

At 10:07, he flipped down the ON CALL visor sign. Drove to an Asian fusion restaurant where lunch for one cost enough to feed a shantytown Malaysian family. Parked in the alley so he faced the restaurant's service door.

10:11: Two cooks walked past his cab and into the restaurant. 10:13: A sixtyish Vietnamese man in a busboy's black shirt and pants took a Saigon second to scan the vehicle crouched near his destination. 10:14: Zlatko strolled into the alley carrying a dish-washer's white apron and a flat expression. Used the restaurant's back door. 10:21: Zlatko appeared in the cab's mirrors, arms by his side, coming toward the blue taxi on a circular route justified, Sami guessed, by the bummed cigarette tucked above non-smoker Zlatko's right ear.

Zlatko got in the back of the cab.

Right behind me! Can't see his hands!

Sami said, *"As-salaam alaykum."*

"Why are you here?" Zlatko's eyes burned in the rearview mirror.

"On the subway, you said you are troubled. We are brothers. I came to help."

"And that is all? No confession?"

"What do either of us have to confess?"

Zlatko shrank in the backseat.

"On the train, I was worried our Ameer has confusion about what is righteous and *halal*. What is *haram* and not permitted. How the Koran forbids killing innocents, women, and children, so the planes that hit the towers, the one crashed in that green field, they must be *haram*. The Pentagon plane, against soldiers, *yes*, *halal*, and civilians there who served the soldiers, unavoidable. Loose ends or contingency casualties. But instead of worrying about our Ameer, I should have paid attention to my own duties."

Zlatko shook his head. "Last night I lost our money envelope."

"*Wait*: You thought *I* stole it?"

"Ours is a wicked world. I saw the bodies of my wife, two daughters, son. Saw what my *neighbors* had done to us Muslims in our Bosnian town while I was out riding my bicycle thinking about the Olympics. . . . Forgive me: I feared this *kuffar* world around us had swallowed your soul. But it is I who lost the money. Have endangered our mission."

"You are not to blame for accidents." Sami let his mercy sink in, then threw out a hook. "Have you told our Ameer?"

"Not yet."

"How much money do you need?"

"All of my end should cost around $950. I've spent about $600. All the rest plus the extra from last night was in the lost envelope."

"I have $147. If I hustle now, my taxi can make the rest."

"You are a true brother! I will be waiting down the block in that grocery store parking lot at 2:05."

As Zlatko left the cab, out of his sleeve popped a restaurant butcher knife.

That's why he sat behind me.

He let Zlatko sweat until 2:19, then raced the taxi into the grocery store lot. Zlatko told him, "Radio Shack on Georgia Avenue."

There Zlatko made Sami wait in the parked taxi. Sami kept a window open to hear the street. An instrumental "Jingle Bells" from a store competed with a man ringing a handheld bell by a red bucket.

Cari Jones defied her dark hair with blonde highlights, wore a black leather trench coat, marched past the taxi telling her cell phone, "Soon as I get there, Mom'll say it's great I have a career, but my baby clock . . ."

Zlatko put packages in the taxi's backseat. Climbed in front with one Radio Shack sack, told Sami to drop him off on a corner different from any the Homeland Security/FBI/outsourced street dogs had trailed him to before they broke off surveillance to avoid spooking the streetwise warrior.

Zlatko pulled two prepaid cell phones from the sack, fished out the manual, saying, "*Yes,* call-waiting, call-conferencing, call-blocking . . ."

He looked at Sami. "In Baghdad, we learned you don't want to be holding the right cell phone when someone dials a wrong number."

After he left Zlatko, Sami drove eleven blocks to find a pay phone. Twenty minutes later as he cruised up North Capitol Street, Sami drove past a waving ebony-skinned lawyer in an Italian suit to pick up a white man who looked like a rumpled bear.

"I wish your Ameer let you guys carry cell phones," said Harry as he settled in the back of Sami's taxi.

"No cell phones. Coded messages on Facebook from computers at libraries, Staples, and Internet cafés."

"But Zlatko just bought two phones. 'Course, it's in the rule book that every black ops honcho, spy runner, and Ameer lies to his button boys."

"Every case officer lies? Even you?"

"I play by my rules." Harry winked. "We've got our geniuses reverse-engineering Zlatko's latest buys from that Radio Shack."

The rearview mirror showed Sami a tan sedan.

"It's Ted," said Harry. "Don't shake him, okay? He's learning. He's got to. FBI, CIA, Uncle Sam's top street shooters are turning in their papers, going private, getting outsource-contracted back to do the same job at twice their government paychecks."

"Private armies fight for private profit. Government is about citizens carrying their public weight."

"When did Sami start caring about how Uncle Sam works?"

"I'm almost straight, remember? After your geniuses report, you'll have the *who, when,* and *how.* You can take down the cell. I can fly free."

Sami fed the taxi into traffic up Constitution Avenue past Smithsonian museums.

A dead pigeon lay in their traffic lane. Sami saw a sunbaked soldier named John Herne standing on the corner, staring at the fallen bird as if it hid a bomb.

"Look at this town," said Harry. "I remember when this was an AM radio burg where white folks were scared to come out after dark and Nixon had his finger on the Doomsday trigger. 'Top dollar' meant a civil service paycheck. Nobody was from D.C. People came here as cause-humpers. Now, crash or no crash, all the big money has a D.C. cash register.

"Some say we're inevitable. Like Rome, only adjusted for the Internet and Mister Glock .40. I say if we create a Sophia Loren like Rome did, let the 'D.C.' of Washington stand for 'Destiny City.'"

"My jihad brothers say the same thing. So do Ted and his evangelical crusaders."

"What do you say?"

"That real people are trapped in those big ideas."

"Yeah, but what about Sophia Loren?"

The two men laughed.

"D.C. is your story, Sami. *Destiny City.* Born and bred for it. Spy life and street action are all you know. What makes you think you can quit?"

Harry's cell phone rang. He took the call. Listened. Clicked off.

Told Sami, "Our geniuses got no idea what Zlatko is building. We're flooding every Radio Shack kinda place with agents and Zlatko's photos to see what he bought before, but it's elbow-to-elbow Christmas rush in those stores."

They rode past a block strung with colored bulbs.

"In this life," said Harry, "you're either doing something or something's getting done to you. What's your deal, Sami?"

Sami let Harry out of the cab, drove to a commercial strip where French and African patois jammed with Spanish. Cruising cars blasted gangsta rap idolized by white Kansas teenagers. Sami parked his cab in the lot of a four-story commercial building.

He checked his watch: 4:29. Ivan usually closed his doctor's office at 5:00 and drove his gold SUV home. Sami scanned ethnic stores, discount furniture barns, a veterinary hospital with a green Dumpster. Told himself he couldn't see flies circling the emerald steel. Wondered where Harry'd set up the surveillance posts. Wondered if they'd called in his presence, if a satellite snapped his picture.

"Understand our new spy biz," Harry had told Sami. "Sure, satellite surveillance of Doc Ivan's office and house is overkill, but it's about buy-in.

"We got something real, but if it's only a Homeland/CIA/FBI-outsourced Argus show, with sixteen major spy shops dancing for the old U.S. of A., we might be weak on bureaucratic muscle. So I partnered my company with a contractor for the National Applications Office to satellite monitor your Ameer. Now NAO'll line up to make sure we get what we want so they can share our credit."

I'm a taxi driver, thought Sami. *I take you where you want to go.*
I'm a spy. I take you where you want to go.

At 4:47, a brown medical transport services van parked at the building. The driver in a white uniform got out to lower the electric motored stairs.

They shuffled out of the building. Some were black, some brown. A wispy blonde girl on crutches swung toward the van. They were all poor. The bottom line mattered as much as any for two women in black burkas that exposed only their eyes.

Last out of the door came Ivan, a doctor who didn't care about health insurance, charged what patients could afford for what he could do. Sometimes, like now, that meant walking a white-haired old lady to the van.

Sami parked behind the van, pulled on a black Detroit Tigers baseball cap to hide his face as he joined his Ameer and the old lady.

"Taxi," said Sami.

Ivan kept the poise of an emergency room boss. "Here you go, Mrs. Callaghan."

The white-haired old lady wrinkled her brow. "But . . . I didn't order a cab."

"You've got a voucher for today," said her doctor. "Remember?"

"I do?"

"Yes."

The white uniformed van driver took his cue from Doc Ivan. The stairs' electric motor whined, the doors shut, and away drove the brown van.

Her doctor said, "Emma, did you drop your gloves in the elevator?"

The old lady looked at her trembling bird hands. "I must have."

"I'll wait with the cabbie. Take your time."

She toddled back inside the building.

"Ameer, I must confess," blurted Sami. He told him about breaking the rules to confront a worried Zlatko and replace the lost money.

"But why are you here now?"

"I fear that Zlatko's vision of what is acceptable for our target and the vision you and I share . . . I fear a conflict of faith. I have seen this before."

"In Beirut," said the Ameer, "where holy martyrs blew up the Marines' barracks and Ronald Reagan slunk away. There we learned Americans will back down. Then sex-crazy Clinton ran from one Black Hawk helicopter crash, missed Osama with missiles."

The Ameer put a fatherly hand on Sami's shoulder. "Sometimes it's easiest for a soldier not to know all, so if his heart is challenged, his conscience is clear. Don't worry about Zlatko. He will do what must be done. His part will not pain his soul. All else is sacrifice to contain this disease called America. Americans fear death. Their overreaction to us will force our misguided Muslim brothers to rally to our true path."

"What of my part, Ameer? I have done so little."

"You are whispered about online." The doctor smiled, so Sami knew the legend birthed by the CIA still lived. "Praise Allah that I work in a building where if you make friends, keys are shared. With my colleagues at the medical imaging office. With two *kuffars* who repair computers that are probably stolen."

Dozens of computers! Untraceable! That's how he makes contacts!

"I dared not put you too close to the operation. If your fame attracted attention. . . . But in two days, we will both be heroes on the run."

The building's glass doors showed Emma tottering toward them.

The Ameer told Sami what to do that night at the *vaquera*'s. Told Sami where to go tomorrow morning.

Emma wiggled her gloved hands. "They were in my pockets!" Sami drove her home, refused a tip of her few silver coins.

He drove to a pay phone. Called Harry, told him about the computers, the Ameer's new orders. Argued for the cell to be rolled up. Got told, *"We're gonna let it ride."* Drove to 13th Street's hilltop panorama of Destiny City, parked on a block of row houses where a Latino grocery store flanked a green door.

He pushed the doorbell for the green door. Made a loud *ring*!

Invisible feet clunked down unseen stairs. The door's glass

peephole darkened as someone looked out. The green door opened. Star-streaked midnight hair curled to her blue sweater. She wore faded jeans. Had a clean jaw, high cheekbones with a puckered scar on her heart side from the punch she'd taken in junior high soccer. The scar gave her lips a perpetual sardonic smile. Those fleshy lips along with her desert tribe Jewish Sephardic tan skin and the *Sinaloensa* Mexican she'd perfected while surfing away the summer before law school fooled people into thinking *Rose* was gringo for *Rosalita*.

"I wasn't expecting anyone," said Rose.

Climbing those stairs behind her rounded blue jean hips, Sami smelled Christmas pine, spices like cumin and chili from the downstairs store, perhaps incense, her musk.

Her apartment's main room held a computer, fax, photo-copy machine. An eviction-salvaged sofa. Two chairs separated by a table where Sami had set his tea the morning he'd been offi-cially waiting for a fax from the Taxi Commission but truly wait-ing for Zlatko to return for credit card applications the *vaquera* had promised him.

Sami's eyes swept through the kitchen to the *closed* door for a room lined with law books, government manuals. The door to her bedroom—*closed*. He refused to fear the closed doors. Refused to wonder whether Harry had bugged all of Rose's rooms.

She stood behind Sami. "Are you here for work?"

"Yes."

Shadows filled the apartment. Her walls and fading-gray-light glass windows kept out sounds of the street. Muffled screams.

He lunged with his hands like a *Muay Thai* strike, caught her face in his prayer grasp, and pressed her against the wall as she met his kiss.

Night took the city.

They sat naked in her bed, propped on pillows, covers drawn up. A lamp glowed.

Rose lit a joint. "Do you think Harry figured this would happen?"

"He's practical."

"For your crew, I'm just an inferior woman you seduced to use, but Harry. . . . Maybe he figures, 'What the hell, let them get some happy.'"

"Maybe," said Sami as he watched her take a hit.

Across town in her Virginia apartment, redheaded Lorna Dumas exhaled burnt tobacco, stared at the blue uniform on her bed, thought, *I gotta quit smoking.*

Upstairs from her green door, Rose asked Sami, "Do you still think of yourself as Muslim?"

"Feels like some God is chasing me."

"Nice dodge." Rose passed him the joint.

Sami took a hit.

She said, "Getting stoned puts you in solid with both your jihad and the FBI."

"I always wanted to be popular. What about you?"

"My mother taught my girlfriends how to give a blow job," said Rose. "Made me promise not to have sex until I knew what the hell I was doing.

"Who the hell ever knows what they're doing? I fell for the wrong guy over and over again, became a kick-ass federal prosecutor who one day found a certain *political* slant to her job, spent two years as a public defender, realized that helping unconnected people work the system was the only way they were ever going to get a fair shake.

"So now, I'm the *vaquera.* Don't speak enough English to fill out an immigration form without fucking yourself? Go to the *vaquera.* Work permits, car registration, insurance, your political asylum application with the photo of you minus your arm that got hacked off in Sierra Leone—*hey,* America is the fill-in-the-blank society.

"Then came Zlatko. Everybody lies, but he lied like an antiabortion murderer I interviewed when I was a prosecutor. Hard-core eyes. Plus no way was he Albanian. I can't trust badges, but the tingles made me call my old pal Harry."

She hit the joint, held it to him. "Zlatko found me through the people who snuck here with him from Mexico, right?"

Sami waved away another hit—

—*fluttering wing* vision vanished like smoke.

"Right," said Rose. "I'm not supposed to know anything."

"Be glad you've got no idea what it's like out there."

"I stipulate to a certain degree of unreality. But I'm no virgin."

Sami said, "I knew this kid. His virgin mission, he gets handed killing three guys. Said he went 'wild in his mind.' That's what it's like out there. You live *behind* the world others see. All alone out there on a street full of invisible gunmen is *you*."

"You adopt survival mechanisms," she said.

"Fuck survival. You beat the other guy.

"Beirut. I'm thirteen. Men drove into the neighborhoods, gave us kids AK-47s. I never thought to ask who the ammo really *really* came from. Barricades cut up my home blocks. Sandbags, barbed wire, fuel barrels. Fuck what our parents said, we were cool and saving our world. I learned to run fast, because I was small, and the fucking snipers' priority was wounding kids because that suckers out rescuers.

"One day, down the block at some other crew's barricade, those guys made an old man step out front, hands in the air. We see he's one of us, a Muslim. They tell him to walk to us. So he does, him and us thinking it's a swap. They let him get 'bout nine feet from our sandbags. Shot him dead.

"We couldn't leave cover to pull his body in, so it laid there. After three days, we had to abandon our barricade. The stench. The flies.

"Two weeks, different barricade, same thing—only now it's a teenage Muslim guy just like me, hands up, had taken three steps toward our spot.

"I nailed him. Head shot." Sami paused. "He was dead as soon as he walked my way. I just got to choose his time and place, his meaning."

Night held the city.

"Is that why you left Beirut?" asked Rose.

"PLO guys I idolized took custody of a sniper we captured, set him free. Started me thinking: *Whose side is anybody really on?* Then my father got a job at the Marine barracks. One of our factions blew it and him up. The Marines took care of my family. Put me in a Detroit high school. Soon as I could, I joined the Corps. *Semper fi.*"

"Me, too," she said.

He leaned into a kiss she captured. She kicked off the covers, cupped his hand over her breast. Seven minutes later, he guided her on top of him, straddling him, arcing over him like a quarter moon as he whispered, *"I see you. I see you."*

Afterward, Rose lay across him. "Don't say anything. Neither of us. Not unless we can say it again and again and again."

"Until," he said. *"Until,* not *unless."*

Their flesh goose-bumped. He reached for the sheet and blanket.

"Are you hungry?" she said.

"Not now. Now you have to fall asleep."

"Why?"

"I have to use your computer when you don't know it."

"Oh," she said.

"But I can spend the night."

And he did, his last waking moment echoing a fluttering wing.

A mile away in her *go-to-sleep* teddy bears bedroom, seven-year-old Amy Lewis whispered to her best friend through a cell phone bought for the adventure, "Gramma says I'll really be going to bed a whole three hours later because the world is round!"

Wake up! Sami bolted upright in Rose's bed. Glided through the dark to her main room, grabbed her phone, tapped in the panic number, got routed to a woken bear who heard Sami whisper, "The Ameer! Keys! Medical imaging office! He's got access to—"

"*Fuck!*" Harry killed their call.

Sami calmed his jackhammering heart. Made himself go back to sleep. Have faith in himself and a bear.

Gray clouds covered the morning sky. Sami drove to where the Ameer had sent Maher. Maher waved. *Too friendly for just a cab*, but this feral kid's street skills had beaten Harry's tails. Maher climbed in front. *Another mistake.* Sami thought: *Where do you live? How do you get money? Did you come up with using Facebook?*

"What's that smell?" said Sami as they drove around the Beltway.

"Sorry, chemicals from the dry cleaners. The Koreans are nice. Took me a month to get the job through that Christian youth hostel."

Maher carried a backpack. "The newspaper calls it the Trackside Slaughter. Ballistics say the gun was also used to shoot a gangbanger from the Clifton Terrace crew. The cops can't figure Latino *and* black bodies."

The future filled Maher's eyes. "We'll be something to write about. Brother," he said, "I know Ameer is worried. But I'm chill. He's so smart! Combining what you've got to do with checking me out while I get the last of my shit, *like*, how tight is that?"

"Very tight." Sami grinned. "Is that how American kids say it?"

"Yeah." Suburbia flowed past the taxi. "Look out there. Redondo Beach. Akron where my cousins live. Here. It's all the same TV shows. Stupid news about dumb rich girls who do nothing but get their pictures taken. The holy Jesus in the

Koran, blessed be His name, what if He were driving with us today, seeing all this meaningless crap? We gotta stop all the ruining. If not us, *who*?"

"We're in the same car, my brother."

The gun shop sat in a Beltway exit mall. A pine wreath decorated the barred door. The clerk behind the glass counter wore a holstered Glock and a red Santa Claus hat.

"Hey, guy!" The clerk smiled at Maher. "Good to see you again."

"Yeah." Maher handed the clerk his California driver's license for routine processing by the law with a five-year backlog.

The clerk filled his eyes with nonblond Sami.

"This is my uncle," explained Maher. "He's Jewish."

"Oh, well *Sha-lum Ha-nooka*."

"Shalom," said Sami.

Maher rented a 1911 Colt .45 automatic and ear protectors, bought four boxes of ammo and a black silhouette from a target display that featured a pistol-pointing, grizzled Arab in a burnoose and bumper stickers proclaiming that an aging, antiwar movie actress should *still* be bombed back to Hanoi.

The store's shooting range had ten lanes, three occupied. Gunfire boomed. As Sami shot holes in their target, Maher dumped three boxes of ammo into his backpack.

"The .45s are the biggest bullets," said Maher, taking his turn on the firing line. He showed no post-traumatic stress syndrome from the last time he'd fired a gun.

As they left the gun shop, the clerk said, "Happy New Year!"

At the next mall, the sporting goods store roared with crazed shoppers. Sami gave a clerk the order printed from Rose's computer. The clerk said, "You know these bikes are unassembled in boxes, right?"

"Cheaper that way."

"It's for orphans," said Maher.

"God bless you." The clerk took their cash so they could skip the line.

"Um," said Maher. "Do you guys sell steel cup protectors? You know. For . . . for down there. For hockey."

"I think they're all plastic."

As they carried three bike boxes to the taxi, Sami said, "*Hockey?*"

Maher shrugged. "Won't happen tomorrow, but when I become a holy martyr, the virgins waiting for me in paradise will get one, too. I wanna be able to have kids."

"You want to have children in paradise?"

"Got to be a better place to raise them than here."

They crammed the bike boxes into the taxi. Drove to a subway stop. Only then did Maher relay the Ameer's orders for that night, *where* to be tomorrow, *what* to do precisely *when*. Before he vanished into the crowd, Maher said, "I love you, brother."

Thirty-four minutes later, Harry rode in the taxi beside Sami and said, "Before dawn, NEST black-bagged Ivan's building— not the Nuclear Emergency *Search* Teams, their shadows whose 'S' stands for *Strike*. They pulled all hazmat out of the medical imaging office, substituted fake material, and broke the machines so nobody will wonder when they don't work. We're still balancing records hacked from the office computers, but it looks like all radioactive material is accounted for. Put that together with your horny teenager looking for a metal cup to shield his balls, and they're probably building a put-together-at-the-last-minute dirty bomb."

"So now it won't be dirty, but it'll still be a bomb."

"Yeah, but even if they augment hydrogen peroxide or chemicals from a dry cleaner with gunpowder from bullets, how big could it be?"

"How many deaths add up to 'big'?"

"We don't think that's the point," said Harry. "We know

what Zlatko is building. I posted what we had on A-Space and Intellipedia, the classified sites, set it up like a game. A dozen nerds came up with an Explosive Magnetic Generator of Frequency. The Soviets perfected them. Both Ivan and Zlatko grew up behind the Iron Curtain. A U.S. general challenged some grad students a few years ago, and they designed an EMGF to fit in a pickup truck with a cost of eight hundred dollars—most of it bought from Radio Shack.

"EMGFs are why you turn off your cell phone when you fly. They don't really 'explode,' they beam a sphere of electronic waves that fries unshielded computers, phones, circuit boards for car engines—"

"That's why I'm supposed to turn off my taxi tomorrow at precisely two p.m.!"

"And why you're parking where they told you. That pull-off by the Potomac is across the freeways from the Pentagon. EMGFs are designed to slam the enemy's command and control centers. They're invisible inside any pickup-sized vehicle. . . . "

"Like the Ameer's SUV," said Sami.

"Assemble an EMGF with an electric motor into your shielded vehicle, drive it—hell, *park it*—outside the Pentagon's secure perimeter, turn it on, fry systems all over a mile-thick spherical zone. We'd be burned all the way to Baghdad and A-stan."

"What about the bomb they think is dirty?"

Harry said, "We figure it's a Baghdad doubletap. They park the EMGF vehicle. The longer the EMGF runs, the more it destroys. When SWAT teams figure out what's going on and blitz the source . . . *boom!* Booby-trapped. Radiation is bonus blood."

"And the cell phones?"

"Maybe one of your crew is gonna be a martyr, stay behind, detonate the booby trap when he sees SWAT closing in. That'd be optimum."

"Frying the Pentagon meets Zlatko's conscience. After they ditch the EMGF vehicle, I'll be the walk-to getaway. If my cab engine gets fried, bikes will still work. Three bikes, four brothers, one stay-behind.

"When do we hit them?" said Sami.

The blue taxi crawled through holiday traffic.

"No!" said Sami.

"After dark, the Pentagon gets ringed by camouflaged snake eaters. Tomorrow when your brothers attack, we got 'em. Odds are, we get two alive for interrogation."

"Take them now!"

"Then we get Ivan, but even you don't know where the other two are. We can't let them run free. And if we take them too soon, we won't find out who they report to."

"They answer to no one but themselves! You said you get that!"

"I do—our bosses don't."

"Get the fuck out of my cab."

On that night before Christmas Eve, Sami assembled three bikes in his apartment. He looked around the mattress-on-the-floor hideaway that his Ameer believed had been made safe from discovery by the *vaquera's* tricks, told himself: *No more lying rooms.*

At 9:30, he broke all the rules, used the breaker box phone outside in the night.

Cold kisses wet his skin. He told Rose, "It's starting to snow."

"Too early for holiday clichés. Can't count on the weather."

"Tomorrow starts a whole new season."

"I'm ready," said Rose.

The city went to sleep.

Cari Jones brushed her streaked blonde hair, saw her black leather coat hung ready to go, decided to try computer dating when she got back.

John Herne packed three different pill bottles for post-traumatic stress syndrome in his soldier's duffel at Walter Reed Hospital.

Lorna Dumas decided to let her red hair swing free on her blue uniform tomorrow and threw her cigarettes down her building's trash chute.

Amy Lewis chose her bestest brown teddy bear for Gramma's.

Morning woke Sami to a snow-dusted town.

At ten a.m., he grabbed the cell phone and Glock. Loaded three bikes into his taxi. *They gotta see what they're expecting.* Called Harry, "Launching." Drove his taxi into Christmas Eve snowstorm traffic.

"It's a mess out there," said the man on news/traffic radio. "Washingtonians have never figured out how to drive in the snow, and we weren't expecting this storm."

Sami flashed on the Beirut radio announcer who daily reported which commuter streets were ruled by snipers.

He eased the blue taxi over slick streets: *Fender benders fuck up ops.*

Windshield wipers washed Sami's view as he drove through a whooshing tunnel, popped up on an interstate threaded along the city. Green metal highway signs arrowed routes for I-395 south to Virginia, for exits to the Jefferson Memorial, federal office complexes, the airport, George Washington Parkway, the Pentagon.

Traffic on the bridge over the Potomac parted for the blue taxi obviously headed to the airport, taking that exit—but then unexpectedly pulling off the main road into a tree-lined turnout where the sign read "Roaches Run Waterfowl Sanctuary."

Bad day to be a bird. Sami parked the taxi away from the only other vehicle in the bird-watcher's roost, a battered car with bumper stickers reading "One Planet, One People" and "Audubon Society." A passenger jet roared overhead. Snowflakes died on the warm blue taxi. A husky man wearing a parka stood at tripod-mounted binoculars aimed at the icy gray river, at the highways that blocked a view of the Pentagon.

Parka Man turned to face the taxi and Sami saw he was a bear.

Harry lumbered to the taxi, got in beside the driver. "Anything—*anything*—from your Ameer, the others?"

"What's wrong?"

"It's nearing noon. Attack time is two p.m. Doc Ivan came to work like always. But his SUV is still in its parking spot. Given the traffic, the weather, the time they'll need to fit in the EMGF and some electric motor—"

"Hit him! Hit him now!"

Harry started to protest—barked orders up his sleeve: "COOK to all units: HRT Alpha: Take down Target One. I say again: Hit Target One now! Go! *Go!*"

The idling taxi grew close. Sami shut off the engine. A passenger jet roared overhead. The bear unzipped his parka. The taxi smelled of bike oil and rubber, fading car heater fumes, salty hope.

Harry's eyes lost focus. He listened to his radio earpiece. Blinked.

"Shit!" Harry radioed, "Core plan! Reset to core plan!"

Told Sami, "All they found in Doc Ivan's office was a scared old lady in an examination robe. She's Muslim, did what the doctor ordered. Ivan walked out of the building right under our eyes inside her full burka, rode that charity van to *poof.*

"S'okay," Harry said. "He's just being cagey. Doesn't know we're on him. He'll keep with the plan. We're set if he comes back for his SUV. They'll attack the Pentagon and we'll nail them. Everything's cool, got FBI execs visiting Muslim leaders here to assure them that the busts are legit. It's okay."

Sami said, "I don't know about them having other vehicles!"

"That's the way a cell works. Nobody knows everything."

"Except the guy you let slip away."

"Life is risk. You don't play it that way, you get played." Harry shrugged. "You gotta go with what you know. That's why we have spies."

They sat waiting in the cold until 12:51—*trigger* (time) *minus 69 minutes*.

A tan sedan pulled into the parking lot. Ted raced to the taxi through sleet. Through the lowered driver's window and the hail of ice pellets he said, "An hour till they're due here. We do this now or I have to pull Sami!"

"*What?*" said both Sami and Harry.

"You're six months overdue for your mandatory drug test. Has to be cleared immediately, or we pull you off. I got a portable kit in the car, on-site processing will clear you so you can stay on—"

"This is bullshit!" yelled Sami. "We've got a terrorist attack!"

"I've got orders," said Ted. "The Hoover Building says I'm fired if I don't get this done right *darn* now."

Harry said, "Okay, Ted. He'll be right over."

The FBI liaison ran for the shelter of his tan sedan.

Sami stared at the bear.

"Go do it. Time like this, we all gotta pee."

"If I go . . . I'm gone."

"*Ahh.*" A jetliner roared overhead. Harry smiled. "Fuck them."

The bear used his cell phone.

"Hey, Jenny." He asked Sami for his real name, Social Security number, CIA identifiers. Relayed them to Jenny. Said, "*Crash RIP.*"

Hung up. Grinned at Sami. "Congratulations. Ted's off your case, but give him what he wants or he could still fuck this up. You've been Rebooted In Place, RIP. Now work for Argus. Twice the salary, half the BS."

Harry sent the dazed spy to the tan sedan.

"Sorry," said Ted as Sami filled a plastic bottle with his urine.

Don't give this holier-than-thou bureaucrat the time of—

"This is so stupid," said Ted. "So what if Argus wants to certify—"

"*This came from Argus?* Harry's company?"

"Well . . . sure. This is their show."

Sami left Ted watching liquid change colors in a bottle. Slammed the door when he climbed in the blue taxi. His expression killed the bear's grin.

"Why?" said Sami.

"You're too good to lose."

"I'm quitting! I'm not working for Argus!"

"Sure you are. It'll take a year commitment to get your ass out of the drug-use sling. And *yeah*, don't worry: I'll protect Rose. Why wouldn't I? One more op. You spy as the holy warrior hero who escaped from the Christmas Eve D.C. bust."

"Fuck you!"

"Fucking costs.

"I know what you're thinking," continued Harry. "Going Beirut on me gets you nothing but Uncle Sam's sniper scopes zeroing your back."

The bear said, "I didn't pick any of this war. But I'm not going to lose."

Snowflakes hit the taxi windshield. A jetliner roared overhead. The bear sighed. *T minus 47 minutes.* The choppy gray river lapped against the riprap of the bird sanctuary. Harry relocated Ted's tan sedan next to the bumper-stickered car. *T minus 17.* Pentagon units reported all clear. A jetliner roared. Ted got out of the tan sedan to look through the tripod binoculars.

Sami yelled, "They're not after the Pentagon!"

"*What?*"

"The Ameer doesn't give a shit about our 'command and control.' He hates our whole thing. He wants fear. To humiliate us. Make us overreact. Maher's expecting to live today. Ivan wants to be a hero on the run. He implied that Zlatko's mission is solo and won't bother his beliefs. Zlatko'd love to hit a target like the Pentagon, but he's not coming here. So that's not it. Three bikes: Ivan, Maher, me. Here!"

Harry touched his radio earpiece. Said, "That al Qaeda media group al Sahab, 'the clouds.' NSA just intercepted an e-mail to them via a D.C. server saying that today will be a great day, to watch the skies."

A jetliner roared overhead.

"They know the taxi!" Sami ran toward the tan sedan.

A bear charged his heels.

A Marine sniper popped out of his hide, his rifle hungry for a target.

Harry crammed himself behind the wheel of the tan sedan, Sami dove in the front seat, and Ted jumped in the back, even though he didn't know why. The tan sedan fishtailed out of the bird sanctuary as Harry yelled, "Told you they were linked!"

"Ivan posted bragging rights, not—just drive! Go, go!"

Christmas Eve afternoon on the way to the airport. Falling snow. Cars surging bumper to bumper on a two-lane, one-way road.

"Get around them!" yelled Sami.

Harry whipped the tan sedan onto the shoulder. Horns honked. They ran over a highway reflector pole. Slid past a parked airport police cruiser. Spinning red lights filled their mirrors.

"Call them off!" yelled Sami.

"No unencrypted radios!" Harry yelled into his sleeve at *T minus 13*. "They could have a police band monitor! Cell phone the airport cops!"

Ted yelled, "What are we looking for?"

"We gotta know it when we see it!" said Sami.

The electronic marquee sign mounted over one-way airport traffic read, "Threat Level Code Orange." The digital clock revealed *T minus 11*.

Ronald Reagan National Airport sits across the river from

the white dome of the Capitol. The "old" terminal is a gray concrete box few airlines use. The air-travel gem is the "new" white stone terminal: one million square feet, three levels, a rectangle shopping mall with three-story windows between thirty-five gates to jetliners. The airport control tower rises from the terminal's far end like a towering rook from chess.

The tan sedan forced its way back into airport traffic.

Harry barked orders up his sleeve.

Wide-eyed Ted braced himself in the backseat.

Ahead at the old terminal, sweeping into the car-clogged road, airport cop, phone pressed to his ear, hand on his holstered pistol, he—

Halts the chasing cop cruiser.

Autos hunt drop-off parking spots. Travelers drag wheeled suitcases. Snow falls.

"Nothing!" yelled Sami. "I see nothing! Go! Go!"

Driving in bumper-to-bumper traffic to the upper level of the new terminal ate two minutes off the clock. Three lanes of vehicles lined the sidewalk.

"Couldn't evacuate this place now!" Harry's eyes scanned the chaos.

"Gotta be here, gotta." Sami stared through the falling snow. Saw—

"Way down at the end! Close to the control tower!"

Parked near the sidewalk. Flashers blinking. A brown van. MEDICAL TRANSPORT SERVICES.

"The stairs' electric motor! They'll use that!"

Out! Sami ran crouched alongside moving cars. Fog blurred the van's windows. Exhaust smogged out the tailpipe: engine running. *Driver will be watching side mirrors.*

Sami dove under the van. The shock of ice slush soaked his pants and shirt as he crawled on his elbows. *Hot muffler!* Gas stench, he crawled to the front tire, rolled out—

He rose like a cobra beside the driver's closed window.

Startled stolen white uniform–wearing Ivan on the other side of that glass.

A woman rolled a hard-shell pink suitcase past Sami. He grabbed it—*"Hey!"*—swung the suitcase through the air. *Bam!* The driver's window cobwebbed into a thousand shards. *Bam!* The pink suitcase knocked the cobwebbed window into the van.

Driver's seat Ivan whirled toward a control box. Sami grabbed the Ameer's lips, pulled him through the shattered window, and slammed him to the slushy pavement. *"Stop! Police!"* Sami kicked the Ameer in the head, drew his Glock, imagined the pull of the trigger, the recoil, the *splat* of brains on wet pavement. *"Alive, Sami!"* yelled Harry. Strangers screamed. *"Police! Drop your weapon!"*

Ted bellowed above the chaos, "FBI! Everyone freeze!"

"No one's in the van!" Sami glared at the traffic cop who'd helped the medical crew park the brown van at the curb. "Was there another guy?"

"They had a patient pickup! With a wheelchair." The cop pointed to the terminal.

"What did he look like?"

"Like a guy! White guy. Blond hair. White uniform. EMT vest."

Ghosts whispered to Sami, *"Diverting the enemy . . . let us attack. Timing."*

"Harry!" Sami yelled to the man cuffing the unconscious Ameer. "It's Maher!"

"Go!" Harry guarded a brown van with a neutralized EMGF near an airport control tower and people-packed jetliners flying through a snowstorm.

"Ted—you know Maher's face—work down from the other end!"

The FBI agent leaped into the tan sedan. Siren wailing, red light spinning, Ted raced back the way they'd come—straight into oncoming one-way traffic.

Sami ran toward the terminal, told the uniformed cop, "Stay away from me!"

Don't blow my cover. I'm a spy. I'm a spy.

Plunging into a sea of shuffling humanity. Shoulder to shoulder. *Move!* Suitcases rolled like roadblocks. Crowd hubbub. Scents of Christmas pine, lemony floor cleaner, sweat, petroleum luggage fabric. Through the bedlam cut ringing phones.

Sami shoved his way toward the other end of the terminal.

Where is he? White uniform. Blond guy. Vest. Pushing an empty wheelchair.

Sami didn't *exactly* know how his brothers packed the wheelchair's tubular frame with gunpowder and particles they thought were radioactive. Wired an IV bag of liquid to the same detonation device Zlatko engineered for the gunpowder. But Sami *knew*.

A digital clock on the wall told him *T minus 1.*

The diversion bomb timed to cover the EMGF transmission. First responders might mistake the brown medical van for one of their own. Let it run as jetliners tumbled through the snowflakes.

Where are you? Move, out of my way! Sami jumped for a glimpse over the teeming crowd. "Watch it!" Somebody bumped him. *There's the terminal wall, the end, the last/first street exit, there's—*

An IV-bagged wheelchair sat by the wall of windows.

Sami leaped onto a planter—*There!* Fifty feet from the wheelchair. Nearing the exit: blond, EMT vest over a stolen white uniform. *Get to him! Con him! Neutralize!*

"Maher!" bellowed Sami.

Quiet filled the moment as if in slow-motion. Maher turned. Saw his brother waving at him above the airport crowd. A quizzical look filled the California blond's face. He reached his right hand inside the vest.

Forty-four feet away, known murderer and terrorist Maher's textbook gesture equaled *gun!* FBI Special Agent Ted Harris drew his service weapon, pushed an old man out of the way, acquired his target—fired three booming shots.

Panic exploded. Screaming. People tried to run. Dive. Hide.

"FBI!" yelled Ted. "FBI!"

Shots one and two blasted Maher off his feet.

His third bullet crashed into a metal heating grate above an exit.

Sami fought through the scared, silent mob toward where Maher sprawled on his back as combat-shuffling toward him came Ted, his eyes on what the suspect had pulled from his vest, still held in his right hand: only a cell phone.

Maher rose on his elbows, vaguely heard *"Don't move!"* Saw his white shirt reddening. Felt *phone* in his right hand. Saw brother Sami scrambling through the huddled crowd to save him. Maher smiled blood. Saw Sami stumble, crawl closer. Maher's right thumb hit speed dial as he raised a weakening left thumbs-up.

Sami screamed, *"No!"*

In the city, Zlatko stood outside a green door, left hand pushing a buzzer while his right hand held a pistol tied to four other murders as he terminated a loose end who ran downstairs to the peephole he'd blurred with street slush.

In Ronald Reagan National Airport, soldier John Herne huddled with blondish, black leather–coated Cari Jones. Beside them was redheaded, blue-uniformed, airline service rep Lorna Dumas pulling Amy Lewis and teddy bear closer to the shelter of an empty wheelchair rigged with a cell phone programmed to block every call. Except one.

They all heard *ring!*

NEIGHBORS

Joseph Finder

"I CAN'T SHAKE the feeling that they're up to something," Matt Parker said. He didn't need to say: the new neighbors. He was peering out their bedroom window through a gap between the slats of the venetian blinds.

Kate Parker looked up from her book, groaned. "Not this again. Come to bed. It's after eleven."

"I'm serious," Matt said.

"So am I. Plus, they can probably see you staring at them."

"Not from this angle." But just to be safe he dropped the slat. He turned around, arms folded. "I don't like them," he said.

"You haven't even met them."

"I saw you talking to them yesterday. I don't think they're a real couple. She's, like, twenty years younger than him."

"Laura's eight years younger than Jimmy."

"He's got to be an Arab."

"I think Laura said his parents are Persian."

"Persian," Matt scoffed. "That's just a fancy word for Iranian. Like an Iraqi saying he's *Mesopotamian* or something."

Kate shook her head and went back to her book. Some girl novel: an Oprah Book Club selection with a cover that looked like an Amish quilt. At the foot of their bed, the big flat-screen

TV flickered a blue light across her delicate features. She had the sound muted: Matt didn't get how she could concentrate on a book with the TV on.

"Also, does he look like a Norwood to you?" Matt said when he came back from brushing his teeth, a few stray white flecks of Colgate on his chin. "Jimmy *Norwood*? What kind of name is *Norwood* for an Arab guy? That can't be his real name."

Kate gave a small, tight sigh, folded down the corner of a page and closed her book. "It's Nourwood, actually." She spelled it.

"That's not a real name." He climbed into bed. "And where's their furniture? They didn't even have a moving van. They just showed up one day with all their stuff in that stupid little Toyota hybrid sardine can."

"Boy, you really have been stalking them."

Matt jutted his jaw. "I notice stuff. Like foreign-made cars."

"Yeah, well, I hate to burst your bubble, but they're renting the house furnished from the Gormans. Ruth and Chuck didn't want to sell their house, given the market these days, and there's no room in their condo in Boca for—"

"What kind of people would rent a furnished house?"

"Look at us," Kate pointed out. "We move, like, every two years."

"You knew when you married me that was how it would be. That's just part of the life. I'm telling you, there's something not quite right about them. Remember the Olsens in Pittsburgh?"

"Don't start."

"Did I or did I not tell you their marriage was in trouble? You insisted Daphne had postpartum depression. Then they got divorced."

"Yeah, like five years after we moved," Kate said. "Half of all marriages end in divorce. Anyway, the Nourwoods are a perfectly nice couple."

Something on TV caught Matt's eye. He fumbled for the

remote, found it under the down comforter next to Kate's pillow, touched a button to bring up the sound.

"—officials tell WXBS *NightCast* that FBI intelligence reports indicate an increased level of terrorist chatter—"

"I love that word, *chatter*," Kate said. "Makes it sound like they bugged Perez Hilton's tea set or something."

"*Shh.*" Matt raised the volume.

The anchorman of the local news, who wore a cheap pin-striped suit and looked as if he was about sixteen, went on, ". . . heightened concerns about a possible terrorist strike in downtown Boston just two days from now." The chyron next to him was a crude rendering of a crosshair and the words "Boston Terror Target?"

Now the picture cut to a reporter standing in the dark outside one of the big new skyscrapers in the financial district, the wind whipping his hair. "Ken, a spokesman for the Boston police told me just a few minutes ago that the mayor has ordered heightened security for all Boston landmarks, including the State House, Government Center, and all major office buildings."

"Isn't it a little loud?" Kate said.

But Matt continued to stare at the screen.

"—speculates that the terrorists might be locally based. The police spokesman told me that their pattern seems to be to establish residence in or near a major city and assimilate themselves into the fabric of a neighborhood while they make their long-range plans, just as law enforcement authorities believe happened in the bombing in Chicago last year, also on April nineteenth, which, though never solved, is believed to be—"

"Yeah, yeah, yeah," Kate said.

"Shh!"

"—FBI undercover operatives throughout the Boston area in an attempt to infiltrate this suspected terrorist ring," the reporter said.

"I love that," Kate said. "It's always a 'ring.' Why not a ter-rorist *bracelet*? Or a necklace."

"This isn't funny," Matt said.

MATT COULDN'T SLEEP.

After tossing and turning for half an hour, he slipped quietly out of bed and padded down the hall to the tiny guest room that served as their home office. It was furnished with little more than a couple of filing cabinets, for household bills and owner's manuals and the like, and an old Dell PC atop an Ikea desk.

He opened a browser on the computer and entered "James Nourwood" in Google. It came back:

Did you mean: James *Norwood*

No, dammit, he thought. I meant what I typed.

All Google pulled up was a scattering of useless citations that happened to contain "James" and "wood" and words that ended in "-nour." Useless. He tried typing just "Nourwood."

Nothing. Some import-export firm based in Syria called Nour Wood, a high-pressure-laminate company founded by a man named Nour. But if Google was right, and it usually was, there was nobody named Nourwood in the entire world.

Which meant that either their new neighbor was really fly-ing under the radar, or that wasn't his real name.

So Matt tried a powerful search engine called ZabaSearch, which could give you the home addresses of just about every-body, even celebrities. He entered "Nourwood" and then selected "Massachusetts" in the pull-down menu of states.

The answer came back instantly in big, red, mocking letters:

No Results Match NOURWOOD
Check Your Spelling and Try Your Search Again

Well, he thought, they've just moved here. Probably too recent to show up yet. Anyway, they were renters, not owners, so maybe that explained why they didn't show up on the database yet in Massachusetts. He went back to the ZabaSearch home page and this time left the default "All 50 States" selected.

Same thing.

No Results Match NOURWOOD

What did that mean, they didn't show up *anywhere* in the country? That was impossible.

No, he told himself. Maybe not. If Nourwood, as he'd suspected, wasn't a real name.

This strange couple was living right next door under an assumed name. Matt's Spidey Sense was starting to tingle.

He remembered how once, as a kid, he'd entered the toolshed in back of the house in Bellingham and suddenly the hairs on the back of his neck stood up, thick as cleats. He had no idea why. A few seconds later, he realized that the coil of rope in the corner of the dimly lit shed was actually a snake. He stood frozen in place, fascinated and terrified by its shiny skin, its bold orange and white and black stripes. True, it was only a king snake, but what if it had been one of the venomous pit vipers sometimes found in western Washington State, like a prairie rattlesnake? Since that day he'd learned to trust his instincts. The unconscious often senses danger long before the conscious mind.

"What are you doing?"

He started at Kate's voice. The wall-to-wall carpet had muffled her approach.

"Why are you awake, babe?" he said.

"Matt, it's like two in the morning," Kate said, her voice sleep-husky. "What the hell are you doing?"

He quickly closed the browser, but she'd already seen it.

"You're Googling the neighbors now?"

"They don't even exist, Kate. I told you, there's something wrong with them."

"Believe me, they exist," Kate said. "They're very real. She even teaches Pilates."

"You sure you have the right spelling?"

"It's on their mailbox," she said. "Look for yourself."

"Oh, right, that's real hard proof," he said, a little too heavy on the sarcasm. "Did they give you a phone number? A cell phone, maybe?"

"Jesus Christ. Look, you have any questions for them, why don't you ask them yourself, tomorrow night? Or I guess it's tonight by now."

"Tonight?"

"The Kramers' cocktail party. I told you about it like five times. They're having the neighbors over to show off their new renovation."

Matt groaned.

"We've turned down their last two invitations. We have to go." She rubbed her eyes. "You know, you're really being ridiculous."

"Better safe than sorry. When I think about my brother, Donny—I mean he was a great soldier. A true patriot. And look what happened to him."

"Don't think about your brother," she said softly.

"I can't stop thinking about him. You know that."

"Come back to bed," Kate said.

FOR THE REST of the night, Matt found himself listening to Kate's soft breathing and watching the numbers change on the digital clock. At 4:58 a.m. he finally gave up trying to sleep. Slipping quietly out of bed, he threw on yesterday's clothes and went downstairs to pee, so he wouldn't wake Kate. As he stood at the toilet, he found himself looking idly out the window, over the café curtains, at the side of the Gormans' house, not twenty feet away. The windows were dark: the Nourwoods were asleep. He saw their car parked in the driveway, which gave him an idea.

Grabbing a pen from the kitchen counter and the only scrap of paper he could find quickly—a supermarket register receipt— he opened the back door and stepped out into the darkness, catching the screen door before it could slam, pushing it gently closed until the pneumatic hiss stopped and the latch clicked.

The night—really, the morning—was moonless and starless, with just the faintest pale glow on the horizon. He could barely see five feet in front of him. He crossed the narrow grassy rectangle that separated the two houses, and stood at the verge of Nourwood's driveway, the little car a hulking silhouette. But gradually his eyes adjusted to the dark, and there was a little ambient light from a distant streetlamp. Nourwood's car, a Toyota Yaris, was one of those ridiculous foreign-made econobox hybrids. It looked as if you could lift it up with one hand. The license plate was completely in shadow, so he came closer for a better look.

Suddenly his eyes were dazzled by the harsh light from a set of halogen floods mounted above the garage. For a sickening moment he thought that maybe Nourwood had seen someone prowling around and flicked a switch. But no: Matt had apparently tripped a motion sensor.

What if they kept their bedroom curtains open and one of them wasn't a sound sleeper? He'd have to move quickly now, just to be safe.

Now, at least, he could make out the license plate clearly. He wrote the numbers on the register receipt, then turned to go back, when he collided with someone.

Startled, Matt gave an involuntary shout, a sort of *uhhh!* sound at exactly the same time as someone said, "Jesus!"

James Nourwood.

He was a good six inches taller than Matt, with a broad, athletic build, and wore a striped bathrobe, unruly tufts of black chest hair sprouting over the top. "Can I help you?" Nourwood said with an imperious scowl.

"Oh—I'm sorry," Matt said. "I'm Matt Parker. Your, uh, next-door neighbor." His mind was spinning like a hamster on a wheel, trying to devise a plausible explanation for why he'd been hunched over his neighbor's car at five in the morning. What could he possibly say? I was curious about your hybrid? Given the Cadillac Escalade in Matt's garage, whose mileage was measured in gallons per mile, not exactly.

"Ah," Nourwood said. "Nice to meet you." He sounded almost arch. He had a neatly trimmed goatee and a dark complexion that made him look as if he had a deep suntan. Nourwood extended a hand and they shook. His hand was large and dry, his clasp limp. "You scared the living daylights out of me. I came out to see if the paper was here yet. . . . I thought someone was trying to steal my car." He had the faintest accent, though hardly anyone else would have picked up on the telltale traces. Something slightly off about the cadence, the intonation, the vowel formation. Like someone born and raised in this country of parents who weren't native speakers. Who perhaps spoke Arabic since infancy and was probably bilingual.

"Yeah, sorry about that, I—my wife lost an earring, and she's all upset about it, and I figured it might have dropped when she came over to visit you guys yesterday."

"Oh?" Nourwood said. "Did she visit us yesterday? I'm sorry I missed her."

"Yep," Matt said. Did Kate say she'd gone over to their house yesterday, or was he remembering that wrong? "Pretty sure it was yesterday. Anyway, it's not like it's fancy or anything, but it sort of has sentimental value."

"I see."

"Yeah, it was the first gift I ever gave her when we started going out, and I'm not much of a gift-giver, so I guess that makes it a collector's item."

Nourwood chuckled politely. "Well, I'll let you know if I see anything." He cocked a brow. "Though it might be a bit easier to look after the sun comes up."

"I know, I know," Matt said hastily, "but I wanted to surprise her when she woke up."

"I see," Nourwood said dubiously. "Of course."

"I notice you have Mass plates—you from in-state?"

"Those plates are brand-new."

"Uh-huh." Matt noticed he didn't say whether he was or wasn't from Massachusetts. Just that the license plates were new. He was being evasive. "So you're not from around here, I take it."

Nourwood shook his head slowly.

"Yeah? Where're you from?"

"Good Lord, where *aren't* I from? I've lived just about every-where, it seems."

"Oh yeah?"

"Well, I hate to be rude, but I have some work to do, and it's my turn to make breakfast. Will we see you tonight at the Kramers' party?"

"I THOUGHT I heard voices outside," Kate said, scraping the last spoonful of yogurt and Bran Buds from her bowl. She looked tired and grumpy.

Matt shrugged, shook his head. He was embarrassed about what had happened and didn't feel like getting into it. "Oh yeah?"

"Maybe I dreamed it. Mind if I finish this off?" She pointed her spoon at the round tub of overpriced yogurt she'd bought at Trader Joe's.

"Go ahead," he said, sliding the yogurt toward her. He hated the stuff. It tasted like old gym socks. "More coffee?"

"I'm good. You were up early."

"Couldn't sleep." He picked up the quart of whole milk and was about to pour some into his coffee when he noticed the date stamped on the top of the carton. "Past the sell-by date," he said. "Any more in the fridge?"

"That's the last," she said. "But it's fine."

"It's expired."

"It's perfectly good."

"*Perfectly good*," he repeated. "Ever notice how you always say something's 'perfectly good' when something's actually not-quite-right about it?" He sniffed the carton but couldn't detect any sour smell. That didn't mean it hadn't begun to turn, of course. You couldn't always tell from the smell alone. He poured the milk slowly, suspiciously, into his coffee, alert for the tiniest curds, but he didn't see any. Maybe it was okay after all. "Just like the Nourwoods. You said they were 'perfectly nice.' Which means you *know* something's off about them."

"I think you drink too much coffee," she said. "Maybe that's what's keeping you up nights."

The *Boston Globe* was spread between them on the small round table, a moisture ring from the yogurt container wrinkling the banner headline:

FBI: Probe Possible Local Terror Plot
Security heightened in high-rises, government buildings

He stabbed the paper with a stubby index finger. "See, that's what's keeping me up nights," he said. "The Nourwoods are keeping me up nights."

"Matt, it's too early."

"Fine," he said. "Just don't say I didn't warn you." He took a sip of coffee. "Why'd they move into the neighborhood, anyway?"

"What's that supposed to mean?"

"Was it for a job or something? Did they say?"

Kate rolled her eyes in that way that always annoyed him. "He got a job at ADS."

"In Hopkinton?" ADS was the big tech company that used to be known by its full name, Andromeda Data Systems. They made—well, he wasn't sure what they did, exactly. Data storage, maybe. Something like that.

"That what he told you?"

She nodded.

"There you go. If he really got a job at ADS, why didn't they move somewhere closer to Hopkinton? That's the flaw in his cover."

She looked at him disdainfully for a long moment and then said, "Can you please just drop this already? You're just going to make yourself crazy."

Now he saw that he was upsetting her, and he felt bad. Softly, he said, "You ever hear back from the doctor?"

She shook her head.

"What's the holdup?"

She shook her head again, compressed her lips. "I wish I knew."

"I don't want you to worry. He'll call."

"I'm not worried. You're the one who's worried."

"That's my job," Matt said. "I worry for both of us."

THE ENGINEERING FIRM where Matt worked was right in downtown Boston, in the tallest building in the city: a sleek sixty-story tower with a skin of blue reflective glass. It was a fine, proud landmark, a mirror in the sky. Matt, a structural engineer by training and an architecture nut by avocation, knew quite a bit about its construction. He'd heard stories about how, shortly after it was built, it would shed entire windowpanes on windy days like some reptile shedding its scales. You'd be walking down the street, admiring the latest addition to the Boston sky-line, and suddenly you'd be crushed beneath five hundred pounds of glass, a hail of jagged shards maiming other passersby. You'd never know what hit you. Funny how things like that could happen, things you'd never in a million years expect. A flying window, of all things! No one was ever safe.

A Swiss engineer even concluded, years after it was built, that in certain wind conditions the tower might actually bend in the middle—might topple right over on its narrow base. How strange, he'd often thought, to be working in such a grandiose landmark, this massive spire so high above the city, and yet be so completely vulnerable, in a glass coffin.

He eased his big black Cadillac Escalade down the ramp into the underground parking garage. A couple of uniformed security guards emerged from their booth. This was a new procedure as of a few days ago, with the heightened security.

Matt clicked off the radio—his favorite sports-talk radio show, the host arguing with some idiot about the Red Sox bull pen—and lowered the tinted window as the older guard approached. Meanwhile, the younger one circled around to the back of the Escalade and gave it a sharp rap.

"Oh, hey, Mr. Parker," the gray-haired guard said.

"Morning, Carlos," Matt said.

"How about them Sox?"

"Going all the way this year."

"Division at least, huh?"

"All the way to the World Series."

"Not this year."

"Come on, keep the faith."

"You ain't been around here long enough," Carlos said. "You don't know about the curse."

"No such thing anymore."

"When you been a Sox fan as long as me, you're just waiting for the late-season choke. It still happens. You'll see." He called out to his younger colleague, "This guy's okay. Mr. Parker is a senior manager at Bristol Worldwide, on twenty-seven."

"How's it going?" the younger guard said, backing away from the car.

"Hey," Matt said. Then, mock-stern, he said, "Carlos, you know, you guys should really check everyone's car."

"Yeah, yeah," Carlos said.

Matt wagged his finger. "It only takes one vehicle."

"If you say so."

But it was true, of course. All someone had to do was pack a car—not even a truck; it wouldn't have to be any bigger than this Escalade—with RDX and park it in the right location in the garage. RDX could slice through steel support pillars like a razor blade through a tomato. Part of the floor directly above would cave right in, then the floor above that, and pretty soon, in a matter of seconds, the whole building would pancake. This was the principle of controlled demolition: The explosives were just the trigger. Gravity did the real work for you.

It always amazed him how little people understood about the fragility of the structures in which they lived and worked.

"Hey," Matt said, "you guys ever get the CCTV cameras at the Stuart Street entrance fixed?"

"Hell didn't freeze over, last I checked," said Carlos.

Matt shook his head. "Not good," he said. "Not in times like these."

The senior guard gave the Escalade a friendly open-handed pat as if sending it on its way. "Tell me about it," he said.

THE FIRST THING Matt did when he got to his cubicle was call home. Kate answered on the first ring.

"No word from the doctor yet?" he asked.

"No," Kate said. "I thought you were him."

"Sorry. Let me know when you hear something, okay?"

"I'll call as soon as I hear. I promise."

He hung up, checked his online office calendar, and realized he had ten minutes before the morning staff meeting. He pulled up Google and entered "license plate search," which produced a long list of websites, most of them dubious. One promised, "Find Out the Truth about Anyone!" But when he entered Nourwood's license plate number and selected Massachusetts, he was shuttled to another page that wanted him to fill out all kinds of information about himself and give his credit card number. That wasn't going to happen. Another one featured a ridiculous photo of a man dressed up to look like someone's idea of a detective, right down to the Sherlock Holmes hat and the big magnifying glass, in which his right eye was grotesquely enlarged. Not very promising, but he entered the license plate number anyway, only to find that Massachusetts wasn't one of the available states. Another site looked more serious, but the fine print explained that when you entered a license plate and your own credit card information, you were "assigned" to a "private investigator." He didn't like that. It made him nervous. He didn't want to be exposed that way. Plus, it said the search would take three to five business days.

By then it would be too late.

He clicked on yet another website, which instantly spawned a dozen lewd pop-up ads that took over his whole screen.

And then Matt noticed his manager, Regina, approaching his cubicle. Frantically he looked for a power button on his monitor but couldn't find one. That was the last thing he needed—for Regina to sidle into his cubicle asking about the RFP, a Request for Proposal, he was late on and see all this porn on his computer screen.

But when she was maybe six feet away, she came to an abrupt halt, as if remembering something, and returned to her office.

Crisis averted.

As he restarted his computer, he found himself increasingly baffled: How could this guy, this "James Nourwood," not appear anywhere on the Internet? That was just about impossible these days. Everyone left digital grease stains and skid marks, whether it was phone numbers, political contributions, high school reunion listings, property sales, corporate websites . . .

Corporate websites. Now there was a thought.

Where was it that "Nourwood" worked again? Ah, yes. The big tech company ADS, in Hopkinton. Or so he had told Kate.

Well, that was simple to check. He found the ADS main phone number. An operator answered, "Good morning, ADS."

"I'd like to speak with one of your employees, please. James Nourwood?"

"Just a moment."

Matt's heart fluttered. What if Nourwood answered his own line? Matt would have no choice but to hang up immediately, of course, but what if his name showed up on Nourwood's caller ID?

Faint keyboard tapping in the background, and then absolute silence. He held his index finger hovered just above the plunger, ready to disconnect the call as soon as he heard Nourwood's voice.

Then again, if Nourwood really did answer the phone, then maybe it wasn't some cover name after all. Maybe there was some benign explanation for the fact that he couldn't be found on the Internet.

His finger hovered, twitched. He stroked the cool plastic of the plunger button, ready to depress it with the lightning reflexes of a sniper. There was a click, and then the operator's voice again: "How are you spelling that, sir?"

Matt spelled Nourwood for her slowly.

"I'm checking, but I don't find anyone with that name. I even looked under N-O-R-W-O-O-D, but I didn't find that either. Any idea what department he might be in?"

Matt's twitchy index finger couldn't be restrained anymore, and he ended the call.

AFTER THE STAFF meeting, he stopped by Len Baxter's office. Lenny was the head of IT in Bristol's Boston office, a bearded, gnomelike figure who kept to himself but had always been helpful whenever Matt had a computer problem. Every day, no matter the season, he wore an unvarying uniform: jeans, a plaid flannel shirt, and a Red Sox baseball cap, no doubt to conceal his bald spot. Everyone had something to hide.

"Mattie boy, what can I do you for?" Lenny said.

"I need a favor," Matt said.

"Gonna cost you." Lenny flashed a grin. "Kidding. Talk to me."

"Can you do a quick public-records search on LexisNexis?"

Lenny cocked his head. "For what?"

"Just a name. James Nourwood." He spelled it.

"This a personnel matter?"

"Oh, no. Nothing like that. He's just some sales guy at ADS who keeps trying to sell us a data recovery program, and I don't know, I get this funny feeling about him."

"I can't do that," Lenny said gravely. "That would be a violation of the Privacy Act of 1974 as well as the Gramm-Leach-Bliley Act."

Matt's stomach flipped over. But then Lenny grinned. "Just messing with you. Sure, happy to." He crunched away at his keyboard, squinted at the screen, tapped some more. "Spell it again?"

Matt did.

"Funny. Not coming up with anything."

Matt swallowed. "You're not?"

Lenny's stubby fingers flew over the keyboard. "Very peculiar," he said. "Your guy isn't registered to vote and never got a driver's license, hasn't purchased any property. . . . You sure he's not a figment of your imagination?"

"Know what? I must have gotten his name wrong. Never mind. I'll get back to you."

"No worries," Lenny said. "Anytime."

MATT WAS HARDLY a party animal. He disliked socializing, particularly with the neighbors. Wherever he lived, he preferred to keep a low profile. Plus, he didn't much like the Kramers. They had the biggest house in the neighborhood and a lawn like a golf course, and every year they resealed their driveway so it looked like polished onyx. They were throwing a party tonight to show off their latest renovation. Matt found this annoying. If you could afford to spend half a million dollars remodeling your house, the least you could do was keep quiet about it.

But this was one party that Matt was actually looking forward to. He wanted to ask the "Nourwoods" a few questions.

The party was already in full swing when he arrived: giddy, lubricated laughter and the smells of strong perfume and gin and melted cheese. He smiled at the neighbors, most of whom he didn't know, said hello to Audrey Kramer, and then caught sight of Kate chatting amiably with the Nourwoods. He froze. Why was she being so friendly to them?

As soon as Kate spied Matt, she waved him over. "Jimmy, Laura—my husband, Matt."

Nourwood was dressed in an expensive-looking blue suit, a crisp white shirt, and a striped tie. He looked prosperous and preening. His wife was small and blond and plain, solidly built, with small, pert features. Next to her husband she looked washed-out. They really didn't look like a married couple, Matt thought. They didn't seem to fit together in any way. Both of them smiled politely and extended their hands, and Matt noticed that her handshake was a lot firmer than her husband's.

"We've met," Nourwood said, his dark eyes gleaming.

"You have?" Kate said.

"Early this morning. He didn't tell you?" Nourwood laughed, showing very white, even teeth. "*Very* early this morning."

Kate flashed Matt a look of surprise. "No."

"Did you ever find your earring?" Nourwood asked Kate.

"Earring?" she said. "What earring?"

"The one Matt gave you—his first gift to you?"

Matt tried to intercept her with a warning look, but Kate gave him no chance. "This guy?" she said. "I don't think he's ever given me a pair of earrings the whole time I've known him."

"Ah," Nourwood said. His eyes bored right into Matt like an X-ray. "I misunderstood."

Matt's face went hot and prickly, and he wondered how obvious it was. He'd been caught in a transparent lie. How was he going to explain what he'd really been doing in Nourwood's driveway at five in the morning without sounding defensive or sketchy? And then he rebuked himself: This guy's a liar and an undercover operative, and *you're* acting like the guilty one?

The two women launched into a high-spirited conversation, like old friends, about restaurants and movies and shopping, leaving the two men standing there in awkward silence.

"My apologies," Nourwood said quietly. "I should have thought before I said anything. We all have things we prefer to keep hidden from our spouses."

Matt attempted a casual chuckle, but it came out hollow and forced. "Oh no, not at all," he said. "I should have told you the whole story." He lowered his voice, confiding. "Those earrings were actually a surprise gift—"

"Ah," Nourwood said, cutting him off with a knowing smile. "Not another word. My bad."

Matt hesitated. Without further elaboration, his new, revised story made no sense: why the pointless lie, how had these imaginary earrings ended up on Nourwood's driveway, all that. But Nourwood either didn't need to hear more—or didn't believe him and didn't *want* to hear more.

Matt's Spidey Sense was tingling again.

Laura and Kate were laughing and talking a mile a minute. Laura was saying something about Neiman Marcus, Kate nodding emphatically and saying, "Totally. Totally."

Instead of trying to salvage a shred of credibility, Matt decided to change the subject. "So how do you like ADS?"

Nourwood stared at him blankly. "ADS?"

"Andromeda Data Systems. You don't work there?" Now he wondered whether Kate might have just heard wrong.

"Oh, right," Nourwood said, as if just now remembering. "It's fine. You know—it's a job."

"Uh-huh," Matt said. Maybe it was Nourwood's turn to get caught in a lie. "You just started there, right?"

"Right, right," Nourwood said vaguely, obviously not eager to talk about it.

"How's the commute?" Matt persisted, moving in for the kill. "You must, like, *live* on the turnpike."

"Not at all. It's not too bad."

There was no question about it: Nourwood didn't work at ADS at all. He was probably afraid to be asked too many questions about the company.

So Matt bore in. "What kind of work do you do?"

"Oh, you don't want to know, believe me," Nourwood said in an offhanded way. His eyes were roaming the room over Matt's shoulders, as if he was desperate for an escape from the grilling.

"Not at all. I'd love to know."

"Believe me," Nourwood said, feigning joviality, though there was something hard in his eyes. "Whenever I try to explain what I do, people fall asleep standing up. Tell me about yourself."

"Me? I'm an engineer. But we're not done with you." Then Matt flashed a mollifying grin.

"I guess you could say I'm an engineer, too," Nourwood said. "A project engineer."

"Oh, yeah? I know a fair amount about ADS," Matt lied. He knew nothing more than what he'd gleaned from a quick glance at their website this morning and skimming the occasional article in the *Globe*. "I'd love to hear all about it."

"I'm an independent contractor. On kind of a consulting project."

"Really?" Matt said, pretending to be fascinated. "Tell me about it."

Nourwood's restless eyes returned to Matt's, and for a few seconds seemed to be studying him. "I wish I could," he said at last. "But they made me sign all sorts of nondisclosure agreements."

Matt wondered whether Nourwood was a harmless king snake or a venomous prairie rattlesnake. "Huh," he said.

"It's just a short-term project anyway," Nourwood went on, his eyes gone opaque. "That's why we're renting."

Matt's stomach flipped over. A short-term project. That was one way of putting it. Of course it was short term. In a couple of days Nourwood's true mission would be finished. Matt cleared his throat, attempted another approach entirely. "You know, it's the weirdest thing, but you look so damned familiar."

"Oh?"

"I could swear I've met you before."

Nourwood nodded. "I get that a lot."

Matt doubted it. "College, maybe?"

"I don't think so."

"Where'd you go to college?"

Nourwood seemed to hesitate. "Madison," he said, almost grudgingly.

"You're *kidding* me! I've got a bunch of friends who went there. What year'd you graduate?"

He caught Kate giving him a poisonous look. She had this astonishing ability to talk and eavesdrop at the same time. In truth, Matt didn't know a single person who'd gone to the University of Wisconsin at Madison. But if Matt could get Nourwood to give him a year of graduation, he'd finally be able to unearth something on this guy.

Nourwood looked uncomfortable. "I didn't really socialize much in college," he said. "I doubt I'd know any of your friends. Anyway, I didn't—I didn't exactly graduate. Long story." A taut laugh.

"Love to hear it."

"But not a very interesting story. Maybe some other time."

"I'll take a rain check," Matt said. "We'd love to have you guys over sometime. What's your cell number?" Of course, Matt had no intention of inviting the Nourwoods over. Not in a million years. But there had to be ways to trace a cell phone number.

"I should have my new mobile phone in a day or two," Nourwood said. "Let me take yours."

Touché, Matt thought. He smiled like an idiot while he scrambled for a response. "You know, it's funny, I'm blanking on it."

"Is that your mobile phone right there, clipped to your belt?"

"Oh," Matt said, looking down, flushing with embarrassment.

"Your number's easy to find on the phone. Here, let me take a look."

Nourwood reached for Matt's phone, but Matt put his hand over it. Just then, Matt felt a painful pinch at his elbow. "Excuse us," Kate said. "Matt, Audrey Kramer needs to ask you something."

"Hope you find your earrings," Nourwood said with a wink that sent a chill down Matt's spine.

"WHAT THE HELL do you think you were doing in there?" Kate said on the walk home.

Matt, embarrassed, snorted softly and shook his head.

"I don't *believe* you."

"What?"

"The way you were interrogating him? That was out-and-out rude."

"I was just making conversation."

"Please, Matt. I know damned well what you were doing. You might as well have put him under the klieg lights. That was way out of line."

"You notice how he was evading my questions?"

"Fine, so let it drop!"

"Don't you get it? Don't you get how dangerous this guy might be?"

"Oh, for God's sake, Matt. You're doing that *Rear Window* thing again. Laura seems perfectly nice."

"There you go: 'perfectly nice.' Like that milk that's about to go bad."

"The milk is fine," she snapped. "And I'm not even going to *ask* what you were doing in front of their house at five in the morning."

A moment passed. The scuff of their footsteps on the pavement. "You still haven't heard back from the doctor, have you?"

"Will you please stop asking?"

"But what's taking him so long?"

"Matt, we've been through this three times before."

"I know," he said softly.

"And we always come through just fine."

"There's always the first time."

"God, you're such a worrier."

"Better safe than sorry. I worry for both of us."

"I know," she said, and she linked arms with him and snuggled close. "I know you do."

THE NEXT MORNING, as Matt was backing the Escalade out of the garage, he glanced over and saw Nourwood getting into his tiny Toyota, and another idea came to him.

Halfway down the driveway, he stopped the car. For a minute or so he just sat there, enjoying the muted throb of the 6.2-liter all-aluminum V-8 engine with its 403 horsepower and its 517 foot-pounds of torque. He watched Nourwood back his crappy, holier-than-thou subcompact out into the street with a toylike whine and then proceed down Ballard to Centre Street.

James Nourwood was going to work, and Matt Parker was going to follow.

Let's see where you really work. Whoever you really are.

He called his manager, Regina, and told her he was having car trouble and would probably be a little late. She sounded mildly annoyed, but that was her default mode.

Matt kept his Escalade a few cars behind Nourwood's Yaris, so Nourwood wouldn't notice. At the end of Centre Street, Nourwood signaled for a right. No traffic light here, just a stop sign, and the morning rush hour was heavy. By the time Matt was able to turn, Nourwood was in the far left lane, almost out of sight, signaling left. That was the way to the Mass Pike westbound. The direction of Hopkinton and ADS headquarters. Maybe he really did work there after all.

Matt followed him around the curve, but then Nourwood abruptly veered into the right lane, onto Washington Street, which made no sense at all. This was a local road. Where was the man going?

When Nourwood turned into a gas station, Matt smiled to himself. Even those damned gas-sipping toy cars needed to fill up from time to time. Matt drove on past the gas station—he couldn't exactly follow him in—and parked along the curb fifty feet or so ahead. Far enough away that Nourwood wouldn't notice but close enough to see him leave.

But then Matt noticed something peculiar in his rearview mirror. Nourwood didn't pull up to a gas pump. Instead, he parked alongside another car, a gleaming blue Ford Focus not much bigger than his own.

Then Nourwood's car door opened. He got out, looked around quickly, then opened the passenger's side door of the blue Ford and got in.

Matt's heart began to thud. Who was Nourwood meeting? The strong morning sun was reflected off the Ford's windows, turning them into mirrors, impossible to see in. Matt just watched for what seemed an eternity.

It was probably no more than five minutes, as it turned out, before Nourwood got out of the Ford, followed by the driver, a slender, black-haired young man in his twenties wearing khakis and a white shirt and blue tie. With crisp efficiency, the two men switched cars. Nourwood was the first to leave, backing the Ford out of the space, then hanging a left out of the gas station onto Washington Street, back the way he'd come.

Matt, facing the wrong way on Washington Street, didn't

dare attempt a U-turn: too much oncoming traffic. There was nowhere to turn left. Frantic, he pulled away from the curb without looking. A car swerved, horn blasting and brakes squealing. Just up ahead on the right was a Dunkin' Donuts. Matt turned into the lot, spun around, and circled back. But the blue Ford was gone.

He cursed aloud. If only he had some idea which way Nourwood was headed. West on the turnpike? East? Or maybe not the turnpike at all. Furious at himself, he gave up and proceeded toward the Mass Pike inbound. He'd surely lost the last chance to flush the guy out: Tomorrow was the big day. In the morning, it would be too late.

As he drove onto the ramp and merged with the clotted traffic on the pike, his mind raced. Why had Nourwood switched cars? Why else except to elude detection, to avoid being spotted by someone who might recognize his vehicle?

The inbound traffic was heavy and sluggish, worse than usual. Was there an accident? Construction? He switched on his radio in search of a traffic report. "—According to a spokesman for the FBI's Boston office," a female announcer was saying. Then a man's voice, a thick Boston accent: "You know, Kim, if *I* worked in one of those buildings downtown, I'd take a personal day. Call it a long weekend. Get an early start on my weekend golf game." Matt switched the radio off.

Just outside the city, the lines were long at the Allston/ Brighton toll plaza, but not at the Fast Lane booths. Matt had never gotten one of those E-ZPass accounts, though. He didn't like the idea of putting a transponder on his windshield, an electronic dog tag. He didn't want Big Brother to know where he was at all times. Sometimes it amazed him how people gave up their right to privacy without a second thought. They just didn't think about how easily tyranny could move in to fill the vacuum. His brother, Donny, back in Colorado—he understood. He was a true hero.

As he glanced enviously over at the Fast Lane, he saw a bright blue car zipping past. The man behind the wheel had dark hair and a dark complexion.

Nourwood.

He was quite sure of it.

Miraculously, Matt had caught up with him on the highway—only to be on the verge of losing him again! Stuck in the slow lane, with three cars ahead of him. The driver at the booth seemed to be chatting with the attendant, asking directions or whatever. Matt honked, tried to maneuver out of the line, but there was no room. Then he remembered that even if he'd been able to get over to one of the Fast Lanes, he couldn't just drive through without a transponder. A camera would take a picture of his license plate and send him a ticket, and that was exactly the kind of trouble he didn't need.

By the time he handed the old guy a dollar bill and a quarter and cleared the booth, Nourwood was gone. Matt accelerated, moved to the left-hand lane—and then, like some desert mirage, caught a glimpse of blue.

Yes. There it was, not far ahead. Nourwood's cerulean blue Ford was easy to spot, because it was weaving deftly in and out of traffic, crazy fast, like Dale Earnhardt at Daytona.

As if he were trying to shake a tail.

Matt's Escalade had far more cojones than Nourwood's silly little Ford. It could do zero to sixty in 6.5, and its passing power wasn't too shabby either. But he had to be careful. Better to stay back, not draw Nourwood's attention. Or get pulled over by the cops: Now *that* would be ironic.

Just up ahead were the downtown exits. Matt normally took the first one, the Copley Square exit. He wondered—the thought dawned on him with a dread that seeped cold into the pit of his stomach—whether Nourwood was headed toward one of the city's skyscrapers to conduct surveillance, as these guys so often did when a terrorist operation was in the works.

Maybe even the Hancock.

Dear God, he thought. Not that. Of all buildings in Boston, not that.

Let Kate scoff at his paranoia. She wouldn't be scoffing when he flushed out this Nourwood, this man with a fake name and a contrived background and all his tricky driving maneuvers.

When Nourwood passed the Copley exit, Matt sighed aloud. Then, still changing lanes, speeding faster and faster, Nourwood passed the South Station exit, too.

Where, then, *was* he going?

Suddenly the blue Ford cut clear across three lanes of traffic and barreled onto an exit ramp. Matt was barely able to make the exit himself.

And when he saw the green exit sign with the white airplane symbol on it, he felt his mouth go dry.

He hadn't seen Nourwood load a suitcase into his car, or any other travel bags. The man was going to the airport, but without a suitcase.

Matt's cell phone rang, but he ignored it. No doubt the officious Regina calling from work with some pointless question.

As the blue Ford emerged from the Callahan Tunnel, a few car lengths ahead of Matt's Escalade, it veered off to the right, to the exit marked Logan International Airport. Nourwood passed the turnoffs for the first few terminals, stayed on the perimeter road, then took the turnoff for central parking. Now Matt was right behind him: living dangerously. If Nourwood happened to look in his rearview mirror, he'd see Matt's Escalade. No reason for Nourwood to suspect it was Matt. Unless, waiting in line to enter the garage, he glanced back.

So at the last minute, Matt swung his car away from the garage entrance and off to the side, letting Nourwood go on ahead. He watched the man's arm snake out—a charcoal gray sleeve, the dark-complexioned hand, the hairy wrist, and the expensive watch—and snatch the ticket. Then Matt followed him inside. He took the ticket, watched the lift gate rise. The ramp just ahead rose steeply: a 15% gradient, he calculated. Nourwood's blue Ford, once again, was gone.

Chill, Matt told himself. He's only going one way. You'll catch up to him. Or see his parked car. But as he wound steadily uphill, tires squealing on the glazed concrete surface, Matt saw no blue Ford. He marveled at the lousy design of this parking structure, all the wasted space under the grade ramps, the curtain walls and the horizontally disposed beams, the petrified forest of vertical columns taking up far too many bays. When he saw how enormous the garage was, how many possible routes Nourwood could have taken on each deck, he cursed himself for not taking the risk of staying right behind the guy. Now it was too late. How many times had he lost Nourwood this morning?

Half an hour later, having circled and circled the garage, up to the roof and back down, he finally gave up.

Matt slammed his fist on the steering wheel, accidentally hitting the horn, and the guy right in front of him at the exit, driving a Hummer, stuck out his tattooed arm and gave him the finger.

FOR THE REST of the day, Matt could barely concentrate on his RFP. Who cared about it, anyway, with what was about to happen? At lunch he dodged an invitation from Lenny Baxter, the IT guy, to grab a sandwich at the deli, preferring to go off by himself and think.

As he finished his turkey club sandwich at Subway, crumpling the wrapper into a neat ball, his cell phone rang. It was Kate.

"The Doctor called," she said.

"Finally. Tell me." His heart started racing again, but he managed to sound calm.

"We're fine," she said.

"Great. That's great news. So, how're you feeling?"

"You know me. I never worry."

"You don't have to," Matt said. "I do it for you."

Back at his cubicle, he found the website for the University of Wisconsin's office of the registrar. A line said, "To verify a degree or dates of attendance" and gave a number, which he called.

"I need to *verify*"—Matt deliberately used the word in order to sound official—"attendance on a job applicant, please."

"Of course," the young woman said. "Can I have the name?"

Matt was surprised at how easy this was going to be. He gave Nourwood's name, heard the girl tap at her keyboard. "All *righty*," she said, all corn-fed Midwestern hospitality. "So you should get a degree verification letter in two to three business days. I'll just need to get—"

"Days?" Matt croaked. "I—I don't have time for that!"

"If you need an immediate answer you can contact the National Student Clearinghouse. Assuming you have an account with them, sir."

"I—we're just—a small office here. And, um, the hiring deadline is today, or it's not going to go through, so if there's any way . . ."

"Oh," the woman said, full of genuine-sounding concern. "Well, let me see what I can do for you, then. Can you hold?"

She came back on the line a couple of minutes later. "I'm sorry, sir, I don't have a James Nourwood. I'm not finding *any* Nourwoods. Are you sure you've got the spelling right?"

AT 6:45 P.M. Matt pulled into his driveway and noticed the blue Ford Focus parked next door. So Nourwood was home, too.

Turning his key in the front door, he realized it was already unlocked. He moved slowly, warily, through the living room, nerves a-jangle, listening, pulse racing. He thought he heard a female cry from somewhere in the house, though he wasn't sure whether it was Kate's or whether it was in fact a laugh or a cry, and then the hollow-core door to the basement came open, the one between the kitchen and the half bath, and James Nourwood loomed in the doorway, a twenty-pound sledgehammer in his hand.

Matt dove at Nourwood and tackled him to the floor. He could smell the man's strong aftershave, tinged with acrid sweat. He was surprised at how easily Nourwood went down. The sledgehammer slid from his grip, thudded onto the carpet. The guy barely put up a fight. He was trying to say something, but Matt grabbed his throat and squeezed it just below the larynx.

Matt snarled, *"You goddamned—"*

A shout came from somewhere close. Kate's voice, high and shrill. "Oh, my God! Matt, stop it! Oh, my God, Jimmy, I'm so sorry!"

Confused and disoriented, Matt relaxed his grip on Nourwood's throat and said, "What the hell's going on here?"

"Matt, get off of him!" Kate shrieked.

Nourwood's olive-complexioned face had gone a shade of purple. Then, unexpectedly, he laughed. "What you must have . . . thought," Nourwood managed to choke out. "I'm—so sorry. Your wife told me to just go down and grab . . . all my tools are in storage." He struggled, was finally able to sit up. "Laura's been nagging me for days to put up a fence around her tomato garden to keep out the chipmunks, and I didn't realize how—how much clay's in the soil here. You can't pound in the stakes without a decent sledgehammer."

Matt turned around, looked at Kate. She looked mortified. "Jimmy, it's all my fault. Matt's been on edge recently."

Now Laura Nourwood was there, too, ice clinking festively in a tumbler of scotch. "What's going *on* here? Jimmy, you okay?"

Nourwood rose unsteadily, brushed off his suit jacket and pants. "I'm fine," he said.

"What happened?" his wife said. "Was it the vertigo again?"

"No, no, no," Nourwood chuckled. "Just a misunderstanding."

"Sorry," Matt mumbled. "Shoulda asked before I jumped you."

"NO, REALLY, IT'S all my fault," Kate said later as they sat in the living room, drinks in their hands. Kate had heated up some frozen cheesy puff pastry things from Trader Joe's and kept passing around the tray. "Matt, I probably should have told you I'd invited them over, but I just saw Laura in her backyard planting out her tomatoes, and we started talking, and it turns out Laura's into heirloom tomatoes, which you know how much I love. And I was telling her that I thought it was probably too early to plant out her tomatoes around here, she should wait for last frost, and then Jimmy got home, and he asked if we had a sledgehammer he could borrow, so I just asked these guys over for a drink. . . ."

"My bad," Matt said, still embarrassed about how he'd over-reacted. But it didn't mean his underlying suspicions had been wrong—not at all. Just in this one particular instance. Nothing else about the man had changed. None of his lies about his job or his college or what he was really doing.

"Tomorrow we'll all laugh about it," Kate said.

I doubt that, Matt thought.

"What do you mean?" said Nourwood. "I'm laughing now!" He turned to his wife, put his big ham hock hand over hers. "Just please don't ask our neighbors for a cup of sugar! I don't think I'm up to it." He laughed loud and long, and the women joined him. Matt smiled thinly.

"I was telling the ladies about my day from hell," Nourwood said. "So my sister Nabilah calls me last night to tell me she has a job interview in Boston and she's flying in this morning."

"Nothing like advance notice," said Laura.

Nourwood shrugged. "This is my baby sister we're talking about. She does everything last-minute. She graduated from college last May, and she's been looking for a job for months, and all of a sudden it's rush rush rush. And she asks can I pick her up at the airport."

"God forbid she should take a cab," Laura said.

"What is an older brother for?" Nourwood said.

"Nabilah's what you'd call a princess," said his wife.

"Really, I don't mind at all," said Nourwood. "But of course it had to be on the same day that my car's going into the shop."

"I think she planned it that way," Laura said.

"But the car dealership couldn't have been nicer about it. They were even willing to bring the loaner to a gas station on Washington Street. But I got a late start leaving the house, and then the kid had all kinds of paperwork he wanted me to fill out, even though I thought we'd gone over all of this on the phone. So there I am on the highway in this rented car, driving to the airport like a madman. Only I don't know where the turn signal is, and come to find out the parking brake is partly on, so the car's moving all jerky, like a jackrabbit. And I don't want to be late for Nabilah, because I know she'll freak out."

"God forbid she might have to wait a couple of minutes for her chauffeur," Laura said acidly.

"So right when I'm driving into the parking garage at Logan, my cell phone rings, and who should it be but Nabilah? She got an earlier flight, and she's been waiting at the airport for half an hour already, and she's freaking out, she's going to be late for the interview, and where am I, and all of this."

Laura Nourwood shook her head, compressed her lips. Her dislike for her sister-in-law was palpable.

"But I've already taken the ticket from the garage thingy, so I turn around, and I have to plead with the man in the booth to let me out without paying their minimum."

"What was it, like ten bucks, Jimmy?" said his wife. "You should have just paid."

"I don't like throwing away money," Nourwood replied.

"You know that. So I race over to Terminal C and I park right in front of arrivals and get out of the car, and all of a sudden this state trooper's coming at me, yelling, and writing me a ticket. He says I'm not allowed to park in front of the terminal. Like I've got a car bomb or something. In this little rented Ford!"

"You do look Arab," his wife said. "And these days . . ."

"Persians are not Arabs," Nourwood said stiffly. "I speak Farsi, not Arabic."

"And I'm sure that Boston cop appreciates the distinction," Laura said. She looked at Matt and shrugged apologetically. "Jimmy hates cops."

Annoyed, Nourwood shook his head. "So as soon as I get back in the car to move it, Nabilah comes out, with like five suitcases—and she's not even staying overnight! So I race downtown to Fidelity, and then I have to floor it to get to Westwood because my eleven a.m. got moved up an hour."

"Don't tell me you got a speeding ticket," Laura said.

"When it rains, it pours," Nourwood said.

"Westwood?" Matt said. "You told me you work for ADS. They're in Hopkinton."

"Well, if you want to get technical about it, I actually work for Dataviz, which is a *subsidiary* of ADS. They just got acquired by ADS six months ago. And let me tell you, this isn't going to be an easy integration. They still haven't changed the name on the building, and they still answer the phone 'Dataviz' instead of 'ADS.'"

"Huh," Matt said. "And . . . your sister—did she go to UW too?"

"UW?" Nourwood said.

"Didn't you tell me you went to Madison?" Matt said. He added drily, "Maybe I misheard."

"Ah, yes, yes," Nourwood said. "James Madison University. JMU."

"JMU," Matt repeated. "Huh."

"That happens a lot," Nourwood said. "Not Wisconsin. Harrisonburg, Virginia."

Then that would explain why the University of Wisconsin had no record of any James Nourwood, Matt thought. "Huh," he said.

"And no, Nabilah went to Tulane," said Nourwood. "I guess we Nouris feel more comfortable in those southern colleges. Maybe it's the warmer climate."

"Nouris?"

"I married a feminist," Nourwood said.

"I'm confused," Matt said.

"Laura didn't want to take my name, Nouri."

"Why should I?" his wife put in. "I mean, how archaic is that? I was Laura Wood my whole life until we got married. Why shouldn't he change his name to James Wood?"

"And neither one of us likes hyphenated names," Nourwood said.

"This girlfriend of mine named Janice Ritter," Laura said, "married a guy named Steve Hyman. And they merged their names and got Ryman."

"That sounds a lot closer to 'Hyman' than to 'Ritter,'" Kate said.

"And the mayor of Los Angeles, Antonio Villar, married Corina Raigosa," Nourwood said. "And they both became Villaraigosa."

"That's brilliant," Kate said. "Nouri and Wood become Nourwood. Like Brad Pitt and Angelina Jolie become Brangelina!"

Nouri, Matt thought. Even if he had gone to the University of Wisconsin, they wouldn't have had a record of a Nourwood.

"Well, but that's just the tabloid nickname for them," Nourwood objected. "They didn't change their names legally."

"Neither did we," Laura Nourwood said.

"When you give me a son, we will," her husband said.

"*Give* you a son?" his wife blurted out. "You mean, when *we* have a *child*. *If* we have a child. I got news for you, Jimmy. You're not back in the old country. You've never even *been* to the old country."

EARLY THE NEXT morning, Matt was glugging the almost-spoiled milk down the sink drain when Kate entered the kitchen.

"Hey! What are you doing? That's perfectly good milk!"

"It tastes sort of suspicious to me," Matt said.

"Now you're getting paranoid about dairy products?"

"Paranoid?" He turned to face her, speaking slowly. "What if I'd been right about them?"

"But you weren't, you big goofball!"

"Okay, fine," Matt said. "We know that *now*. It's just that I couldn't quite shake the feeling that they were . . ."

"Undercover FBI agents?"

"They just had that vibe. And when I think about Donny, doing five consecutive life sentences in supermax back in Colorado just because he dared to fight for freedom on our native soil, you know? I just get the willies sometimes."

"Man, you're always jumping at shadows." She handed him a small red plastic gadget. "Here's the LPD detonator the Doctor sent over. I told you he'd come through."

"I hope the Doctor is absolutely certain this one's going to work. Remember Cleveland?"

"That won't happen again," she said. "The Doctor wasn't running that operation. If there's one thing the Doctor knows, it's explosives."

"What about the RDX?"

"The Escalade's already packed."

"Sweetie," Matt said, and he gave her a kiss. "How early did you get up?"

"Least I could do. You've got a long day ahead of you. You're taking the Stuart Street entrance, right?"

"Of course," he said. "All four of us are. No CCTV camera there."

"So, we'll meet up in Sayreville tonight?" Kate said.

"As planned."

"We're going to be Robert and Angela Rosenheim."

"That almost sounds like one of those blended names," Matt said.

"It's what the Doctor gave us. We'd better get used to saying it. Okay, *Robert*?"

"Bob. No, let's make it Rob. Are you Angela or Angie?"

"Angie's okay."

"Okay." He paused. "But what if I *had* been right about the neighbors? Because one of these times I'm going to be. You know that."

"Well," Kate said, almost sheepishly. "I did take the precaution of letting the air out of their tires."

EAST OF SUEZ,
WEST OF CHARING CROSS ROAD

John Lawton

UNHAPPINESS DOES NOT fall on a man from the sky like a branch struck by lightning, it is more like rising damp. It creeps up day by day, unfelt or ignored until it is too late. And if it's true that each unhappy family is unhappy in its own way, then the whole must be greater than the sum of the parts in Tolstoy's equation, because George Horsfield was unhappy in a way that could only be described as commonplace. He had married young, and he had not married well.

IN 1948 HE had answered the call to arms. At the age of eighteen he hadn't much choice. National Service—the draft—the only occasion in its thousand-year history that England had had peacetime conscription. It was considered a necessary precaution in a world in which, to quote the U.S. Secretary of State, England had lost an empire and not yet found a role. Not that England knew this—England's attitude was that we had crushed old Adolf, and we'd be buggered if we'd now lose an empire—it would take more than little brown men in loincloths . . . okay, so we lost India . . . or Johnny Arab with a couple of petrol bombs or those Bolshie Jews in their damn kibbutzes—okay, so we'd cut and run in Palestine, but dammit man, one has to draw the line somewhere. And the line was east of Suez, somewhere east of Suez, anywhere east of Suez—a sort of movable feast really.

George had expected to do his two years square-bashing or polishing coal. Instead, to both his surprise and pleasure, he was considered officer material by the War Office Selection Board. Not too short in the leg, no dropped aitches, a passing knowledge of the proper use of a knife and fork, and no pretensions to be an intellectual. He was offered a short-service commission, rapidly trained at Eaton Hall in Cheshire—a beggar man's Sandhurst—and put back on the parade ground not as a private but as Second Lieutenant HG Horsfield RAOC.

Why RAOC? Because the light of ambition had flickered in George's poorly exercised mind—he meant to turn this short-service commission into a career—and he had worked out that promotion was faster in the technical corps than in the infantry regiments, and he had chosen the Royal Army Ordnance Corps, the "suppliers," whose most dangerous activity was that they supplied some of the chaps who took apart unexploded bombs, but, that allowed for, an outfit in which one was unlikely to get blown up, shot at, or otherwise injured in anything resembling combat.

GEORGE'S EFFORTS NOTWITHSTANDING, England did lose an empire, and the bits it didn't lose England gave away with bad grace. By the end of the next decade a British prime minister could stand up in front of an audience of white South Africans, until that moment regarded as our "kith and kin," and inform them that "a wind of change is blowing through the continent." He meant, "the black man will take charge," but as ever with Mr. Macmillan, it was too subtle a remark to be effective. Like his "you've never had it so good," it was much quoted and little understood.

George did not have it so good. In fact, the 1950s were little else but a disappointment to him. He seemed to be festering in the backwaters of England—Nottingham, Bicester—postings relieved only, if at all, by interludes in the backwater of Europe known as Belgium. The second pip on his shoulder grew so slowly it was tempting to force it under a bucket like rhubarb. It was 1953 before the pip bore fruit. Just in time for the coronation.

They gave him a few years to get used to his promotion—he boxed the compass of obscure English bases—then Lieutenant Horsfield was delighted with the prospect of a posting to Libya, at least until he got there. He had thought of it in terms of the campaigns of the Second World War that he'd followed with newspaper clippings, a large corkboard, and drawing pins when he was a boy—Monty, the eccentric, lisping Englishman, versus Rommel, the old Desert Fox, the romantic, halfway-decent German. Benghazi, Tobruk, El Alamein—the first land victory of the war. The first real action since the Battle of Britain.

There was plenty of evidence of the war around Fort Kasala (known to the British as 595 Ordnance Depot, but built by the Italians during their brief, barmy empire in Africa). Mostly it was scrap metal. Bits of tanks and artillery half-buried in the sand. A sort of modern version of the legs of Ozymandias. And the fort itself looked as though it had taken a bit of a bashing in its time. But the action had long since settled down to the slow motion favored by camels and even more so by donkeys. It took less than a week for it to dawn on George that he had once more drawn the short straw. There was only one word for the Kingdom of Libya—*boring*. A realm of sand and camel shit.

He found he could get through a day's paperwork by about eleven in the morning. He found that his clerk-corporal could get through it by ten, and since it was received wisdom in Her Majesty's Forces that the devil made work for idle hands, he inquired politely of Corporal Ollerenshaw, "What do you do with the rest of the day?"

Ollerenshaw, not having bothered either to stand or salute on the arrival of an officer, was still behind his desk. He held up the book he had been reading—*Teach Yourself Italian*.

"*Come sta?*"

"Sorry, corporal, I don't quite . . ."

"It means, 'How are you, sir?' In Italian. I'm studying for my O level exam in Italian."

"Really?"

"Yes, sir. I do a couple of exams a year. Helps to pass the time. I've got Maths, English, History, Physics, Biology, French, German, and Russian—this year I'll take Italian and Art History."

"Good Lord, how long have you been here?"

"Four years, sir. I think it was a curse from the bad fairy at my christening. I would either sleep for a century until kissed by a prince or get four years in fuckin' Libya. 'Scuse my French, sir."

Ollerenshaw rooted around in his desk drawer and took out two books—*Teach Yourself Russian* and a Russian-English, English-Russian dictionary.

"Why don't you give it a whirl, sir? It's better than goin' bonkers or shaggin' camels."

George took the books, and for a week or more they sat unopened on his desk.

It was hearing Ollerenshaw through the partition—"*Una bottiglia di vino rosso, per favore*"—"*Mia moglie vorrebbe gli spaghetti alle vongole*"—that finally prompted him to open them. The alphabet was a surprise, so odd it might as well have been Greek, and as he read on he realized it was Greek, and he learned the story of how two Orthodox priests from Greece had created the world's first artificial alphabet for a previously illiterate culture by adapting their own to the needs of the Russian language. And from that moment George was hooked.

Two years later, and the end of George's tour of duty in sight, he had passed his O level and A level Russian and was passing fluent—passing only in that he had just Ollerenshaw to converse with in Russian and might, should he meet a real Russki for a bit of a chat, be found to be unequivocally fluent.

Most afternoons the two of them would sit in George's office in sanctioned idleness speaking Russian, addressing each other as "comrade," and drinking strong black tea to get into the spirit of things Russian.

"Tell me, *tovarich*," Ollerenshaw said, "why have you just stuck with Russian? While you've been teaching yourself Russian I've passed Italian, Art History, Swedish, and Technical Drawing."

George had a ready answer for this.

"Libya suits you. You're happy doing nothing at the bumhole of nowhere. Nobody to pester you but me—a weekly wage and all found petrol you can flog to the wogs—you're in lazy bugger's heaven. You've got skiving down to a fine art. And I wish you well of it. But I want more. I don't want to be a lieutenant all my life, and I certainly don't want to be pushing around dockets for pith helmets, army boots, and jerry cans for much longer. Russian is what will get me out of it."

"How d'you reckon that?"

"I've applied for a transfer to Military Intelligence."

"Fuck me! You mean MI5 and all them spooks an' that?"

"They need Russian speakers. Russian is my ticket."

MI5 DID NOT want George. His next home posting, still a lowly first lieutenant at the age of twenty-nine, was to Command Ordnance Depot Upton Bassett on the coast of Lincolnshire—flat, sandy, cold, and miserable. The only possible connection with things Russian was that the wind, which blew bitterly off the North Sea all year round, probably started off somewhere in the Urals.

He hated it.

The saving grace was that a decent-but-dull old bloke—Major Denis Cockburn, a veteran of World War II, with a good track record in bomb disposal—took him up.

"We can always use a fourth at bridge."

George came from a family that thought three-card brag was the height of sophistication but readily turned his hand to the pseudo-intellectual pastime of the upper classes.

He partnered the major's wife, Sylvia—the major usually partnered Sylvia's unmarried sister, Grace.

George, far from being the most perceptive of men, at least deduced that a slow process of matchmaking had been begun. He didn't want this. Grace was at least ten years older than him and far and away the less attractive of the two sisters. The major had got the pick of the bunch, but that wasn't saying much.

George pretended to be blind to hints and deaf to suggestions. Evenings with the Cockburns were just about the only damn thing that stopped him from leaving all his clothes on a beach and disappearing into the North Sea forever. He'd hang on to them. He'd ignore anything that changed the status quo.

Alas, he could not ignore death.

When the major died of a sudden and unexpected heart attack in September 1959, seemingly devoid of any family but Sylvia and Grace, it fell to George to have the grieving widow on his arm at the funeral.

"You were his best friend," Sylvia told him.

No, thought George, I was his only friend, and that's not the same thing at all.

A string of unwilling subalterns was dragooned into replacing Denis at the bridge table. George continued to do his bit. After all, it was scarcely any hardship, he was fond of Sylvia in his way, and it could not be long before red tape broke up bridge nights forever when the army asked for the house back and shuffled her off somewhere with a pension.

But the breakup came in the most unanticipated way. He'd seen off Grace with a practiced display of indifference, but it had not occurred to him that he might need to see off Sylvia, too.

On February 29th, 1960, she sat him down on the flowery sofa in the boxy sitting room of her standard army house, told him how grateful she had been for his care and company since the death of her husband, and George, not seeing where this was leading, said that he had grown fond of her and was happy to do anything for her.

It was then that she proposed to him.

She was, he thought, about forty-five or -six, although she looked older, and whilst a bit broad in the beam was not unattractive.

This had little to do with his acceptance. It was not her body that tipped the balance, it was her character. Sylvia could be a bit of a dragon when she wanted, and George was simply too scared to say no. He could have said something about haste or mourning or with real wit have quoted Hamlet, saying that the "funeral baked meats did coldly furnish forth the marriage table." But he didn't.

"I'm not a young thing anymore," she said. "It need not be a marriage of passion. There's much to be said for companionship."

George was not well acquainted with passion. There'd been the odd dusky prostitute out in Libya, a one-night fling with an NAAFI woman in Aldershot . . . but little else. He had not given up on passion, because he did not consider that he had yet begun with it.

They were married as soon as the banns had been read, and he walked out of church under a tunnel of swords in his blue dress uniform, the Madame Bovary of Upton Bassett, down a path that led to twin beds, Ovaltine, and hairnets worn overnight. He had not given up on passion, but it was beginning to look as though passion had given up on him.

SIX WEEKS LATER, desperation led him to act irrationally. Against all better judgment he asked once more to be transferred to Intelligence and was gobsmacked to find himself summoned to an interview at the War Office in London. London . . . Whitehall . . . the hub of the universe.

Simply stepping out of a cab so close to the Cenotaph—
England's memorial to her dead, at least her own white dead, of
countless imperial ventures—gave him a thrill. It was all he
could do not to salute.

Down all the corridors and in the right door to face a lieutenant colonel, then he saluted. But, he could not fail to notice,
he was saluting not some secret agent in civilian dress, not Bull-
dog Drummond or James Bond, but another Ordnance officer
just like himself.

"You've been hiding your light under a bushel, haven't you?"
Lieutenant Colonel Breen said when they'd zipped through the
introductions.

"I have?"

Breen flourished a sheet of smudgy-carboned typed paper.

"Your old CO in Tripoli tells me you did a first-class job
running the mess. And I think you're just the chap we need
here."

Silence being the better part of discretion, and discretion
being the better part of an old cliché, George said nothing and
let Breen amble to his point.

"A good man is hard to find."

Well—he knew that, he just wasn't wholly certain he'd ever
qualified as a "good man." It went with "first-class mind" (said
of eggheads) or "very able"(said of politicians) and was the
vocabulary of a world he moved in without ever touching.

"And we need a good man right here."

Oh Christ—they weren't making him mess officer? Not again!

"Er . . . actually, sir, I was under the impression that I was
being interviewed for a post in Intelligence."

"Eh? What?"

"I have fluent Russian, sir, and I . . . "

"Well, you won't be needing it here . . . ha . . . ha . . . ha!"

"Mess officer?"

Breen seemed momentarily baffled.

"Mess officer? Mess officer? Oh, I get it. Yes, I suppose you will be, in a way, it's just that the mess you'll be supplying will be the entire British Army 'East of Suez.' And you'll get your third pip. Congratulations, Captain."

Intelligence was not mentioned again except as an abstract quality that went along with "good man" and "first-class mind."

SYLVIA WOULD NOT hear of living in Hendon or Finchley. The army had houses in north London, but she would not even look. So they moved to West Byfleet in Surrey, onto a hermetically sealed army estate of identical houses, and as far as George could see, identical wives, attending identical coffee mornings.

"Even the bloody furniture's identical!"

"It's what one knows," she said. "And it's a fair and decent world without envy. After all, the thing about the forces is that everyone knows what everyone else earns. Goes with the rank, you can look it up in an almanac if you want. It takes the bitterness out of life."

George thought of all those endless pink gins he and Ollerenshaw had knocked back out in Libya, and how what had made them palatable was the bitters.

George hung up his uniform, went into plain clothes, War Office Staff Captain (Ord) General Stores, let his hair grow a little longer, and became a commuter—the 7:57 a.m. to Waterloo, and the 5:27 p.m. back again. It was far from Russia.

Many of his colleagues played poker on the train, many more did crosswords, and a few read. George read, he got through most of Dostoevsky in the original, the books disguised with the dust jacket from a Harold Robbins or an Irwin Shaw, and when he wasn't reading stared out of the window at the suburbs of south London—Streatham, Tooting, Wimbledon—and posh "villages" of Surrey—Surbiton, Esher, Weybridge—and imagined them all blown to buggery.

The only break in the routine was getting rat-arsed at the

office party a few days before Christmas 1962, falling asleep on the train, and being woken by a cleaner to find himself in a railway siding in Guildford at dawn the next morning.

It didn't feel foolish—it felt raffish, almost daring, a touch of Errol Flynn debauchery—but as 1963 dawned, England was becoming a much more raffish and daring place, and Errol Flynn would soon come to seem like the role model for an entire nation.

IT WAS ALL down to one person, really—a nineteen-year-old named Christine Keeler. Miss Keeler had had an affair with George's boss, the top man, the minister of war, the Rt. Hon. John (Umpteenth Baron) Profumo (of Italy), MP (Stratford-on-Avon, Con.), OBE. Miss Keeler had simultaneously had an affair with Yevgeni Ivanov, an "attaché of the Soviet embassy" (newspeak for spy)—and the ensuing scandal had rocked Britain, come close to toppling the government, led to a trumped-up prosecution (for pimping) of a society doctor, his subsequent suicide, and the resignation of the aforementioned John Profumo.

At the War Office, there were two notable reactions. Alarm that the class divide had been dropped long enough to allow a toff like Profumo to take up with a girl of neither breeding nor education, whose parents lived in a converted wooden railway carriage, that a great party (Conservative) could be brought down by a woman of easy virtue (Keeler)—and paranoia that the Russians could get that close.

For a while Christine Keeler was regarded as the most dangerous woman in England. George adored her. If he thought he'd get away with it he'd have pinned her picture to his office wall.

IT WAS POSSIBLE that his lust for a pinup girl he had never met was what led him into folly.

The dust had scarcely settled on the Profumo affair. Lord

Denning had published his report entitled unambiguously "Lord Denning's Report" and found himself the author of an unwitting best seller when it sold four thousand copies in the first hour and the queues outside Her Majesty's Stationery Office in Kingsway stretched around the block and into Drury Lane, and the country had a new prime minister in the cadaverous shape of Sir Alec Douglas-Home, who had resigned an earldom for the chance to live at No. 10.

George coveted a copy of the Denning Report, but it was understood to be very bad form for a serving officer, let alone one at the ministry that had been if not at the heart of the scandal then most certainly close to the liver and kidneys, to be seen in the queue.

His friend Ted—Captain Edward Ffyffe-Robertson RAOC—got him a copy, and George refrained from asking how. It was better than any novel—a marvelous tale of pot-smoking West Indians, masked men, naked orgies, beautiful, available women, and high society. He read it and reread it, and since he and Sylvia had now taken not only separate beds but also separate rooms, slept with it under his pillow.

About six months later Ted was propping up the wall in George's office, having nothing better to do than jingle the coins in his pocket or play pocket billiards whilst making the smallest of small talk.

Elsie the tea lady parked her trolley by the open door.

"You're early," Ted said.

"Ain't even started on teas yet. They got me 'anding out the post while old Albert's orf sick. What a diabolical bleedin' liberty. Ain't they never 'eard of demarcation? Lucky I don't have the union on 'em."

Then she slung a single, large brown envelope onto George's desk.

"I see you got yer promotion then, Mr. 'Orsefiddle. All right for some."

She pushed her trolley on. George looked at the envelope.

"Lieutenant Colonel HG Horsfield."

"It's got to be a mistake, surely?"

Ted peered over.

"It is, old man. Hugh Horsfield. Half-colonel in Artillery. He's on the fourth floor. Daft old Elsie's given you his post."

"There's another Horsfield?"

"Yep. Been here about six weeks. Surprised you haven't met him. He's certainly made his presence felt."

With hindsight George ought to have asked what Ted's last remark meant.

Instead, later the same day, he went in search of Lieutenant Colonel Horsfield, out of nothing more than curiosity and a sense of fellow feeling.

He tapped on the open door. A big bloke with salt-and-pepper hair and a spiky little moustache looked up from his desk.

George beamed at him.

"Lieutenant Colonel. HG Horsfield? I'm Captain HG Horsfield."

His alter ego got up and walked across to the door and, with a single utterance of "Fascinating," swung it to in George's face.

Later, Ted said, "I did try to warn you, old man. He's got a fierce reputation."

"As what?"

"He's the sort of bloke who gets described as not suffering fools gladly."

"Are you saying I'm a fool?"

"Oh, the things only your best friend will tell. Like using the right brand of bath soap. No, I'm not saying that."

"Then what are you saying?"

"I'm saying that to a highflyer like Hugh Horsfield, blokes like us who keep our boys in pots and pans and socks and blankets are merely the also-rans of the British Army. He deals with the big stuff. He's Artillery after all."

"Big stuff? What big stuff?"

"Well, we're none of us supposed to say, are we? But here's a hint: think back to August 1945 and those mushroom-shaped clouds over Japan."

"Oh. I see. Bloody hell!"

"Bloody hell indeed."

"Anything else?"

"I do hear that he's more than a bit of a ladies' man. In the first month alone he's supposed to have shagged half the women on the fourth floor. And you know that blonde in the typing pool we all nicknamed the Jayne Mansfield of Muswell Hill?"

"Not her, too? I thought she didn't look at anything below a full colonel."

"Well, if the grapevine has it aright she dropped her knickers to half-mast for this half-colonel."

What a bastard.

George hated his namesake.

George envied his namesake.

IT WAS SOMEONE'S birthday. Some bloke on the floor below whom he didn't know particularly well, but Ted did. A whole crowd of them, serving soldiers in civvies, literally and metaphorically letting their hair down, followed up cake and coffee in the office with a mob-handed invasion of a nightclub in Greek Street, Soho. Soho—a ten-minute walk from the War Office, the nearest thing London had to a red-light district, occupying a maze of narrow little streets east of the elegant Regent Street, south of the increasingly vulgar Oxford Street, north of the bright lights of Shaftesbury Avenue, and west of the bookshops of the Charing Cross Road. It was home to the Marquee music club, the Flamingo, also a music club, the private boozing club known as the Colony Room, the scurrilous magazine Private Eye, the Gay Hussar restaurant, the Coach and Horses pub (and too many other pubs ever to mention), a host of odd little shops where a nod and a wink might get you into the back room for purchase of a faintly pornographic film, a plethora of strip clubs, and the occasional and more-than-occasional prostitute.

He'd be late home. So what? They'd all be late home.

They moved rapidly on to Frith Street and street by street and club by club worked their way across toward Wardour Street. The intention, George was sure, was to end up in a strip joint. He hoped to slip away before they reached the Silver Tit or the Golden Arse and the embarrassing farce of watching a woman wearing only a G-string and pasties jiggle all that would jiggle in front of a bunch of pissed and paunchy middle-aged men who confused titillation with satisfaction.

He'd been aware of Lieutenant Colonel Horsfield's presence from the first—the upper-class bray of a barroom bore could cut through any amount of noise. He knew HG's type. Minor public school, too idle for university, but snapped up by Sandhurst because he cut a decent figure on the parade ground. Indeed, he rather thought the only reason the army had picked him for Eaton Hall was that he, too, looked the officer type at a handsome five feet eleven inches.

As they reached Dean Street, George stepped off the pavement meaning to head south and catch a bus to Waterloo, but Ted had him by one arm.

"Not so fast, old son. The night is yet young."

"If it's all the same to you, Ted, I'd just as soon go home. I can't abide strippers, and HG is really beginning to get on my tits, if not on theirs."

"Nonsense, you're one of us. And we won't be going to a titty bar for at least an hour. Come and have a drink with your mates and ignore HG. He'll be off as soon as the first prozzie flashes a bit of cleavage at him."

"He doesn't?"

"He does. Sooner or later everybody does. Haven't you?"

"Well . . . yes . . . out in Benghazi . . . before I was married . . . but not . . ."

"It's okay, old son. Not compulsory. I'll just be having a couple of jars myself, then I'll be home to Mill Hill and the missus."

It was a miserable half hour. He retreated to a booth on his own, nursing a pink gin he didn't much want. He'd no idea how long she'd been sitting there. He just looked up from pink reflections and there she was. Petite, dark, twentyish, and looking uncannily like the dangerous woman of his dreams: the almost pencil-thin eyebrows, the swept-back chestnut hair, the almond eyes, the pout of slightly prominent front teeth, and the cheekbones from heaven or Hollywood.

"Buy a girl a drink?"

This was what hostesses did. Plonked themselves down, got you to buy them a drink, and then ordered house "champagne" at a price that dwarfed the national debt. George wasn't falling for that.

"Have mine," he said, pushing the pink gin across the table. "I haven't touched it."

"Thanks, love."

He realized at once that she wasn't a hostess. No hostess would have taken the drink.

"You're not working here, are you?"

"Nah. But . . ."

"But what?"

"But I am . . . working."

The penny dropped, clunking down inside him, rattling around in the rusty pinball machine of the soul.

"And you think I . . ."

"You look as though you could do with something. I could . . . make you happy . . . just for a while I could make you happy."

George heard a voice very like his own say, "How much?"

"Not up front, love. That's just vulgar."

"I haven't got a lot of cash on me."

"S'okay. I take checks."

SHE HAD A room three flights up in Bridle Lane. Clothed she was gorgeous, naked she was irresistible. If George died on the train home he would die happy.

She had one hand on his balls and was kissing him in one ear—he was priapic as Punch. He was on the edge, seconds away from entry, sheathed in a frenchie, when the door burst open, his head turned sharply, and a flashbulb went off in his eyes.

When the stars cleared, he found himself facing a big bloke in a dark suit clutching a Polaroid camera and smiling smugly at him.

"Get dressed, Mr. Horsfield. Meet me in the Stork Café in Berwick Street. You're not there in fifteen minutes this goes to your wife."

The square cardboard plate shot from the base of the camera and took form before his eyes.

He fell back on the pillow and groaned. He'd know a Russian accent anywhere. He'd been set up—trussed up like a turkey.

"Oh . . . shit."

"Sorry, love. But, y'know. It's a job. Gotta make a livin' somehow."

George's wits were gathering slowly, cohering into a fuzzy knot of meaning.

"You mean they pay you to . . . frame blokes like me?"

"'Fraid so. Prozzyin' ain't what it used to be."

The knot pulled tight.

"You take money for this!?!"

"O'course. I'm no commie. It's a job. I get paid. Up front."

He had a memory somewhere of her telling him that was vulgar, but he sidestepped it.

"Paid to get you out of yer trousers, into bed, do what I do till Boris gets here."

"What you do?"

"You know, love . . . the other."

"You mean sex?"

"If it gets that far. He was a bit early tonight."

A light shone in George's mind. The knot slackened off, and the life began to crawl back into his startled groin.

"You've been paid to . . . fuck me?"

"Language, love. But yeah."

"Would you mind awfully if we . . . er . . . finished the job?"

She thought for a moment.

"Why not? Least I can do. Besides, I like you. And old Boris is hardly going to bugger off after fifteen minutes. He needs you. He'll wait till dawn if he has to."

WALKING TO BERWICK Street, along the whore's paradise of Meard Street, apprehension mingled with bliss. It was like that moment in Tobruk when Johnny Arab had stuck a pipe of super-strength hashish in front of him and he had looked askance at it but inhaled all the same. The headiness never quite offset and overwhelmed the sheer oddness of the situation.

In the caff a few late-night "beatniks" (scruffbags, Sylvia would have called them) spun out cups of frothy coffee as long as they could and put the world to rights—while Boris, if that really was his name, sat alone at a table next to the lavatory door.

George was at least half an hour late. Boris glanced at his watch but said nothing about it. Silently he slid the finished Polaroid—congealed as George thought of it—across the table, his finger never quite letting go of it.

"This type of camera only takes these shots. No negative. Hard to copy, and I won't even try unless you make me. Do what we ask, Mr. Horsfield, and you will not find us unreasonable people. Give us what we want, and when we have it, you can have this. Frame it, burn it, I don't care—but if we get what we want, you can be assured this will be the only copy and your wife need never know."

George didn't even look at the photo. It might ruin a precious memory.

"What is it you want?"

Boris all but whispered, "Everything you're sending east of Suez."

"I see," said George, utterly baffled by this.

"Be here one week tonight. Nine o'clock. You bring evidence of something you've shipped out—show willing as you people say—and we'll brief you on what to look for next. In fact, we'll give you a shopping list."

Boris stood up. A bigger bugger in a black suit came over and stood next to him. George hadn't even noticed this one was in the room.

"Well?" he said in Russian.

"A pushover," Boris replied.

The other man picked up the photo, glimmed it, and said, "When did he shave off the moustache?"

"Who cares?" Boris replied.

Then he switched to English, said, "Next week," to George, and they left.

George sat there. He'd learned two things. They didn't know he spoke Russian, and they had the wrong Horsfield. George felt like laughing. It really was very funny—but it didn't let him off the hook. . . . Whatever they called him, Henry George Horsfield RAOC or Hugh George Horsfield RA . . . they still had a photograph of him in bed with a whore. It might end up in the hands of the right wife or the wrong wife, but he had no doubts it would all end up on a desk at the War Office if he screwed up now.

HE GOT BUGGER all work done the next day. He had sneaked into home very late, left a note for Sylvia saying he would be out early, caught the 7.01 train, and sneaked into the office very early. He could not face her across the breakfast table. He couldn't face anyone. He closed his office door, but after ten minutes decided that that was a dead giveaway and opened it again. He hoped Ted did not want to chat. He hoped Daft Elsie had no gossip as she brought round the tea.

At five-thirty in the evening he took his briefcase and sought out a caff in Soho. He sat in Old Compton Street staring into his deflating frothy coffee much as he had stared into his pink gin the night before. Oddly, most oddly, the same thing happened. He looked up from his cup and there she was. Right opposite him. A vision of beauty and betrayal.

"I was just passin'. Honest. And I saw you sittin' in the window."

"You're wasting your time. I haven't got the money, and after last night . . ."

"I'm not on the pull. It's six o'clock and broad bleedin' daylight. I . . . I . . . I thought you looked lonely."

"I'm always lonely," he replied, surprised at his own honesty. "But what you see now is misery of your own making."

"You'll be fine. Just give old Boris what he wants."

"Has it occurred to you that that might be treason?"

"Nah . . . it's not as if you're John Profumo or I'm Christine Keeler. We're small fry, we are."

Oh God, if only she knew.

"I can't give him what he wants. He wants secrets."

"Don't you know any?"

"Of course I do . . . everything's a sodding secret. But . . . but . . . I'm RAOC. Do you know what that stands for?"

"Nah. Rags And Old Clothes?"

"Close. Our nickname is the Rag And Oil Company. Royal Army Ordnance Corps. I keep the British Army in saucepans and socks!"

"Ah."

"You begin to see? Boris will want secrets about weapons."

"O'course he will. How long have you got?"

"I really ought to be on a train by nine."

"Well . . . you come home with me. We'll have a bit of a think."

"I'm not sure I could face that room again."

"You silly bugger. I don't work from home, do I? Nah. I got a place in Henrietta Street. Let's nip along and put the kettle on. It's cozy. Really it is. Ever so."

How Sylvia would have despised the "ever so." It would be "common."

Over tea and ginger biscuits she heard him out—the confusion of two Horsfields and how he really had nothing that Boris would ever want.

She said, "You gotta laugh, ain't yer?"

And they did.

She thought while they fucked—he could see in her eyes that she wasn't quite with him, but he didn't much mind.

Afterward, she said, "You gotta do what I have to do."

"What's that?"

"Fake it."

George took this on board with a certain solemnity and doubt.

She shook him by the arm vigorously.

"Leave it out, captain. I'd never fake one with you."

THE BEST PART of a week passed. He was due to meet Boris that evening and sat at his desk in the day trying to do what the nameless whore had suggested. Fake it.

He had in front of him a shipping docket for frying pans.

FP1 Titanium Range 12 inch. Maximum heat dispersal.
116 units.

It was typical army-speak that the docket didn't actually say they were frying pans. The docket was an FP1, and that was only used for frying pans, so the bloke on the receiving end in Singapore would just look at the code and know what was in the crate. There was a certain logic to it. Fewer things got stolen this way. He'd once shipped thirty-two kettles to Cyprus, and somehow the word *kettle* had ended up on the docket and only ten ever arrived at their destination.

He could see possibilities in this. All he needed was a jar of that newfangled American stuff, Liquid Paper, which he bought out of his own money from an import shop in the Charing Cross Road, a bit of jiggery-pokery, and access to the equally newfangled, equally American Xerox machine. Uncle Sam had finally given the world something useful. It almost made up for popcorn and rock 'n' roll.

Caution stepped in. He practiced first on an interoffice memo. Just as well—he made a hash of it. "Staff Canteen Menu, Changes to: Subsection Potato, Mashed: WD414" would never be the same again. No matter, if one of these yards of bumf dropped onto his desk in the course of a day, then so did a dozen more. He'd even seen one headed "War Office Gravy, Lumps in."

He found the best technique was to thin the Liquid Paper as far as it would go and then treat it like ink. Fortunately, the empire had only just died—or committed hara-kiri—and he had in his desk drawer two or three dip pens, with nibs, and a dry, clean, cut-glass inkwell that might have graced the desk of the assistant commissioner of Eastern Nigeria in 1910.

And—practice does make perfect. And a copy of a copy of a copy—three passes on the Xerox—makes the perfect into a pleasing blur.

"Titanium" was fairly easily altered to "Plutonium."

A full stop was added before "Range."

"12 inch" became "120 miles."

He stared, willing something to come to him about "Maximum heat dispersal," and when nothing did concluded it was fine as it was. And 116 units sounded spot-on. A good, healthy number, divisible by nothing.

He looked over his handiwork. It would do. It would . . . "pass muster," that was the phrase. And it was pleasingly ambiguous.

FP1 Plutonium. Range 120 miles. Maximum heat dispersal.
116 units.

But what if Boris asked what they were?

BORIS DID, BUT by then George was ready for him.

"FP means Field Personnel. And I'm sure you know what plutonium is."

"You cheeky bugger. You think I'm just some dumb Russki? The point is, to what aspect of Field Personnel does this document refer?"

George looked him in the eye, said, "Just put it all together. Add up the parts and get to the sum."

Boris looked down at the paper and then up at George.

Whatever penny dropped, George would roll with it.

"My God. I don't believe it. You bastards are upping the ante on us. You're putting tactical nuclear weapons into Singapore!"

"Well," George replied in all honesty. "You said it, I didn't."

"And they shipped in January. My God, they're already there!"

George was emboldened.

"And why not—things are hotting up in Vietnam. Or did you think that after Cuba we'd just roll over and die?"

And then he kicked himself. Was Vietnam, either bit of it, within 120 miles of Singapore? He hadn't a clue.

Mouth, big, shut.

But Boris didn't seem to know either.

He pushed the Polaroid across the table to him. This time he took his hand off it.

"You will understand. We keep our word."

George doubted this.

And then Boris reached into his pocket, pulled out a white envelope, and pushed that to George.

"And I am to give you this."

"What is it?"

"Five hundred pounds. I believe you call it a monkey."

Good God—here he was betraying his country's canteen secrets, and the bastards were actually going to pay him for it.

He took it round to Henrietta Street.

He didn't mention it until after they'd made love.

And she said, "Bloody hell. That's more'n I make in a month," and George said, "It's more than I make in three months."

They agreed. They'd stash it in the bottom of her wardrobe and think what they might do with it some other time.

As he was leaving for Waterloo, George said, "Do you realize, I don't know your name."

"You din' ask. And it's Donna."

"Is that your real name?"

"Nah. S'my workin' name. Goes with my surname, Needham. It's like a joke. Donna Needham. Gettit?"

"Yes. I get it. You're referring to men."

"Yeah, but you can call me Janet if you like. That's me real name."

"I think I prefer Donna."

IT BECAME PART of the summer. Part of the summer's new routine.

He would ring home about once a week and tell Sylvia he would be working late.

"The DDT to the DFC's in town. The brass want me in a meeting. Sorry, old thing."

Considering that she had been married to a serving army officer for twenty years before she met George, Sylvia had never bothered to learn any army jargon. She expected men to talk bollocks, and she paid it no mind. She accepted it and dismissed it simultaneously.

George would then keep an appointment with Boris in the Berwick Street caff, sell his country up the Swanee, and then go round to the flat in Henrietta Street.

Even as his conscience atrophied, or quite possibly because it atrophied, love blossomed. He was absolutely potty about Donna and told her so every time he saw her.

Boris didn't use the Berwick Street café every time, and it suited both to meet at Kempton Park racecourse on the occasional Saturday, particularly if Sylvia had gone to a whist drive or taken herself off shopping in Kingston-upon-Thames. Five bob each way on the favorite was George's limit. Boris played long shots and made more than he lost. It was, George thought, a fair reflection of both their characters and their trades.

As the weeks passed, George doctored more dockets, pocketed more cash—although he never again collected five hundred pounds in one go (Boris explained that this had been merely to get his attention), every meeting resulted in his treachery being rewarded with a hundred or two hundred pounds.

Some deceptions required a bit of thought.

For example, he found himself staring at a docket for saucepans he had shipped to Hong Kong from the makers in Lancashire.

SP3 PRESTIGE Copper-topped 6 inch. 250 units.

Prestige was probably the best-known maker of saucepans in the country. He couldn't leave the word intact—it was just possible that even old Boris had heard of them.

But once contemplated, his liar's muse came to his rescue, and it was easily altered to read

FP3 P F T Cobalt-tipped 6 inch. 250 units.

He'd no idea what this might mean, but, once in the caff with two cups of frothy coffee in front of them, as ever, Boris filled in most of the blanks.

Yes, FP meant what it had always meant. He struggled a little with P F T, and George waited patiently as Boris steered himself in the direction of Personal Field Tactical, and as he put that together with cobalt-tipped, his great Russian self-righteousness surfaced with a bang.

"You really are a bunch of bastards, aren't you? You're fitting handheld rocket launchers with missiles coated with spent uranium!"

Oh, was that it? George knew cobalt had something to do with radioactivity, but quite what was beyond him.

"Armor-piercing, cobalt-tipped shells? You bastards. You utter fockin' bastards. Queensberry rules, my Bolshevik arse!"

Ah . . . armor-piercing, that was what they were for. George hadn't a clue and would have guessed blindly had Boris asked.

"Bastards!"

After which outburst Boris slipped him a hundred quid and called it a long 'un.

Midsummer, George got lucky. He was running out of ideas, and somebody mentioned that the army had American-built ground-to-air missiles deployed with NATO forces in Europe. A truck-mounted launcher that went by the code name of *Honest John*. It wasn't exactly a secret, and there was every chance Boris knew what *Honest John* was.

It rang a bell in the great canteen of the mind. A while back, he was almost certain, he had shipped fifty large stew pots out to

Aden, bought from a firm in Waterford called Honett Iron. It was the shortest alteration he ever made, and lit the shortest fuse in Boris.

"Bastards!" he said yet again.

And then he paused, and in thinking, came close to unraveling George's skein of lies. George had thought to impress Boris with a fake docket for a missile that really existed, and it was about to blow up in his face.

"Just a minute. I know this thing, it only has a range of fifteen miles. Who can you nuke from Aden? It doesn't make sense. Every other country is more than fifteen miles away. There's nothing but fockin' dyesert within fifteen miles of Aden."

George was stuck. To say anything would be wrong, but this was one gap Boris's fertile imagination didn't seem willing to plug.

"Er . . . that depends," said George.

"On what?"

"Er . . . on . . . on what you think is going on in the er . . . 'fockin' dyesert.'"

Boris stared at him.

A silence screaming to be filled.

And Boris wasn't going to fill it.

George risked all.

"After all, I mean . . . you either have spy planes or you don't."

It was enigmatic.

George had no idea whether the Russians had spy planes. The Americans did. One had been shot down over the Soviet Union in 1960, resulting in egg-on-face as the Russians paraded the unfortunate pilot alive before the world's press. So much for the cyanide capsule.

It was enigmatic. Enigmatic to the point of meaninglessness, but it did the trick. It turned Boris's inquiries inward. Meanwhile, George had scared himself shitless. He'd got cocky and he'd nearly paid the price.

*   *   *

HE LOBBED ANOTHER envelope of money into the bottom of Donna's wardrobe. He hadn't counted it, and neither of them had spent any of it, but he reckoned they must have about two thousand pounds in there.

"I have to stop," he said. "Boris damn near caught me tonight."

TWO DAYS LATER, George opened his copy of the *Daily Telegraph* on the train to work, and page one chilled him to the briefcase.

Russian Spy Plane Shot Down Over Aden

He had reached Waterloo and was crossing the Hungerford Footbridge to the Victoria Embankment before he managed to reassure himself with the notion that because it had been shot down, the USSR still didn't know what was (not) going on in the "fockin' dyesert."

He told Donna, the next time they met, the next time they made love. He lay back in the afterglow and felt anxiety awaken from its erotically induced slumber.

"You see," he said, "I had to tell Boris something. There's nothing going on in the 'fockin' dyesert.' But the Russians launched a spy plane to find out. On Boris's say-so. On my say-so. I mean, for all I know the Vietcong are deploying more troops along the DMZ, the Chinese might be massing their millions at the border with Hong Kong. . . . This is all getting . . . out of hand."

Donna ran her fingers through his hair, brought her lips close to his ear, with that touch of moist breath that drove him wild.

"Y'know, Georgie, you been luckier than you know."

"How so?"

"Supposin' there really had been something going on out in the 'fockin' dyesert'?"

"Oh Christ."

"Don't bear thinkin' about, do it? But you're right. This is all gettin' outta hand. We need to do something."

"Such as?"

"Dunno. But, let me think. I'm better at it than you are."

"Could you think quickly. Before I start World War III."

"Sssh, Georgie. Donna's thinkin'."

"IT'S LIKE THIS," she said. "You want out, but the Russkies have enough on you to fit you up for treason, and then there's the Polaroid of you an' me in bed an' your wife to think about."

"I got the Polaroid back months ago."

"You did? Good. Now . . . thing is, as I see it, they got you for selling them our secrets 'bout rockets an' 'at out east. Only you gave 'em saucepans and tea urns. So what have they really got?"

"Me. They've got me, because saucepans and tea urns are just as secret as nukes. I'm still a traitor. I'll be the Klaus Fuchs of kitchenware."

"No. You're not. The other Horsfield is, 'cos that's who they think they're dealing with."

George could not see where this was headed.

"We gotta do two things, see off old Boris and put the other Horsfield in the frame. Give 'em the Horsfield they wanted in the first place."

"Oh God."

"No . . . listen . . . Boris thinks he's been dealing with Lieutenant Col. Horsfield. What we gotta do is make the colonel think he's dealing with Boris . . . swap him for you and then blow the whistle."

"Or let the whistle blow," said George.

"How do you mean?"

"If I understand that cunning little mind of yours aright, you mean to try and frame Horsfield."

"S'right."

"I know HG. He's a total bastard, but he can't be scared or intimidated. We make any move against him, he catches even a whiff of Russian involvement, he'll blow the whistle himself."

"Y'know. That's even more than I hoped for. Let me try for the full house then. Is he what you might call a ladies' man?"

"How do you mean?"

"Well, no offense, Georgie, but you was easy to pull. If I was to try and pull HG, what would he do?"

"Oh, I see. Well, if office gossip is to be believed, he'd paint his arse blue and shag you under a lamppost in Soho Square."

"Bingo," said Donna. "Bingo bloody bingo!"

THEY DIPPED INTO the wardrobe money for the first time.

"I can't do this myself, and I can't use the room in Bridle Lane. I'll pay a mate to do HG, and I know a house in Marshall Street that's going under the wrecking ball any day now. It'll be perfect. I'll get a room kitted out so it looks like a regular pad and then we just abandon it. The gray area is knowing when we might get to HG."

"It's Ted's birthday next week. Bound to be a pub and club crawl. I could even predict that at some point we'll all be in the same club you found me in."

"What would be HG's type?"

"Now you mention it . . . not you. He goes for blondes, blondes with big . . . "

"Tits?"

"Quite."

"Okay, that narrows it down. I'll have to ask Judy. She'll want a ton for the job and another for the risk, but she'll do it."

TED'S BIRTHDAY BASH coincided with George's Boris night at the Berwick Street caff. Something was going right. God knows, they might even get away with this. "This"—he wasn't at all sure what "this" was. He knew his own part in this, but the initiative had now passed to Donna. She had planned the night's activity like a film script.

He slipped away early from Ted's party. Ted was three sheets to the wind anyway. HG was in full flight with a string of smutty stories, and the only risk was that he might get off with some woman before Judy pulled him. As he was leaving, a tall, busty blonde, another Jayne Mansfield or Diana Dors, cantilevered by state-of-the-art bra mechanics into a pink lamb's wool sweater that showed plenty of cleavage and looked as solid as Everest, came into the club. She winked at George and carried on down the stairs without a word.

George went round to Bridle Lane.

It was a tale of two wigs.

Donna had a wig ready for him.

"You and Boris are about the same size. It's just a matter of hair color. Besides, it's not as if HG will get a good look at you."

And a wig ready for herself. She was transformed into a pocket Marilyn Monroe.

He hated the waiting. They stood at the corner of Fouberts Place, looking down the length of Marshall Street. It was past nine when a staggering, three-quarters pissed HG appeared on the arm of a very steady Judy. They stopped under a lamppost. He didn't paint his arse blue, but he groped her in public, his hand on her backside, his face half-buried in her cleavage.

George watched Judy gently reposition his hand at her waist and heard her say, "Not so fast, soldier, we're almost there."

"We are? Bloody good show."

George hated HG.

George hated HG for being so predictable.

Donna whispered.

"Ten minutes at the most. Judy'll pull a curtain to when he's got his kit off. Now, are you sure you know how to work it?"

"It's just a camera like any other, Donna."

"Georgie—we only got one chance."

"Yes. I know how to work it."

When the curtain moved, George tiptoed up the stairs, imagining Boris doing the same thing all those months ago as he prepared to spring the honey trap.

At the bedroom door he could hear the baritone rumble of HG's drunken sweet nothings.

"S'wonderful. S'bloody amazing. Tits. Marvelous things. If I had tits . . . bloody hell . . . I'd play with them all day."

Then kick, flash, bang, wallop . . . and HG was sprawled where he had been, and George was uttering Boris's lines in the best Russian accent he could muster.

"You have ten minutes, Colonel Horsfield. You fail to meet me in the Penguin Café in Kingly Street, this goes to your wife."

He was impressed by his own timing. The Polariod shot out of the bottom of the camera just as he said "wife."

HG was staring at him glassy-eyed. Judy grabbed her clothes and ran past him hell-for-leather. Still, HG stared. Perhaps he was too drunk to understand what was happening.

"You have ten minutes, Colonel. Penguin Café, Kingly Street. *Das vidanye.*"

He'd no idea why he'd thrown in the *"das vidanye"* perhaps a desperate urge to sound more Russian.

HG said, "I'll be there . . . you commie fucking bastard. I'll be there."

Much to George's alarm, he got up from the bed, seemingly less drunk, bollock-naked, stiff cock swaying in its frenchie, and came toward him.

George fled. It was what Donna had told him to do.

Down in the street, George arrived just in time to see Judy pulling on her stilettos and heading off toward Beak Street. Donna took the Polaroid from him, waved it in the air, and looked for the image.

"Gottim," she said.

George looked at his watch. Didn't dare to raise his voice much above a whisper.

"I must hurry. I have to meet Boris."

"No. No, you don't. You leave Boris to me."

This wasn't part of the plan. This had never been mentioned. "What?"

"Go back to the party."

"I don't . . . "

"Find your mates. They must be in a club somewhere near. You know the pattern: booze, booze, strippers. Find 'em. Ditch the wig. Ditch the camera. Go back and make yourself seen."

She kissed him.

"And don't go down Berwick Street."

DONNA STOOD AWHILE on the next corner, watched as HG emerged and saw him rumble off in the direction of Kingly Street. Then she went the other way, toward Berwick Street, and stood behind one of the market stalls that were scattered along the right-hand side.

She could see Boris. He was reading a newspaper, letting his coffee go cold and occasionally glancing at his watch. He was almost taking George's arrival for granted, but not quite.

She was reassured when he finally gave up and stood a moment on the pavement outside the caff, looking up at the stars and muttering something Russian. Really, he wasn't any taller than George, just a bit bigger in the chest and shoulders. What with the wig and flashbulb going off, all HG was likely to say was "some big bugger, sort of darkish, in a dark suit, didn't really get a good look I'm afraid."

That was old Boris, a big, dark bugger in a dark suit.

Her only worry was that if Boris flagged a cab and there wasn't one close behind, she'd lose him. But it was a warm summer evening: Boris had decided to walk. He set off westward, in the direction of the Soviet embassy. Perhaps he needed to think.

Was he going to shop George for one no-show or was he going to roll with it, string it and George out in the hope of keeping the stream of information flowing?

Boris crossed Regent Street into Mayfair and headed south toward Piccadilly. He seemed to be in no hurry and paid no attention to cabs or buses. Indeed, he seemed to pay no attention to anything, as though he was deep in thought.

She matched her pace to his, trying to stay in shadow, but Boris never looked back. In Shepherd Market he turned into one of those tiny alleys that dot the northern side of Piccadilly, and she quickened her step to get to the corner.

The light vanished. A hand grabbed her by the jacket and pulled her into the alley. The other hand pulled off her wig, and Boris's voice said, "Don't take me for a fockin' fool. Horsfield doesn't show and then you appear in a silly wig, trailing after me like a third-rate gumshoe. What the fock are you playing at?"

It was better than she'd dared hope for. She'd been foxed all along to work out how to get him alone, this close, in a dark alley. And now he'd done it for her.

She pressed her gun to his heart and shot him dead.

Then she leaned down, tucked the Polaroid into his inside pocket, put her wig back on, walked down to Piccadilly and caught a number 38 bus home.

THE FIRST GEORGE heard was from Daft Elsie, pushing her trolley round just after eleven the next morning.

"Can't get on the fourth floor. Buggers won't let me. Some sort of argy-bargy going on. I ask yer. Spooks and spies. Gotta be a load of old bollocks, ain't it?"

"Two sugars, please," said George.

"And I got these 'ere jam don'uts special for that Colonel 'Orsepiddle. 'Ere, love, you have one."

"So," he tried to sound casual, "it all revolves around the good colonel, does it?"

"Let's put it this way, love. 'E's doin' a lot of shoutin'. An' it's not as if he whispers at the best of times."

So—HG wasn't so much blowing the whistle as shouting the odds.

After lunch Ted dropped in, dropped the latest, not-yet-late-final-but-almost edition of the *London Evening Standard* onto his desk.

George pulled it toward him.

Soviet Embassy Attaché Shot Dead in Mayfair.

George said nothing.

Ted said, "Could be an interesting few weeks. Russkies play hell. Possibly bump off one of ours. A few expulsions, followed by retaliatory expulsions. . . . God I'd hate to be in Moscow right now."

"What makes you think we did it? I mean, do we shoot foreign agents in the street?"

"Not as a rule. But boldness was our friend. I gather from a mate at Scotland Yard that they're clueless. No one saw or heard a damn thing. Anyway . . . change the subject . . . what was up with you last night? Throwing up in the bogs for an hour. Not like you, old son."

"Change it back—does this have anything to do with the hoo-ha going on on the fourth floor?"

"Well, let me put it this way. Be a striking bloody coincidence if it didn't."

IT BECAME RECEIVED wisdom in the office that the Russians had tried to set up HG and that he would have none of it. Less received, but much bandied, was the theory that rather than keep the meeting with the man attempting blackmail, HG had simply rung MI5, who had bumped off the unfortunate Russki on his way across Mayfair. That one Boris Alexandrovich Bulganov was found dead within a few yards of MI5 HQ in Curzon

Street added to veracity, as did a rumor that he'd had a photograph of HG in bed with a prozzie in his pocket. Some wag pinned a notice to the canteen message board offering ten pounds for a copy but found no takers.

Ted was profound upon the matter, "Always knew he'd end up in trouble if he let his dick do the thinking for him."

It became, almost at once, a diplomatic incident. Nothing on the scale of Profumo or the U2 spy plane, but the Russians accused the British of assassinating Boris, whom they described as a "cultural attaché." The British accused the Russians of attempting to blackmail HG Horsfield, whose name never graced the newspapers—merely "unnamed high-ranking British officer"—and George could only conclude that neither one had put the dates together and worked out that they had been blackmailing *an* HG Horsfield for some time, but not *the* HG Horsfield. If they'd swapped information, George would have been sunk. But, of course, they'd never do that.

HG's "reward" was to be made a full colonel and posted to the Bahamas. Anywhere out of the way. Why the Bahamas might need a tactical nuclear weapons expert was neither here nor there nor anywhere.

George never heard from the Russians again. He expected to. Every day for six months he expected to. But he didn't.

SIX MONTHS ON, Boris's death was eclipsed.

George arrived home in West Byfleet to find an ambulance and a crowd of neighbors outside his house.

Mrs. Wallace, wife of Jack Wallace, lieutenant in REME—George thought her name might be Betty—came up oozing an alarming mixture of tears and sympathy.

"Oh, Captain Horsfield . . . I don't know what to . . . "

George pushed past her to the ambulance men. A covered stretcher was already in the back of the ambulance and he knew the worst at once.

"How?" he asked simply.

"She took a tumble, sir. Top o'the stairs to the bottom. Broken neck. Never knew what hit her."

George spent an evening alone with a bottle of scotch, ignoring the ringing phone. He hadn't loved Sylvia. He had never loved Sylvia. He had been fond of her. She was too young, a rotten age to go . . . and then he realized he didn't actually know how old Sylvia was. He might find out only when they chipped it on her tombstone.

Grief was nothing—guilt was everything.

Decorum ruled.

He did not go to Henrietta Street for the best part of a month. He wrote to Donna, much as he wrote to many of his friends, knowing that the done thing was the notice in *The Times*, but that few of his friends read *The Times* and that the *Daily Mail* didn't bother with a deaths column.

When he did go to Henrietta Street, he cut through Covent Garden, fifty yards to the north, and bought a bouquet of flowers.

"You never brought me flowers before."

"I've never asked you to marry me before."

"Wot? Marriage? Me an' you?"

"I can't think that 'marry me' would imply anything else."

And having read the odd bit of Shakespeare in the interim, George quoted an approximation of Hamlet on the matter of baked meats, funerals, and wedding feasts.

"Sometimes, Georgie, I can't understand a word you say."

She was hesitant. The last thing he had wanted, though he had troubled himself to imagine it. She said she'd "just put the kettle on," and then she seemed to perch on the edge of the sofa without a muscle in her body relaxing.

"What's the matter?"

"If . . . if we was to get married . . . what would we do? I mean we carried on . . . once we got shot of the Russians, we just carried on . . . as normal. Only there weren't no normal."

George knew exactly what she meant, but said nothing.

"I mean . . . oh . . . bloody nora . . . I don't know what I mean."

"You mean that serving army officers don't marry prostitutes."

"Yeah . . . something like that."

"I have thought of leaving the army. There are opportunities in supply management, and the army is one of the best references a chap could have."

The kettle whistled. She turned it off but made no move toward making tea.

"Where would we live?"

"Anywhere. Where are you from?"

"Colchester."

Colchester was the biggest military prison in the country—the glasshouse, England's Leavenworth. Considered the worst posting a man could get. He'd never shake off the feel of the army in Colchester.

"Okay. Well . . . perhaps not Colchester . . ."

"I always wanted to live up north."

"What? Manchester? Leeds?"

"Nah . . . 'Ampstead. I'd never want to leave London . . . 'specially now it's started to . . . wotchercallit? . . . swing."

"Hampstead won't be cheap."

"I saved over three thousand quid from the game."

"I have about a thousand in savings, and I inherited more from Sylvia. In fact about seven and a half thousand pounds. Not inconsiderable."

Not inconsiderable—a lifetime of saving roughly equivalent to a couple of years on "the game."

"And of course, I'll get a pension. I've done sixteen years and a bit. I'll get part of a pension now, more if I leave it, and at thirty-five I'm young enough to put twenty or more years into another career."

"And there's the money in the bottom of the wardrobe."

"I hadn't forgotten."

"I counted it. Just the other day I counted it. We got seventeen hundred and thirty-two pounds. O'course there been expenses."

Donna was skirting the edge of a taboo subject. George was in two minds as to whether to let her plunge in. Who knows? It might clear the air.

"I give Judy two hundred. And there was money for the room . . . an 'at."

George bit, appropriately, on the bullet.

"And how much did the gun cost you?"

There was a very long pause.

"Did you always know?"

"Yes."

"It didn't come cheap. Fifty quid."

In for a penny, in for a pound.

Marry without secrets.

George cleared his throat.

"And of course, there's the cost of your return ticket to West Byfleet last month, isn't there?"

He could see her go rigid, a ramrod to her spine, a crab-claw grip to her fingers on the arm of the sofa.

He hoped she'd speak first, but after an age it seemed to him she might never speak again.

"I don't care," he said softly. "Really I don't."

She would not look at him.

"Donna. Please say yes. Please tell me you'll marry me."

Donna said nothing.

George got up and made tea, hoping he would be making tea for two for the rest of their lives.

FATHER'S DAY

John Weisman

20 JUNE 2004, 0312 hours. It had to be close to a hundred degrees when Charlie Becker, retired Army Ranger and current spy, rolled out of the blacked-out Humvee. He hit the ground like he'd been body-slammed. He was lucky not to have separated his shoulder.

Screw it. What was pain? *Just weakness leaving the body.*

Charlie scuttled crablike off the highway into the ditch and rolled over the closest dune—rolled so he wouldn't leave any telltale infidel boot tracks—into the soft sand of the rough scrub-brush desert.

Weapons check. He patted himself down in the spectacles, testicles, watch, and wallet mode. Pistol, knives, four M4 mags, four Sig mags. Flexicuffs, marking pen, duct tape, digital camera. Everything was where it had to be. He made sure the mag in his M4 carbine hadn't been jarred loose by the impact, took the suppressor out of the padded pouch on his tactical vest, and twisted it over the flash-hider.

Comms check. He ran his hand from the mike mounted even with his lower lip to make sure the connection on the back of his left ear-cup hadn't shaken loose. Then he flipped the night vision goggles down, rolled onto his back (ensuring, as he did, that a healthy portion of Iraq's fine-grit sand slipped down the back of his shirt), and watched as the three APCs and eight Humvees disappeared down Route Irish, fading into the moonless night on their way to Forward Operating Base Falcon.

Now it begins. Charlie flipped the NVGs up and just lay there. Except he wasn't just lying there. He was a human antenna dish, a sponge sucking up every external sensation he could absorb. Ears keened, jaw dropped, he listened.

A dog barked somewhere off to Charlie's north. Through the amplified stereo hearing protectors he heard the convoy engines grinding. Other than that: quiet.

Not good. Logic dictated there should be crickets chirping in the sunflower field bordered by thorny scrub and mangy palm trees on whose edge he was lying. But there was no hint of them. Which told Charlie the critters were still nervous about his arrival. Which meant he had a few more minutes to go before he could think about moving.

To his right, the barest wisp of hot breeze caused the dry trees to rustle like cellophane. He brought his left arm up and focused on his watch. The muted display told him he'd left the Humvee two minutes, forty-five forty-six forty-seven seconds ago.

How time flies when you're having fun.

I am getting too old for this crap, thought Charlie. *I'm fifty-two. I have a remarried ex-wife, an Irish girlfriend, a son at West Point, a beautiful daughter newly wed to a Ranger captain, and in six months I'm going to be a grandfather. Maybe they'll name the kid after me. Hell, it's fricking Father's Day. I should be home, practicing how to dandle Charlie Junior on my knee.*

The fistful of sand down his sweaty back began to itch.

Probably ticks in it, Charlie thought.

Or fleas.

Or baby camel spiders.

Last deployment he'd e-mailed his girlfriend Irish Beth a picture captioned "Charlie and the Uninvited Guest." Jose'd tossed a dead camel spider into his hide as a joke and caught Charlie's *holy shit, dude* reaction on the Nikon Coolpix. Some joke. Adult camel spiders were a foot and a half end to end, and their bites burned like acid.

For an instant he saw Beth's face. Then he thought about her breasts. About how good it felt caressing the shamrock tattoo on her fine, dancer's butt.

He blinked behind his clear, prescription Oakleys. Put Beth out of his mind. Wiped her image clean away. Charlie Becker was in his thirty-fourth year of warfare and he understood. *You can think about Beth, or you can do your job. But you can't do both.*

Charlie reached into his left cargo pocket, extracted the do-rag, made a hood, pulled the Palm Treo PDA out of his vest, rolled onto his side, punched in his code, and hit the display button so he could receive streaming video from the remotely piloted Predator vehicle loitering overhead.

He squinted at the screen. There he was—a flashing triangle on the side of Highway 8. Three other triangles blinked at two-hundred-yard intervals to his south. Jose was closest. Then Fred. Then Tuzz Man. Charlie cracked a brief smile. *Four triangles in the Triangle of Death. Who says Allah doesn't have a sense of humor?*

He shut the screen down, stowed the rag, closed his eyes so he'd get his night vision back faster, and lay there, listening to the night sounds and totting up the positive and negative aspects of twenty-first-century netcentric warfare. Predators were perfect examples of good news/bad news to operators like Charlie. This one was controlled from eleven time zones away—Nellis Air Force Base outside Las Vegas to be precise. Launched from Kuwait ten hours ago, it would circle until he'd completed the mission. An eye in the sky watching his back.

That was the good news. The bad was that anybody with the right clearances could sit in Tampa or Langley and watch Charlie trying to shake the shit out of his shirt. Which meant that even as he lay here, some supergrade desk jockey holding a

Starbucks grande and munching an organic cranberry bran muffin back at CIA headquarters was right now second-guessing his every fricking move, just waiting to summon the lawyers.

Still, there were techno-advantages that Charlie, a veteran of Jurassic-era warfare, had lacked in such antediluvian venues as Desert One, Grenada, Honduras, Panama, and Somalia. The Treo, for example. The Treo was linked to a secure satellite network. It gave Charlie the capability to look at real-time video. That's how he knew that tonight's target, Tariq Zubaydi, a local with probable ties to Abu Musab al-Zarqawi and al Qaeda in Iraq, was at home and tucked into bed. He'd watched as Tariq's guests left the house shortly after 2300 hours. Saw the lights go out just after midnight. Bingo.

0344 HOURS. THE four men linked up in a clump of papyrus by a yardwide canal smelling of brackish water and human waste. The staff sergeant trail boss of the convoy out of which they'd bailed assumed they were Special Forces working a direct action mission. That's because they'd shown up at Camp Liberty with their own sterile Humvee, asked for the convoy's honcho by name, and knew the convoy number, code name, its route to Mahmudiyah, and contingency plan call sign. Not to mention the fact that they wore Army-issue uniforms with subdued infrared-readable American flags. The plate carriers holding their ceramic body armor and spare mags bore Velcro'd name tags but no other designators. The whole picture, the sergeant would testify later, read Special Forces on a black op. In neon.

But Charlie and his companions weren't Soldiers. They were civilians. Charlie was a GS-14. Jose and Fred, retired Ranger sergeants, and Tuzzy, a former Marine gunny, were 13s. Their business cards, name tags, photo IDs, and e-mail addresses (all under aliases) identified them as employees of the Army Research Laboratory, whose on-paper headquarters was three floors of offices and the bug-proof conference rooms called

SCIFs in an anonymous four-story building on Wilson Boulevard in Rosslyn, Virginia.

In point of fact, they were all CIA, and those three floors were where Ground Branch, the so-called action group of CIA's grotesquely named SAD—Special Activity Division—was headquartered. The National Clandestine Service's pooh-bahs at Langley had "relocated"—their term—Ground Branch to one of CIA's satellite offices, because they claimed it would maintain better operational security. Charlie, a lanky former master sergeant who had been in Ground Branch since his retirement after twenty-five-plus years with the 75th Ranger Regiment in 2001, knew better. *It's CIA's fricking caste system. NCS ostracized Ground Branch because they consider themselves royalty and don't want to have to eat in the same cafeteria as a bunch of gun-toting knuckle-draggers.*

The prime witness supporting Charlie's theory was as close as Nicola's pod. Nicola Rogers was Deputy Branch Chief/ Insurgency/Baghdad and Charlie's GS-15 boss. To Charlie, she represented everything wrong with CIA. She'd been in-country for 92 of her 120-day deployment without setting foot beyond the Green Zone, except to be driven to Camp Victory to shop, eat pizza, or do karaoke night.

A tall, lithe, thirty-six-year-old chemically blonde women's studies graduate of Vassar, Nicola was a Southeast Asia economic analyst on loan to the clandestine service. She'd volunteered for Baghdad because she was on the cusp of promotion to Senior Intelligence Service (SIS) rank, and there was a rumor currently caroming through Langley's corridors that CIA's GS-15 promotables needed an Iraq tour to demonstrate they were team players.

Charlie often wondered whose team Nicola was on. It certainly wasn't his. He guessed she was filling out her résumé so once she got her SIS she could resign and become a civilian contractor, pulling in a third of a mil–plus for doing the same job she was now doing for $110,256.

Moreover, like the vast majority of the 378 officer-bureaucrats assigned to Baghdad Station or CIA's bases in Mosul, Arbīl, Basra, and Kirkuk, Nicola spent almost zero time gathering intelligence. She frittered away most of the day staring at her screen reading and answering senseless memos from Langley; playing computer games; downloading music, podcasts, and TV shows from iTunes; or composing whiny e-mails to her fiancé, a Yale Law grad in CIA's Office of Legal Counsel. Two or three times a week she'd allow Charlie admittance to her hallowed "secure office pod," look at him like he was a dirty Kleenex, and lecture about how warfare increased global warming and victimized women.

And virtually every time Charlie suggested something imaginative he could do out beyond the wire, she'd launch chaff. Nicola's First (and only) Law of Intelligence Physics went:

$$\text{Operations} = \text{Risks} = \text{Problems}$$

Zero ops therefore equaled zero problems. That philosophy was why Charlie was fond of saying that what CIA needed most these days was a 500-psi enema, starting with the director of central intelligence and ending with Nicola and all like her.

What kept Charlie going was that despite BGAlbatross, which was the CIA-style digraph code name by which he referred to Nicola, he'd had a number of successes. In fact, over the past couple of months Charlie and his seven-man Archangel paramilitary team had made a sizable dent in AQI, intel shorthand for Abu Musab al-Zarqawi's al Qaeda in Iraq terror organization of pro-Saddam Sunni insurgents, fanatic Islamist beheaders, and common dirtbag criminals.

In April he'd disrupted a Sunni network bringing foreign AQI fighters from Syria, killing six and capturing three. In May he'd ID'd an AQI mole working in the Green Zone, captured him, and flipped him. Made him a penetration agent—who led Team

ARCHANGEL to a safe house where they killed five of AQI's top-tier support cell personnel. And over the past three weeks he'd intercepted and waxed four of Zarqawi's couriers. Even better, he'd seized their laptops, pen drives, and cell phones intact.

It's amazing, Charlie thought, *how much information bad guys keep that they shouldn't.*

Tonight he'd score again. Happy Father's Day. Six days ago, a Sunni calling himself Tariq Zubaydi the grocer had shown up in the Green Zone bearing a DVD.

Tariq, who hadn't bathed in a while and smelled strongly of garlic, told the Blackwater gunsel working the security desk that the disc had been brought to his store by a stranger who'd told him, "There are those who know you speak English, and you will cooperate and take this to the Americans in the Green Zone or you will disappear."

It took two hours until Tariq was finally passed down the food chain to Nicola.

BGAlbatross locked Tariq in an interrogation room and slipped the DVD onto her laptop—a stupid thing to do Charlie thought, given the fact it could have been virus-rich—started to screen it, got physically ill after about thirty seconds, and summoned Charlie. "You watch. You like this kind of stuff."

The Iraqi had delivered an AQI snuff video. A thirteen-minute compilation of the beheadings of Fabrizio Quattrocchi, the Italian national killed on April 14, and Nick Berg, an American murdered on May 11. But there was new material, too: the bloody execution of Hussein Ali Alyan, a Shia Lebanese national, killed June 12, only forty-eight hours earlier. It hadn't even made Al Jazeera yet.

Nicola insisted on grilling Tariq herself. Charlie was relegated to watching from behind two-way glass. She got nowhere of course, because (a) she didn't know a fricking thing about interrogation, and (b) she was noticeably turned off by Tariq's BO.

Charlie, who'd graduated not only the Army's interrogation school at Fort Huachuca, Arizona, but also the FBI's advanced interrogation techniques and criminal profiling courses at Quantico, Virginia, fumed and made detailed notes. He also did a quick wash of Tariq Zubaydi's name through Baghdad Station's insurgent database and came up dry. But dry meant nothing. Baghdad Station's files were notoriously incomplete and—more to the point—Tariq was good.

Charlie focused. The Iraqi'd obviously had tradecraft training. He was careful about his body language. And when Nicola pressed him, he did what any good operator would do when challenged: He deflected, redirected, flattered. His grocery was on the verge of bankruptcy. It was so dangerous to come here. He admired the Americans.

BGAlbatross's head bobbed up and down like one of those rear-window doggy dolls. Charlie watched Tariq read her like the proverbial book. And when her doe eyes finally told Tariq *I feel your pain*, Tariq set the hook. He explained his only son was a cripple—he'd lost his leg in a bombing—and his wife had cancer.

Tears welling, he asked for three thousand dollars and ten cartons of French cigarettes so he could send his family to safety in Amman. He'd use the cigarettes to bribe the border guards.

Nicola rummaged for a Kleenex.

Charlie: *Oh, fuck me.*

And so, ignoring her dagger looks, Charlie stepped into the interrogation room and took over. He told Tariq in the passable Arabic he'd learned at language school in Monterey and polished during a fourteen-month tour training Special Forces in Qatar, "Read my lips, *habibi*, no name, no money."

In fifteen minutes Charlie bargained the cash down to one hundred dollars and the cigarettes to two cartons. That accomplished, he insisted on the name of the messenger who'd delivered the video.

Tariq looked past Charlie's Saddam Hussein mustache deep

into his cold blue eyes, factored in the scars on Charlie's face and his knuckles, understood he was dealing with a pro, and coughed up the name Abu Hadidi and a physical description. Yes, it was a war name and a probably phony description. But small victories are small victories. More important, it set a quid pro quo precedent for future meetings.

Through it all, Nicola sat dumbstruck. She'd never known Charlie was the only Ground Branch operator in Baghdad fluent in Arabic, because she'd never bothered to ask him anything about himself.

Tariq's gaze passed slowly from Charlie to Nicola and back to Charlie, and when Charlie caught the Iraqi's subtle yet unmistakable contempt, he almost laughed out loud. The Iraqi was obviously thinking the same thought as Charlie: *Had this worthless woman learned nothing in spy school?*

Charlie kept everybody waiting while he collected the cash and doctored one of the cartons, affixing a Radio Frequency ID transponder (RFID) that CIA's techno-wizards concealed within an inventory sticker. So when Tariq departed the Green Zone, Charlie, the well-worn galabia he referred to as a man-dress over his body armor, was waiting with Jose, who could pass for Egyptian, in one of ARCHANGEL's battered Toyota pickup trucks. The RFID's transmissions allowed him to trail Tariq's filthy Nissan across the river, through the Sunni market on Karada Kharidge, then along a leisurely, meandering course—Charlie and Jose decided Tariq was running an SDR, or surveillance detection route—that ultimately led southwest into the Sunni Triangle of Death to the squalid city of Mahmudiyah.

But not Mahmudiyah itself. Tariq turned off Highway 8 north of the big canal, near a cluster of villas marked on Charlie's maps as Insurgent Central. The development had been built in 1991 for Republican Guard officers and their families, and Charlie had long suspected it was a transit zone for AQI kidnap victims.

Jose gave Tariq about a klik's lead, while Charlie surreptitiously shot video with his cell phone. One point eight kliks past a walled cluster of villas that had once housed top Baath Party officials, Tariq pulled onto a rutted dirt road, drove east over a fetid, yardwide canal, and two hundred meters later pulled up next to a two-story, stone-faced villa with a clothesline on its flat roof, the easternmost structure of a three-house compound. Between the houses, the canal, and the Baath Party villas sat tilled fields of desiccated sunflowers. From one thousand meters away, Charlie squinted through binoculars as Tariq unlocked a heavy wrought-iron grille door and disappeared.

"If I was Abu Musab al-Zarqawi that's exactly the kind of place I'd stash people," Charlie told BGALBATROSS when he got back. "I should check this guy out."

She gave Charlie a nasty look. "You already did." Hell, she was pissed he'd even trailed Tariq in the first place (although she downloaded his photos fast enough).

When he asked for Predator surveillance she said, "No way" and ostentatiously swiveled toward her computer screen.

Dismissed, Charlie returned to the shipping container he called home, turned up the air-conditioning, drank half a six-pack, and imagined how lovely it would be to sell Nicola Rogers to the Hells Angels. Then he pulled off his clothes, ran through the shower, crawled into his rack, and thought about Irish Beth.

Four days later, Friday, 18 June, while Charlie was working a source on lower Hilla Road, Tariq returned. The Iraqi asked for Nicola by name and demanded four thousand dollars.

Nicola paid him every penny and even apologized for Charlie's behavior. The reason: Tariq brought two "proof of life" videos. The first showed a South Korean, thirty-three-year-old Kim Sun-il, who had been kidnapped not twenty-four hours previously. A tearful, terrified Kim begged his hooded captors not to kill him.

The second was also a gem: new video of Keith Matthew Maupin. Maupin, a Soldier from Ohio, had been captured when his convoy was ambushed by AQI two months previously. There'd been no sign of him since the week after his capture. In this video, Maupin was kneeling, an AK to his head, with three gunmen standing behind him.

When Charlie got back they screened the DVD half a dozen times, Nicola murmuring "holy shit" like a mantra.

Charlie was impressed, too, but wary. "Did you polygraph Tariq?"

"No, I did not polygraph Tariq." Nicola was visibly annoyed by the question. "C'mon, Charlie, this is pure gold. Besides, there was no time to box him."

You numskull, thought Charlie, *you* make *the fricking time.* Charlie frowned. The timing—Tariq's sudden appearance and these 24-karat videos—was almost too good to be true. Charlie knew from experience that when things *appeared* too good to be true, they often *were* too good to be true. His skepticism was wasted on Nicola, who told him he should take yes for an answer and then ordered him out so she could tell her boss what had dropped into her lap.

Charlie copied the DVD, went back to his shipping container, and spent the afternoon memorizing every tiny detail. He noted every crack and stain in the walls, every irregularity in the marble floors, even the cabriole leg of an armchair barely in the frame of the Maupin video. He froze the picture, zooming in long enough to identify a fleur-de-lis pattern on the chair's upholstered apron.

Two and a half hours later, a beaming Nicola showed Charlie the opening screen of a PowerPoint entitled "Hostages in Iraq: A New and Important Development from Nicola Rogers." Nicola was ecstatic: Baghdad's chief of station had forwarded Nicola's package to Langley as flash traffic. But that wasn't all. She'd received an e-mail from the deputy chief of Iraq Group at headquarters saying he was putting her in for a cash bonus.

When Charlie gave her a quizzical look, she showed him all

twenty-one screens. She'd composed a piece of fiction explaining how she'd developed Tariq Zubaydi as her AQI penetration agent. She'd used Charlie's surveillance photos to illustrate the narrative. Charlie, unnamed, was described as "an American operative."

"Well," she said, misreacting to Charlie's scowl, "he *is* my agent. I told him to bring me—and only me—every DVD they give him. He promised he would. I only paid him after he agreed."

Charlie felt like puking. Or quitting. Going the contractor route himself. He and Beth had talked about it. She'd been in favor. It was Charlie who'd hemmed and hawed like he had a flawed gene. The same gene that kept him at the Regiment for almost twenty-six years. The same gene, when he was offered a quarter mil by one of the private intelligence outsourcers, made him turn them down and apply to CIA, where the Brahman at human resources told Charlie even with his code word clearances he was lucky to get a GS-14 salary because he didn't have a college degree.

So here he was, still a cog in the federal machine. BGAlbatross tells lies and gets a bonus. *And what does operative Charlie have to show for his scars?* A master sergeant's pension, the Silver Star, the two Purple Hearts, the Combat Infantryman's Badge, the Combat Jump Wings, and the four rows of ribbons in the shadow box on his living room wall is what.

And yet . . . and yet . . . when he actually accomplished something—taught a young Ranger tradecraft that might save his life someday, killed or captured a high-value target, worked a source who got him one step closer to Abu Musab al-Zarqawi—to Charlie, that *mattered*. Duty. Honor. Country. That mattered, too. Later, he'd tell Jose, "I'm fricking old-fashioned is why. A dinosaur, that's me."

So Charlie didn't puke. Or quit. Instead, he stuck his desert-booted foot in the figurative door and browbeat Nicola until she approved Predator surveillance of *bayt* Tariq Zubaydi.

With Nicola's support, there was a bird overhead by 1830 hours. Charlie watched real-time, noting the half-dozen-plus vehicles that visited Tariq's house over an eight-hour stretch. Got a look at some of the individuals. Washed the identifiable pictures not through Baghdad Station but Langley's Big Pond photo database and its newest VEIL (Virtual Exploitation and Information-Leveraging) software. And came up with a couple of palpable hits.

At 0320 hours he woke Nicola and made his sales pitch: Tariq's knowledge of tradecraft, his unique access to real-time information, and his links to known bad guys all made him a viable target.

"It's the duck rule," Charlie insisted.

Just after 0400 hours, wilting under Charlie's barrage, Nicola grudgingly admitted that Tariq quacked like a duck and was therefore probably more than just a grocer who spoke some English.

"That's right—that's why we gotta pick him up."

"Impossible, Charlie."

She was so fricking consistent. But this time there was way too much at stake to let her have her way.

"Nicola, don't be obstructionist. This guy knows stuff. I saw it in the interrogation room. He knows people. I saw it in the Predator surveillance. We gotta grab him."

"If we do, I'll lose him as my agent. I won't get any more videos."

Geezus. Did she see nothing? "He's not *your* agent. He's probably Zarqawi's agent. He's a walk-in. An unvetted walk-in, no less. He's probably target-assessing us for AQI."

"An AQI agent?" Nicola's eyes narrowed. "But I told Langley . . ."

"Let me bring him in—you can box him. Then he's vetted. Then we flip him. Double him back against AQI, like I did Faiz."

She looked at him blankly.

"The mole. Remember?"

Nicola's eyes lost focus. She squirmed, her body language telling Charlie she was nervous her lies would be discovered. So he switched gears. "Y'know, I'm convinced Kim and Maupin are in Tariq's neighborhood."

BGAlbatross crossed her arms. "Headquarters says AQI warehouses hostages in Fallujah, not Baghdad."

"HQ could be wrong." Charlie played off her quizzical look. "Fallujah? It's complicated and risky. Think about the logistics. Moving Kim north with all our coalition roadblocks and thousands of troops, secreting him, making the video, and then getting it back to Tariq? And all in less than twenty-four hours?"

She pursed her lips. "You have a point . . . I guess."

He paused. "C'mon, let me bring Tariq in."

He saw she was weakening.

"For chrissakes, Nicola, if we can pinpoint just one hostage."

"But the consequences, Charlie."

"Nicola, think about the consequences of *not* doing this."

"*Not* doing?"

"An old sergeant major used to tell me, 'The main thing is to keep the main thing the main thing.'"

When her expression told Charlie she had no idea what he was talking about, he spelled it out. "Our main thing is hostages, right?"

"Uh-huh."

"What if bringing Tariq in resulted in retrieving a hostage? Or some solid information about where a hostage—hostages— are being kept?"

Nicola calculated the odds. Then: "You can go. But I'm writing a memo to the file that this is being done against my better judgment because I believe your operation to snatch my

valuable agent—which is how headquarters thinks of Tariq—
is too risky. After all, Charlie, your operation could compro-
mise him."

20 JUNE 2004, 0410 hours. It took Charlie less than fifteen seconds to pick the lock on Tariq's wrought-iron security gate. He
eased it open and, with Fred's infrared flashlight focused on the
vintage lock of the front door, he picked that, too. Charlie's op
plan was basic. They'd made a silent approach. Charlie mounted
an infrared flasher, visible from a thousand yards away, above the
front door. Now they'd make entry stealthily, suppress any resistance, restrain Tariq, then follow up with a thorough SSE—a
sensitive site exploitation—to discover any goodies Tariq might
have lying around. Like his cell phones, his laptop, his PC hard
drive, or any notes, phone messages, memos, or photographs.

Charlie would signal Harlan and Paul, who were in an
ARCHANGEL truck two kliks north. They'd ID the house by its
infrared flasher. Charlie's team would bundle Tariq into the
truck, pile in themselves, and haul butt to Baghdad in plenty of
time for a Father's Day breakfast of Egg McMuffin at the Camp
Victory Mickey D's. It was textbook. Classic.

0411. Charlie eased the inner door open. The beam of Fred's
IR flashlight swept the entry. He saw no trip wires or other
booby traps. His left index finger pressed the switch of the IR
SureFire attached to his M4 and painted the low-ceilinged foyer
left-right, right-left, his eyes leading the muzzle.

All clear. He, Jose, and Fred started forward. Tuzz would
remain outside, making sure they weren't interrupted.

0412. The three men soundlessly cleared the sparsely furnished living room, then moved into the dining area.

That's where the hair on the back of Charlie's neck stood up.
Something's wrong.

He couldn't put a face on it, but his instincts were screaming
oougah-oougah, dive, dive, dive.

Screw 'em. Back to work. Kitchen: clear. Jose's upturned thumb told them that the small laundry room was okay, too.

The ground floor was safe.

0413. Charlie started upstairs. For someone packing sixty pounds of gear he moved with the nimbleness of a ballet dancer. He was climbing the marble stair treads one at a time when he stopped abruptly.

Realized what was wrong.

Realized he'd been an idiot. "Shit."

He backed down the stairs, headed for the kitchen.

Jose: "What's up, boss?"

"This, dude." Charlie's gloved left index finger swept the small kitchen table. Even through the NVGs, the trail of dust was clear.

"And this." He went to the fridge. Opened it. It was empty. Pulled the curtains aside and looked under the sink.

Nothing. No knives, forks, or spoons in the drawers under the counter. No dishes in the cupboards. No food in the pantry. No laundry in the washroom. No signs of life.

Tariq Zubaydi didn't live here. Nobody lived here. This was a safe house.

There was no wife, no crippled kid. *Of course* Tariq was good; *of course* he'd had training. Tariq was fricking AQI. A disinformation agent, just as he'd told Nicola.

Charlie shook his head, disgusted at Nicola's naïveté and his own obtuseness. *Abu Hadidi.* That was the war name the sonofabitch had coughed up. It was probably his own fricking war name. *How dumb can I be?*

Charlie took a good look at the living room. A faux Persian was centered in the room. Atop it sat a couch, a coffee table, and two armchairs. The two lamps were attached to timers.

He dispatched Jose and Fred upstairs. They returned ninety seconds later to confirm what Charlie already knew: The place was empty.

0417. Charlie examined the furniture. Christ, there was something familiar about the armchair. The cabriole leg. He'd seen it in the Maupin video. Even through the green-tinged monochrome of his NVGs he could make out the faded fleur-de-lis pattern. *AQI videoed Keith Maupin in this house.* Tomorrow he'd come back with a forensics team to search for DNA.

"We're on to something." They moved the couch and chairs. Rolled the rug. And discovered exactly what Charlie thought they'd discover: a two-foot-square plug of plywood inlaid into the marble floor.

Then: gunfire. Unmistakable. AKs. Simultaneously: Tuzzy's suppressed M4 and his voice in Charlie's ears: "Hostiles. Two groups, I count eight muzzle flashes."

"Fred, cover with Tuzz," Charlie said into the mike. Then Charlie pinged Paul in the truck. "Get your asses up here."

He pulled the Treo out. The infrared picture from the Predator showed one-two-three-four-five-six-seven-eight-nine-ten hostiles coming in a flanking movement, four from the west, the rest from the south. Bad news: They'd been suckered. And capture was not a viable option here.

Charlie hit the rapid dial. The Treo flamed out—dropped signal. He ran to the doorway, rolled outside, disregarding the AK rounds impacting the stone facade above his head, and tried again. On his flanks, Tuzz and Fred were proned out, squinting through NVGs, squeezing off two-shot bursts.

It seemed an age, then the phone connected. In an even voice, Charlie said, "This is ARCHANGEL."

"ARCHANGEL, Ops," came the reply. It was the operations center at the Combined Joint Special Operations Task Force.

Charlie spoke in shorthand. "SITREP hostiles. Running Bear." SITREP stood for situation report and Running Bear was the code word for tonight's contingency plan—CONPLAN in mil-speak.

"Running Bear CONPLAN," the voice on the other end

confirmed. There was a five-second pause while ARCHANGEL's position was retrieved from the Predator's GPS display and his coordinates were punched into a computer. Then: "Fourteen minutes, ARCHANGEL." That's how long it would take for the pair of Apache attack choppers circling Camp Taji to reach Charlie.

"Roger that." Charlie rolled onto his side and tapped Fred on the back. "Fourteen minutes, dude." Then he stowed the Treo and scurried back into the living room on all fours. He pulled his combat Emerson from its sheath and shoved the blade tip between plywood and marble. Damn, it was tight. "Hoser—gimme a hand here."

The two of them removed the plug.

Revealing a ladder.

Leading to a tunnel.

Leading who fricking knew where.

Nowhere good.

0420. Charlie focused the IR flashlight into the hole. The tunnel floor was nine, maybe ten feet below. Quickly, he started to shrug out of his gear. He'd made that mistake once—got himself wedged so tightly he'd had to cut himself loose. Almost got himself killed.

He peeled down to basics: body armor, mags, knife, pistol, flashlight, NVGs, and commo kit. Jose started to do the same. Charlie waved him off. Charlie was a master sergeant, and master sergeants led by example. "Twelve minutes until cavalry gets here, dude. You stay with Fred and Tuzz. If I need you I'll call."

Jose picked his M4 off the floor. "Stay safe, boss."

"No other way." Charlie rolled onto the ladder, tested the rungs, and when they held, eased his way down.

At the bottom, he scanned through his NVGs. Checked the compass on his watchband. The tunnel went north, and as far as he could see it was unoccupied. But the damn thing was just over a yard wide and less than four feet high.

Charlie stood five-eleven. *Geezus H. My back and my fricking legs are going to kill me by the time I get through this.* Charlie looked up. Jose's bearded face peered down at him, green through the NVGs.

"You okay, boss?"

"Couldn't be better, dude." He gave his teammate an upturned thumb, then swiveled, squatted, and put his M4 in low ready. Gave himself a burst of IR light, saw nothing but air, and duckwalked forward.

0426. Charlie was having trouble breathing. He hadn't gone two hundred feet, yet his lats felt as if they'd been napalmed. His fifty-two-year-old back screamed *Yo, geezer, give me a fricking rocking chair and a screen porch. Yeah, well,* he thought, *Rangers lead the way.*

Lead the way even when you knew it could get you hurt. The way he'd felt jumping at five hundred feet over Grenada. The way he'd felt in Mogadishu. The way he felt now. This is what he *did.*

A hundred feet ahead, the tunnel veered left—west. It looked to be about a forty-five-degree turn. Charlie edged closer to the left wall so as to give himself cover. That's where I'd set the ambush if I was them.

He halted. Brought out the do-rag and Treo, covered his face and head, and fired it up, only to confirm there was no reception down here. That was another bad-news element of twenty-first-century netcentric warfare: It is signals dependent. Block the signal, you defeat the system.

He stowed the PDA. Pressed the transmit button on the radio twice.

Immediately Jose's voice came back at him: "Boss?"

Charlie hit the transmit switch twice again, telling Jose he was okay. At least the radios were working.

0429. He figured he was about three-quarters to the first villa west of Tariq's safe house. Thing was, he wasn't sure what he'd do when he got there.

He was missing something here. They had to know he'd find the tunnel. Had to know he'd come after them. Had to know he wasn't without resources. In—he checked his watch—four and a half minutes the Apaches with all their firepower would be on-site to rip these scumbags new assholes.

0431. Muscles burning, he eased into the curve, moving inch by inch, his NVGs scanning floor, walls, ceiling.

Nothing.

But something deep inside Charlie still made him bring the M4 up. His right thumb eased the safety downward. He was surprised by the loudness of the metallic click as it snapped into the fire position.

Scan and breathe. Eyes open, he kept a sight picture through the NVG-capable Aimpoint.

He moved forward soundlessly, his boots heel-toe, heel-toe on the packed earth, trigger finger indexed, touching the side of the M4's magazine well.

He paused to control himself. Took a deep breath.

Okay. What was the main thing here?

That's the key, Charlie thought. *The main thing is to keep the main thing the main thing.*

And then, as he cleared the bend, Charlie saw something thirty feet ahead that could be the main thing.

A teenage kid. Facing Charlie. Propped up against a wooden crate, kind of sitting on his hands. The kid wasn't wearing a shirt but sported a pair of the baggy pajama bottoms that young Iraqi boys wore before they transitioned to blue jeans.

The left leg of the kid's pj's was cut off above the knee, revealing an ugly, raw stump.

One of the main things about this could-be main thing was that the kid wore an American helmet and stared back at Charlie through its NVGs. On the front of the helmet cover, Charlie read the name MAUPIN.

As unfatherly as it might have been, Charlie's first instinct was to shoot the kid preemptively. Then he thought better of it. But he kept the Aimpoint's dot on the kid's bare chest.

He advanced, the kid staring at him.

From ten feet away, Charlie asked in Arabic, "What's your name, boy?"

"Rachid."

Charlie nodded. "Where'd you get the helmet, Rachid?"

The kid's voice was so subdued he might have been on painkillers. "From my father."

Always ask a question to which you know the answer. Charlie gave it five seconds. "Who's your father, Rachid?"

"My father is Tariq."

That was when Charlie realized what the real main thing was. That the real main thing was Charlie. Charlie, who'd put one big fricking dent in AQI's operations.

"Show me your hands, Rachid."

Shrugging, the kid brought them out. Each adolescent hand held a single alligator clip attached to a pair of wires. The wires ran under the boy to the crate. Two short pieces of wood dowel separated the tips.

As Charlie watched, the kid squeezed the clips. The dowels tumbled in slo-mo onto the tunnel floor.

I should have shot him, Charlie thought. *I should have killed him even though he's someone's son, because the fathers here are fricking nuts.*

Rachid looked at Charlie with the same sort of blank stare Charlie had seen on khat-eaters in Somalia.

"My father says to tell you Happy Father's Day."

In the heartbeat between the time Rachid released the clips and the tunnel disintegrated in a violent orange fireball, Charlie thought he saw the kid smile.

CASEY AT THE BAT

Stephen Hunter

"NO, NO," SAID Basil St. Florian. "Bren guns. We need the Bren guns. It is simply undoable without Bren guns. Surely you understand."

Roger understood but he was nevertheless unwilling.

"Our wealth is in our Bren guns. Without Bren guns, we are nothing. Pah, we are dust, we are cat shit, do you see? Nothing. NOTHING!"

Of course he said *"Rien,"* for the language was French as was the setting, the cellar of a farmhouse outside the rural burg of Nantilles, département Limousin, two hundred miles south and east of Paris. The year was 1944, and the date was June 7. Basil had just dropped in the night before, with his American chum.

"Do you not see," Basil explained, "that the point in giving you Brens was to wage war upon the Germans, not to make you powerful politically in the postwar, after we have pushed Jerry out? Communists, Gaullists, we do not care, it does not matter, or matter *now*. What matters now is that you have to help us push Jerry out. That was the point of the Bren guns. We gave them to you for that reason, explicitly, and no other. You have had them eighteen months, and you have never used them once. The war will be over, we will push Jerry out, the Gaullists will take over, and we will demand our Brens back, and if we don't get them, we will send Irishmen to get them. You do not want Irishmen interested in you. No good can come of it. It's my advice to use the Brens, help us push Jerry, become glorious heroes, happily give up the Brens, then defeat the Gaullists in fair, free elections."

"I will not give you Bren guns," said Roger, "and that is final. Long live Comintern. Long live the Internationale. Long live the great Stalin, the bear, the man of steel. If you were in Spain, you would understand this principle. If you—"

Basil turned to Leets.

"Make him see about the Brens. Dear Roger, listen to the American lieutenant here. Do you think the Americans would have sent a fellow so far as they've sent this one just to tell you lies? I understand that you might not trust a pompous British foof like me, but this fellow is an actual son of the earth. His pater was a farmer. He raises wheat and cows and fights red Indians, as in the movies. He is tall, silent, magnificent. He is a walking myth. Listen to him."

He turned to his chum Leets and then realized he had, once again, forgotten Leets's name. It was nothing personal, he just was so busy being magnificent and British and all that, so he couldn't be troubled by small details, such as Yank names.

"I say, Lieutenant, I seem to have forgotten the name. What was the name again?" He thought it was remarkable that the name kept slipping away on him. They had trained together at Milton Hall on the river Jedburgh in Scotland for this little picnic for six or so weeks, but the name kept slipping away, and whenever it did, it took Basil wholly out of where he was and turned his attention to the mystery of the disappearing name.

"My name is Leets," said Leets in English, accented in the tones of the middle plains of his vast homeland, the Minnesota part.

"It's so strange," said Basil. "It just goes away. Poof, it's gone, so bizarre. Anyhow, tell him."

Leets also spoke French with a Parisian accent, which was why Roger, of Group Roger, didn't care for him, or for Basil. Roger thought all Parisians were traitors or bourgeoisie, equally culpable in any case, and that seemed to go twice for British or American Parisians. He didn't know that Leets spoke with a Parisian accent because he'd lived there between the ages of two and nine while his father managed 3M's European accounts. No, Leets's father was not a farmer, not hardly, and had certainly never fought red Indians; he was a rather wealthy business executive now retired, living in Sarasota, Florida, with one son, Leets, in occupied France playing cowboys with the insane, another a naval aviator on a jeep carrier that had yet to reach the Pacific, and still a third 4-F and in medical school in Chicago.

Roger, namesake and kingpin of Group Roger, turned his fetid little eyes upon Leets.

"I can blow the bridge," said Leets. "It's not a problem. The bridge will go down; it's only a matter of rigging the 808 in the right place and leaving a couple of time pencils stuck in the stuff."

But Basil interrupted, on the wings of an epiphany.

"It's because you're all so similar," he said, as if he'd given the matter a great deal of Oxford-educated thought. "It has to do with gene pools. In our country, or in Europe on the whole, the gene pool is much more diverse. You see that in the fantastic European faces. Really, go to any city in Europe, and the variety in such features as eye spacing, jawline, height of forehead, width of cheekbones is extraordinary. I could watch it for days. But you Yanks seem to have about three faces between you, and you pass them back and forth. Yours is the farm boy face. Rather broad, no visible bone structure, pleasant, but not sharp enough to be particularly attractive. I fear you'll lose your hair prematurely. Your people do have good, healthy dentition, I must give you that. But all the plumpness on the face. You must eat nothing but cake and candy. It goes to your face and turns you rather clownish, and it's wizard-hard keeping you apart. You remind me of at least six other Americans I know, and I can't remember their names either. Wait, one of them is a chap called Carruthers. Do you know him?"

Leets thought this question rhetorical, and in any event it seemed to tucker Basil out for a bit. Leets turned back to the fat French communist guerrilla.

"We can kill the sentries, I can rig the 808 and plant the package, and it doesn't even have to be fancy. It's simple engineering; anyone could look at it and see the stress points. So: Pop the tab on the time pencil and run like hell. The problem is that the garrison at Nantilles is only a mile away, and the minimum time I can get the bridge rigged is about three minutes because we have to go in hard. When we shoot the sentries, it'll make a noise, because we don't have suppressors. The noise will travel and the garrison will be alerted. Meanwhile, I have to get down and lash the package just so on the trusses. They'll get there before I'm done. So my team will get fried like eggs if we're still rigging when they show. That's why we need the Brens. We've only got rifles and Stens and my Thompson, and we can't build enough volume of fire to hold them off. I need two Brens on the road from Nantilles with a lot of ammo to shoot up the trucks as they come along. You can't disable a truck with a Sten. Simple physics: The Sten shoots a nine-millimeter pistol bullet and it doesn't penetrate metal. Sometimes it even bounces off of glass. The Bren .303 is a powerful rifle- and machine-gun round which will penetrate the sheet metal of truck construction, damage the motor, rip up the wiring and tubing, as well as rupture the tires. It will pierce the wood construction of the truck bed and hit the men it carries. It can also lay down heavy, powerful fields of fire that will drive infantry back. That's what it's for; that's why the British gave you the Brens."

"The lieutenant knows a lot about guns, doesn't he?" said Basil. "I'm rather alarmed, to be honest. It seems somewhat unwholesome to know that much about such a macabre topic."

"*Non!*" said Roger, spraying them with garlic. He was a butcher, immense and sagacious. He'd fought on the Loyalist side in Spain, where he was wounded twice. He was almost grotesquely valiant and fearless, but he understood the primitive calculus of the politics: The Brens were power, and without power Group Roger would be at the mercy of all other groups, and that was more important than the prospect of 2nd SS Panzer Division Das Reich using the bridge to rush tanks to the Normandy beachhead, as intelligence predicted they would surely do.

"My dear brother-in-arms Roger," said Basil, "the bridge will be blown, that I assure you. The only thing in doubt is whether Lieutenant Beets—"

"Leets."

"Leets, yes, of course, whether Lieutenant Leets and his team of maquis from Group Phillippe will make it out alive. Without the Brens, they haven't a chance, do you see?"

"Phillippe is a pig, as are all his men," said Roger. "It is better for them to die at the bridge and spare us the effort of hunting them down to hang after the war. That is my only concern."

"Can you say to this brave young American, 'Leftenant Beets, you must die, that is all there is to it'?"

"Yes, it's nothing," said Roger. He turned to Leets with uninterested eyes. "'Leftenant Beets, you must die, that is all there is to it.' All right, I said it. Fine. Good-bye, sorry and all that, but policy is policy."

He signaled his two bodyguards, who after rattling their Schmeissers dramatically film-noir style, rose and began to escort him up the cellar steps.

"Well, there you have it," said Basil to Leets. "Sorry, but it looks like your number is up, leftenant. You get pranged. Sad, unjust, but inescapable. Fate, I gather. Yours not to reason why, et cetera et cetera. Do you know your Tennyson?"

"I know that one," said Leets glumly.

"I suppose one could simply not go. I think that's what I'd do in your shoes, but then I'm not the demo man, you are. I'm the head potato, so I'll supervise quite nicely from the treeline. As for you, if you decide not to go, it would be embarrassing, of course, but in the long run, it probably doesn't make much difference whether the bridge goes or not, and it seems silly to waste a future doctor of all the fabled Minnesotans on such a local Frenchy balls-up between de Gaulle's smarmy peons and that giant, stinking, garlic-sucking red butcher."

"If I catch it," said Leets, "I catch it. That's the game I signed up for. I just hate to catch it because of some little snit between Group Roger and Group Phillippe. Stopping Das Reich is worth it; helping Roger prevail over Phillippe is not, and I don't give a shit about FFI or FTP."

"Yet they can't really be separated, can they? It's always so complicated, haven't you noticed? Politics, politics, politics, it's like chewing gum in the works—it gets in everywhere and mucks up everything. Anyhow, if you like, I'll write your people a very nice letter about what a hero you were. Would you like that?"

As with much of what Basil said, the words were pitched in a key of meaning so exquisite Leets couldn't exactly tell if they were serious or not. You could never be sure with Basil; he frequently said the exact opposite of what he meant. He seemed to live in a zone of near-comedy in which nearly every damned thing was "amusing" and he took great pleasure in saying the "shocking" thing. The first thing he said to Leets all those weeks ago at Milton were, "It's all a racket, you know. Our richies are trying to wipe out their richies so they can get all the nig-nog gold; that's what it's *really* all about. Our job is to make the world safe for nig-nog gold."

"Jim Leets," Leets had said, "Sigma Chi, N.U. '41."

Now Basil said, "I can, however, in my tiny British pea brain, concoct one other possibility."

"What's that?"

"Well, it has to do with a radio."

"We don't have a radio."

The radio was lashed to Andre Breton's body which, unfortunately, had hit the earth at about eight hundred miles an hour when Andre's parachute ripped in half on the tail spar of the Liberator that had dropped them the night of the invasion. Neither the radio nor Andre had been salvageable, which is why Team Casey was down 33 percent strength before its other two-thirds landed under their chutes a minute or so after Andre had his accident.

"The Germans have radios."

"We're not Germans. We're good guys, remember? Captain, sometimes I think you don't take this all that seriously."

"I speak German. What else is necessary?"

"This is crazy. You'll never—"

"Anyway, here's my idea. I cop a German uniform tomorrow, and walk into the garrison headquarters at eleven a.m. With my command presence, I will send Jerry away. Then I will commandeer his radio and put in a call. A fellow owes me a favor. If his groundwork is solid, it just might work out."

"Jerry will put you up against a wall at 11:03 and shoot you."

"Hmm, good point. Possibly if Jerry is distracted."

"Go ahead, I'm all ears."

"You blow something up. I don't know, anything. Improvise, that's what you chaps are so good at. Jerry runs to see. While Jerry's got his knickers in a wad, I enter the garrison headquarters, all snazzed up, Jerry-style. It's easy for me to commandeer the radio, make my call. Five minutes and I'm out."

"Who are you trying to reach on radio?"

"A certain fellow."

"A fellow where?"

"In England."

"You're going to radio England? From a German command post in occupied France?"

"I am. I'm going to dial up Roddy Walthingham, of the Signals Intelligence Branch, in Islington. He's some kind of mucky-muck there and there are sure to be lots of radios about."

"What can he do?"

"You didn't hear this from me, chum, but it's said he's one of the pinks. Pink as in red. Same team, just different players, for now. Joe for king, that sort of thing. Anyhow, he's sure to know somebody who knows somebody who knows somebody in the big town."

"London?" asked Leets, but Basil just smiled, and Leets realized he meant Moscow.

So Basil turned himself into a passable German officer with little enough trouble. The uniform came from an actual officer who had been killed in an ambush in 1943, and his uniform kept in storage by the maquis against the possibility of just such a gambit. It smelled of sweat, farts, and blood. It was also a year out of date in terms of accoutrements, badges, and suchlike, but Basil knew or at least believed that with enough charisma he could get through anything.

And thus at eleven a.m., as Leets and three maquis from Group Phillippe prepared to blow up a deserted farmhouse half a mile out of town the other way from the bridge, Basil strode masterfully to the gate of the garrison HQ of the 113th Flakbattalion, the lucky Luftwaffers who controlled security there in Nantilles. The explosion had the predictable effect on the Luftwaffers, who panicked, grabbed weapons and other equipment, and began running toward the rising column of smoke. They were terrified of a screwup because it meant they might be transferred somewhere actual fighting was possible.

Basil watched them go, and when the last of several ragtag groups had disappeared, he strode toward the big communications van next to the château, with its thirty-foot radio mast adorned with all kinds of Jerry stylistics; this one had a triangle up top. These people!

It helped that the officer whose uniform he wore had been a hero, and a lot of ribbons and badges decorated his breast. One, in particular, was an emblem of a tank, and underneath it hung three little plates of some sort. The other stuff was the usual mishmash of bold colored ribbons and such, and it all signified martial valor, very impressive to the distinctly nonmilitaristic Luftwaffers who hadn't run to the blasts and didn't know skittles about such stuff but recognized what they took to be the real McCoy when it appeared.

Basil got to the radio van easily enough and chased the duty sergeant away by proclaiming himself Major Strasser—he'd seen *Casablanca*, of course—of Abwehr 31, top secret.

He faced a bank of gear, all of it rather H. G. Wellesian in its futuresque array of dials, switches, knobs, gauges, and such forth set in shiny Bakelite.

The transceiver turned out to be a 15W S.E., a small, complete station with an output power of 15 watts, just jolly super and what the doctor ordered. The frequency range embraced those used by the British and the mechanics for synchronization between transmitter and receiver was very advanced.

He faced the thing, a big green box opened to show an instrumentality. Two dials up top, a midpoint dial displaying frequency, the tuner below, and below that buttons and switches and all the foofah of radioland. Had he a course on it somewhere in time? Seems he had, but there was so much, it was best to let the old subconscious take over and run the show.

It was very Teutonic. It had labels and sublabels everywhere, switches, dials, wires, the whole German gestalt in one instrument, insanely well ordered yet somewhat overengineered in a vulgar way. Instead of "On/Off" the switch read literally, "Makingtobroadcast/Stoppingtobroadcast Facilitation." A British radio would have been less imposing, less a manifesto of purpose, but also less reliable. You could bomb this thing and it would keep working.

The machine crackled and spat and began to radiate heat. Evidently it was quite powerful.

He put on some radio earphones, hearing the noise of static to be quite annoying, found what had to be a channel or frequency knob, and spun it to the British range.

He knew both sides worked with jamming equipment, but it wasn't useful to jam large numbers of frequencies, so more usually they played little games, trying to infiltrate each other's communications and cause mischief. He also knew he should flip a switch and go to Morse, but he had never been a good operator. He reasoned that the airwaves today were totally filled with chatter of various sorts and whomever was listening would have to weigh the English heavily, get interpretation from analysts, and alert command, and the whole process had to take days. He decided just to talk, as if on telly from a club in Bloomsbury.

"Hullo, hullo," he said each time the crackly static stopped.

A couple of times he got Germans screaming, "You must use radio procedure, you are directed to halt, this is against regulations," and turned quickly away, but later rather than sooner, someone said, "Hullo, who's this?"

"Basil St. Florian," Basil said.

"Chum, use radio protocol, please. Identify by call sign, wait for verification."

"Sorry, don't know the protocol. It's a borrowed radio, do you see?"

"Chum, I can't—Basil St. Florian? Were you at Harrow, '28 through '32? Big fellow, batsman, six runs against St. Albans?"

"Seven, actually. The gods smiled on me that day."

"I went down at St. Albans. I was fine leg. I dismissed you, finally. You smiled at me. Lord, I never saw such a striker."

"I remember. Such, such were the joys, old man. Who knew we'd meet again like this? Now, look here, I'm trying to reach Islington Signals Intelligence. Can you help?"

"I shouldn't give out information."

"Old man, it's not like I'm just anybody. I remember you. Reddish hair, freckly, looked like you wanted to squid me on the noggin. Remember how fierce you were, that's why I winked. I have it right, don't I?"

"In fact, you do. All these years, now this. Islington, you say?"

"Absolutely. Can you help?"

"I'm actually wizard-keen on these things. It took a war to find out. Hmm, let me just do some diddling, they'd be John-Able-6, do you see? I'm going to do a patch."

"Thanks ever so much."

Basil waited, examining his fingernails, looking about for something to drink. A nice port, say, or possibly some aged French cognac? He yawned. Tick-tock, tick-tock, tick-tock. *When* would the fellow—

"Identify, please."

"Is this John-Able-6?"

"Identify, please."

"Basil St. Florian. Looking to speak with your man Roddy Walthingham. Put him on, there's a good lad."

"Do you think this is a telephone exchange?"

"No, no, but nevertheless I need to talk to him. Old school chum. Need a favor."

"Identify, please."

"Listen carefully: I am in a bother and I need to talk to Roddy. It's war business, not gossip."

"Where are you?"

"In Nantilles."

"Didn't realize the boys had got that far inland."

"They haven't. That's why it's rather urgent, old man."

"This is very against regulations."

"Dear man, I'm actually at a Jerry radio and at any moment, Jerry will return. Now I have to talk to Roddy. Please, play up play up and play the game."

"Public school then. I hate you all. You deserve to burn."

"We do, I know. Such officious little pricks, the lot of us. I'll help you light the timbers after the war and then climb into them, smiling. But first, let's win it. I implore you."

"Bah," said the fellow, "you'd best not put me on report."

"I shan't."

"All right. He's right next door. Hate him too."

In a minute or so, another voice came over the earphones.

"Yes, hullo."

"Roddy, it's Basil. Basil St. Florian."

"Basil, good God."

"How're Diane and the girls?"

"Rather enjoying the country. They could come back to town, since Jerry hardly flies anymore, but I think they like it out there."

"Good for them. Say, Roddy, need a favor, do you mind?"

"Certainly, Basil, if I can."

"I'm to go with some boys tonight to set off a firecracker under a bridge. Nasty work, they say it has to be done. 'Ours not to reason why,' all that."

"Sounds fascinating."

"Not really. Hardly any wit to it at all. You know, just destroying things, it seems so infantile in the long run. Anyhow, our cause would be helped if a gang in the area called Group Roger, have you got that, would pitch in with its Brens. But it's some red-white thing and they won't help. I thought you had Uncle Joe's ear—"

"Basil! Now really! People may be listening."

"No inference or judgment meant. I tell no tales, and let each man enjoy his own politics and loyalties, as I do mine. That's what the war's all about, isn't it? Let's put it this way: If *one* had Uncle Joe's ear, *one* might ask that Group Roger in Nantilles vicinity pitch in with Brens to help Group Phillippe. That's all. Have you got that?"

"Roger, Brens, Phillippe, Nantilles. I'll make a call."

"Thanks, old man. Good-bye."

"No, no, you say *over and out*."

"Over and out, then."

"Ciao, friend."

Basil put the microphone down, unhooked the earphones from around his head, and looked up into the eyes of two sergeants with Schmeissers and a lieutenant colonel.

LEETS LOOKED AT his Bulova. It had been an hour, no, an hour and a half.

"I think they got him," said his No. 1, a young fellow called Leon.

"Shit," said Leets, in English. He was at a window in the upper floor of a residence fifty yards across from the gated château that served as the 113th Flakbattalion's headquarters and garrison. He held an M1 Thompson submachine gun low, out of sight, and wore a French rain slicker, rubbers, and a plowman's rough hat.

"We can't hit it," said Leon. "Not four of us. And if we got him out, on the surprise aspect of it, where'd we go? We have no automobile to escape."

Leon was right, but still Leets hated the idea of Captain Basil St. Florian perishing on something so utterly trivial as a bridge in the interests of one Team Casey that existed out of a misbegotten SOE/OSS cooperative plan, silly, cracked, and doomed as all get out. Strictly a show, thought up by big headquarters brainiacs with too much spare time, of no true import. He knew it; they all knew it and had known it in all the hours in Areas A and F and whatever, disguised golf clubs mostly, where they'd trained before deployment to the god-awful food at Milton Hall. As the Brit had said, it probably didn't make any difference anyhow. He cursed himself; he should have just planted the charges without the Brens and taken his chances on the run to the woods. Maybe the Krauts wouldn't have been quick enough out of the gates to get there and lay down fire before he rigged his surprises. Maybe it would have been a piece of cake. But you couldn't tell Basil St. Florian a thing, and when the man got an idea in his head, it crowded out all other concerns.

"Look!" said Leon.

It was Basil. He was not alone. He was surrounded by adoring young men of the 113th Flakbattalion and their commanding officer who were escorting Basil to the gate. Basil made a brief, theatrical bow, shook the commander's hand, and turned and smartly strode off.

It took a while for him to reach the outskirts of town, but when he hit the rendezvous, Leets and the maquis, by backstreets and fence-jumping, were already there.

"What the hell?"

"Well, I reached Roddy. Somehow. He's to make certain arrangements."

"What took you so long?"

"Ah, it seems the previous owner of this uniform had an illustrious career. This little trinket"—he touched the metallic emblem of a tank with its three tiny plates affixed serially beneath—"signifies a champion tank destroyer on the Eastern Front. The Luftwaffers wanted to hear war stories. So I ended up giving a little performance on the best ways to destroy a T-36. Good God, I hope none of the fellows—they seemed like good lads—try that sort of thing on their own against a Centurion. I just made it up. Something about the third wheel of the left tread being the drive wheel, and if you could hit that with a Panzerfaust, the machine would stop in its tracks. Could there be a third wheel? And I don't believe I specified left from which perspective. All in all, it was a rather feeble performance, but the London *Times* critics weren't around, just some dim Hanoverian farm boys drafted into the German air force."

"You made the call? You got through?"

"Why, it worked better than our trunk lines. No operator, no interference. It was as if Roddy was in the same room. Amazing, these technical things. Now, what's for dinner?"

IT SELDOM WORKED as well as it did that night, perhaps using up the last of Team Casey's good luck. At any rate, Roddy moseyed out of the radio shack. It was rainy in Islington and everybody was keen about invasion news. Would our boys be pushed back? Or would they stay, and was this the beginning of the end?

So nobody paid much attention to a short, fat man with an academic's somewhat diffident habit of moving and being. Roddy drew his mackintosh tight about him, pulled his deerstalker down about his ears to keep the surprising June chill out, and nodded at the duty officer. His specialty was coding, and he was actually damned good at it, if thought by all a trifle odd. He wandered about as if there wasn't a war on, and by now everyone accepted that his weirdness and inability to deal with military security matters were a part of his genius and must be accepted. Actually, it was good cover for his real job, which was straight penetration for GRU Section 7, foreign intelligence.

He crossed the busy street to a druggist's and looked for the phone. He found it occupied and waited smilingly as a woman finished her call, then departed. He entered, dropped a tuppence, and waited. It rang three times. He hung up. The phone rang twice, then ceased. Roddy redialed the number.

"Hullo, is that you?"

"Of course, Roddy. Who else could it be?"

Roddy's conversational partner was Major Boris Zyborny, code name RAFTER, in charge of penetration of the British main target and Roddy's controller. He worked in deep cover in the Polish Free Republic Democratic Army liaison office, doing something or other unclear, while keeping tabs on all his boys and girls for Red Army intelligence.

Roddy said, "I need a favor. An old school chum."

"One of ours?"

"No."

"He's to be ignored. He's meaningless. Enjoy his company, mourn his death if it happens, but keep him out of the equation."

"A *good* friend. I want to help him."

Roddy explained, and seven minutes later, Major Zyborny was on the long-range radio to Moscow GRU, where someone eventually tracked down a partisan director named Klemansk, a former Comintern agent who'd magically escaped the purges (he was in a Spanish prison awaiting execution at the time) and now commanded Activity Sphere 3, Western Europe, for GRU. Klemansk took some convincing, and in the end agreed because Zyborny assured him that Roddy was important and could only become more important and doing little things like this for him would keep him happy for the long, hard years ahead.

So Klemansk got on Activity Sphere 3's radio hookup, and via Paris, reached Group Roger on the matter of the Bren guns.

THE GERMANS OF course monitored all this information, as their radio intelligence and intercept systems were superb. However, it was buried in endless tons of other intercepted information, as the invasion had upped radio traffic to nearly torrential levels. It was beyond human capacity to analyze and interpret all of it, and by priority, it was decanted into categories depending on urgency. Since a bridge outside Nantilles was way down the list, the intercepts didn't get the attention they clearly deserved until June 14, 1944, by which time the obscure drama of Team Casey, the 113th Luftwaffe Flakbattalion, 2nd SS Panzer Division Das Reich, and Groups Roger and Phillippe had long since played out.

★　　　★　　　★

LEETS APPLIED THE last of the burnt cork to his face. Burning corks had turned out to be no picnic. Back at Area 5 in the Catoctins, everybody had assured the trainees that burning cork was a piece of cake, but no one ever managed to explain how to do it. Major Applegate told stories about hunting Mexicans on the Arizona border with the border patrol, and how they'd always corked their faces when serious business was set for the evening, but he never ever explained exactly how to burn the goddamned cork. Leets had singed the hair off his fingers before he struck on the idea of wedging the cork into a doorway, holding it there by pressuring the door against it with his foot, and burning it with candle flame. It oxidized slowly, stupidly, and resentfully, but finally he had enough and managed to do a reasonable job of masquerading his fat, broad, uninteresting, and very white American face against the darkness.

HE WAS NOW ready, though he felt more like the football player he'd been than the soldier he was, so packed with gear very like the shoulder and thigh pads that had protected him in Big Ten wars. He had a Thompson gun and seven mags with twenty-eight .45s in each, the mags in a pouch strapped to his web belt, as were six Gammon grenades, Allways fuzes packed with half a stick of the green plasticky Explosive 808, all ready to have their caps unscrewed, their linen lines secured, and then be tossed to explode on impact. They smelled of almonds, reminding him of a candy bar he had once loved in a far-off paradise called Minnesota. He had a wicked, phosphate-bladed M3 fighting knife strapped to his right outside lace-up Corcoran jump boot, which was bloused neatly into his reinforced jump pants, an OD cotton slash-pocketed jump jacket, almost like Hemingway's safari coat, over his wool OD shirt with his silver first lieutenant's bars and the crossed rifles of Infantry, as he'd been a member of the 501st of the 101st before his French got him recruitment by OSS, a Colt .45 on the web belt, seven in the mag, two more mags on a pouch on the web, and a black watch cap pulled low over his ears so that he looked like one of the lesser Our Gang members. He also carried a satchel full of Explosive 808, also smelling pungently of almonds and, let's see, was that it, oh yes, time pencils, that is, Delay Switch No. 10, a tin of five of them in the satchel with the 808 for quick deployment.

The plan: The Luftwaffers had wisely used French labor to cut down the forest around the bridge, so it was basically coverless, nude land on the approach, studded with evergreen stumps that were stout enough to stop all vehicles that ran on tires. Stealth was impossible, too, in the arc lights the Germans had mounted that blazed away all night long. There was no danger from the six 88-millimeter flak guns sandbagged around the bridge, since they were dedicated, meaning permanently mounted in antiaircraft trajectories to defend the bridge from Allied air attack, and so out of the picture tactically, and were unmanned at night, as no Typhoons or Jugs would risk a run in the dark. But there were at least six sentries, a sergeant of the guard and four or five riflemen, at each end of the bridge.

So stealth was out. Rather, in a rattly old Citroën, Leets and his three FFI maquis would approach the bridge and when called to halt at close range open fire. They would shoot the sentries, Gammon bomb the guardhouse, and lay down fire on the men at the other end of the bridge, and Leets would hop out to the center, monkey-climb over, plant the 808, and wedge in the already primed time pencils, and then they'd run like hell to the woods two hundred yards away. If reinforcements from Nantilles got there before they made it to the woods, they'd be dead friggin' ducks, as the Germans, even incompetent Luftwaffers, could hose them down with MG-42 fire from the guns mounted on the trucks, while the men gave chase with Mausers and Schmeissers.

That's where the Brens came in. The Brens could drive the trucks back, even destroy them, and scatter the easily frightened

Luftwaffers. The whole thing turned on the Brens. The two Brens were the wanted nail that doomed the horse that lost the squad that let down the battalion that defeated the army that ruined the war.

"Great news, chum," said Basil. "You have Brens!"

"What?"

"Hmm, it seems that Roger had a change of mind, or perhaps an order from higher HQ. In any event, even as we speak, Roger and his two Bren gun teams are setting up on the slope overlooking the road from Nantilles, three hundred yards beyond the bridge."

"Do we know that for a fact?"

"Chum, if Roger says they're there, then they're there."

"I wish I could actually see the guys." But he looked at the Bulova he wore upside down on his wrist and saw that it was 0238 British War Time, so it was time to go.

"Okay," he said, "then let's blow this son of a bitch."

"Good attitude. I'll be with the other boys in the woodline. We'll lay down fire from our end."

"You can't see well enough to do any good, and that goddamn little peashooter"—Leets indicated the Sten Machine Carbine hung around Basil by a sling, a tubular construction that looked as if it had been designed by a committee of very dull plumbers, a 9-millimeter burp gun that fired too fast when it fired at all, and then its bullets did little good when they got there if they got there at all—"won't frighten anyone."

"Beets, I can't help it that their guns are so much better than ours. We make do with what is. We do our bit, that's all."

"Yeah, yeah. Well, let's go then. Batter up!" Leets said bitterly. He stormed to the Citroën for his drive to battle. But then he remembered his manners.

"Sorry, captain. I'm a blowhard, I know. Just venting because I'm scared shitless. Anyhow, thanks, what you did was swell, it was, I don't know—"

"Stop it, Beets. Just go blow up your silly bridge."

"Captain, one last thing. Who the hell are you? Where are you from? How do you know so much? What are you doing here? Surely you're too old, too advanced, too brilliant for all this running around. You should be a general or something. You look forty. Who *are* you?"

"Long, long story, chum. Blow the damned bridge and we'll have a chat."

ENTER MILLIE BEEMAN. Millie, from Millicent, from the Beemans, you know, *the* Beemans of the North Shore. Millie was a lovely girl, clever as the devil. She graduated with high marks from Smith but never bragged or acted smart, got her first job working as a secretary at *Time* in Manhattan for the awful Luce and his hideous wife, spent some time on a Senate staff (her father arranged it), and then when war came, she gravitated toward the Office of Strategic Services just as surely as it gravitated toward her. People knew where they belonged, and organizations knew what kind of people belonged in them, so General Donovan's assistants fell in instant love with the willowy blonde who looked smashing at any party, smoked brilliantly, and had languid, see-through-anything luminosity in her eyes. Everyone loved the way her hair fell down to her shoulders; everyone loved the diaphanous cling of a gown or blouse to her long-limbed, definitely femalesque torso; everyone loved her yards and yards of legs, her perfect ankles well displayed by the platform of the heels all the girls wore.

By '43 she'd transferred to London station at 72 Grosvenor in Mayfair, under Colonel Bruce, one of whose assistants she'd become, and wore the uniform of a second lieutenant in the WACs. She was in charge of the colonel's social calendar, important since one of the common jests of the time was that OSS actually stood for Oh So Social. She answered his phones or placed his calls, but it was more than that. She also knew the

town, in the sense of "knew the town," and so was able to pri-
oritize. The colonel was hopeless and said yes to every invitation
in the days before she arrived on station. She knew who was in,
who out, which receptions it was important to be seen at, which
could be safely ignored, which generals were in the ascension,
which in the decline, which FFI liaison officers could be trusted,
which should be avoided, which journalists were helpful, which
were not, who could be blackmailed, ignored, betrayed, dumped,
manipulated, or insulted and, by contrast, who could be trusted,
used, counted on, confided in, who had access, represented the
kind of people we like and need, and so forth and so on. She was
indispensable, she was ruthless, she was efficient, she was beautiful and brilliant at once, and she was the third-ranking NKVD
agent in OSS, the star of INO (Foreign Intelligence Section) who
had been trained at SHON, Shkola Osobogo Naznacheniya, the
Special Purposes School, in Balashikha, fifteen miles east of the
Moscow Ring Road, when everybody thought she was rusticat-
ing in the Hamptons.

Millie sniffed something was up at six p.m. that evening,
when Colonel Bruce's mood immediately brightened. The issue
of the day had been Operation Jedburgh, by which three-man
teams of OSS/SOE/FFI agents had parachuted behind the lines
to wreak havoc on German communications and transportation
lines in the immediate wake of the Normandy show. So far, no
good. No teams had hit a target, many had drifted apart in the
descent and failed to link up with maquis units whom they were
supposed to lead, and several had never acknowledged arrival by
radio and were considered combat-lost. It was looking like a
washout, and Colonel Bruce knew he was meeting with Sir
Colin Gubbins, head of SOE, and that Gubbins would blame the
muck-up on the American third of the units. It was *so* important
that the teams do well!

But around six, an SOE liaison informed the colonel that
radio intercepts strongly suggested one team was in position

and would strike tonight at midnight against a bridge on Das Reich's route to the beachhead.

"Millie, do you see? This is what we need."

It was a great issue with OSS that it was considered immature, inferior, and amateur in comparison to the far savvier British intel outfits, and it drove General Donovan mad.

"Yes, sir."

"Oh, the boys," said Colonel Bruce. "Those wonderful, wonderful boys, they make me so proud. Here's to Casey's turn at bat!"

Millie, of course, was not privy to code names and didn't know which groups were operating where; she just scooped up all available information and turned it over to her KGB INO control, a fellow named Hedgepath who'd been big in WPA before the war and was now big in the Office of War Information, the propaganda unit, where he was some sort of chief of psychological operations or something like that, reporting directly to Mr. Sherwood. She adored Hedgepath, because of course he was one of the few men on earth who didn't yield to and couldn't be budged by her blandishments, charms, and beauty; she had no way of knowing he was a sexual deviate and therefore immune to such.

She called him from a phone in Accounting Section, feeling utterly secure, because no one monitored internal calls between American entities such as 72 Grosvenor and the London OWI headquarters nearby. It was Kate Jesse's phone, and Kate thought she used it to speak to a secret lover, an RAF bomber pilot. Kate's problem: She read *Redbook* magazine too earnestly.

"Hullo," said Hedgepath.

"Millie here."

"Of course, my dear. Report, please."

She reiterated what she had learned that day: the colonel's schedule, his incoming calls, reports, office tidbits, expenditure, the nuts and bolts of it. Finally she mentioned some kind of show that was set for the evening and the colonel's curious explosion of glee, "Casey's turn at bat."

"Oh, baseball," said Mr. Hedgepath. "I loathe baseball. It's mostly standing around, isn't it? Awfully boring. Who's this Casey?"

"It's from a famous poem. 'Mighty Casey' they call him, a sort of Babe Ruth figure. All hopes are on him. It's very dramatic."

"Who knew there was drama in baseball?"

"At any rate, 'Casey at the Bat' is about a hero's chance to win the big game. As I recall, he fails. In America, it's regarded a tragedy. I think Casey has to do with something they're calling Operation Jedburgh."

Jedburgh?

"Hmm," said Hedgepath. He knew from NKVD Moscow Center that the terrible Zyborny had sent a flash to GRU earlier, but Center wasn't completely able to penetrate the GRU code and knew only that the subject of the message was a Brit-Yank-Frenchy thing called Operation Jedburgh, some silly blowing-up of structures that would have to be expensively rebuilt after the war. But Control did not want GRU operating with impunity anywhere, and the two agencies cordially hated each other. NKVD Moscow Center was suddenly interested in Operation Jed, not as part of the war against the Germans, which it knew was won, but in the war against GRU for postwar operational control of the intelligence mechanism.

"Urgent you penetrate Jed," Moscow had ordered.

"My dear Miss Beeman," said Mr. Hedgepath. "Can you focus tonight on this 'Casey' thing? There's a lot of interest in it. Possibly flirt it up with one of the cowboys and get me some information soonest? I'd like to pop a line to Our Friends before bedtime if possible."

Millie sighed. She knew exactly what she had to do. Drinks with Frank Tyne, a horrible man who was all swagger and bluster. He'd been in and out of France for two years now and it was rumored had actually killed several Germans. More to the point, he adored her and had been asking her out for weeks.

Tonight, his dreams came true.

LEETS WAS HAVING some trouble breathing. His stomach was edgy, his fingers felt like greasy sausages from someone else's body, and he wanted only to sleep. He'd felt this way before games sometimes. He'd been a tight end usually, because of his size, a blocker, but there were a few plays in the book that designated him as receiver, and he both loved and hated that opportunity. You could become a hero. You could become a goat. It all happened in a split second in front of fifty thousand yelling maniacs cram-packed into Dyche Stadium or some other Big Ten coliseum. Once, memorably (to him at any rate) he caught a touchdown ball on a freakish, lucky, thing-of-beauty pass that he'd ticked with a finger, popped into the air, and snatched while himself falling. He was a hero who knew he'd been lucky and secretly felt he didn't deserve the Monday of acclaim he'd gotten. It was his favorite memory; it was his worst memory. It came to him now in both formats.

The car rolled onward. No wonder they called them coffee-grinders, a little turtle of a thing powered seemingly by batteries. *Chut-chut-chut* it went. Leon drove. Leets was in the passenger's side with the Thompson. In the backseat, in fetal positions, were Jerome and Franc, good guys, kids really, all with Stens. They'd have trouble getting out, so it was up to Leets, really. He'd deliver the first blows for freedom in this part of France. He felt sick about it, but it was increasingly obvious that it didn't matter how he felt, as what would happen would happen, and if the Brens were there, thank God and Basil St. Florian, and if they weren't, Dad would be so upset.

A bottle was produced. It came to Leets with a small glass. He poured some bitter fluid, man, it kicked like a mule, JESUS

CHRIST! he gasped for breath, poured another tot, and held it over for Leon to gulp down.

"Vive la France!" said Leon, completing the transaction.

"Vive la France!" came the salute from the rear.

Vive my ass! thought Leets.

They entered the cone of Luftwaffe arc light, and immediately the two sentries at the gate raised hands and began to scream, "HALT! HALT! HALT!" They were kids also, a little panicked because no cars ever emerged from the darkness out of nowhere, and they themselves didn't know what to do, open fire or run and get a sergeant. Their helmets and weapons looked too big.

It was murder. It was war but it was still murder.

Leets rolled from the Citroën and put three into each boy from the hip at a range of about ten yards. The Thompson seemed to point itself, so hungry to kill, and under his feathery trigger control convulsed spastically three times in a tenth of a second, then three times more in another tenth of a second, leaking incandescence and noise, and the boys were gone. He brought the gun to his shoulder, zeroed in on the guardhouse through the aperture sight to the blade at muzzle and feathered off the rest of the magazine, holding the butt tight into his shoulder, watching the wood and dust splinter and leap as the rounds struck and ripped, glass shattered, and a door broke, punctured, and fell. Sensations: the harsh percussion of the detonating cartridges, the weirdness of the empty brass poppity-popping out of the breach in a glinting arc, the substantiality of the bolt sliding through the receiver at thunderbolt speed, the dazzle of the muzzle flash, the acrid stench of burning powder, the spurt and drift of the gun smoke.

The gun empty, he reached into his pouch pocket and pulled out an already primed Gammon. With a thumb he pinned the little floppy lead weight at the end of the Gammon linen against the side of the bag, feeling the slight squishiness of the clump of 808 inside, cranked slightly to the right to the classic QB pose so he could come off his right foot, and launched a tight spiral toward the guardhouse fifty feet away, following through Otto Graham–style. As the bomb sailed through the air, its weighted linen wrap unfurled, and when it separated it popped a restraining pin free inside the Allways fuze, arming that gizmo to detonate on impact. That was the genius of the Gammon; when armed it was volatile as hell, but it always went off.

Great throw, the guardhouse went in a blaze of light and percussion, making Leets blink, stagger, have a momentary loss of reality. His men were next to him, emptying Stens into the wreckage and at fleeing German figures.

"Un autre," said Leon, another.

Leets got another grenade out, pinned the weight, and this time put more arm into it. It sailed into the darkness, where presumably Germans still cowered, perhaps unlimbering weapons, but the explosion was larger than the last—the Gammon power depended wholly upon how much 808 was packed about the Allways, and evidently Leets had been a little overexcited on this one.

Dust rose, half the lights went out, burning pieces of stuff flew through the air, it was all the chaos and irrationality of an explosion. Hearing was gone for the night. Leets paused for a second to get another magazine into his Thompson, made sure the bolt was back, and raced forward into the madness.

"THEY MUST BE so brave," said Millie Beeman to poor, hopelessly in love Frank Tyne. Frank was some kind of Maine ex-cop of French-Canadian extraction (hence his French), a husky guy, not liked by any of the crowd. He was crude, direct, horny, stupid, supposedly a hero but so full of himself.

"Good guys. See, the deal is, it was time to show Jerry some action. The general knew that. So these teams, they were put together as an opportunity for the outfit to show its stuff."

"And tonight's the night?"

"Tonight's the night," Frank said, with a wicked gleam in his eyes that suggested that maybe he was assuming tonight was the night in more ways than one.

They sat in the bar of the Savoy, amid smoke, other drinkers, and trysters.

"Frank, you should be so proud. It's your plan, after all. You're really doing something. I mean, so much of it is politics, society, canoodling, and it has nothing to do with the war. I just get depressed sometimes. Even Colonel Bruce, oh, he tries hard, he's such a darling, but he's so ineffectual. You, Frank. *You* are stopping the Nazis. That is so important. Somebody has to do the fighting!"

She touched Frank's wrist, and smiled radiantly, and watched the poor schlub melt. Then, fighting the sudden rush of phlegm to his throat, he said, "Look, let's get out of here."

"Frank, we shouldn't. I mean—"

"Miss Beeman—Millie, may I call you Millie?"

"Of course."

"Millie, it's the night of the warrior. We should commemorate it. Look, let's go back to my office; I have a little stash of very fine Pikesville rye. We can have some privacy. It'll be a great night, and we can wait for news of Team Casey's strike to come in and celebrate."

Millie played up the I'm-considering look, going through several *yes-why-not*s and several *no-no-it's wrongs*, before seeming to settle on the yes-why-not.

"Yes, why not?" she said, but he was already pulling on his raincoat over his uniform.

LEETS REACHED THE center of the span, when a volley of rifle shots kicked dust and splinters up. He flinched, realized he wasn't hit, recovered. The fire surely came from the other end of the bridge, where a small security force had been cowering, uncertain what to do. Fortunately the Luftwaffers were as poor at marksmanship as they were at aggression, and so all the shots missed flesh. Leets answered with another long burst from the Thompson, while his comrades chipped in with Stens.

"Throw some bombs," he ordered, while he himself went to the railing of the span, looked over it.

It was not an impressive bridge. It was, in fact, a rather pathetic bridge. But it would do well enough to support the weight of a thirty-ton Tiger II tank, a column of which under the auspices of SS Das Reich now headed toward it on the road to Normandy. Leets had seen the structure at daylight: two buttresses, heavy logs, no apparent stone construction except at the base. He simply had to detonate enough 808 where the truss met the span to disconnect the support; the span would collapse of its own, or at least cave in enough to prevent passage of the heavy German vehicles; it needn't be pretty or dramatically satisfying. A little tiny bang would be fine, just enough to get a little bit of a job done.

He knelt, slipped the Thompson off its sling and the satchel of 808 to the ground. He reached into it, pulled out a tin of the SOE-issue Time Pencils ("Switch, Delay, No. 10," as the tin ever so helpfully read) and beheld the five six-inch-long brass tubes, each with a tin-wrapped nodule at the end. The problem with them, goddammit, was that as clever as they were, they were somewhat retarded in their firing rate. Supposedly they were set to fire a primer in ten minutes, but just as often they went in eight or nine or eleven or twelve. It was a matter of how quickly the acid in a crushed ampoule ate through a restraining wire, which, when it yielded, allowed the spring-driven needle to plunge into the primer, which went bang, causing the larger, encasing 808 to go bang.

So Leets took them out now, all five of them, discarded the tin, and stomped hard on the proper end of the pencils. Immediately a new odor arrived at his nose, that of the just-released cupric acid as it sloshed forward from the shattered vials in five

pencils and began to chew at the metal. He wanted them cook-
ing now, eating up the time so that when he and the boys fled, the
Germans didn't have a chance to pull the pencils free. He put
them in the bellows pocket of his jump pants, buttoning it tightly.

He squirmed over the railing, eased himself down, flailed
with a foot for mooring on the truss, found it, and carefully
squinched down until he was beneath the bridge span.

Suddenly he heard a racket far-off. Oh Christ, he almost let
go and plummeted twenty-five feet to the sluggish streambed
below. Were they shooting at him? But then he recognized
the glorious workman's hammerlike bashing of the Bren gun,
knowable because of its wonderfully slow rate of fire that enabled
gunners to stay longer on target than our poor Joes with their
faster-shooting BARs.

Goddamn, good old Basil! Basil, you snotty, arrogant, unim-
pressible, cold-blooded aristo, goddamn you, you got me my
Brens, and maybe I will get out of this one alive.

Vive le Basil!

Brimming now with excitement and enthusiasm, he called
up to Franc, "808, comrade!"

Franc leaned over, holding the satchel; it was a stretch, Franc
dangling the satchel by its strap off the edge of the bridge, Leets
clinging to the truss, grasping at the thing, which seemed somehow just out of reach, but in what seemed a mere seven hours,
he finally snared it securely and pulled it in.

He was monkey-clinging to the truss now, his feet secure on
a horizontal spar, crouched under the span, where it was damp
and pungent, where no man had been in fifty years or so. He
tried to find a way to attach the satchel itself, but in wedging it
against junctures, he could never feel it secure enough to consider planted. Ach. It was so awkward. Christ, his muscles ached
everywhere, and he could feel gravity sucking at his limbs, urg-
ing him downward into the muck below.

Finally, he managed to moor the satchel between his knees.

Then, holding on with one hand, he unsheathed his M3 knife from his boot sheath and cut the canvas strap on the satchel. Now what to do with the knife? He couldn't quite find the angle to get it back into the sheath, so he tried to slide it into his belt, and of course at a certain point it disappeared and hit the water below.

Goddamn! He hated to lose a good knife that way. It was odd how annoyed he was at the loss of the knife.

Anyway, he liberated the satchel from between his knees, wedged it into the truss, and used the long strap to bind it securely. He pawed at the gathered, crunched material to find a passage to the explosive, and at last his fingers touched the sticky, gummy green stuff. He smelled almonds. He felt as if he were at a mixer at the Alpha Chi Omega house and the house-mother had put little dishes of almonds out, to go with the punch, when all anybody wanted to do was get out of there and head down to Howard Street for some hooch. Now he reached into his bellows pocket, careful since it was at a radical angle and the pencils could easily slip out. But one by one, he removed a pencil and jammed it into the wad of 808 nested in the satchel nested in the bridge.

They always said: Use two to make sure. He used all five and made certain in his orthodox Midwestern way that each one was secure and driven in deep enough so that gravity wouldn't pull it out.

God, I did it, he thought.

It seemed to take an hour to clamber back up to the bridge span itself, and Franc and Leon pulled him, while the third maquis hammered away with the Sten periodically.

On the span he was elated, yet also exhausted.

"Whoa," he said in English, "wouldn't want to do that job over." Then, reverting to French he said, "Friends, let's get the hell out of here!"

He grabbed his Thompson and ran back down the bridge, past the blown-out guardhouse, deserted, sandbagged gun pits with their silent 88s pressing skyward, the wreckage and small fires from the Gammons; now it was only a question of the long run up the hill to the treeline in the darkness, waiting for the boom from the . . .

That's when he noticed the Brens were no longer firing.

That's when he saw a German truck scuttling over the crest of the road, and it began to disgorge troops, many of them, while up top, a soldier unlimbered an MG-42.

IT WAS SPREAD out before her on Frank Tyne's desk: Operation Jedburgh.

She could see all the locations for the teams and all their targets, laid out across all of France, all the boys who'd gone in with darkened faces and knives between their teeth. Teams Albert and Bristol, Charles and David, Teams Edward and Francis, and on and on to Teams Xylophone and Zed, with the mission to set Europe ablaze.

"Oh, Frank," she said. "And to think, you thought it up. That's your plan. Those magnificent men, fighting and killing, and all under your direction."

Frank swelled a bit, then turned modest.

"Sweetie, you have to understand, I didn't think it up on my own. I mean, it was a true team effort, and it involved logistics and liaison between three entities; I was just part of the team that put the players on the field, that's all. It's my bit. Nothing dramatic. I don't want you thinking I'm a hero. The kids are the heroes."

Her eyes scanned the map with incredible intensity, and if dumbbell Frank had had a whisper of sense in his brain he would have noted how inappropriate her concentration was, but of course he was way gone. He was over the edge. His dick was as big as a wine bottle.

"Ooooo!" she squealed girlishly. "What's this one? Casey. At Nantilles."

"You must have heard the name in the air. Casey's on for tonight. There's a bridge, Casey's going to hit it, take it down, ka-boom!"

"Such heroes."

"If there's room for heroics. First you have to get through the bullshit—oh, excuse me—the bull crap about politics. France is not only fighting the Germans, but the French themselves are always trying to skew this way or that for political advantage after the war." He wanted to show her what an insider he was. "Casey was hung up for some reason, because a commie guerrilla outfit wouldn't give them support. Somehow the Brits managed to get it all the way to Moscow and back, and the commies were ordered to pitch in." He smiled smugly, loosened his tie, took another swig of rye.

"And it's happening tonight?"

He looked at his watch, worn commando-style upside down on his wrist.

"Real soon now. We should know by dawn."

"It's so exciting."

"Millie, whyn't you come over here on the couch and we'll relax for a bit, have a few more drinks? Then I'll wander down to Radio and see if anything's come in on Casey."

"Oh, Frank," she said. She sunk down on the old sofa that comprised his office furniture, beside the desk and the battered filing cabinets and the safe, and snuggled close to him and felt him groping to get his beefy arms around her.

"Oh, Millie, Millie, God Millie, if you only knew, Jesus Millie, I've had the same feeling for you you have for me. I'm so glad the war has brought us together, oh Millie."

She smiled, and when he closed his eyes to kiss her, she brought a handkerchief full of knockout drops to his nostrils and felt him struggle, then go limp.

She got up quickly, went to the map, marked the coordinates

for Nantilles and Casey's operational area and then realized of course they would know all this. The big info was that a red group had agreed to assist the Jeds, which meant assist the FFI. She knew NKVD would go through the roof on that one! It felt so wrong to her, so unjust. If you helped FFI, then the war would have been for nothing; when it was over, it would just go back to what it had been before, with big money ruling everything and the little guy squashed to nothingness and all the bullies and all the rich scum and all the boys who'd pawed her at Smith—brutal, smelly, drunken Frank Tynes—all those men would be triumphant, and what, really, what would have been the point? The only hope was the Soviet Union, the greatness of Uncle Joe, the justice of a system that didn't depend on exploitation but that enabled man to be all that he could be, noble and giving, generous and loving. That was a world worth fighting for, and if she didn't have a gun, she had a telephone.

She picked it up and dialed, knowing that nowhere on earth would anyone see anything suspicious about Frank Tyne of OSS calling David Hedgepath of the Office of War Information at 10:14 p.m. on the night of June 8, 1944.

LEETS DID A quick tumble through the facts as he thought them to be and concluded that yes, Team Casey had a chance.

Luftwaffe troops were basically antiaircraft gunners, their rifle marksmanship and combat aggression had to be somewhat deficient. They wouldn't understand elevation or deflection fire at moving targets. It was dark; untrained, unblooded troops didn't care for the dark. They weren't sure where they were going, and at best they'd put in a half-effort, each fellow thinking, "I don't want to be the one guy who dies tonight."

"Okay," he said to the maquis, "we'll go ahead by leapfrogging. As each guy runs, the other three pour fire on Les Boches. When you hold on them, aim a man high, or your rounds won't reach the target. Shoot, move, don't stop no matter what. We spread out, try and go about fifty yards per spurt. Up top they'll be covering us. We don't need the damn Brens; we're fine."

"Fuck that fat Roger," said Leon. "He is pig filth, swine, a screwer of mothers and babies."

"That communist shit, the reds should be rounded up after the war and—"

"We will visit Roger, I promise you," said Leets. "Now come on, guys, let's get a move on."

Franc went first, then was passed by Leon, and finally Jerome. Leets crouched behind a sandbag revetment and had a wild, insane heroic impulse. Maybe I should stay here, cover them, and keep the Krauts off until the bridge blows.

Then he thought, Fuck that.

He was moving, was past Franc, past Leon, almost to Jerome, moving through fire that was sporadic at best, now and then licking up a spit of dust in the general area, and he'd heard nothing blazing by his ears, indicative of the fact that Jerry had zeroed on them.

The flare popped, freezing him.

Flares? These clowns have flares?

He looked back to the bridge and beheld with horror the reality that two more trucks had arrived, in the dappled camouflage coloring of 2nd SS Das Reich, and watched as from each truck spilled lean, toughened Panzergrenadiers in their camouflage tunics, hardened by years on the Eastern Front, a unit noted and feared far and wide as the finest of the SS Divisions. These characters carried the new Stg-44, something the Germans called an "attack rifle," which fired a shortened 8mm round with accuracy and a high rate of fire. Oh, fuck, they could really lay fire with that sonofabitch.

Another flare popped, and then another, and the whole scene lit up, this puny French river valley, he and his three maquis racing uphill toward a treeline through a landscape of flickering shadow, as the descending parachute flares caught on the stumps of the so recently cut pines and threw blades of darkness this way and that, like scythes, the Germans still two hundred yards away but coming strong, the camouflaged Panzer-grenadiers racing through and past the confused young Luft-waffers, and now, suddenly, from the ridgeline, a long arc of tracer as the MG-42s tried to range the target.

We are screwed, he thought. This is it.

The bridge went.

It wasn't the blossoming, booming movie explosion so famil-iar from the Warner Bros. backlog agitprop films, but more of a disappointingly insubstantial percussion, lifting a large volcano of smoke and dust from the structure in the aftermath of a flash too brief for anyone to see. Leets stole a moment in the fading parachute flare to examine his legacy: The bridge, as the dust cleared, was not downed, leaving a gap as if a mouth had been punched front-teethless, but the roadway span hung at a grotesque 45-degree angle, torquing downward, meaning the truss Leets had 808'ed had gone, but the other one held. It would take days to repair, or to detour around, and those would be days with no 2nd SS Das Reich at Normandy.

He stood, dumped a mag a man high at the nearest parade of SS Panzergrenadiers, and shouted to his guys, "Go, go, go, go!"

Franc took the first hit. He just slumped, tried to get up, then sat, then lay down, then curled up.

"Go, go, go!" screamed Leets, dumping another mag. He had three left.

Of the two maquis, Leon, the youngster, made it closest to the treeline, but then a new flare popped and the German fire found him and put him in a beaten zone, and no man survives the beaten zone.

Jerome didn't make it nearly as far, and Leets was unclear, for he ran himself through a sleet of light and splinter as the Ger-mans tried to bring him down, but in the second before he was hit he saw Jerome jack vertically from his runner's crouch and go down hard as gravity took hold of his remains.

The bullet struck Leets in the left buttock, blowing through his hip. Man, did he go down, full of spangles and fire flashes and lightning bugs and flies' wings. His mind emptied; all visible movement ceased in the universe, and it went silent—I am dead, he thought—but he blinked himself alive again and saw SS coming up hard in the light of a new flare, holding their fire, for they wanted someone alive for the info before the execution, and he cursed himself for throwing out the strychnine tablet he'd been issued.

The pain was immense, and he tried to make it go away by rushing a mag change, lifting the ever-loyal, faultless best friend of the Thompson gun, and running another mag, seeming to drive them back or down or whatever.

He was twenty-four.

He didn't want to die.

He tried to get through another mag change but dropped the heavy weapon. He got a Gammon bomb out but couldn't get the cap unscrewed. He pulled out his .45, jacked the slide, held it up stupidly without aiming, blinked in the bright light of another flare just overhead and squeezed off a few pointless rounds.

The gun locked back. He saw two Panzergrenadiers quite close with their fancy new rifles and was amazed that at this ultimate moment his lifelong interest in firearms reasserted itself, and he thought for just a second how *interesting* it would be to ring one of those cool babies out at a range, then take it apart lovingly, taking notes, figuring out what made it go, running tests on the ammo. It would be so damned *interesting*.

Then the two Germans sat down, as if embarrassed.

A wave of explosions wiped out the reality that was but a few yards ahead of him.

"There, there, Beets, chum," said Basil. "The fellows are here with a stretcher. I see a bit of bone, but any horse doctor can set that."

"Basil, I, what, get out of here, oh, for—"

But Basil had turned and was busy running mags through his Sten, as around him, the other maquisards fired whatever weapons they had.

Somehow Leets was on a stretcher and being humped at speed the remaining few yards to the treeline.

"Basil, I—"

"There's the good chap. Beets, these fellows will take good care of you. Get Leftenant Beets somewhere to medical aid. Get him out of here."

"Basil, you come, too, come on, Basil, we got the bridge, we can—"

"Oh, someone has to stay to discourage these fellows. They seem so stubborn. But I'll be along in a bit. We'll have that chat. Good luck, Beets, and Godspeed."

Basil turned and disappeared back into the forest. For Leets, it became an ordeal of not passing out as the maquis heaved his sorry ass along a dark path until he seemed to be being slid into some kind of vehicle, and then he did in fact pass out. Neither he nor any other of the man's army of friends, lovers, and acquaintances ever saw Basil St. Florian again.

ON JUNE 9TH, 1944, Major Frank Tyne, U.S.A. attached to OSS, found a florist who would deliver, and he had a bouquet of mums and roses sent to Millie at 72 Grosvenor, Mayfair, office of Colonel David K. E. Bruce.

He got no response.

Finally, on the 11th, he got his nerve up, parked himself on her floor, and finally caught a glimpse of her rushing from one office to another.

"Millie!"

"Oh, Frank."

"Millie, did you get my flowers?"

Millie seemed both nonplussed and busy. She was clearly anxious to flee but stayed and faced him with a somewhat tense, unpleasant face.

"Yes, Frank, I got them. They were very nice. Who knew there were florists in London in wartime?"

"Wasn't easy to find one. Listen, Millie, I wanted to apologize about the other night. Really, I don't know what came over me. I'm so glad I passed out before I did anything inappropriate. I'm just hoping you'll see a way to forgive me. It would mean so much."

"Frank," she touched his hand. "It's fine. Everyone had too much to drink. Please, don't worry about it."

"Thanks. Say, I was wondering if—"

"Frank, there's so much going on now that we're ashore. The colonel's going to the front soon on instructions from General Donovan."

"Yes, I know, I've heard—"

"So his scheduling is a nightmare."

"Sure, Millie, maybe sometime."

"Maybe. Say, what happened to Casey, if I may ask?"

"You didn't hear?"

"Just rumors. Not happy ones."

"No. They hit the bridge, did some damage, maybe cost elements of Das Reich a day or two, but they were wiped out, along with the French maquis group. Then Das Reich shot fifty hostages. So it was no good, really, a waste. OWI's going to try to do something with Casey. Maybe a short little movie for the home folks, 'The Heroes of the Bridge at Nantilles,' something like that."

"It's so sad," she said. "Sometimes there's no justice in this world."

Stephen Hunter would like to thank Helge Fykse, LA6NCA, of Norway, for information on German radio technology.

MAX IS CALLING

Gayle Lynds

VIENNA WAS COLD that spring, and dreary. The sixteenth- and seventeenth-century buildings of the Innere Stadt stood like sentinels against time, cloaked in a chilly mist. Dressed in rain gear, businesspeople and students, *hausfrauen* and *doktoren* hurried through pools of yellow lamplight, umbrellas bobbing. Only the cafés and pubs could be counted upon for gaiety. The last refuge, they were bustling of course. The rich aromas of coffee and beer scented the gray air.

Watching carefully all around, two men in dark trench coats moved quickly past St. Stephen's Cathedral, its Romanesque entrance alight. The old city of Strauss and Mahler, Freud and Klimt felt like a dream, an exciting dream to one of the pair—Bayard Stockton. But then he was with Jacob "Cowboy" Crandell, a Langley undercover legend, in a city storied for its espionage.

As Bay had learned, the Viennese were a melancholy lot, relentlessly self-absorbed with their glorious past of the Hapsburg empire. Flamboyant fatalism, some called it. But then they had survived the Nazis and the Cold War to become the political ground zero of east and west, north and south. Some seventeen thousand diplomats operated in the city, a full one percent of the population—and about half had links to intelligence services.

They worked at embassies and global agencies such as OPEC, the IAEA, and the UN. From business to government, Langley wanted to know what they were thinking, who was on the take, who was in line to get the next contract, and the peccadilloes, peculiarities, and vulnerabilities of all players and potentials. Naturally, Vienna was awash with foreign agents. The freewheeling ones occasionally murdered in broad daylight, while the authorities, who often knew them, looked the other way. As it had historically, Vienna handled everything diplomatically, especially when a political connection existed.

Bay loved it. Fresh from Langley's grueling training courses, he had been there two exhilarating months. He was young for the business, only twenty-five, a wiry man not quite six feet tall. His collar was up against the frigid damp, and a black beret covered his head, wavy red hair showing beneath. There was nothing unusual about his smooth face, his blue eyes, or his shaved chin, which was just the way he liked it. In his pocket was an unmarked envelope containing 5,000 euros—about $6,250— which made anonymity even more important tonight.

"Stop walking like an athlete," Cowboy rumbled under his breath. "Dammit, boy, you should've learned that in CIA 101. Rolling off your feet shows the strength of your muscles and your training. The Viennese are always looking around, which means they're going to check you out. Don't give them a reason to remember you. What were you—a runner? The one hundred?"

Bay blinked. In his enthusiasm for being with Cowboy and his mission tonight he had forgotten himself. "Yeah, the hundred." And free weights, of course. But he did not mention that. He flattened his feet, tightened his joints.

Cowboy's cool blue eyes appraised him. Then he dipped his big head in a short nod. He seldom gave compliments, so Bay was pleased with the nod.

"Hell, this is a beautiful antique burg." Cowboy was peering around at the buildings, grande dames decked out in soaring pediments, ornate rococo, and regal porticoes. Hands dug into his coat pockets, he was fifty-two years old, a tall, rangy man with a neutral expression. His brown hair, broad face, and rimless eyeglasses were wet, but he seemed immune to what would annoy the rest of humanity, which Bay admired. From the wilds of Wyoming, Cowboy wore Tony Lama snakeskin cowboy boots. They were incidental to his nickname. The real reason was his shoot-from-the-hip boldness, which occasionally got him into trouble but more often resulted in success. Close-mouthed and adaptable, he knew the city like the veins in his hands and was the most productive of the station's case officers, handling an impressive twenty assets.

As they walked, his boots clicked on the cobblestones. To Bay, they sounded like exotic music in this very correct city.

"Operating here is like being inside a museum, punctuated by boredom, of course," Cowboy instructed. "The lull before the storm. I used to believe I could die happy in my Jaguar. Now I know Vienna's the place. What do you think?"

"It's terrific." Bay shot him a grin.

When a new officer arrived at his first station, he was customarily given a desk job for several weeks to read and analyze reports, recorded conversations, and streams of satellite data. Once he was familiar with that, he was assigned to shadow experienced officers for hands-on training. Bay had worked with two good ones and been pretty successful so far. Then Herb Rutkowski, the head of station, had called him into his office this afternoon to give him special instructions and the good news his next assignment was with Cowboy Crandell.

"Tell me about Max, sir."

As they turned the corner, they passed the Mozart statue, and Cowboy said, "It was four months ago, Christmas season on the Kärntner Strasse. The stores were busy, a lot of people coming and going. I felt a tug on my pocket and grabbed. The hand was gone, but a torn piece of paper was left inside. Of course, that was the first contact—a list of four names. All were Chechen informants, just as the note claimed. There was also a phone number, which the station traced. It belonged to a disposable cell; the owner was unidentifiable. So I figured what the hell . . . I dialed the number, and the man who answered told me to call him Max, and he'd give me more intel for a price. All his contacts with me have been through disposable cells. Wily bugger, but his intel's been good."

"Is Max a Chechen?"

"Damn right he is. Never seen his face, and don't have a clue who he really is."

"Is that unusual?"

"Not here. Most of my assets are unknowns, but these Chechens are the best at it. Austria's got one of the most liberal refugee programs in the EU, so about twelve thousand are living in the city. Mostly they're from the two wars against Russia. A lot aren't legal. They were guerrilla fighters and soldiers and don't have a war or any good way to earn a living, so they've invaded the criminal underworld. Made it a hell of a lot more dangerous in the process. Besides the usual thievery and break-ins, they act as bodyguards, smugglers, strong-arm tacticians, and assassins. Not a postcard picture of Vienna. It drives the authorities nuts, especially when one country hires them to screw another country."

"How will my blind date work?"

As they strode along, a frown crossed Cowboy's face. Instantly it was gone. "Max gives me a location and the time to arrive. Then he phones to tell me exactly where to meet. You'll go in with the five grand. He'll give you a piece of paper folded down to nothing, which is his latest report. You'll give him the dough. It's always dark, and he doesn't like to talk. Herb says you speak Russian, but good luck trying to have a conversation with him."

"I understand, sir."

"I hope you do."

Pedestrians pushed past them. The edge of an umbrella nearly spiked Bay's head. He glanced over his shoulder to make certain it was unintentional. When he turned back, a tall woman dressed in a short red skirt, flesh-colored tights, very high heels, and a formfitting black jacket was sauntering down a building's steps, smiling widely. Her red lips were so shiny they seemed to reflect light. Although she held a small collapsible umbrella overhead, her long golden hair hung limp from the mist.

"Cowboy," she purred in German, "it has been a long time. Who is this nice young gentleman with you?" She sidled up to Bay and ran her free hand down over his trench coat and inside to pat his shirt. Her breath smelled of peppermint toothpaste.

Bay grinned.

"Having a slow evening, Estelle?" There was a devilish light in Cowboy's eyes as he answered in German. "This is my new friend, Bay. You have any info, feel free to pass it to him. He won't mind."

"Oh?" She stared into Bay's eyes, her hand pressing against his heart.

He could feel it pound.

"I would like to give him 'information,'" she decided.

"I'll just bet you would," Cowboy said. "We've got to be going, Estelle. Behave yourself."

Estelle gave a pretty nod and backed off. "Have a nice evening."

But as they walked away, Cowboy said to Bay, "Give me five euros."

Bay reached inside his trench coat. And spun on his heel. He ran back to Estelle, who was trotting up her steps.

He grabbed her arm and felt big, hard muscle. "Nice trick. Hand over my wallet."

Estelle turned and pouted. "I don't know—"

Bay's voice turned steely as he saw the prominent Adam's

apple. "Don't fuck with me. You know what I can do to you. Give it to me. Now."

Her long black lashes lowered and raised. "You're so mean. Oh, all right." She took the wallet from her jacket pocket.

He snatched it and jogged off. Ahead, Cowboy was striding along without a look over his shoulder.

When he caught up, Bay said, "Okay, I get it. Estelle's a guy."

Cowboy laughed loudly. "You're lucky you found out the easy way." Then as they rounded the corner, he looked sharply at him. "Herb says you're a hotshot. Ivy League, top of your class at the Farm, six languages. Grew up in Europe. What I see is eagerness and idealism, not that that's the end of the world. I'm just warning you this is no glamour gig. It's exhausting, nerve-numbing, and frustrating. The days are over of putting on your tux for an embassy party every night to try to get buddy-buddy with some East Bloc official so you can convince him his ideology sucks and he should play on our team. Now you've got to infiltrate the tenements, the mud huts, the terrorist cells. Vienna's as close to the old Cold War days as you'll get, and it's not very."

"Then why are you so successful?"

Cowboy chuckled. "Charm." His expression grew serious as he continued, "The word is out I pay, and I keep my mouth shut. Chechen informants won't take a piss unless they're sure they can do it in secret."

"With so many assets, you must handle a lot of money. Do you ever have trouble getting it for them?"

"As long as they deliver, Langley will. Tonight's money is for Max's last piece of intel. In it he claimed the Lebanese were paying the French tens of millions of dollars in contracts in exchange for nuclear technology, starting with a seventy-megawatt commercial atomic reactor and a smaller research reactor. Apparently they're already building both."

"Jesus. Lebanon aiming for nuclear capabilities? That's fucking terrifying." Bay already knew about it, but Herb had instructed him to pretend he did not. According to Herb, Cowboy was so intent on keeping his unknowns happy that he did not press them for more information when he should. Bay's job tonight was to try to get Max to reveal how he had found the intel so the station could back-check it.

"Yeah, I can just see Hezbollah cackling about it in the Bekaa Valley," Cowboy said with relish. "I'd love to be in Jerusalem when Mossad gets the news. The Israelis will go nuts. They'll start polishing the jet to bomb it, and Washington will go into a paroxysm trying to calm them down until they can confirm or disprove it from other sources."

"Max's intel could be wrong."

"Exactly. That's why we're paying him only five thousand euros."

"And if it's accurate?"

"Max gets a big bonus. As for tonight, he'll either have more about that, or else he's got something new for me. Limo drivers, housekeepers, babysitters, secretaries—all of them are sources for a good informant. The problem for us in the professional spy game is it's harder than hell to get to them ourselves. That's how much the world's changed." Cowboy paused. "I'll be honest with you. I don't like that Herb wants you to do the meet. I've never been ordered to let someone else handle one of my assets. This is your first time, right?"

"Right," Bay said. "Are your other assets as productive as Max?"

"Some are. Some aren't."

"It's incredible how many you have."

"I know what I'm doing. I hope like hell you do, too. This is where we wait."

They stopped alongside the tall paned-glass windows of Café Militant. Cowboy pulled open the brass-handled door, and they stepped into a spacious, high-ceilinged room from the extravagant past. The brass fixtures glittered, the crystal chandeliers glowed with soft light, and the marble-topped tables shone. Although nearly every table and booth was filled, the place emanated a kind of happy solitude. That was Vienna for you— the populace was together but alone. Teaspoons tinkled and newspapers rustled as patrons glanced up.

The liveried waiter approached, very erect, gold-rimmed menus in hand.

"*Servus, Herr Ober,*" Cowboy greeted him in German with the perfect inflections of a native Austrian.

Satisfied that the unexpected would not intrude, the patrons returned to their reading. The waiter straightened approvingly and led them across the aged parquet floor to a velvet-upholstered booth. It was faded royal purple.

Without a glance at the offered menu, Cowboy solidified his credentials: "*Tsvoh melanges, bitte.*" He ordered the coffees using the colloquial word for two, *tsvoh*, instead of *tsvai*.

With an approving lift of his head, the waiter vanished. Cowboy took out his cell phone and laid it on the table, preparing to receive the call from Max. The device was actually a Secure Mobile Environment Portable Electronic Device—an SME-PED computer handheld. With it one could send classified e-mail, access classified networks, and make top secret phone calls. Created under guidelines of the National Security Agency, it appeared ordinary, like a BlackBerry, and while either on or off secure mode could be operated like any smart phone with Internet access. All the covert officers carried the handhelds.

"Not all of your assets are unknowns surely," Bay said. "I'd heard you were a master at recruiting."

"When I was working in West Berlin in the old days, we used a system called the BAR code. BAR stood for 'befriend, assess, recruit.' Sounds simple, but it can be blown in a heartbeat. To give you an example, I remember one potential who was a file clerk in the East German embassy—he had access we liked. He also had a mistress with three children in addition to a wife with two kids. Debt up to his nose hairs. One of my people had gotten him to pull a couple of inconsequential files for money. This was the point at which he could go either way—back off and risk we'd rat him out, which he probably figured we wouldn't, or go in deeper for a lot more money, which would've been a death sentence if he were caught. So I had my man bring him to a safe house. As soon as he stepped inside the door, I walked across the room with a big-ass smile, my hand outstretched, and introduced myself by saying, 'My friends call me Cowboy.' The guy's shoulders relaxed, and a silly grin filled his face. I expressed sympathy for a man with so many family obligations, talked about how each of his children had a right to a first-rate education and wouldn't it be great if they could all escape to the West. I *respected* the guy. By the time we'd finished off a bottle of Stoli vodka, the guy was ready to pawn his soul." He sighed happily. "Ah, for the good old days."

The waiter arrived with two frothy, milky coffees.

Cowboy reached for his. "Viennese roasts can't compare to the Illys and Lavazzas of the world, but they're still damn good."

Bay liked melanges, too. He sipped the hot drink.

Cowboy checked his Rolex.

"Is Max late?" Bay wondered.

"Relax." As Cowboy drank deeply, his cell phone rang. He snatched it up and read the screen. "Max is calling."

Bay nodded casually while his heart rate sped.

Cowboy listened, then spoke into the handheld in Russian, "Give the boy your report, and he'll pay you just the way I do. This is out of my hands, Max, but he'll take good care of you. Where do you want to meet?" He ended the connection. "He's unhappy I won't be there, but he wants the money. You won't have a problem. Remember, show him respect. That's the answer for the Chechens. Threaten him, and you'll get a shiv up your ribs."

"I don't have any reason to threaten him."

"I know you don't, but it's what he thinks that matters." Cowboy left euros on the table, and they walked out of the café. On the street, he relayed the directions. "Herb is an ass. He should never have put you in this position. I'll be waiting for you."

Edgy, Bay walked off through the lamplight. Down the street a door opened, and the mournful sound of a jazz saxophone wafted out. Rain droplets floated ghostlike in the night air. Passing an alley, he peered into the darkness. Empty.

He continued on and turned the corner. Six shops later, he came to another alley. Glancing along the street, he assessed the few walkers. There were no cars in the pedestrianized Innere Stadt.

At last he entered the alley. Brick buildings towered on either side, and trash cans stood next to padlocked doors. There were lights high on the buildings, but as he progressed deeper into the dark passageway, the lights were shattered. Chest tight, he could not see well enough to spot anything. He took out a tiny flashlight and beamed it onto the cobblestones.

"Stop," a voice ordered in Russian. It was deep, gravelly. "You are?"

"Cowboy sent me, Max," Bay answered in Russian. Then he remembered Cowboy's story about West Berlin. "My friends call me Bay." He smiled warmly and stretched out his hand. He could just make out a tall, shadowy form.

The shadow was motionless. "Turn off your light and resume approaching."

As he walked again, Bay let his hand drift down. "I was in Chechnya a few years ago. The mountains are even more beautiful than Switzerland's. Are you from Grozny? I ate at the Hollywood restaurant there. Great food." What he did not say was most of the patrons were armed, and closing time was dicey. "I'm sorry you're in exile. We'd like to help you and your family. If you don't want to go back to Chechnya, we can arrange papers for you to have a better life here in Vienna or somewhere else."

But Max did not rise to the BAR code conversational bait. "I am wearing infrared glasses," he warned. "I am watching you. Do not remove your weapon. Give me the money."

Bay felt the comforting weight of the 9-millimeter Browning holstered in his armpit. "I'm sorry, but no, Max. First tell me how you found out about Lebanon's nuclear projects, then I'll give you the cash." He started to reach into his trench coat pocket.

"Stop!" Max ordered.

"You want to be paid, don't you?"

The voice lowered menacingly. "Continue."

Bay took out the fat envelope and held it up. "It's all here. Five thousand beautiful euros."

"Show me—slowly."

Bay opened the envelope, fanned out the cash, then returned it to the envelope. "Tell me about the Lebanese, and of course give me the intel you brought for Cowboy."

"The Lebanese are not my friends as Cowboy is, so I have written the information for him."

Heels clicked on the cobblestones toward Bay. A gloved hand extended. But instead of offering the promised small folded note, the hand ripped away Bay's envelope.

Without thinking, Bay reacted. He slammed a *kagi-zuki* hook punch toward Max's chest, but Max was already backing off. The blow fell short as Max pivoted and smashed a foot in an expert *yoko-geri* side snap kick into Bay's side, the sharp heel bruising. As Bay lashed back, a second blow from the foot struck his temple. He fell hard, his head hitting the cobblestones.

As if from a great distance, he heard Max warn, "I work only with Cowboy, boy."

In pain, Bay tried to speak, to roll over, to get up. His mind swam. He heard someone moan, then realized it was he. A wave of nausea swept through him.

*   *   *

WIPING SWEAT FROM his face, Bay limped back around the corner. He ached everywhere, and his head throbbed. But his brain was clearing. The good news was no ribs were broken. And that was the only good news. He did not like what he was thinking.

There were few people out now. He passed the first alley, heading toward the Café Militant. A sense of eerie desertion filled the street. As he neared the café, the looming figure of Cowboy, peering through his damp eyeglasses, stepped out of a dark doorway and joined him. The jovial expression on his face vanished as he took in Bay's appearance.

"What in hell happened to you?" Cowboy said.

"You were right. Max was unhappy not to be working with you tonight."

"You didn't insult him, did you? Chechens are thin-skinned."

"No, and I didn't threaten him either. The bottom line is Max didn't give me any intel. He took the money, beat on me, and split."

"Christ! What in hell have you done. He was one of my best assets! I told Herb this wasn't a good idea. Fucking Herb. He should've been sent back to Langley long ago to some desk job where he couldn't screw up an operation!"

"I did get some good information *about* Max." Bay spoke slowly to be certain Cowboy understood every word.

"What?"

"His identity."

Cowboy stared. His broad face stretched in surprise. "Jesus, who is he?"

"Give me back the five thousand euros, Cowboy."

"What in hell are you talking about?" he demanded.

"Your boots. The sound of them on the cobblestones. The hard heel that slammed into my side and skull."

"You're delusional. Max rattled your brain."

"Then there are your unknown assets who're needing small

fortunes of money every month," Bay continued grimly. "Your Jaguar. Your Rolex watch. The fact that 'Max' knew I had a weapon. When I finally peeled myself off the ground, I felt along the back of the alley. There's a door that opens onto the alley on this street. You ran down it to get to the meet before I did. *You're* Max, you asshole."

Bay saw Cowboy's hand twitch, and there was a sudden movement of air. Instantly Bay reached for his Browning, but almost invisibly Cowboy's Glock had appeared. The taller man took one step back and pointed it at Bay's heart.

"Now I know how you got that Phi Beta Kappa key," Cowboy rumbled. "Smart little shit, aren't you. Take your hand out of your coat."

As they stood facing each other on the lonely street, Bay felt fresh sweat bead up on his forehead. Slowly he removed his hand and lowered it to his side. "I'll bet you've been making up all your unknowns' intel—including the story about Lebanon. How could you do that?"

Cowboy blinked. "God knows the cops won't care if I erase you. By now they may have already identified you as being with the station—"

"Why, dammit!"

Emotions played across Cowboy's face, finally settling into chilly neutrality. "Goethe said something like this—the most important things aren't always to be found in the files. We make up history as we go along, and only a few of the million or so viewpoints ever make it into the files *or* the history books. You're wondering how I 'could do it,' so I'll tell you about Nick Shadrin. You know the name?"

Bay shook his head. Nerves on fire, he tried to figure out how to take down Cowboy or at least escape.

But Cowboy's gaze was alert, and his pistol steady. "Shadrin was a Soviet defector back in the fifties. His real name was

Nikolai Artamonov, and he became a spy for us. Then in the late seventies he vanished here in Vienna. Some said he died accidentally from too much chloroform when the KGB kidnapped him. Others said it was natural causes and we buried him quietly to hide it from the KGB. But the story I like was he'd been KGB all along. After twenty years acting secretly against us, his mission was over, and he wanted to return to his family in Moscow. Mossad found out and cut a deal with the KGB to not blow the operation if they'd exchange some key Jewish dissidents being held in the Gulag. Imagine it. The Vienna Woods. The dead of winter. A cluster of shriveled Jews, the KGB and Mossad weaponized to their fangs, and Nick Shadrin. To this day they're still covering up the exchange. Neither wants us to know our foe and supposed friend conspired to serve their own interests and give us a black eye. So here's the point. History's an imaginary construct. It's half-truths and lies. If you're on the front lines and paying attention, you get hit with deep disappointment. At the same time, you're freed. You realize it's just a game, and the objective of every game is to separate the winners from the losers. That's why I do it."

Now Bay understood. "What you're really saying is there are no rules for you."

"Or for you either. You're young. I'll teach you everything I know and give you a cut. Pretty soon you'll have your own string of unknowns. You'll learn to maneuver. How to make the best plays. If you want to end up at the top of the mountain at Langley, I can help with that, too."

Bay had a sick taste in his mouth. "You poor, sorry bastard."

Cowboy's head snapped back as if he had been slapped. His finger tightened on the trigger.

"Go ahead, shoot," Bay dared. "I'd rather be dead than do what you do. You could've stayed one of the best. What a contribution you could be making! Disappointed? Hell, you're not disappointed. You quit, then you turned. You're a *failure*."

An ironic smile spread across Cowboy's face. "Ah, another case where history will be written more than one way. But then Vienna's the place. You have a lot to learn, but I suspect you're the type who'll do it." He turned on his heels and ran east.

"Stop, Cowboy!" Bay hurtled after him, his head throbbing. "Come back to the station with me. It'll be better for you if you're the one who tells Herb. Cowboy, stop!"

Although Cowboy was in his fifties, his long legs ate up the distance, while Bay ached with every stride. His muscles were weak. Pushing himself, he drew on his years as a runner, but Cowboy remained ahead.

At the Parkring, cars roared past. Their headlights were cones of white light, their taillights bloody streams of red. Cowboy jumped into a dark green Jaguar XK8 parked at the curb. Even at a distance, Bay could hear the power of the engine as it revved. Still running, he watched as the car slid into traffic. But then the Jaguar suddenly shot out from the congestion, careening off at an angle.

"No!" Bay bellowed.

Bolting up over the curb, the car smashed into a thick telephone pole. The hood cracked open, and white steam rose wraithlike around it. The ear-bleed noise of the blasting horn filled the air. As traffic slowed, a police siren began to scream. Pedestrians gathered around until Bay could no longer see the Jaguar.

Breathing heavily, he pushed through the crowd. The horn was quiet, and a police car was stopped at the curb. Angrily he wiped his sleeve across his wet face. The driver's door to the Jag was open, and a policeman was leaning inside.

"How is he?" Bay asked in German.

The policeman stepped back. "Do you know him, sir?" Although his tone and demeanor were polite, Bay detected wariness.

"He's Jacob Crandell, a political officer at the U.S. consulate.

I work there, too. How is he?" he repeated as he stared inside. Cowboy was no longer leaning on the horn, his body relaxed back against the seat. His head lolled to the side, and his glasses were crooked on his nose, one lens cracked. His eyes were closed. Blood spilled from a corner of his mouth, but oddly he was smiling.

"I'm sorry to tell you, sir, I could find no pulse," the policeman said. "I've called for an ambulance. Please show me your identification."

Woodenly he took out his wallet and handed it over.

As the policeman wrote, Bay tried to feel the pavement under his feet, the mist against his skin, smell the exhaust in the air.

A second policeman joined the first. "Who is it?"

"Cowboy Crandell," the first one said. "I'd been wondering what he was up to." He returned Bay's billfold.

"Good, then this is an easy case. A traffic accident."

They did not look at Bay. They did not want to be given another reason, Bay realized.

"Yes, a traffic accident," said the other. "Very straightforward."

Bay silently slid back into the crowd and walked away. As the traffic of the Parkring thundered, his mind roamed over the evening, remembering Cowboy's stories, advice, and gruff kindness. Cowboy had always lived on the edge, which was fine, but then he had died from it as if it were a disease. Still, he had died the way he wanted.

Hell, this is a beautiful antique burg. . . . Operating here is like being inside a museum, punctuated by boredom, of course. The lull before the storm. I used to believe I could die happy in my Jaguar. Now I know Vienna's the place.

Bay dug his hands into his trench coat pockets and headed back into the Innere Stadt. He passed busy cafés and noisy pubs. People milled on the street, deciding where to find their next dose of gaiety in the gray night. As he walked, he could hear

Cowboy's voice: *You have a lot to learn, but I suspect you're the type who'll do it.* Bay smiled to himself, realizing he was keeping his movements nondescript, just as Cowboy had said to do. With cold fingers he wiped tears from his eyes. Then he glanced covertly around and faded into the crowd.

THE INTERROGATOR

David Morrell

WHEN ANDREW DURAND was growing up, his father never missed an opportunity to teach him tradecraft. Anything they did was a chance for the boy to learn about dead drops, brush contacts, cutouts, elicitation, and other arts of the espionage profession.

Not that Andrew's father spent a great deal of time with him. As a senior member of the Agency's Directorate of Operations, his father had global responsibilities that constantly called him away. But when circumstances permitted, the father's attention to Andrew was absolute, and Andrew never forgot their conspiratorial expeditions.

In particular, Andrew recalled the July afternoon his father took him sailing on the Chesapeake to celebrate his sixteenth birthday. During a lull in the wind, his father told him about his graduate-student days at George Washington University and how his political science professor introduced him to a man who turned out to be a CIA recruiter.

"It was the Cold War years of the nineteen fifties," his father said with a nostalgic smile as waves lapped the hull. "The nuclear arms race. Mushroom clouds. Bomb shelters. In fact, my parents installed a bomb shelter where we now have the swimming pool. The thing was deep enough that when we tore it out later, we didn't need to do much excavating for the pool. I figured handling the Soviets was just about the most important job anybody could want, so when the recruiter finally ended the courtship and popped the question, I didn't need long to decide. The Agency had already done its background check. A few formalities still remained, like the polygraph, but before they got to that, they decided to test my qualifications for the job they had in mind."

The test, Andrew's father explained, was to make him sit in a windowless room and read a novel. Written by Henry James, published in 1903, the book was called *The Ambassadors*. In long, complicated sentences, the first section introduced a middle-aged American with the odd name of Lambert Strether, who traveled to Paris on some kind of mission.

"James has a reputation for being difficult to read," Andrew's father said. "At first, I thought I was being subjected to a practical joke. After all, what was the point of just sitting in a room and reading? After about a half hour, music started playing through a speaker hidden in the ceiling, something brassy by Frank Sinatra, 'I've Got You Under My Skin.' I remember the title because I later understood how ironic it was. Another brassy Sinatra tune followed. Then another. Abruptly, the music stopped, and a male voice I'd never heard before instructed me to put the book in my lap and describe what was happening in the plot. I replied that Strether worked for a rich woman in a town in New England. She'd sent him to Paris to learn why her son hadn't returned home after a long trip abroad. 'Continue reading,' the voice said. The moment I picked up the novel, another brassy Sinatra tune began playing.

"As I turned the pages, I was suddenly aware of faint voices behind the music, a man and a woman. Their tone was subdued, but I could tell they were angry. At once, the music and the voices stopped.

"'What's happening in the book?' the voice asked from the ceiling.

"I answered, 'Strether's worried that he'll lose his job if he doesn't persuade the son to go home to his mother.'

"'Lose only his job?' the voice asked.

"'Well, the rich woman's a widow, and there's a hint that she and Strether might get married. But that won't happen if Strether doesn't bring her son home.'

"'There were people talking behind the music.'

"'Yes. A man and a woman.'

"'What were they discussing?'

"'They were supposed to meet at a restaurant for dinner. But the man arrived late, claiming last-minute responsibilities at his office. His wife believes he was with another woman.'

"'Continue reading,' the voice said."

Andrew remembered listening to his father explain how the test persisted for hours. In addition to the music, two and then three conversations took place simultaneously behind the songs. Periodically, the voice asked about each of them (a woman was fearful about an impending gall-bladder surgery; a man was angry about the cost of his daughter's wedding; a child was worried about a sick dog). The voice also wanted to know what was happening in the densely textured novel.

"Obviously, it was an exercise to determine how much I could be aware of at the same time, or whether the examiner could distract me and get under my skin," Andrew's father said. "It turned out that my political science teacher had recommended me to the Agency because of my ability to hold various thoughts at once without being distracted. I passed the test and was initially assigned to hotbed cities like Bonn, which in those days was the capital of West Germany. Pretending to be an attaché, I made chitchat at crowded embassy cocktail parties while monitoring the voices of foreign diplomats around me. No one expected state secrets to be revealed. Nonetheless, my superiors were surprised by the useful personal details I was able to gather at those diplomatic receptions: who was trying to seduce whom, for example, or who had money problems. Alcohol and the supposed safety of the chaos of voices in a crowded room made people careless. After that, I was promoted to junior analyst, where I rose through the ranks because I could balance the relative significance of various crises that erupted simultaneously around the globe."

The waves lapped stronger against the hull. The boat shifted. The memories made Andrew's father hesitate. Drawn into the past, he took a moment before glancing toward clouds moving across the sky.

"Finally, the wind's picking up. Grab the wheel, son. Check the compass. Take us southwest toward home. By the way, that James book, *The Ambassadors*? After all my effort, I was determined to finish it. In the end, it turned out that Strether's experience in Paris was so broadening that he felt he'd become smarter, aware of everything around him. But he was wrong. The rich woman's son gained his trust, only to make a fool of him. Despite all his awareness, Strether returned to America, where he assumed he'd lose everything."

"FOUR DAYS," ANDREW promised the somber group in the high-security conference room. He was thirty-nine and spoke with the authoritative tone of his father.

"Is that a guarantee?"

"I can possibly get results sooner, but definitely no later than four days."

"There's a time element," a grim official warned, "the probability of smallpox dispersal in a subway system during peak hours. Ten days from now. But we don't know the exact time or which country, let alone which city. Our people apprehended the subject in Paris. His fellow conspirators were with him. One escaped, but the rest died in a gun battle. We have documents that indicate what they set in motion—but not the particulars. Just because they were in Paris, that doesn't rule out another city with a major subway system as the target."

"Four days after I start, you'll have the details," Andrew assured them. "Where's the subject being rendered?"

"Uzbekistan."

Andrew's beefy neck crinkled when he nodded. "They know how to be discreet."

"They ought to, given how much we pay them."

"But I don't want any foreign interrogator involved," Andrew emphasized. "Thugs have unreliable methods. A subject will confess to anything if tortured sufficiently. You want reliable information, not a hysterical confession that turns out to be baseless."

"Exactly. You're completely in charge."

"In fact, there's no reason why this needs to be an extraordinary rendition." Andrew's use of "rendition" referred to the practice of moving a prisoner from one jurisdiction to another, a common occurrence in the legal system. But when the rendition was "extraordinary," the prisoner was taken out of the legal system and placed where the normal rules no longer applied and accountability was no longer a factor. "The interview could just as easily take place in the United States."

"Unfortunately, not everyone appreciates the difference between torture and your methods, Andrew. A jet's waiting to fly you to Uzbekistan."

ANDREW'S FATHER HAD been heavyset. Andrew was more so. A big man with a large chest, he resembled a heavyweight boxer, an impression that frequently made a detainee's eyes widen at first sight of him. With his deep, raspy voice, he exuded a sense of menace and power, causing his subjects to feel increasing dread, unaware that Andrew's true power came from numerous psychology courses taken at George Washington University, where he had earned a master's degree under a created identity.

A burly American civilian guard greeted him at a remote Uzbekistan airstrip next to a concrete-block building that was the rendering facility, the only structure in the boulder-dotted valley.

Andrew introduced himself as Mr. Baker.

The guard said he was Mr. Able. "I have the subject's documents ready for you. We know his name and those of his relatives, where they live and work, in case you want to make him talk by threatening to kill people he loves."

"That won't be necessary. I'll hardly ever speak to him." A cold wind tugged at Andrew's dark suit. When working, he always dressed formally, another way of expressing authority.

Escorted by Mr. Able, he passed through the security checkpoint, then entered the facility, which had harsh overhead lights and a row of doors with barred windows. The walls were made from unpainted cinder blocks. Everything felt damp.

"Your room's to the right," Mr. Able told him.

Andrew's travel bag contained four days of clothes, the maximum he would need. He set it on the concrete floor next to a cot. He barely looked at the stainless-steel sink and toilet. Instead he focused on a metal table upon which sat a laptop computer. "The other equipment should have arrived."

"It's been installed. But I don't know why we needed to bother. While we waited for you, my men and I could have put the fear of God into him."

"I can't imagine how that's possible when he's convinced God's on his side. Is the interpreter ready?"

"Yes."

"Reliable?"

"Very."

"Then let's get started."

*　　*　　*

ANDREW WATCHED Mr. Able unlock a metal door. Holding a .45-caliber Glock pistol, the guard and two others armed with identical pistols entered the cell and aimed at the prisoner. Andrew and the interpreter stood in the open doorway. The compartment was windowless, except for the barred opening in the door. It felt damper than the corridor. The echo was sharp.

A short, gaunt Iraqi man was slumped on the concrete floor, his back against the wall, his wrists shackled to chains above his head. In his midthirties, he had a thin, dark face and short, black hair. His lips were scabbed. His cheeks were bruised. Dried blood grimed his black shirt and pants.

As if dazed, the subject stared straight ahead, not reacting to Andrew's entrance.

Andrew turned toward Mr. Able, his stark expression making clear that he'd sent explicit instructions not to abuse the prisoner.

"That happened when the team grabbed him in Paris," the guard explained. "He's lucky he didn't get killed in the gun battle."

"*He* doesn't think so. He wants to die for his cause."

"Yeah, well, if he doesn't talk, we can arrange for him to get his wish," Mr. Able said. "The thing is, as much as he'd like to be a martyr, I'm sure he didn't intend for any suffering to be involved." The guard faced the prisoner. "Isn't that right, chum? You figured you'd jump over the agony and get straight to the virgins in paradise. Well, you were wrong."

The prisoner showed no reaction, continuing to look straight ahead. As an experiment, Andrew raised his arm above his head and pointed toward the ceiling, but the prisoner's eyes didn't follow his broad gesture. They remained so resolutely fixed on the opposite wall that Andrew became convinced the subject wasn't as dazed as he appeared.

"Translate for me," Andrew told the interpreter, then concentrated on the prisoner. "You have information about a soon-to-occur attack on a subway system. This attack will probably involve smallpox. You will tell me exactly when and where this attack will take place. You'll tell me whether the attack does involve smallpox and how the smallpox was obtained. You'll tell me how the attack will be carried out. The next time you see me, you'll tell me all of these things and anything else I wish to know."

The prisoner kept staring straight ahead.

When the interpreter finished, Andrew pointed toward a narrow cot bolted to the floor along one wall. He told Mr. Able, "Remove it. Leave a thin blanket. Unshackle him. Lock the room. Cover the window in the door."

"Look, is all this really necessary?" the guard complained. "Just give me two hours with him and—"

Andrew left the cell.

THE WAY HE *avoids eye contact,* Andrew thought. *He's been warned about some types of interrogation.*

Like most intelligence operatives, Andrew had received training in the ways humans processed information. According to one theory known as neuro-linguistic programming, most people were either sight-oriented, sound-oriented, or touch-oriented. A sight-oriented person tended to favor language that involved metaphors of sight, such as "I see what you mean." From an observer's point of view, that type of person tended to look up toward the left when creating a thought and to look up to the right when remembering something. In contrast, a sound-oriented person tended to use metaphors such as "I hear what you're getting at." When creating a thought, that type of person looked directly to the observer's left and, when remembering something, looked directly to the right. Finally, a touch-oriented person favored metaphors such as "I feel that can work." When that type of person looked down to the left or the right, those movements, too, were revealing.

People were seldom exclusively one type, but through careful observation, a trained interrogator could determine the sense orientation an individual favored. The interrogator might ask, "What city will be attacked?" If a sound-oriented prisoner glanced directly to the left and said, "Washington," that statement was a created thought—an invention. But, if the prisoner glanced to the right and said the same thing, that statement was based on a memory. Of course, the prisoner might be remembering a lie he was instructed to tell. Nonetheless, through careful observation of eye movements, a skilled interrogator could reach reasonably certain conclusions about whether a prisoner was lying or telling the truth.

The trouble was, this particular prisoner obstinately refused to look Andrew in the eyes.

Hell, he knows about neuro-linguistic programming, Andrew thought. *He's been warned that his eye movements might tell me something about his mission.*

The sophistication made Andrew uneasy. To consider these fanatics as ignorant was a lethal mistake. They learned exponentially and seemed dangerously more complex every day.

He couldn't help thinking of the simplicity of an interrogation technique favored during his father's youth in the 1950s. Back then, a prisoner was injected with Sodium Pentothal or one of the other so-called truth serums. This relaxed a detainee to such a degree that his mental discipline was compromised, in theory making him vulnerable to questioning. But the process was often like trying to get information from a drunk. Fantasy, exaggeration, and fact became indistinguishable. Needing clarity and reliability, interrogators developed other methods.

IN HIS ROOM, Andrew sat at his desk, activated the laptop computer, and watched an image appear. Transmitted from a hidden camera, it showed the prisoner in his cell. In keeping with Andrew's instructions, the cot had been removed. The barred opening in the door was covered. A thin blanket lay on the concrete floor. The subject's arms had been unshackled. He rubbed his chafed wrists. Now that he was alone, he confirmed Andrew's suspicions by looking around warily, no longer fixing his gaze toward a spot on a wall.

Andrew pressed a button on the laptop's keyboard and subtly increased the glare of the overhead lights in the cell. The change was so imperceptible that the subject couldn't notice. During the next four days, the intensity would continue to increase until the glare was blinding, but no moment in the gradually agonizing change would be perceptible.

Andrew pressed another button and reduced the cell's temperature a quarter of a degree. Again, the change was too small for the prisoner to notice, but during the next four days, the damp chill in the compartment would become extreme.

The subject sat in a corner with his back against the wall. In a moment, his eyes closed, perhaps in meditation.

Can't allow that, Andrew thought. He pressed a third button, which activated a siren in the prisoner's cell. On the screen, the prisoner jerked his eyes open. Startled, he looked up at the ceiling, where the siren was located. For now, the siren was at its lowest setting. It lasted only three seconds. But over the next four days, at unpredictable intervals, it would be repeated, each time louder and longer.

The prisoner would be given small amounts of bread and water to keep his strength at a sufficient level to prevent him from passing out. But the toilet in his cell would stop functioning, his wastes accumulating, their stench adding to his other sensory ordeals.

Andrew was reminded of the story his father had told him long ago on the sailboat. In his father's case, there had been various increasing challenges to his perceptions. In the prisoner's case, there would be increasing *assaults* to his perceptions. He would soon lose his sense of time. Minutes would feel like hours, and hours would feel like days. The intensifying barrage of painful stimuli would tear away his psychological defenses, leaving him so overwhelmed, disoriented, and worn down that he'd reveal any secret if only he could sleep.

THE PRISONER LASTED three and a half days. The sporadic faint siren eventually became a prolonged wail that forced him to put his hands over his ears and scream. Of course, his scream could not be heard amid the siren. Only the O of his mouth communicated the anguished noise escaping from him. The eventual searing glare of the lights changed to a pulsing light-dark, light-dark strobe effect that made the prisoner scrunch his eyes shut, straining to protect them. The thin blanket he'd been allowed was merely an attempt to give him false hope, for as the cold intensified, seeping up from the concrete floor and into his bones, the blanket gave him no protection. He huddled uselessly under it, unable to stop shivering.

AGAIN, MR. ABLE and the other two guards entered the cell. Again, Andrew and the interpreter stood in the open doorway.

The prisoner twitched, this time definitely affected by Andrew's size.

"When and where will the attack occur?" Andrew asked. "Does the attack involve smallpox? If so, how did your group obtain it? How will the attack be carried out? Tell me, and this is what I'll do." Andrew took a remote control from his suit-coat pocket and pressed a button that lowered the lights to a pleasant glow.

"I'll also shut off the siren," Andrew said. "I'll make the room's temperature comfortable. I'll allow you to sleep. Wouldn't it be wonderful to sleep? Sleep is the greatest pleasure. Sleep will refresh you."

Hugging himself to keep from shaking, the prisoner confessed. Because he hadn't slept for almost four days, the information wasn't always clear. Andrew needed to rephrase questions and prompt him numerous times, on occasion reactivating the siren and the throbbing lights to jolt his nerves. In the end, Andrew learned all that he wanted, and the prisoner no longer avoided looking at him. With a beseeching gaze, the desperate man told him what he needed, and the movement of his red, swollen, sleep-deprived eyes told Andrew that he wasn't lying.

The target was New York City. The attack did involve smallpox. In four days, at five p.m. on numerous subway platforms, aerosol canisters that looked like hair-spray dispensers would be taken from backpacks. Their tops would be twisted, then returned to the backpacks. Their pressurized air would be vented through a tube in each backpack, dispersing the virus among the crowd. The victims wouldn't know about the attack until days later when symptoms of the disease began to appear, but by then, the victims would have spread the virus much farther.

As Andrew hurried toward a scrambler-equipped satellite radio to report what he'd learned, he heard muffled screams coming from another cell. Water splashed. Disturbed by the significance of the sounds, Andrew ran to an open doorway through which he saw a man strapped to a board. The board was tilted so that the man's head was lower than his feet. His head was in a brace so that he couldn't turn it from side to side. He was naked, except for his underwear. His features were covered by a cloth, but the brown color of his skin matched that of the prisoner Andrew had interrogated, making Andrew conclude that this man, too, was an Iraqi.

Mr. Able stood over this new prisoner, pouring water onto his covered face. The prisoner made a gagging sound. He squirmed desperately, barely able to move.

"Our team in Paris caught the guy who escaped," the guard

told Andrew, then poured more water over the prisoner's face. "He arrived while you were questioning the other prisoner."

"Stop," Andrew said.

"You took almost four days. At the start, I told you I could get someone to confess in two hours. But the truth is, all I really need is ten minutes."

What Andrew watched helplessly was called waterboarding. The immobilized prisoner was subjected to a heavy stream of water over his face. The soggy cloth on his nose and mouth added to the weight of the water and made breathing even more difficult. The cloth covered his eyes and increased his terror because he couldn't see to anticipate when more water would strike him. The incline guaranteed that the water would rush into his nostrils.

Unable to expel the water, the prisoner kept gagging, relentlessly subjected to the sensation of drowning. Andrew knew of cases in which prisoners did in fact drown. Other times, panic broke their sanity. Intelligence operatives who allowed themselves to be waterboarded in an effort to understand the experience were seldom able to bear even a minute of it. Those prisoners who were eventually set free reported that the panic they endured created lifelong traumas that made it impossible for them to look at a rain shower or even at water flowing from a tap.

In this case, the prisoner thrashed with such force that Andrew was convinced he would dislocate his limbs.

"Okay, asshole," Mr. Able said through a translator. He yanked the drenched cloth from the victim's face.

Andrew was appalled to see a section of plastic wrap stretched over the prisoner's mouth. The only way the man could breathe was through his nose, from which water and snot erupted as he fought to clear his nostrils.

"Here's your chance not to drown." The guard yanked the

plastic wrap from the prisoner's mouth. "Which subway system's going to be attacked?"

The prisoner spat water. He gasped for air, his chest heaving.

"Speak up, jerk-off. I haven't got all day."

The prisoner made a sound as if he might vomit.

"Fine." Mr. Able stretched the plastic wrap across the prisoner's mouth. He threw the dripping cloth over his face, picked up another container of water, and poured.

With his feet tilted above him, the prisoner squirmed and gagged insanely as water cascaded onto the smothering cloth and into his nostrils.

"One last time, pal." Again, the guard yanked the cloth and the plastic wrap from the prisoner's face. "Answer my question, or you'll drown. What subway system's going to be attacked?"

"Paris," the prisoner managed to say.

"You won't like it if I find out you're lying."

"*Paris.*"

"Wait right there, chum. Don't go away." The guard left the prisoner strapped to the board and proceeded along the corridor to the man in the other cell.

"No," Andrew said. He hurried after the guard, and what he saw when he reached the cell filled him with dismay. Guards had stripped the first prisoner and strapped him to a board, tilting his head down. A cloth covered his face.

"Stop," Andrew said.

When he tried to intervene, two other guards grabbed him, dragging him back. Frantic, Andrew strained to pull free, but suddenly the barrel of a pistol was rammed painfully into his back, and he stopped resisting.

"I keep getting radio calls from nervous, important people," Mr. Able said. "They keep asking what the hell's taking so long. A lot of people will die soon if we don't get the right information. I tell those nervous, important people that you've got your special way of doing things, that you don't think *my* way's reliable, that you think a prisoner'll tell me anything just to make me stop."

"It's true," Andrew said. "Panic makes him so desperate he'll say anything he thinks you want to hear. The information isn't dependable. But *my* way strips away his defenses. He doesn't have any resistance by the time I finish with him. He doesn't have the strength to lie."

"Well, Mr. Baker, waterboarding makes them too terrified to lie." The guard began pouring water over the prisoner's face. It took less time than with the other man, because this prisoner was already exhausted from the sensory assaults that Andrew had subjected him to. He struggled. He gagged. As water poured over his downward-tilted face, rushing into his nostrils, he made choking sounds beneath the smothering cloth.

"What subway system's going to be attacked?" Mr. Able demanded.

"He already told me!" Andrew shouted.

"Well, let's hear what he answers *this* time." The guard ripped the cloth and a strip of plastic wrap from his mouth.

"Paris," the prisoner moaned.

Andrew gaped. "No. That's not the answer he gave me. He told me New York City."

"But now he says Paris, and so does the other guy. Paris is where they got captured. Why else would they be there if they weren't going to attack it? Enough time's been wasted. Our bosses are waiting for my report. We don't need you here. I'm the interrogator they should have hired."

"You're making a mistake."

"No, *you* made the mistake when you took so damned long. We can't waste any more time."

Andrew struggled to pull away from the guards who held his arms so tightly they made his hands numb, restricting the flow of blood. "Those people you want to impress—tell them the target's either New York *or* Paris. Tell them to increase surveillance at *all* the major subway systems but to emphasize New York and Paris. Four days from now. Thursday. Five p.m. local time. The attackers will wear backpacks. They'll have hairspray canisters inside the backpacks. The canisters hold the smallpox."

"I haven't started questioning these maggots about the other details," Mr. Able said. "Right now, I just want to let everybody know the target area."

"When they confessed to you, they never looked at you!" Andrew shouted.

"How the hell could they look at me when their heads were braced?" Mr. Able demanded. "I was standing to the side."

"Their eyes. They should have angled their eyes toward you. They should have used their eyes to beg you to believe them. Instead they kept staring at the ceiling, the same way the first prisoner stared at the wall when I got here."

"You expect me to believe that NLP shit? If they look to the left, they're making things up. If they look to the right, they're remembering something. So they look at the ceiling to keep me from knowing if they're lying or not."

"That's the theory."

"Well, suppose what they're remembering is a lie they rehearsed? Left. Right. None of it means anything."

"The point is *they* think it means something. That's why they won't look at you. After three and a half days, when the man I interrogated was ready for questioning, he couldn't stop looking at me. His eyes wouldn't stop pleading for me to let him sleep. And he always looked to the right. Maybe he remembered a lie, but at least, his eyes didn't tell me he was inventing something. The men you waterboarded, though, when they confessed, they didn't give you a chance to learn *anything* from their eyes."

"But . . ." A sudden doubt made Mr. Able frown. "If you're right, the only way that would work . . ."

". . . is if they were waterboarded other times. As part of their training," Andrew said. "Once they adjusted to it, their trainer could condition them to control their eyes."

"But the panic's overwhelming. No one would agree to be waterboarded repeatedly."

"Unless they welcome death."

The stark words made the guard cock his head, threatened by Andrew's logic.

Apparently the other guards reacted the same way. Confused, they released him. Feeling blood flow into his arms, Andrew stepped forward. "All these prisoners want is to die for their cause and go to paradise. They're not afraid of death. They welcome it. How can waterboarding make them panic?"

A long moment passed. Mr. Able lowered his gaze toward the water and scum on the floor. "Report whatever the hell you want."

"I will in a moment." Andrew turned toward the other guards. "Who stuck the pistol into my back?"

The man on the right said, "I did. No hard feelings."

"Wrong." Andrew rammed the palm of his hand against the man's face and shattered his nose.

FOUR DAYS LATER, shortly after five p.m. eastern standard time, Andrew received a radio message that five men with backpacks containing smallpox-dispersal cans had been arrested as they attempted to enter various sections of the New York City subway system. A weight seemed to fall from his chest. For the first time in a long while, he breathed freely. After the confidence with which he'd confronted Mr. Able, he'd begun to be troubled by doubts. So many lives depended on his skills. Given the sophistication of the prisoners, he'd been worried that, for once, he might have been fooled.

He was in Afghanistan now, conducting another sensory-assault interrogation. As before, the person usually in charge resented his intrusion and complained that he could get results much faster than Andrew did.

Andrew ignored him.

But on the eve of the third day of the interrogation, when Andrew was sure that his prisoner would soon lose all his psychological defenses and reveal what Andrew needed to know, he was again reminded of his father. He sat before the computer on his desk, watching the image of the prisoner, and he recalled that his father had sometimes been asked to go to the Agency's training facility at Camp Peary, Virginia, where he taught operatives to extend the limits of their perceptions.

"It's like most things. It involves practice," his father had explained to Andrew. "For old times' sake, I made my students read *The Ambassadors*. I tried to distract them with blaring music. I inserted conversations behind the music. A layer at a time. After a while, the students learned to be more aware, to perceive many things at once."

As Andrew studied the computer screen and pushed buttons that flashed the blinding lights in the prisoner's cell while at the same time causing a siren to wail, he thought about the lesson that his father had said he took from that Henry James novel.

"Lambert Strether becomes increasingly aware as the novel progresses," Andrew's father had told him. "Eventually, Strether notices all sorts of things that he normally would have missed. Undertones in conversations. Overtones in the way someone looks at someone else. All the details in the way people dress and what those details say about them. He becomes a master of consciousness. The sentences dramatize that point. They get longer and more complicated as the novel progresses, as if matching Strether's growing mind. I get the sense that James hoped those complicated sentences would make the reader's mind develop as Strether's does. But this is the novel's point, Andrew. Never forget this, especially if you enter the intelligence profession, as I hope you will. For all his awareness, Strether loses. In the end, he's outwitted. His confidence in his awareness destroys him. The day you become most sure of something, that's the day you need to start doubting it. The essence of the intelligence profession is that you can never be aware enough, never be conscious enough, because your opponent is determined to be even more aware."

Andrew kept watching the computer screen and the agony of his prisoner as lights flashed and sirens wailed. Abruptly, he pressed buttons that turned off the lights and the siren. He wanted to create ten minutes of peace, ten minutes in which the prisoner would be unable to relax, dreading the further assault on his senses. It was a hell that the prisoner would soon do anything to end.

Except, Andrew thought.

The day you become most sure of something, that's the day you need to start doubting it. His father's words echoed in Andrew's memory as he thought about his conviction that the only sure method of interrogation was his own. But was it possible that . . .

A threatening idea wormed into Andrew's imagination. An operative could be trained to add one perception onto another and then another until he or she could monitor multiple conversations while reading a book and listening to brassy music.

Then why couldn't an operative of a different sort be trained to endure deepening cold, throbbing lights, and wailing sirens for three and a half days without sleep? The first time would be agony, but the agony of the second time would perhaps be less because it was familiar. The third time would be a learning experience, testing methods of self-hypnotism to make the onslaught less painful.

Watching the prisoner's supposed anguish, Andrew felt empty. Could an enemy become that sophisticated? If they learned NLP in order to defeat it, if they practiced being water-boarded in order to control their reactions to it, why couldn't they educate themselves in other methods of interrogation in order to defeat *those*? Any group whose members blew themselves up or infected themselves with smallpox to destroy their enemies and thus attain paradise was capable of anything.

Andrew pressed buttons on his computer keyboard and caused the strobe lights and siren to resume in the prisoner's cold cell. Imagining the blare, he watched the sleepless prisoner scream.

Or was the prisoner only pretending to have reached the limit of his endurance? Andrew had the troubling sense that the man on the screen was reacting predictably, almost on schedule, as if the prisoner had been trained to know what to anticipate and was behaving the way an interrogator would expect.

But how can I be sure? Andrew wondered. *How much further do I need to push him in order to be confident he isn't faking? Four and a half days? Five? Longer? Can anyone survive that and remain sane?*

Andrew recalled his father telling him about one of the most dramatic interrogations in American espionage. During the 1960s, a Soviet defector came to Washington and told the CIA that he knew about numerous Soviet moles in the U.S. intelligence system. His accusations resulted in investigations that came close to immobilizing the Agency.

Soon afterward, a second Soviet defector came to Washington and accused the first defector of being a double agent sent by the Soviets to paralyze the Agency by making false accusations about moles within it. In turn, the first defector claimed that the second defector was the true double agent and had been sent to discredit him.

These conflicting accusations finally brought American intelligence operations to a standstill. To break the stasis, the second defector, who'd been promised money, a new identity, and a consulting position with the Agency, was taken to a secret confinement facility where he was interrogated periodically for the next five years. Most of that time was spent in solitary confinement in a small cell with a narrow cot and a single lightbulb in the ceil-ing. He was given nothing to read. He couldn't speak to anyone. He was allowed to bathe only once a week. Except for the pas-sage of the seasons, he had no idea what day or week, month or year it was. He tried making a calendar, using threads from a blanket, but each time he completed one, his guards destroyed it. His boarded window prevented him from ever breathing fresh air. In summer, his room felt like a sweatbox. For five hundred and sixty-two days of those five years, he was questioned intensely, sometimes around the clock. But despite his pro-longed ordeal, he never recanted his accusation, nor did the first defector, even though their stories were mutually contradictory and one of them must have been lying. Nobody ever learned the truth.

Five years, Andrew thought. *Maybe I'm being too easy. Maybe I need more time.*

Suddenly wishing for the innocent era of Sodium Pentothal, he pressed another button and watched the prisoner wail.

It seemed the man would never stop.

SLEEPING WITH MY ASSASSIN

Andrew Klavan

I KNEW WHY she had come—of course I did—but I fell for her anyway—of course. That was what she'd been designed for and who I was, who they'd made me. I didn't even question it much, to be honest. I'd come to hate philosophizing of that sort by then. Endless discussions about nature versus nurture or fate versus free will. In the end, what are you even talking about really? Nothing: the way words work, the way the human brain puts ideas together—what we're capable of conceiving, I mean, not the real, underlying truth of the matter. I'm sure there's some logic to a person's life and all that. Some algorithm of accident and providence and inborn character that explains it. Maybe God can work it out, if he exists and has a calculator handy. Maybe even he shrugs the whole thing off as a pain in the celestial ass.

But for me, in the event, it was more poetry than philosophy or math. I saw her and I thought, "Ah, yes, of course, that's who they *would* send, isn't it?" She was death and the past and my dreams incarnate. And I fell for her, even knowing why she'd come.

I HAD PREMONITIONS of the end as soon as I read about the train wreck. I saw it on the *Drudge Report* over my morning coffee and suspected right away it was one of ours. A computer glitch on the D.C.–New York corridor. A head-on collision, twenty-seven dead, no one, seemingly, to blame. They were still digging bodies from the smoking wreckage when the FBI announced it wasn't terrorism. A likely story. Of course it was terrorism. By afternoon and through the two days following, various Islamist groups were claiming credit by way of various YouTube videos featuring various magi with greasy beards and colorful noses and utterly ridiculous hats. That was a likely story, too. Those hate-crazy clowns—they didn't have the network for it, not in this country.

Which meant it was a genuine riddle. Because we *did* have the network, but we had no cause.

I WORRIED AT it for a day or two, trying to sort out the possibilities. Stein was our man on the eastern railways, and I suppose, after so many decades of silence and unknowing, he might have just flipped and pressed the button. But he was always a stolid character, unlikely to go rogue. And anyway, instinct told me this was something else, something more disturbing. It had the smell of genuine catastrophe.

Finally, the anxiety got to be too much for me. I decided to take a risk. I couldn't contact Stein himself, of course. If we weren't active, it would be a useless danger. If we were, it would mean death to us both. Using my cover, I called a contact at the Agency instead—a threat analyst in the New York office—and he and I took a lunchtime stroll around the hole in the ground where the World Trade Center used to be.

There was nothing particularly strange about this. There are plenty of gabby spooks around. You'd be surprised. A lot of these guys are just overeducated bureaucrats playing *Spy vs. Spy*. They graduate with an ideology and maybe some computer skills but no real sense of evil whatsoever. Secrecy doesn't mean that much to them. Gossip is the only real talent they have—and the only real power they have—and they know you have to give to get. Buy them a drink and they'll spill state secrets like your Aunt May talking about Cousin Jane's abortion: all raised eyebrows and confidential murmurs and theoretically subtle hints you'd have to be an idiot not to understand.

But Jay—I'll call him Jay—was different. He'd been in Afghanistan, for one thing. He'd seen the sort of things people do to one another on the strength of bad religion or through the logic of misguided ideas or just out of plain monkey meanness. He knew the moral universe was not a simple machine in which you pour goodness in one end and goodness reliably comes out the other. All this made him better at his job than the academic whiz kids, more circumspect, more paranoid and thoughtful, less likely to make an easy trade for information. Subtlety, in fact, was the whole point for him. The unsaid thing that left open a world of possibilities. Which was his world—because, the way Jay saw it, you never really knew.

We were on the walkway beside the wreckage pit, moving in slow, measured steps amid a quick, jerky, time-lapse lunch crowd. We were shoulder to shoulder, our eyes front. Both of us in overcoats, both of us with our hands in our pockets. It was a biting October day.

Jay made the slightest gesture with his head toward the damage. Not dramatic at all—barely perceptible. But just enough to answer my objections to blaming the *jihadis*, just enough to say, *They did that, didn't they?*

"That was different," I said. Muttering, tight-lipped. "Primitive. Plus they got lucky. Plus we were stupid then."

"Oh, we're stupid now," he said with a laugh. "Believe me."

"Still."

He looked at me as we walked along—looked until I turned and read his eyes. I saw that he was puzzled, too; he smelled catastrophe, too.

"You know something?" he asked me.

I shrugged. I didn't. "There was some chatter before the fact," I said. "They knew it was on the way."

This was just a guess, but I felt sure it was a good one. It was the only reason I could think of why the YouTube wise men in their absurd hats should have had any measure of credibility with Jay at all. I could tell by his reaction that I'd gotten it right. There *had* been chatter. They *had* known.

Jay pursed his lips and let out a breath, a whispered whistle. We both faced front again. I saw him nodding from the corner of my eyes, confirming my suspicions.

"So why are there no fingerprints?" he wondered aloud.

WELL, EXACTLY. THAT was the question. Because the Arabs leave fingerprints. They pretty much have to. They pretty much *want* to, but even if they didn't, they would. Because they don't have the network. They aren't implanted, integrated, invisible the way we are. How could they be? Think of our preparation, the time we had to establish ourselves here. Time enough, in fact, so that the whole point and purpose of us passed away.

Which brought me right back where I'd started. They had the cause but not the network. We had the network but not the cause. I couldn't make any sense of it, and it had me worried. I kept circling around it in my mind as I walked uptown on Broadway toward my office.

It was a long walk in the brisk, wistful weather. Soon enough, the useless round of reasoning wore itself out, and I wasn't thinking at all anymore but had drifted instead into daydreams.

I'd always been like that, a dreamer, all my life. Lately, though, the quality of the dreams had changed. There was an aspect of compulsion to them, maybe even of addiction. They'd acquired a disturbing and ambient realism, too. I was there sometimes almost more than I was here. I *wanted* to be there more. I found a kind of peace when I was dreaming that I never had otherwise.

It was always about the Village. Always about Centerville. Not memories of my childhood, mind you. I had those, too, but the daydreams were something different, something more pathetic really, when you consider it. In the daydreams, I was in my hometown again but as a man in his early thirties, say, a man some quarter century younger than I am now but some fifteen years older than I was when I left the Village for good. I suppose, if you wanted to get psychological about it, you could say I was imagining myself at my father's age, the age my father was when I was little. But I think, more to the point, I was dreaming about myself at an age when I was still romantic but not unrecognizably young, more like myself than a seventeen-year-old but vigorous enough to play the handsome hero of a love story.

That's what they were, my daydreams: love stories. Their plots are too childish and embarrassing to go into at length, but a few details give their flavor. The setting played a major role: Centerville's green lawns and trim clapboard houses, the Stars and Stripes waving above the verandas, the bikes and trikes rattling along the sidewalks. Churches, parks and ponds, and elm-shaded walkways. And the school, of course, the gray, shingled, all American elementary school. The world of my boyhood, in other words.

She—the girl, the love interest—was variously named Mary or Sally or Jane. Smith was always her last name. Mary or Sally or Jane Smith. She was always very prim and proper—sometimes shy, sometimes warm and outgoing, but always proper and modest as good women were back there, back then. That, I think, was the heart of what I pined for. Not the Village's peaceful lawns and houses—or not *only* its lawns and houses and tree-lined walks—but the sweetness of its women, their virginity or at least their virtue or at least what I had thought as a boy was their virtue and had so admired and desired and loved.

The rest of the daydream—the plot—was, as I say, all

nonsense. I would be some romantic figure just home from some war or adventure, usually with a dashing scar on my cheek to show for it. There would be misunderstandings and separations, physical heroism sometimes and finally reconciliation, even marriage, even, if I was dreaming at leisure in the solitude of my apartment, a wedding night. Insipid, adolescent scenarios, I know, but it would be difficult to overstate how engrossed I could become in them, how soothing it was to me to return in my mind to the innocence and peace of that American small-town setting, circa 1960, to reexperience the virtue and propriety of women in the days before radicalism and feminism and sex on demand. That old and innocent America, all gone now, all forever gone.

Walking home from Ground Zero that day, I was so immersed, in fact, that I reached the middle of Washington Square Park before I came back to myself—and then I woke to my surroundings with a sort of breathless rush, a threatening flutter of panic. I stood still by the dry, leaf-littered fountain. I stood with my hands in my pockets and scanned swaths of landscape to the right and the left of the marble arch. Then I turned around and scanned the paths behind me. I had the unnerving sense that I was being followed or watched. I was almost sure of it. My eyes went over the faces of the few people sitting on the benches, the few sitting on the rim of the fountain, and the several others passing on the walks beneath the naked trees. I had the feeling that I had seen someone I knew or recognized, that it was that that had jolted me out of my daydreaming fugue state.

But there was no one. After another moment or two, I moved on. I was rattled, but uncertain what to make of it. On the one hand, my spycraft had grown rusty from long disuse, and I was doubtful it could be trusted. On the other hand, I hated even to entertain the thought that this train wreck and its riddles might mark a return to the paranoia of the bad days.

*   *   *

THE BAD DAYS, as I still thought of them, came in the early nineties, after the system collapsed and the wall came tumbling down. Communication with our controls, always infrequent, had ceased entirely and, forbidden to make contact with one another, we were completely in the dark. Sleepers—any under-cover operatives, but sleepers especially—are always in danger of losing their sense of purpose, of becoming so immersed and identified with the culture they've infiltrated that they become estranged from their motherland and their mission. But now our purpose was lost *in fact*; our motherland and mission were gone well and truly. What's the point of a Soviet pretending to be an American once the Soviet Union no longer exists?

That little conundrum was inner hell enough, believe me, but then the deaths began. Three of us in the space of a year and a half. David Cumberland, the movie director, collapsed on top of a terrified starlet after he or she or his dealer or personal assistant or someone, the investigators never determined who, misjudged the ratio of morphine to cocaine in one of his speedballs. Then Kent Sheffield went out the window of a Paris hotel in the wake of rumors he'd embezzled some of his clients' investments. And finally, Jonathan Synge, one of the first of the Internet billionaires, went down with his twenty-six-foot sailboat in the choppy waves outside the Golden Gate. All of which could have been coincidental or could have meant that the network was blown and the Americans were mopping up or that our own masters were getting rid of us, covering their tracks in light of the new situation. The uncertainty only added to the terror of it.

And the terror, I will not lie, was awful. There was no information, no contact, nothing but the deaths and the waiting. I was rudderless and ceaselessly afraid. My discipline collapsed. I started drinking. My marriage, such as it was, unraveled into a series of affairs and violent arguments and "discussions" that were even more vicious arguments in disguise. I couldn't tell Sharon the truth, of course, so our fights were always off the point and only served to increase my isolation.

"It was bad enough when you were just cold and silent, but now you're disgusting," she said to me. I was coming through the door in the dark of first morning. She was standing in the bedroom doorway in a pink nightgown, her arms hugged tight beneath her breasts. Her face was haggard and grim. She was a competent, sophisticated woman, but anger made her look weak and humorless. As long as we'd been minimally civilized with each other, her company—the mindless conformity of her expectations, the low normalcy of her social-climbing ambitions, just her reliable, undemanding presence day to day—had been some sort of comfort to me. Now even that was gone.

"Let me at least close the door," I said. "The whole building doesn't have to hear you."

"Jesus. I can smell her on you from here."

"So you wash the smell of them off first. What does that make you? The Virgin Mary?" Naturally, it wasn't what I wanted to say. I wanted to tell her about the never-ending fear and silence and the loneliness that made the fear and silence worse. I wanted to cry out to her that my whole purpose in life was gone and that I had known it was gone for years, but now that I could read all about it on the front page there was no denying it to myself any longer. I wanted to fall on my knees and bury my face in her belly and cling to her like a stanchion in high winds and tell her oh, oh, oh, I didn't want to die, not now when it had all become so useless and not like this, hustled into the center of some drab tabloid scenario by a pair of deadpanned experts in faked suicides and accidents, my extermination just another job.

"Oh, and don't give me that look," I said to her instead— even though she had turned her face away now to hide her crying. "We don't even make any sense anymore, do we? I mean, what's the point? Why shouldn't I cheat? What the hell am I getting out of it? It isn't as if you keep house or bring me my drinks and slippers. You're not the mother of my children. . . . "

"Whose fault is that?" she said raggedly, in a tearful rage.

"You work, you make as much money as I do. It isn't as if you need me the way a man wants to be needed. Women . . ." I waved a hand in the air, too drunk to form the thought I wanted, something about the way it used to be, what women were like, what marriage was like in the good old days. "You're just a roommate with a vagina," I finished finally. "As if that's supposed to count for everything. Well, I like a different vagina from time to time, if that's all it comes down to, so sue me. . . ."

The phone rang, interrupting this learned disquisition on modern social mores. Both Sharon and I reared up and stared at the instrument, indignant, as if it were some underling who had dared to break in on important business between us. If a couple can't rip each other to shreds in peace at four in the morning, what's the world coming to?

It rang again. Sharon said, "Go on and talk to your whore." Then she whirled in her pink nightgown and stormed back into the bedroom, slamming the door behind her.

"My whore doesn't have our number," I said—but only softly, because Sharon was no longer there to be hurt by it. Meanwhile, I was thinking *What the hell?* A wrong number? A neighbor complaining about the noise? The signal to set off a disaster or a harbinger of my own assassination? What? I was trying to talk myself out of the less pleasant scenarios, but it was no good. When the phone rang again, I tasted fear, chemical and sour, in the back of my throat.

I stepped to the lampstand by the sofa, took up the handset. Listened without a word.

"I can't stand it anymore," a terrified voice said at once.

"Who is this?" But I already knew—I could guess anyway.

"I don't care about the protocol." He was whining shamelessly. I could practically hear him sweat. "What good is protocol to me? We can't just sit here and be picked off one by one. We have to do something."

"You have the wrong number," I said.

I hung up. I stood in the center of the room and stared at nothing and swallowed the sour taste in my mouth. I was suddenly fully sober.

THAT WAS ALMOST—was it possible?—yes, almost twenty years ago. And that night—that was the worst of it. Whatever their cause, the deaths among us stopped at three. As time went by with no contact and no further disasters, the paranoia faded almost away.

Twenty years. Twenty years of silence and unknowing, the network an orphan, the regime that spawned it gone. The mission? It became a vestigial habit of thought, like some outmoded quirk of inclination or desire acquired in childhood but useless to or even at odds with adult life. I went on as I was trained to go on *because* I had been trained and for no other reason. What had once been the purpose of my every movement became more like a neurotic superstition, an obsessive compulsion like repeatedly washing the hands. I maneuvered my career and cultivated my contacts with an eye to sabotage, positioned myself where I could do the most damage. But there was no damage to do, and no point in doing it. And I didn't want to anyway. Why would I? Why would I hurt this country now?

Don't get me wrong. It wasn't that I had come to love America. I didn't love America. Not this America, weak and drab and stagnant. Its elites in a self-righteous circle jerk and its fat farm fucks muttering "nigger" and its niggers shrunken to bug-eyed skeletons on the watery milk of the government tit. Corrupt politician-alchemists spinning guilt and fear into power. Depraved celebrities with no talent for anything but self-destruction. And John Q. Public? Turn on the television and there he was, trying to win a million dollars on some hidden-camera game show by

wallowing in the slime of his own debauchery. That was enter-
tainment now—that was culture—that was art. And then the
women. Go out on the street and there they were, barking *fuck*
and *shit* into their cell phones. Working like men while their
men behaved like children, playing video games and slapping
hands and drinking beers with their baseball caps on sideways,
then trudging sheepishly home with a "yes, dear," to their grim,
sexless fuck-and-shit mommy-wives. There was no spirit in the
land. No spiritual logic to lead anyone to love or charity. Nothing
for the soul to strive for but welfare bread and online circuses. A
Rome without a world worth conquering. I did not love this
America; no. If I was loyal to anything, it was the country I had
known in childhood. The innocent small-town community with
its flags and churches and lawns. The women in their virtue and
their skirts below the knee. The fathers in their probity and suits
and ties. I loved the pride in liberty back then—not the liberty of
screwing whom you wanted and cursing whatever curses—but
the liberty born of self-reliance and self-control. The Village—I
loved the Village. I loved Centerville. And Centerville was gone.

All the same—all the same, what was left of it—what was left
of this country here and now—was still a relative paradise of
comfort and convenience. What else was there left to care about
but that? Revolution? Whatever came of revolution but slavery
and blood? No. I had my routines, I had my successful business,
the restaurants I enjoyed, my golf games, my sports on TV, my
occasional women. Why—in the name of what forsaken
cause?—would I do damage to such a pleasant ruin of a place to
live and die in as this?

So when I sensed our hand in the train wreck, I just felt my
comforts threatened, frankly. I was unnerved—worried almost
to the point of panic—to think that I might lose my easy, pleasant life.

What else was I supposed to feel, given the realistic possibilities?

*   *   *

I SPENT THE next several days after my meeting with Jay in virtual isolation in my apartment, trolling the Internet obsessively, searching for answers. Stein had been put in charge of the internal investigation now, so there was nothing like trustworthy information from any of the official sources. But there were clues. At least I thought there were. I thought I sensed traces of the truth lying right out in the open, right there in the daily news. A resurgence of Russian arrogance despite plummeting oil prices. A cat-and-canary silence in the Middle Eastern capitals despite all the outlying wise men beating their breasts. It all made for a sort of faint, wispy, curling smoke trail of reasoning if you knew how to see it, how to follow it. The implications were too horrible for me to face directly, but I must've understood them at some subconscious level all the same, because my anxiety grew more unbearable every day. Protocol or no, the impulse to try to contact Stein himself was almost irresistible.

I might've done it, too, if I hadn't remembered Leonard Densham.

It was Densham who had called me that early morning twenty years ago—that morning of my fight with Sharon. His was the whining, sweaty voice on the phone: *I can't stand it anymore. We have to do something.* He had always been the weak link, always, even when we were boys back in Centerville. The last to take a dare, the first to seize on an excuse for cowardice. He should've been eliminated then, but he had peculiar aptitudes when it came to rockets and satellites and so on, the big things at the time. In fact, he had ended up at the Department of Defense, working on the global navigation satellite system. But he was a weak link all the same. He should have been left behind.

As the days went by—those obsessive, anxiety-ridden days in my apartment, at my computer—I became convinced that he— Densham—was the one who had been following me in Washington Square Park. It made sense. If there was danger, uncertainty, anxiety, it made sense that Densham would be the first to break, the first to make contact, now as before. I became convinced that I had actually seen him in the park and subconsciously recognized his face, that it was that that had brought me out of my reverie.

Assuming I was right, I didn't think he would be hard to find. If he was following me, he must've been looking for a chance to make a safe approach. All I needed to do was give him the opportunity.

I chose a place called Smoke—a small smoking club amid the old brick warehouses on the lower west side. Nothing but two rows of cocktail tables in a narrow room of red carpet and red walls and black curtains with no windows behind them. The light was low and the music was loud: impossible to wire, difficult to observe. I went there three days running, arriving in the early evening before the crowds. I sat at the table nearest the back, where I could see everyone who came and went. Each day, I smoked one long Sherman and had one glass of malt and left.

On the third day, just as my smoke burned down to the nub, Densham pushed through the door and came hurrying down the center aisle toward my table.

Once upon a time, I would have said he had gone mad. No one really uses that word anymore. There are syndromes now and pathologies. Schizophrenia and bipolar disorder and this disorder and that. I suppose the notion that someone could just lose touch with reality is problematic in an age when no one is quite certain reality even exists. But Densham was something, all right: delusional, paranoid, anxiety-ridden, fevered, a raging whack job—make up your own diagnosis.

You only had to look at him to see it. It was bone-cold outside—there were snow flurries—and the club was poorly heated. I had sat through my drink with my overcoat on. But Densham? The sweat was gleaming on his face when he came in. His hair was limp and shiny with it. His eyes burned. His fingers worked constantly. He sat across from me at the small round table, bent over, rocking slightly with his fingers working so that he seemed to be playing an invisible clarinet in the empty air.

The waitress was a pretty young thing in a white blouse and black skirt and black stockings, but he barely glanced at her. He brushed her away at first, in fact, with those fiddling fingers, and only called her back to him and ordered a beer as an afterthought—so as not to look suspicious, I guess. Likewise, he shook his head when I opened my box of Shermans to him— and then quickly held my wrist before I could withdraw it. He took a cigarette and leaned into my plastic lighter so that, even through the smell of smoke, I caught a whiff of something on him, some vintage feminine perfume that touched me somehow.

"Calm down," I murmured to him as I held the flame. "You'll only draw attention to yourself. Just calm down."

I lit a fresh cigarette for myself as well, and we both sat back and drew smoke. Densham tried frantically to smile and seem relaxed. It just made him look even crazier.

"You understand what they've done, don't you? Can you see it?" The moment he spoke, the clues and my suspicions began to fall into place. But before I could put them all together, he leaned forward again, hot-eyed and urgent, his fingers drumming the table spasmodically. And he said, "They've sold us. They've sold the network."

My stomach dropped and my thoughts became clear. "To the Arabs."

"Of course, to the Arabs! Who else would . . . ?"

The waitress brought his beer, and he fell back against his chair, sucking crazily on his cigarette until he choked and coughed. I watched the girl's skirt retreating. Then, more calmly than I felt, I said, "That's ridiculous, Densham. Pull yourself together. Look at you. You're falling apart."

"Of course I'm falling apart! I didn't come here to blow things up for a bunch of camel-fucking madmen!"

"Quiet! For God's sake."

He clapped his cigarette hand to his mouth as if to hush himself.

"It doesn't make sense," I said. "What would they sell us *for*?"

Densham gave a jerky shrug, his hand fluttering up into the air now like a butterfly on a string, the cigarette trailing smoke behind. "Oil. What else? The price of oil. That's all they have left now, after all the fine philosophy they fed us. They need a lift in the price of oil—and fast. And what do they have to sell in return that the Arabs want? Us! The network."

I laughed, or tried to make a noise like laughter. "You're crazy. You're making this up."

"I'm not making it up. I deduce it."

"You can deduce anything. It may just be a train crash, Densham. For God's sake."

He stared at me, searched me with that peculiar power of insight crazy people have. "You know it. You know I'm right, don't you?"

I hid behind my drink. "Ah! Things go through your mind when you're on edge. It happens to all of us."

"I think Stein must have gone over."

"What? Gone over to whom?"

"The Americans!" he hissed. "Else why haven't they killed him like they did Cumberland and the others? Or arrested him at least?"

I didn't bother to answer him this time. I saw how it was with him now. He had sat at home in whatever life he had these twenty years and stewed in his terrors and suspicions, and now every outlandish theory seemed like the plain truth to him, every worst-case scenario seemed the obvious fact of the matter. He was like one of those people who call into radio shows at night to talk about flying saucers and government conspiracies.

He saw it all clearly and everyone else was blind. He was mad, in other words.

"You'll see. You'll see," he said. "We're activated. Activated *and* blown. In a week, a month, a year, we'll each get the call to serve the jihad. Refuse it, and our masters hurl us out a window. Accept it, and the Americans run us down with a car in some alley. We're dead either way." He laughed bitterly.

I'd had enough. I reached for my wallet. "You're out of your mind. You've been stewing in your own juices. You need to get out more. Get a good psychiatrist. Whatever you do, don't come near me again."

"I'm not going to do it! You understand? Camel-fucking madmen. I won't do it. That's not what I agreed to."

I shrugged. "We were children. None of us ever agreed to anything."

"Maybe the Americans can use me," Densham went on. "*They'll* spare me. Why not? They spared Stein, didn't they? Americans have always been sentimental that way. They'll see how it is. They'll see I have something to live for now. Finally. Something to live for . . . "

"Shut up. Would you shut up? Pull yourself together. Damn it!"

I threw some cash down on the table and stood. Densham looked up at me as if he only now remembered I was there. He nibbled at the end of his cigarette like a squirrel nibbling on a nut. He seemed small and furtive and ashamed.

"Do you ever miss it?" he said.

"What are you talking about?" I said irritably. I stood there, buttoning my overcoat. "Miss what?"

"The Village. Centerville. *I* miss it sometimes. I miss it a lot."

I looked away from him, embarrassed. It was as if he'd read my daydreams. "Don't be ridiculous," I said. "There's nothing to miss."

"There is to me." He gave another pathetic little laugh, a sob almost. "I loved it. It's the only thing I ever did love really."

"We all . . . idealize our childhoods."

"No. No," he repeated earnestly. "That life, that way of life. That's what we should've been fighting for all along."

I felt my face go hot. I stared down at him as if he were saying something incredible, something I hadn't thought myself a thousand times. "Fighting for?" I said, trying to keep my voice down. "How could we fight for it? It wasn't even real."

"It was real to me."

I sneered, disgusted by him—disgusted because he seemed just then to me to be my own pathetic Inner Man made flesh.

"Get yourself some help, Densham," I said.

He laughed or sobbed again. I left him there and strode across the room to the door.

HIS DEATH MADE the news, small splashes on the inside pages of the tabloids, likewise small but more stately obituaries in the broadsheets, and then, inevitably, links online. Instapundit was where I found it. They linked to a *New York Post* story: *Satellite Pioneer in Shocking SM Suicide.* Densham had been found hanging from the clothes rod in his closet strangled with his own belt and dressed in bizarre leather corsetry and other paraphernalia. A fatal wardrobe malfunction during an otherwise quiet evening of autoerotic asphyxiation—so said the local constabulary.

As murder, it was art—if it *was* murder. That was the genius of it. How could you know for sure? But I knew. At least, I thought I knew. I read the story with my stomach in a tailspin. I recognized it right away as the end of peace of mind for me, the end of what was left of my peace of mind. What sort of mental breakwater would stand against the flood of paranoia now? No. There was no getting away from it: The bad days had returned.

How awful suspense is! Worse than any actual catastrophe. How often have you heard a cancer patient tell you, "The worst part was waiting for the test results." Worse than the cancer itself: the waiting, not knowing, afraid. Awful. And there were days of it now, weeks of it, months.

Maybe that was also part of the reason I fell in love with her. Not just what she looked like and how she behaved and what she represented. That was all in the mix, of course. But maybe I was also just grateful—so grateful—that she had finally arrived.

BY THEN, THE dark, snowy winter had given way to a spring so mild it seemed a kind of silent music. I forced myself to go out of doors just to experience it, just to feel the air. The wistful air. Truly, just like a strain of half-remembered music. Even in New York with the heat of its traffic, its noises and smells, you couldn't feel that air without a softness opening in you, a sense of longing for the past—whatever past it was you happened to long for. I, of course, walked the city streets and dreamed of Centerville, dreamed myself into love stories set in the Village. It was the only relief I had from the suspense, the heavy winter cloud of waiting, unknowing and afraid.

I was lost in those dreams even as she approached me. I was in a coffee shop, at the window counter, my hand limp around the cardboard cup as I gazed unseeing at the storefront glass.

"Do you mind if I sit here?" she said. She had a beautiful voice. I noticed it right away. It was clear and mellow with diction at once flowing and precise. It was the way that women used to speak when they thought about how they *should* speak, when they trained themselves to speak like ladies.

I looked up and she was lovely. Maybe twenty years younger than I, in her thirties. Poised, but not with that brusque, mannish confidence I so often see in women today. Consciously graceful rather, as if her grace was a thing she did for people, a gift she gave them. Her whole style was graceful and vaguely old-fashioned in a sweet, pretty way. Shoulder-length blonde hair in a band. A blue spring dress wide at the shoulders, nipped at the waist, and ending modestly over the knee. I caught the scent she was wearing, and it was lovely, too, graceful and old-fashioned, too. I thought I knew it from somewhere but couldn't remember where.

"Do you mind if I sit here next to you?"

"Not at all," I said to her—but at the same time, my eyes swept the room and I saw there were plenty of tables open, plenty of other places she could sit.

She saw my eyes, read my thoughts. "There was a man outside," she told me. "Following me, making remarks. I thought if I sat next to you, if it seemed as if we knew each other . . ."

What happened next happened very quickly, my brain working things out, my emotions responding, all in a cascading flash. My first reaction was instinctive, automatic. An attractive woman had asked for my protection: I was warmed and immediately alert to the possibility of romance. But in the next moment—or in the next segment of that moment—it was all so quick—I remembered where I'd smelled that perfume before. It was the same scent I'd caught coming off Densham in the club when he had leaned toward me so I could light his cigarette. *I have something to live for now,* he had told me. *Finally. Something to live for.*

My eyes went to her eyes—her pale blue eyes—and I thought, *Ah, yes, of course, that's who they* would *send, isn't it?* And what was, I suppose, horrible—horrible and yet mesmerizing somehow—was that I saw she saw my thought, I saw she saw that I understood everything, and I saw that *she* understood, understood that it didn't matter to me, that it was to her advantage, in fact, because I wanted her, welcomed her.

She was death and the past and my dreams incarnate, and I was in love with her already. I always had been.

* * *

YOU WOULD THINK what followed would have been more or less bizarre, but it wasn't. Not to me. Every lover at the start is in a kind of fiction anyway. The restraint, the things held back, the best foot forward. Even this latest generation of whores and boors must have some courting ritual or other before they go at it like monkeys and then wander off to nurse their hangovers. Every mammal has its manners, its method of approach.

So the fact that she and I never acknowledged the reality of our situation didn't seem to me as strange as all that. We dined together and went to the movies and took long walks in Central Park and took drives into the country to see the spring scenery, just like anyone. We talked more or less at random about what we enjoyed and what we'd seen and what we ought to do. I told her about my business, which offered secure storage and online backup for the computer files of major corporations and government agencies. She told me about teaching English as a second language to visitors and immigrants. That was a nice touch: I was a wealthy entrepreneur, and she was a do-gooder, just getting by. It gave me all kinds of opportunities to take care of her, to play the man. She liked that, being taken care of. She liked for me to open the door for her and stand when she entered a room and hold her chair when she sat down. She accepted these tokens of gentlemanly respect with grace but also with gratitude. She had a way of nestling in my kindnesses, of luxu-riating in my protection and the vulnerability it allowed her. She had a way of looking up at me in expectant deference when there was a decision to be made so that I felt helpless to make any decision but the one that would ultimately please and shel-ter her. She was all softness and beauty, and I found myself tend-ing to her as if she were the last flower left in an otherwise stony world.

As for the past—as for talking about the past: We shared only fragments of it in those first days, fragments at intervals now and then, and if my memories were distortions and hers were lies, how different were we from anyone in the early stages of attraction?

We became lovers in the prettiest way, the gentlest and most graceful way, only after weeks and weeks of courtship and subtle seduction and slow surrender. I wish I had the words to describe the sweetness of her reticence, her modesty, and the measured yielding of her modesty to her passions and to mine. You want to tell me it was all inauthentic? False? A performance? As the kids say nowadays: Whatever! Have such things ever been anything *other* than a kind of performance, a kind of dance? An art form, if you will. And what's art but a special sort of falsehood, a falsehood by which we express the inexpressible truth about ourselves and about the human condition?

Well, that was the way I thought about it anyway—as a kind of art, a kind of story we were telling with our lives, a kind of lovely dance. Right up until the moment of climax, right up until the moment I came, holding her naked in my arms and thanking God—really, thanking God—for the late-life blessing of her. And then it all crumbled in my mind to ashes. What is it, I wonder, about the male orgasm that vaporizes every standing structure of sentiment and enchantment?

An hour later I sat bitterly in the dark, smoking a Sherman by the open window, staring balefully at the shape of her asleep on the bed. The taste of the cigarette brought my meeting with Densham back to me. His squirrelly, nervous voice beneath the smoke and music . . .*We're activated. Activated* and *blown. In a week, a month, a year, we'll each get the call to serve the jihad. Refuse it, and our masters hurl us out a window. Accept it, and the Americans run us down with a car in some alley. We're dead either way.*

She stirred in the shadows and murmured my name. Then, finding me there at the window framed by the relative light of the night city, she propped herself up on an elbow. "Are you all right, sweetheart?"

"Which was it?" I said to her. "Did he take the mission or refuse it?"

"What? Who?"

"Densham. He said he was going to turn them down and trust in the protection of the Americans. But I don't think he would have had the courage in the end. Once he was actually confronted with the choice, it would've been easier just to go along." The words came out of me in a low, tumbling rush. "He would've told himself that he was all wrong about the Americans, that they had no clue about us, that that's why Stein had gone along and gotten away with it scot-free. He could've convinced himself of anything if he thought it meant being with you. You were all he wanted, what he was living for. And there you were, all the while, waiting patiently, watching to see what he knew, who he spoke to, which way he'd turn. Just like you're doing with me."

She didn't answer. She didn't say, *I don't know what you're talking about.* It was chilling. She didn't even bother to pretend.

"I suppose that means that you *are* with the Americans," I said. "He took the mission and you had to stop him. . . . Or, who knows, maybe you're one of ours. Maybe he *did* refuse and that's why you did it. . . ."

"What time is it?" she murmured. "I'm sorry—I'm still asleep. Whatever it is, we can talk in the morning. Come back to bed and be with me."

Eventually, the mood passed and I did.

STRANGELY, AS MUCH as I was expecting the final call, it came unexpectedly. Because I was that lost in her, that immersed in the living dream of our romance. Hours and days at a time, I would forget the call was coming, though I always knew. When it finally did come, nothing could have been further from my mind.

We were in the park. It was an early summer's day. We were

eating lunch at the café overlooking the lake. I was telling a funny story about a website I had sold to a teenage millionaire who had dropped out of high school and had all the money in the world but no manners whatsoever. She was laughing in the most charming and flattering way, graciously covering her mouth with one hand. I was thinking how lovely, how truly lovely she was and what a joy.

The phone in my jacket pocket began to vibrate. Normally, of course, I wouldn't have answered during lunch, but this was the third time it had gone off in as many minutes.

"Excuse me," I said to her. "It might be an emergency at my office." I believed it, too. That was how completely submerged I was in our fairy tale.

I fetched out the cell phone and held it to my ear and even then, even when I heard the cantata in the background, it was a moment before I understood. Bach 140: the first part of the signal. And then a voice said, "George?" which was the other part.

"I'm sorry, you have the wrong number," I responded automatically.

"Oh, sorry, my mistake," the man said. The music was cut short as he hung up.

I slipped the phone back into my pocket, my eyes on her the whole time now.

"Wrong number?" she said finally. Just like that, completely natural, completely believable.

And in the same way, the same tone, almost believing it myself, I answered, "Yes. Sorry. Now what was I saying?"

AS WE WALKED back to my apartment, I found myself saddened more than anything, saddened that it was over. Though the light of the summer day stayed bright through the late afternoon, it had acquired, I noticed, an aura of emotional indigo, a brooding border of darkness that I remembered seeing in my college days when I had walked a lover to the train station for what I knew to be the last time. Now I held her cool hand in mine and glanced down from time to time at her fresh, upturned face and listened to that flowing, ladylike diction as she chattered about this or that future plan—and I ached for every passing minute, every minute that brought us closer to the end.

"Why don't you pour us some wine?" I said, as I helped her with her coat in the foyer. "I just have to check my e-mail for a moment."

I went into the study, consciously cherishing the domestic noises she made moving around the kitchen. I switched on the computer.

Our procedures had last been updated more than twenty years ago. They still included quaint arrangements like drop points and locker keys and corner meetings. I doubted that sort of thing was operational anymore and, as it turned out, I was right. They had sent the material straight to my computer: an untraceable packet that simply appeared as an icon on the desktop when I turned the machine on. I didn't read the whole code. Just enough to see what it was. A virus I could spread through my backup apparatus so that my clients would lose some of their files. Then, when they went to restore the files through my service, they would be rewritten with instructions that would plant minor, undetectable but ultimately devastating glitches throughout entire systems. It was, in other words, a cyber time bomb that would hobble key security responses at essential moments and render the nation helpless to defend against . . . whatever it was our camel-fucking friends were planning to do. At a glance, the business seemed quite elegant and devastating. But I think what struck me most about it was its clinical and efficient realism. It was as devoid of romance as a bad news X-ray. It pushed the whole notion of romance out of my mind.

Maybe that's why I seemed to see her afresh when I walked back into the living room. There she stood now in the center of the floor with our wineglasses, one in each hand. Wearing a pleated skirt and a buttoned blouse and a pearl necklace against her pink skin. It was the first time she seemed simply fraudulent to me. Beautiful, but fraudulent. Like a satire of a fifties house-wife. Not even that. A satire of a television program about a fifties housewife. The sight of her brought a bitter taste of irony into my mouth and into my mind, and as I took a glass from her, I smirked into those wonderful eyes—while they regarded me with nothing I could detect but wide, blue innocence.

I sat in my favorite easy chair. She sat on the rug at my feet. That, too, in my suddenly prosaic mood, struck me as some-what overintentional: a patent construct, a cynical tableau of a woman modest in her youth doting on a somewhat older man in his authority.

All the same, I held my glass down to hers and she lifted hers to mine and we clinked them together. I sipped and sighed.

"I was raised," I said, "in a town called Centerville." I don't know why I felt I had to tell her this, but I did. It was the last act of the play, I guess. The only way I could think to keep it going just a little longer.

She did her part as well. She put her head on my knee and gazed up at me dreamily as I stroked her hair. "Yes," she said. "You've mentioned it. In Indiana, you said."

"Yes. Yes. It was supposed to be in Indiana, a small town in Indiana. But, in fact, of course, it was in the Ukraine some-where. Surrounded by these vast wheat fields. Quite beautiful really. Quite typically American. They wanted us to grow up as typical Americans. That's what the place was made for. Even as they trained us for what we were going to do, they wanted us to develop American habits of manner and mind so we could be slipped into the places they prepared for us, so we wouldn't stand out, you know, wouldn't give ourselves away."

She was very good. Quiet and attentive, her expression unreadable. She could've been thinking anything. She could've simply been waiting for the sense of it to be made clear.

"The problem was, of course, that our intelligence services . . . well, let's say they never had much of a sense of nuance. Or a sense of humor, for that matter." I laughed. "No, never a lot in the way of humor, that's for sure. They constructed the place out of self-serious field reports and magazine articles they accepted without question and programs they saw on TV. Especially the programs they saw on TV, those half-hour situation comedies that were so popular in the fifties, you know, about small-town family life. They developed the whole program around them. Trained our guardians and teachers with them. Reproduced them wholesale in their plodding, literal Russian way, as the setting for our upbringing. As a result, I would say now, we grew up in an America no actual American ever did. We grew up in the America America wanted to be or thought of itself as or . . . I don't know how you would express it exactly. It was a strange dichotomy, that's for sure. Brutal psychologically, in some ways. We were planted as children in the middle of the American Dream and then taught that it was evil and had to be destroyed. . . ."

I sipped my wine. I stroked her hair. I gazed into the middle distance, talking to myself more than anything now, musing out loud, summing up, if you will. "But it was . . . my childhood. You know? I was a boy there. There were, you know, friends and summer days and snowfalls. Happy memories. It was my childhood."

"You sound as though you miss it," she said.

"Oh, terribly. Almost as if it had been real." I looked down at her again. Her sweet, gentle, young and old-fashioned face. "As I love you. As if *you* were real."

She sat up. She took my hand. "But I *am* real." I was surprised. It was the first lie she'd ever told me—aside from everything, I mean. "You see me, don't you? Of course I'm real."

"I'm not going to do it," I told her. "You can tell whoever sent you. I've already deleted the code." Now, again, she simply waited, simply watched me. I stroked her cheek fondly with the back of my hand. "I've given it a lot of thought. It was difficult to know how to approach it actually. Should I try to outguess you, determine what would activate your protocol? Or try to figure out the right and wrong of the matter—though I suppose it's a little late for that. In the end, though . . . in the end, you know what it was? It was a matter of *authenticity*. Of all things. But really, I mean it. When I was younger, I tried to figure out: Who am I? Who was I meant to be? Who *would* I have been if none of this had ever happened? But what good is any of that? Thinking that way? We all have histories. We all have childhoods. Accidents, betrayals, cruelties that leave their scars. We're none of us how we were made. So I thought, well, if I can't be who I am, let me at least be what I seem. Let me be loyal to my longings, at least. Let me be loyal to the things I love. Even if they are just daydreams, they're mine, aren't they? Let me be loyal to my dreams."

She didn't answer. Of course. And the look on her face remained impossible to decipher. I found myself appreciating that at this point. I was grateful for it, though her beauty broke my heart.

I took a final sip of wine and set the glass down on a table and stood. I touched her face a final time, my fingers lingering, then trailing across the softness of her cheek as I moved away.

I didn't turn to her again until I reached the bedroom doorway. And then I did stop and turn and I looked back at her. She made a nice picture, sitting on the rug, her feet tucked under her and her skirt spread out around her like a blue pool. She had followed me with her eyes and was watching me, and now she smiled tentatively.

"Look at you," I said, full of feeling. "Look at you. You were never more beautiful."

And as I turned again to leave the room, I added tenderly, "Come to bed."

THE HAMBURG REDEMPTION

Robert Wilson

WAKING UP, HITTING his head on the low shelf of his hangover smacked him back into the pillow with a groan. No sooner conscious than the images flickered through the gate of his mind. He sat up with a vomital lurch and vised his head in his considerable hands. He squeezed with his eyes tight shut, and mind wide open.

"Get back," he said to himself. "Back inside, you fuckers."

A clock set in the headboard told him it was 4:06. A record. He hadn't slept beyond 3:30 in months.

"Where the hell am I?" he thought, aware that he was talking to himself more and more these days because it helped to keep his mind at bay.

He got to his feet, a little dizzy. He was naked. Didn't remember undressing. Used to finding himself fully clothed, sometimes on the bed, other times on the bathroom floor in a sweat.

He slid open the thick, weighted blind covering the window. Night greeted him. The only immediately visible light came from the blue block letters that seemed to hang unsupported in the blackness:

FLEISCH GROSSMARKT

A heave from his stomach gushed a hot liquid memento of the savagery of last night's drinking into his throat. He couldn't swallow enough to rid his gullet of the acid. He gasped as if drowning.

"Hamburg," he said, his lips moving, no sound. "I'm in Hamburg."

He'd come here because it was home, where he'd spent the first twelve years of his life before his father, a scientist, had moved to the United States in 1964, just six months after they shot JFK. His father, who had turned his back on the collective guilt of his homeland, had embraced America and had taught him to do the same. And he had. My God, had he embraced that country. He'd hugged it so close he'd become part of the apparatus that protected it against any unseen enemy. And now? He shuddered as if a train had passed beneath him and gripped the windowsill. The guilt was rocking his foundations. Not just the guilt at what he had done, but the guilt at what he was going to do. He breathed in, steadied his thoughts by concentrating on the physical.

The hotel, yes, the hotel, it came back to him because he hadn't been too drunk when he arrived, was a converted water tower in the Sternschanzenpark. He twisted his head round a little and saw the lights of the huge TV tower off to the left. He nodded as these certainties emerged. His feet firmed up on the carpet. Strange how comforting chain hotels had become to him, although this colossal nineteenth-century cylinder, with its cavernous entrance, had a moving metal walkway up to the raw brick reception, with sound effects of dripping water, which had so unnerved him that he'd had to grip the moving rubber banister with both hands.

No headache yet, just queasiness and a vast thirst. He opened the minibar, took a bottle of water from the cube of light, and drank it down. Tears came to his eyes. His brain had started to work in unusual sequences, and instead of the usual horrific scenes he had to work at to suppress, he saw cool, still water, mountain streams, the innocence of his seven-year-old daughter in perfect, uninterrupted sleep. He knew now he would be unlikely ever to see her again. Hence the tears. Not wholly sentimental. The water *was* cold.

"What are you doing over there?"

The voice from the other side of the dark room went through him like a cold spear. He even tottered back the few inches to the wall. Someone else is in the *room*? The stupid logic resounded.

A movement.

"Don't turn the light on," he said quickly, an order.

"I'm just reaching for my water . . . OK?"

Female voice. Perfect English. Very slight German inflection. What the hell is *she* doing here? He sniffed the air. No smell of woman.

"You don't remember a thing, do you?" she said.

Nothing from him.

"Hey, dark matter," she said in a hoarse whisper. "Black hole. You don't remember a thing, do you?"

"No," he said. "Who *are* you?"

"Leena," she said. "Who are *you*?"

"Didn't I give you a name?"

"*A* name," she said. "You've got different ones for each port of call?"

Silence. An even worse start to the usual horror of consciousness.

"You *did* tell me your name," she said. "But why wouldn't you?"

"I don't know," he said, trying to think which one he would have used.

"Roland Schafer," she said. "Your surname means 'shepherd' in Old German. Did you know that?"

He did. An image of his father flashed through his mind:

shepherding him and his sister to the International School, where they were being prepared for the American educational system. He had his hands on their heads. He could even remember the pressure of his father's touch, and rather than being comforted by it, he felt strangely ashamed.

"And what sort of a name is Leena?" he asked.

"It's short for Marleena."

"Like Dietrich?"

"Nearly. You're showing your age now, Roland," she said. "We met in a bookshop. Do you remember that?"

"No, I don't," he said, but he did; he just had to play things carefully for the moment.

"You did drink a lot. I mean, really a lot," she said. "I almost had to carry you back here."

"Where do *you* live?"

"Not far, but it was very cold last night, and once I got you up here and undressed and into bed I thought . . . what the hell?"

"What the hell *what*?"

"I might as well sleep here," she said. "Can I turn on the light yet?"

"I haven't got a towel."

"I've seen it all, Roland," she said, and clicked on the standard lamp, which cast a light onto the empty armchair next to him. He slid into it, ran his hands through his gray, wire-wool hair. Shook his face free of any tells.

Her hair was long and blonde. She was maybe just touching thirty, which was all he could tell from the darkness of her corner. She threw off the duvet. Her nudity startled him. Upturned nipples. She swung her body around, picked up something from the floor, and fiddled with it while his view was obscured by her naked back.

"I've got to pee," she announced, and walked past him without the slightest self-consciousness.

She was nearly muscular with defined shoulders and her

breasts in no need of a bra. Her abdominal muscles were well delineated above black panties. The mechanics of her thighs' sinews were evident, and her buttocks had a declivity at the side. Only as she headed to the bathroom did he see a slight difference between her right and left leg.

"Were you an athlete?" he asked.

"I was," she said, and disappeared.

His paranoia cut in sharply. Who is she? What is she doing here? Who sent her? Do they know something?

She returned, throwing him a towel, and got back into bed. This time, because he knew where to look, he saw that her right leg was a prosthetic from the knee down.

"The surgeons didn't think I'd ever walk again," she said. "But they always say that to make you more determined."

"Did we cover this last night?" he asked.

"You know, you drank nearly a whole bottle of grappa single-handed."

"Grappa?"

"It wasn't an Italian restaurant, if that's what's confusing you."

Memory wipe. Too much of that lately. Pity it only wiped the present clean but not one bit of the past.

"I *used* to be an athlete," she said. "Before the car accident."

"Track and field?" he guessed.

"Not bad," she said. "I was a pole-vaulter. You look like someone who keeps himself in good condition . . . or at least used to."

"Yes," he said. "I do weights. I used to play football."

"You should get back on them before it's too late," she said.

"You're going to have to tell me what happened from the top," he said. "I don't remember a goddamn thing."

"I remember it *all*," she said. "That's my problem. Photographic memory. I even remember *unconsciousness*—the four days of coma I had after the car accident, although that wasn't too bad because they were the best four days of my life. They had to wrench me out of that world and back into this one."

"Why?" he asked, surprised to find himself interested.

"Because I was loved by a man for the first time in my life."

"Did you know him?"

She blinked at the question because she'd always assumed it.

"Yes," she said. "I felt I'd known him my whole life."

"Then he must have been your father," he said, letting the paranoia kick back in again, didn't want to drop his defenses this early in the game.

"You didn't notice the leg last night, either," she said, swerving away from the ugly little ditch he'd opened up in front of her, "but I was wearing trousers. You did notice other things, though."

"What?" he asked, looking at her closely.

She threw back the duvet again, crawled to the corner of the bed nearest him, and pulled her hair away from the left side of her face.

"Remember?"

He didn't and he would have done. She had a dent in the left side of her head, and there was scar tissue in front of her left ear around the temple. She traced a line with her finger that went across her left eye.

"It's glass," he said.

"They wanted to reconstruct the dent but I'd had enough of operations by then," she said, sitting back on her heels. "Fifteen on my arms, legs, face, *and* brain. I said I'd wear my hair long. Have you ever had sex with an amputee?"

"I'm not operational in that department at the moment," he said.

"You're in the military," she said.

"What makes you think that?"

"'I'm not operational in that department,'" she repeated. "And you didn't answer my question. Two classic military conversational gambits."

"I'm off sex," he said. "And I've never had a physical relationship with somebody who's lost a limb. Was your father in the military?"

"My father?" she said, and paused as if she could categorize him in a number of ways. "My father was the chief executive officer and owner of Remer Schifffahrtsgesellschaft mbH & Co. KG, Hamburg."

"Was?"

"He's dead."

"Do you like older men?" asked Schafer, more calculating now. She cocked her head to one side, sized him up.

"I like them," she said, shrugging, so that her breasts quivered. She fell backward and rolled under the duvet as if for protection. These questions about her father got under her skin.

"When did you have this car accident?" he asked.

"Four years ago. I was twenty-six, married, a successful businesswoman driving to work, and I got hit by a bus from the side. I was four days in a coma, six months in the hospital. I had to learn to walk and talk again."

"Your English is perfect."

"I was married to an Englishman. It was strange, because after the accident I had to work at my German."

"And the Englishman didn't love you?"

"You listen to people, Roland. I noticed that last night. And you say things that other people might think, but would never dream of voicing."

"But, crucially, I don't remember."

"You're right. He didn't love me."

"He left you?"

"After the accident."

"That was bad."

She shrugged.

"Who looked after you?" he asked. "Your parents?"

"My mother and her boyfriend."

"Was your father already dead?" asked Schafer, unable to resist his instinct to pursue a weakness, and she nodded. "How long ago was that?"

"Four years."

"So . . . before your accident."

She brought her knees up defensively.

"You know, you sound like someone who has to ask a lot of questions . . . for your work," she said. "But you're not a journalist."

"Why do you think that?"

"You don't stroke me to get your answers," she said. "And you're brutal."

"Sorry," he said. "It's been a long time since I ended up naked in a hotel room with a woman who's as good as a stranger, with one leg, one eye, and me with no recollection of how we got here."

"So when *was* the last time that happened to you?" she asked quizzically.

They nearly laughed, like people for whom humor had become an offshore island. He felt strangely calm, which he hadn't for some time. His instinct was telling him he could relax, which was making him paradoxically more vigilant.

"When we left the restaurant, you asked me to come back to your hotel with you," she said, "because you *thought* you were being followed."

"I said *that* to you?"

"Yes, and amazingly, I still came back with you."

"I've been a little paranoid lately."

"You mean it isn't true?"

"What do *you* think?" he said, squeezing some derision into his voice.

"I don't know. I don't disbelieve people just because they're a bit weird because . . . I'm a bit weird myself. I know what it's like to be disbelieved."

"At least you've got a good excuse."

"In the bookshop, we were on a sofa by the window and, when you weren't staring into my head like my neurosurgeon, you were looking up and down the street as if your life depended on it."

He blinked. No recollection.

"We were at a reading," said Leena, to be helpful. "By an American writer called James Hewitt."

"I know him. He writes spy fiction."

"There were about twenty of us in the audience," she said. "You drank two glasses of wine before the reading and another during it."

"You were keeping an eye on me."

"I like older guys," she said. "Afterwards, I asked if you'd read James Hewitt and I bought you a glass of wine."

"What were *you* doing there?"

"The owner of the bookshop rents one of my apartments. He invites me to readings, especially the ones with foreigners because of my English."

"And after the reading?"

"Ten of us crossed the street to a restaurant where they'd laid on a late table for us. It was about ten-thirty."

"We all sat together?"

"You were opposite me. I was next to James Hewitt. One of his friends was on your left, a musician with a long blond pony-tail. You told him you played the alto sax."

That jerked him back in his chair. Nobody knew that. Not even his second and third wives. Nor his ex-colleagues in the Company. He hadn't played music for more than twenty-five years.

"So you're a woman of independent means," he said, to cover his shock. "Did Daddy leave you a fortune?"

"You see what I mean? You listen in a way that nobody else listens and then you ask *that* question. You're brutal. What do you *do*, Roland?"

"I'm a businessman."

"Only if you're what my ex-husband would have called 'a bullshit merchant.'"

"What work did you used to do that journalists had to stroke you?"

"Don't think I don't know your game," said Leena, tapping the side of her head. "I ran my own coffee import company from the age of twenty-one. I created a whole new way of packaging coffee. I was young and beautiful—an exciting combination for the media. Tell me about your military training."

"How did your father die, Leena?"

"He shot himself."

The wind buffeted against the building. The lamp hummed.

"What are you doing here?" he asked, softening, taking to her more now as the possibility of her being a Company recruit diminished. "A beautiful, wealthy woman in a hotel room with some sap who's old enough to be your father."

She stared at him with unblinking, fathomless eyes.

"I recognize damage," she said.

The wall with a painting on it went grainy in his vision. The towel felt rough in his lap. He winced at a twinge in his side.

"Because you've been damaged yourself," said Schafer uneasily. "I can see that."

"The worst damage is never visible," she said.

"Why did your husband leave you?" he asked, swerving away from her insight.

Tucked under the duvet, she looked at him like a small child, but with the eyes of a troubled adult.

"I wasn't alone in the car," she said quietly.

With that he was conscious of a terrible pain cornered in the room.

"My four-year-old son was in the backseat and he took the full force of the impact. He died instantly."

Silence, with a heightened awareness of the two of them

naked in a room in the water tower while the world obliviously churned out its future beyond the window. He wanted to say something, but realized there was nothing to be said. He didn't know what he would do with himself if his daughter died, let alone if he felt in some way responsible for it. He wasn't sure how he was going to cope with her absence, given that by next week she would be unlikely to speak to him ever again. But at least she wouldn't be dead.

"You're the first person, outside the small circle of people I used to call my friends, that I've told that to," she said.

"Why me?"

"Something's ruined you in the same way that I've been ruined."

"How do you know?"

"I'm an expert in guilt," she said. "I recognize all the symptoms."

He knew now why he was calm. Her recognition made him feel that he belonged again. His eyes were suddenly full. He blinked fast and swallowed to quell the emotion. And with that last attempt at control, a fatigue so profound it couldn't possibly have been physical overwhelmed him, and he dropped into a lethal sleep.

TWO MEN SAT in a coffee shop a stone's throw away from the Sternschanzenpark. They were gray men, made grayer by the cold and the coats that they were wearing. The older man, Foley, was skimming a report that the younger one, Spokes, had just produced entitled "Marleena Remer."

"Did she inherit?" asked Foley.

"She got his sixty percent of the shipping company, the house in the country, and his apartment in the city, plus twenty million euros."

"So she doesn't have to work."

"Her head injuries were severe," said Spokes. "There was talk of brain damage and psychological problems. Her accountant sold the coffee company for her while she was still in the hospital."

"Have you got a tax return?"

"There's an income from the shipping company, but most comes from property. She lives in the top two floors of an apartment building which she owns, renting out the other apartments. She has a rental income of just under a million euros and investment income of about half that."

"That doesn't sound so brain damaged to me."

"Maybe not, but there's something 'off' about her," said Spokes.

"Tell me," said Foley, tossing the report.

"Ali, from the Moroccan teahouse on Susannenstrasse, has a daughter who cleans the apartment building's communal spaces and Marleena's condo. She says there's a private elevator to Marleena's quarters so she knows exactly who goes up there," said Spokes. "And Leena, as she's known, gets frequent visits from a number of older men in their fifties and sixties. Same ones, some regular, some not so regular. All times of day and night."

"She's brain damaged enough to turn hooker?"

"Maybe," said Spokes, shrugging. "She underwent three neuro ops and she's on antidepressants, sleeping pills, and painkillers, which is what she has in her medicine cabinet, according to the cleaner."

"What's Schafer getting into now?" muttered Foley.

"Ali's daughter cleans today. Leena will text her the elevator codes, which she changes later on."

"Someone will have to go up there with her," said Foley. "Get the Turk to join her."

"Arslan?" said Spokes. "Isn't that a bit . . . radical?"

"He's just going to take a look at things," said Foley. "But if we need him to be 'radical,' at least he knows the place. That way we limit the number of people who know about this."

"You think it's going to come to that?"

"People far more senior than I am have their jobs riding on the outcome of this," said Foley. "And I've just heard from London that Schafer's English buddy, Damian Rush, gets into Hamburg at eight-forty-five."

"Under his own name?"

"He's only a journalist now."

"I'd better get out to the airport."

"Look," said Foley, nodding out toward the park.

They sipped their coffees as Marleena Remer walked past in an ankle-length, fur-collared black coat, a black fur hat, and gloves.

"You wouldn't know it," said Foley into his coffee.

SCHAFER WOKE UP in the armchair, his head pounding so hard he kept absolutely still while he checked the room. There was a note on the towel in his lap. Leena, an address on the Schanzenstrasse, a telephone number, and a message: "Call me. I think we can help each other." He checked his watch. 8:30. He'd slept for more than three hours. Unheard of in his state. He was more rested than he'd been in months.

As a wise, old operative he should have been uneasy about her, but instead he felt something he couldn't quite define: almost like first love, but without the innocence. He stood, grunting under the pummeling his brain was taking.

The window revealed a bleak dawn. FLEISCH GROSSMARKT still shone blue, but a building was taking shape beneath it as the bare branches of the trees by the railway tracks flailed in the wind. Patches of green showed through the snow. His eyes came to rest on the window ledge on which there were sharp wire spokes. On the seventh floor they weren't there to stop people getting in.

He slurped down three Tylenol with water from the sink in the bathroom. He showered and dressed. In a sudden return of his occupational paranoia he made a meticulous search of his room and found nothing, which was as he'd expected, but it left him unnerved, too. He went down to breakfast. It was going to be a long, hard day.

A bowl of muesli. Fried bacon, *blutwurst*, and eggs. Ham and cheese on rye. Four sweet coffees and some pastries. He was going to need some insulation out there. Zero, with an ugly wind coming from the North. He went straight out, wearing a thick sweater under a reversible coat—blue showing, brown not. He also had a couple of hats and some spectacles—a few basic tools to disguise himself.

In this sort of weather he'd have normally taken the U-Bahn from Schlump into the Gänsemarkt, but he wanted to see what sort of resources the Company had at its disposal, so he opted for a walk in the park around the deserted Japanischer Garten. It was cold *and* damp, and his trousers stiffened up like cardboard before he'd even crossed the road beneath the TV tower.

Since 9/11 and the discovery of the Hamburg cell the Company had developed plenty of immigrants—Turks, Moroccans, Iranians—for basic footwork: listening in at the mosques and sniffing around the Koran schools. The Company wouldn't want too many of them to know that they were being used to tail an ex-colleague, but it wouldn't have to worry about loyalty from those who did.

The café in the park was closed, the chairs stacked and the umbrellas under wraps, waiting for spring, which seemed a long way off. The water features below had been drained so that they wouldn't freeze over. The plants in huge stone half-eggs had been bagged against the frost. The park, as he'd suspected, was empty of people.

Schafer spotted his first tail at the Stephansplatz U-Bahn station ahead of him. A square-headed guy, probably from the Maghreb, who was standing at the entrance of the station, freezing cold, making a show of reading a newspaper. He led him down Dammtorstrasse to the Gänsemarkt. He used to come to this square as a kid with his mother, although it was a triangle and there had never been any geese; it had always been a big part of his family life at Christmas. The lights were on in the huge arched windows of Essen & Trinken, and there was some snow gone to ice on its green copper roof. Schafer quickly lost his tail in the station, saw him looking up and down the wrong platform as he boarded the train to Jungfernstieg.

Coming out of the underground Schafer turned his back on the gray, choppy expanse of the Binnenalster Lake and counted across the buildings from left to right. Third building. Fourth row of windows. Second along. The blind was down. Damian telling him he had company. What did he expect? He'd been arrogant to think that they could pull this off unnoticed. He went to the S-Bahn station and left a chalk mark on the inside of the right-hand steel support. Plan B.

He took a walk down the Alsterfleet canal by the side of the Rathaus. He wanted to see the Elbe but drifted onto the Altstadt square in front of the neorenaissance facade of the nineteenth-century town hall, which looked black and Gothic in the gloom. Back in 1962, at the age of ten, he'd stood here with his parents for a remembrance service to the three hundred victims of the North Sea flood. He recalled the great sadness of the adult crowd on that day, which as a child he hadn't been able to comprehend. He felt more emotional about it now than he had then.

When he arrived at the river Elbe, which was flat as sheet iron at this point, he began to wonder what he was doing. He stared across the water, at the cranes ranked along the port quays, with eyes that had always kept the secrets they'd seen. Now he was going to blow it all open, and he realized there was something valedictory about his movements around his old town.

He got on a train at the Landungsbrücken station. First things first, he had to collect what he was supposed to pick up last night at the reading before the woman, Leena, had thrown everything into disarray. He headed back out to Schlump. Was this any sort of a job for a grown man? Endlessly going around in circles, finding different ways to check your back?

Now that he was on the train and certain that he was free of tails, he took stock. The drinking was out of control—that was clear. He tried to retrace the scene in the bookstore last night, but he still couldn't remember meeting Leena. How could he forget that? She was the whole reason he'd left without what he'd gone in there for. But he did realize *that*. He *had* come out empty-handed . . . hadn't he? His certainty wavered in his paranoid mind. Was that why he was so anxious to get to the bookstore? Why he'd searched his room? To make sure he hadn't picked up, taken the material back to his hotel room, and let Leena walk away with it this morning? He knew it hadn't happened like that. For a start, she wouldn't have been there when he woke up. He'd definitely aborted the mission. But he had to work his way back through the fog, blankness, and memory obliteration of booze to get to it.

The train clattered into St. Pauli and a minute later lunged out. He caught sight of himself in the glass of the window. It wasn't the heavy pouches under his eyes and the depth of the lines from his nose to the corners of his mouth that disturbed him. It was more that he didn't quite recognize himself, had to put his hand up to his face to make sure it was him. This was what losing your moral center did to you. This was what betraying your country did to you.

And with that terrifying admission he got to the point. He had *not* gone to the toilet in the bookstore. He'd been so disturbed by Leena coming on to him, certain that she was a honey trap, that he hadn't dared to go in there even to relieve himself.

At Schlump he walked fast, an icy wind at his back, to the bookstore. He sat down with a cup of coffee and a German copy of James Hewitt's latest novel. Last night's chairs and microphones had been cleared away, and the floor area was now reoccupied by tables laden with books.

He heard the door open. The shop emptied as the two members of staff and a customer left for a smoke on the front step. Schafer went to the toilet, locked the door, lifted the seat, stood on the rim, and, using a penknife, unscrewed the extractor fan housing high up by the ceiling. His most trusted courier had left the black plastic bag that he now found inside the fan. It contained a folded sheet of paper and a memory stick, which he pocketed. He refitted the extractor fan housing, cleaned off the rim of the toilet, flushed, and, leaving the seat raised, went back to resume his reading. The staff returned. The customer flicked his cigarette and moved off.

Schafer appeared to read a couple of chapters while he was actually thinking about Leena. The note. "I think we can help each other." With his paranoia subsiding he was sure, once again, that she was not a honey trap. Quite apart from the "come on" of the note being far too strong, she was too quirky for the average Company operative and her story too powerfully authentic to be anything other than the truth. The note made him think that maybe, given that the Company would know about her by now, she could be of some help in Plan B. He slotted the piece of paper into his book, which he paid for.

He backtracked and crossed the Sternschanzenpark to the hotel, where he knew he'd be followed again. Back in his room he entered Leena's number into his cell phone memory. He tore her note in half, leaving only the message part as the bookmark and left it inside the novel on the bedside table. He screwed up the other half and put it in his pocket.

He took some tape from his suitcase and opened the plastic bag he'd taken from the bookshop toilet. He checked that it was the memo to private contractors that he'd stolen six weeks earlier. He wasn't mentally up to checking the contents of the memory stick on his laptop, but he confirmed that the small mark he'd engraved on the plastic casing was still there. He put the paper and stick back in the plastic bag and sealed it with tape. He wanted to deliver the two pieces of evidence together, personally, because he was going to supply a commentary to the devastating pictures on the memory stick to Rush. Given that he was sealing his fate and that of others, including his fellows on the assignment, his Company superiors, and senior officers in the Pentagon, he should have realized they wouldn't make it easy for him.

Using the stairs, he found that the maids were cleaning the rooms on the tenth floor. He walked past their two trolleys and saw that while one of them wore her passkey around her neck, the other preferred to keep hers tied to the trolley handle on a piece of elastic. He watched them from behind the central elevator shaft as they moved clockwise around the circular landing. When they started vacuuming, he made his move. He unthreaded the passkey and opened one of the rooms they'd already cleaned, number 1015. He slotted a coin in between the door and frame to keep it open and returned the passkey to the trolley. Fifteen minutes later the maids moved up to the eleventh floor.

Schafer let himself into the empty room, looked around. There was no need to be clever about this. He lifted the only painting in the room from the wall. The frame was deep enough to take the memory stick. He taped the plastic bag onto the back and replaced the painting. He left the room, went back down to his own, took a piece of notepaper, and wrote out a classified ad in German. This was for Plan C, in case B messed up. He checked the time: 12:30. Half an hour to get back into town for lunch.

Of the twenty people on the platform at Schlump, the Company man stood out. There was no training ground for these people. By the time he'd hit thirty-five he'd done a decade of this sort of work in Berlin.

He wanted his tail with him this time. They took the train to Jungfernstieg and walked along the front, with the wind whipping off the lake so that it was a relief to turn down Grosse Bleichen and an almost erotic experience to walk into the warmth of the Edelcurry restaurant. Three minutes early. He took a table deep in the restaurant and ordered a pilsner. The combination of last night's alcohol and this morning's adrenaline had put a tremble in his right hand. The beer corrected it, improved his spirits. He reminded himself to act happy.

Thomas Lüpertz was the son of Schafer's father's best friend. They'd done exchanges between families so that Thomas could learn English and Roland could maintain his German. The adolescent friendship had been cemented when Schafer ended up on a posting to Hamburg after his first marriage had bust up in the early 1980s. The two men hadn't seen each other for several years. It didn't matter. They had a great time eating currywurst and drinking beer. They laughed about life's absurdities. He asked Lüpertz to do him a favor, gave him the classified ad he'd written, and asked him to put it in the Hamburger *Abendblatt* and pay for it. His old friend didn't even question it.

Just after two o'clock Lüpertz left without taking his copy of *Die Zeit*, which he'd slapped on the chair next to him on his arrival. Schafer took the newspaper to the toilet with him. He had a long pee, all that beer, and spent time washing his hands. He returned to his seat and ordered a coffee. He drank two more over the next hour while reading the newspaper.

The gloom was gathering for an early winter nightfall as he came out onto the street. His tail was looking very cold. He walked down to Axel-Springer-Platz and called Leena on his cell phone.

"You said we could help each other," he whispered.

"Who is this?" she asked, missing a beat.

"How many offers of help do you leave on drunks in hotel rooms?"

"Per week?"

He laughed. For real. It had been a long time.

"I'm the drunk from the Water Tower Hotel, room seven thirteen."

"I'm with my accountant at the moment," she said. "Why don't you come to my place around seven o'clock?"

"I'll be there."

"I'll text the elevator codes to this number."

She hung up.

He caught a train to Landungsbrücken, switched to the underground, and got out at Sternschanze, leaving his tail on the train. It was dark as he walked up to the hotel, and his feet crunched on ice.

Back in his room he lay on the bed, burping currywurst. The news was full of the ongoing financial meltdown and President-elect Obama's announcement that he would close Gitmo. Couldn't happen sooner. He'd done his time down there. Depressed the hell out of him. He switched to Bloomberg, where all the presenters seemed too desperate for good news in a recession that had only just begun. He felt remarkably calm given that a new world order was taking shape less than seventy years after the last one, while he was getting down to the serious business of betraying his country.

The television annoyed him. He turned it off and stared at the receding ceiling, letting fragmented thoughts of his third wife come to him. She was slipping away. Their separation and his drinking had brought them to a state of alienation he couldn't bear. All that was left was the little girl. They'd called her Femi, the Egyptian for "love." But that wasn't going to be enough to keep them together. It had been the one thing that had pushed them apart. His wife had quit work, and he'd had to come out of retirement to fund it, but he hadn't wanted to go back into the Company because he'd heard it had all gone bad in the 1990s.

The stress rose in his chest. He rolled off the bed to the mini-bar and sucked down a miniature of vodka and a scotch. He went back to the bedside table, opened James Hewitt's novel, and shook his head in dismay. They couldn't even put the book-mark back in the right page.

His cell phone vibrated, Leena sending him the elevator codes.

THEY WERE SITTING in the front of the Moroccan tea shop on Susannenstrasse; it was five in the afternoon. Any view of them from the street was obscured by the ranks of hookahs piled up in the window. Foley wasn't impressed by the report that Spokes had just given him. He sensed the situation was getting out of control, could feel the weight of a heavy decision gathering on his shoulders.

"Damian Rush checked into the Park Hyatt," said Spokes. "He's been out at the port most of the day, seems to be doing an article on the collapse of the German manufacturing miracle."

Foley said nothing in reply, drummed his fingers on the table.

"Lüpertz is in his office, and Ms. Remer is back in her condo," said Spokes.

"I'm going to tell you this so you know what's happening here and perhaps that will help you understand what we're going to have to do? All right?" said Foley. "Schafer and Rush were together in Rabat."

He now had Spokes's full attention.

"After the July bombings in London, MI5 was desperate for intelligence and MI6 sent Rush to ask some questions for them. He and Schafer worked together on some of the interrogations."

"Right. I didn't think it was a coincidence that they were here together in Hamburg."

"And that Rush left MI6 over a year ago and is now a journalist."

Spokes fell silent.

"When Schafer's contract was terminated along with the others', I went to Rabat to close down the 'black site' just after the November election," said Foley. "That was when I discovered that the private contractors' memo was missing. And six weeks' work later, by process of elimination of the other two members of Schafer's Rabat squad, here we are in Hamburg with Schafer and Rush."

Spokes could sense Foley hardening with each of these revelations.

"They still have to meet," said Spokes.

"I know that. And physical meetings and material exchanges are the most dangerous moments for operatives," said Foley, quoting to Spokes from the manual. "And what do you think Schafer is doing about that, with all his field experience from the days of the Berlin Wall?"

"He's trying to confuse us."

"He's not trying. He is," said Foley. "We lost him last night and we lost him again this morning. He knows we can't ask the Germans for help and we've got limited reliable resources at our disposal. So he's spreading us thin on the ground. We're already watching three corners: Rush, Lüpertz, and the wild card, Marleena Remer."

Spokes had suspected it would come to this. It was the nature of cover-ups. Once containment looked hopeless there was only one other course of action.

"What did the Turk find this afternoon?" asked Foley.

"The elevator opens out into her apartment on the top floor," said Spokes, on automatic. "There are two bedrooms with en suite bathrooms, a walk-in closet for her clothes and shoes, a kitchen, dining room, a huge L-shaped living room, where he left the listening device, and an office. On the other half of that floor there's an art gallery with around twenty works in it. More interesting is what's below. That just consists of a room within a room."

"And?"

"It was locked. Arslan said the door looked serious and the walls were made out of brick."

"Has the cleaner ever been in there?"

"No, and she only does the six-foot walkway around the room when Marleena tells her to."

"Anything else in her apartment?"

"No safe," said Spokes. "Arslan mentioned that she had two spare legs of slightly different colors in the walk-in closet. That's it."

"Are those elevator codes still operational?"

"We intercepted an SMS from Leena to Schafer giving new codes."

"Tell the Turk to come and see me."

THE ELEVATOR TO the Park Hyatt hotel dropped into an upmarket shopping mall, which meant that the Turk did not have to wait outside in subzero for the Englishman to make an appearance at six o'clock that evening.

Rush embarked on a circuitous route to the Hauptbahnhof before doubling back past the St. Jacobi and St. Petri churches and ended up going down into the Jungfernstieg station. The Turk didn't want there to be any chance of Rush seeing him in such a well-lit place. He hovered for a minute before the Englishman came back up with a copy of the Hamburger *Abendblatt* under his arm. Arslan watched Rush from the station as he headed up the Ballindamm on the side of the road where the buildings were. Arslan tracked him from across the street under the trees next to the Binnenalster Lake. Rush went into the Café Wien, took a table, stripped off his coat and woolen hat, went to light a cigarette, remembered just in time, and put it back in the packet.

The Turk paced the walkway beneath the trees, nervous and trying to keep warm. This was going to be his only opportunity. It was very dark under there, and the branches clacked overhead. The intense cold meant that there was no one around. Even the traffic, in the early evening on a day of business, was light. He watched as Rush ordered a coffee and read the newspaper in the well-lit café. The Englishman seemed to be studying columns of figures, something like the stock market numbers.

Rush took out his cell phone, looked around him, decided against it. Too many people. He paid the waiter for the coffee, put his coat and hat back on. He still had his cell in his hand.

The wind was cutting, and the Englishman winced as he came out of the Café Wien. He looked back up the street and then across the bridge between the two lakes. Arslan willed him to cross the street which, when the lights changed, he did. Rush walked between the trees before moving out to the railing above the steepish bank down to the water's edge. He lit a cigarette under the lapel of his coat and made his phone call. Arslan moved quickly, using the trees for cover. Just as Rush closed down his cell, the Turk was on him, hit him with a savage blow across the side of the neck that tipped the Englishman over the rail and down the bank. Arslan vaulted the rail and scrambled down to the water's edge, where Rush had come to rest. He heaved him into the icy water and held him under. There was a brief struggle, and it was all over. He kicked him out into the lake, picked up Rush's cell phone, and threw it in after him.

IT WAS A short walk from the hotel to Leena's condo on Schanzenstrasse. Schafer was excited at the prospect of seeing her again. It had been dark for nearly two and a half hours by the time he set off, just before seven o'clock. He picked up a tail waiting for him under the bridge. It didn't bother him.

He entered the elevator codes and went up to her apartment. The doors opened onto a wooden floor and Leena in a black miniskirt, boots over the knee, black tights, a long-sleeved black top, and a necklace of stainless steel lozenges. Her blonde hair was piled high, and makeup disguised the scar tissue on the side of her face.

He wasn't sure of the etiquette of the moment. Their strange earlier intimacy *and* mutual nudity called for more than a handshake. Leena kissed him on the cheek. Her lips made light contact with the corner of his mouth with electric effect. She led him by the arm to the huge window at the back of the apartment, which overlooked the old city toward the lake. The TV tower loomed to the left. They stared at the glittering city. He enjoyed the pressure of her hand on his bicep. He had an odd feeling that she was about to make him an outlandish offer, like: "All this for your soul." She sat him on the sofa, offered him a drink. He took a scotch on the rocks. She joined him with what looked like a glass of water.

"You're looking better than you did this morning," she said.

"It's been a while since I've slept like that," he said. "I've been thinking about what you told me."

"I don't need to know."

"I meant about being able to help each other."

"I told you my expertise," she said. "I think you're an expert, too."

"I don't feel like an expert in anything."

"You ask questions and you listen."

"Doesn't everybody?"

"Nobody listens these days, unless you're talking about *them*, and even then they're selective about what they hear," she said. "I thought, at first, you might be a policeman. A detective, you know, used to asking questions and listening . . . and thinking all the time. Conservative and ordered, hierarchical, but also seeing horrifying things and dealing with evil people."

"I'm not a cop," he said. "I'm a bullshit merchant, remember?"

"That's *part* of your job," she said. "Just to keep people from knowing who you really are."

His face did not betray a single emotion. He sipped his scotch slowly.

"You've had three wives?" she said.

"The middle one only lasted a few months."

"And you're away a lot."

"How would you know?"

"You're not as American as most Americans," she said. "You've assimilated the cultures you've been involved with. You speak German and other languages."

"Russian and Arabic," he said, nodding.

"And you're fifty-. . . . six years old?"

"Fifty-seven."

"There's something of the old warrior about you, Roland."

"Did you say, 'cold warrior'?"

"I recognize you, I mean your type."

"Was your father in the military?"

"Before he went into business," said Leena, "he was in intelligence. It was one of the reasons he was so successful and it was also why my mother left him."

"And why was that?"

"She never quite knew who she was with."

"Did she remarry?"

"A plumber," said Leena. "And she knows exactly where she stands with him."

"Yes," said Schafer, "plumbers are safer than spies and more useful around the house. Did your father shoot himself because your mother left him?"

Leena shook her head slowly, as if her father's suicide had something to do with Schafer.

"What was it?"

"I don't know for certain," said Leena. "And my mother couldn't tell me anything. But two weeks after his funeral I had a visit from a woman who told me that her husband and my father had worked together in Berlin in 1979. Her husband had never come back. She implied that my father had something to do with it. It was complicated by the fact that she wanted money. She might have seen me as someone easy to exploit. That's certainly what my ex-husband thought."

"Did you see her again?"

"A year ago. I'd done a bit of research among my father's 'friends' by then, and I'd found that there was some doubt as to his loyalty. Nothing that could be proved, but there were questions about where the capital came from to start up his shipping company," she said. "I gave the woman some money."

"Was he ever politically motivated?"

"Never," she said. "You're not a spy anymore though, are you?"

"What makes you think that?"

"Last night. It wasn't an act. I don't think a spy would risk getting that drunk. My father used to drink himself senseless, but only on his own."

"I don't work for anybody anymore," said Schafer. "I used to be a spy some years ago, and then the Wall came down and I retrained."

"As what?"

"An interrogator."

"And the Arabic, was that all about the war on terror?"

"No, my third wife's Egyptian," said Schafer. "She speaks English, but I thought it would be fun to learn her language. We use Arabic in the house."

"Children?"

"One daughter. Unexpected. My wife had been told she couldn't conceive and at thirty-eight she suddenly became pregnant. She quit her job. I came out of retirement."

"As an ex-interrogator who speaks fluent Arabic," said Leena. "When was that?"

"2002."

"Perfect timing."

"I didn't want to go back into the Company, so I joined a private security outfit. They paid more. I could get triple-time if I went to Afghanistan or, later, Iraq."

"Abu Ghraib?"

"I was there, but not down in the cells with the 372nd Military Police Company," said Schafer defensively. "The idea was to earn as much as I could as quickly as possible and get back to my retirement."

"So they didn't include a course on how money works on the human brain?" said Leena.

"How's that?"

"The more you make, the more you need, the more you want."

Schafer sipped his drink, shrugged. He felt something like the discomfort of incipient piles.

"So," she said, "your spying days are over. Your interrogating days are finished. You don't work for anybody anymore. You should be back in your retirement. So what are you doing in Hamburg, Roland?"

Silence. Not even traffic noise penetrated the density of the glazing. An invisible clock ticked somewhere. Maybe it was in his head. He didn't know precisely why, something to do with their earlier intimacy and his strange, retrospective day, but he decided to do something uncharacteristic: to reveal himself.

"I'm atoning for my sins," he said.

"That's a strange thing to be doing *here*," said Leena. "You'd be better off in Westphalia with Our Lady of Aachen for that kind of thing."

"I was born in Hamburg," said Schafer. "My parents moved to the States when I was twelve years old. Then I worked here in the eighties. It seemed like the perfect place to come to remember who I used to be."

"And what are these sins?"

Schafer was surprised to find himself in exactly the mode he tried to engender in his interrogees: confessional. And he knew how she'd got him there. Because he wanted it.

"The company I was working for offered me a special assignment. It was a lot of money," said Schafer. "You've heard of 'extraordinary rendition'?"

Leena nodded.

"I operated in a number of 'black sites' in Eastern Europe."

"What are they?"

"Places where terror suspects who'd been 'extracted' on the 'extraordinary rendition' program could be interrogated, using an 'alternative set of procedures,'" said Schafer, the sweat coming up on his palms. "It had been decided that the Third Geneva Convention did not apply to prisoners in the war on terror."

"You don't have to use military speak in here," she said. "I was brought up on collateral damage."

"After the London bombings in July 2007 I was offered another assignment that was so secret it was only referred to by its code name: Wordpainter. There were three of us. We were referred to as the Truth Squad. We were all outside contractors and we were given a special memo."

His heart had gone into overdrive, and he was suddenly finding it difficult to get enough air. He sucked on the whiskey.

"The memo broadened the 'alternative set of procedures,' allowing us to use 'extremely harsh techniques' to extract vital information from 'high-value detainees.'"

"What does that actually mean?" she asked. "The Bush administration had a talent for euphemism."

"Electric shocks, heat, fire, bastinado, strappado, extreme humiliation . . . anything that pushed the limits of human tolerance. You know," said Schafer, after a long, ruminative drink, "once you've decided that torture is okay it's inevitable that boundaries get pushed."

"Presumably you were paid extra to do all that?" she said.

"Seventy thousand dollars a month."

He breathed in heavily, as if he had a weight on his chest. The phone rang. An answering machine cut in after seven rings. No message. The phone rang again. Still no message. It rang once more.

"I'm going to have to take that," said Leena. "It's one of my clients."

She took the call in her office, closed the door. She came back out to explain that she was going to be a while and that he would have to entertain himself. She pointed him to the art gallery, poured him more whiskey.

"Client?" he said. "Are you an analyst or something?"

"I told you, I'm an expert on the nature of guilt," she said from the doorway to her office. "I know how to relieve its symptoms and what the consequences are if it's ignored."

He stayed on the sofa for a while, as if pinned by that statement and exhausted by his own revelations. Then his edginess got to him, and he socked down the scotch and went for another. He grabbed a handful of ice and poured a measure to the brim. He walked the length of the window, asking himself whether this had been a big mistake. Had his vulnerability this morning made him read too much into how he'd felt about her? He stared out of the huge panel of glass at a vast dark patch within the heart of the city. What *did* he feel about her? He wasn't attracted to her, not sexually. Did he think she had some answers? Could she help him understand?

He drifted away from the window, let himself into the art gallery. It was pitch black, with no visible cityscape. He flicked the switch. Only lights illuminating paintings came on. The windows were blacked out. He drifted through the maze of works. He wasn't much interested in modern art. Too conservative. Didn't get it. These were bleak landscapes. Large, white, unframed canvases with something gray and indistinct happening, or rather not happening, in various quarters. The only portrait was at the far end of the gallery. An old man in a business suit was

sitting in a chair within some kind of cage. He was holding on
to the arms and screaming. It made him shiver.

At the end of the gallery was a door, which gave him notions
of escape. It opened onto stairs going up to the roof and down
to the floor below. He went down, drink in hand, the ice tinkling
against the glass. Another door opened onto a wide, wooden-
floored corridor with a view of the city visible at the end. The
lighting was utilitarian neon. He walked down the corridor,
checked around the corner, realized there was a room set within
the entire floor of the condo. Maybe, given her superb physical
shape, it was her gym.

His palms were sweating again as he reached for the door
handle, opened it. The air inside was cold and smelled of damp
and something unpleasant like effluent. The surface of the floor
was different; it had the grittiness of rough concrete. As he felt
for a switch, the door clicked shut.

The strobe of fierce neon thrashed four images onto his
retina. Ropes and pulleys over a large puddle. A metal frame in
front of a cinder block wall. A bed with straps hanging from it.
An uncoiled hose. Even before the neon had settled he fell to the
floor unconscious.

SOMEONE WAS STROKING his face with a wet washcloth and
running a hand through his hair. It was so lulling it put him in
mind of being pushed in a pram under trees. He came to,
stripped to the waist, broken glass on the floor. The concrete bit
into his back. His vision was blurred, but he could make out a
face above him. His vision slowly cleared. Leena rested his head
on the floor and took a seat on a stool at his feet. She was wearing an orange boilersuit, of the sort prisoners wore in Gitmo.

"What is this, Leena?" he asked, seeing blood on his chest.

"You fainted, dropped your glass of whiskey, cut your head
and hand as you went down, and bled all over your shirt," she
said. "You must be familiar with this sort of room."

"What is this?" he asked, turning his head to take in his surroundings.

"I call it a return to equilibrium," said Leena.

"It's a treatment room for your clients?"

"I help people, mainly men, who feel that they have such a disproportionate amount of power to control the lives of others that they experience overwhelming sensations of guilt. By reducing them to a state of powerlessness, through the infliction of pain and humiliation, I return balance to their minds. This reduces their suicidal tendencies and, in some cases, reinvigorates their sense of belonging within the human race."

"And who are your clients?"

"Mainly captains of industry, politicians, military men, policemen, and the odd prison governor, but no interrogators," she said. "Or is that being too euphemistic? The idea is to face up to things, after all. I've never had any paid torturers among my clients."

"I told you I'm atoning for my sins," said Schafer. "I'm dealing with my guilt in my own way. I'm going to reveal myself to the world for the man that I am, for the work that I've done in the name of my government. I'm condemning myself by media. Do you think my wife will have me back? Do you think she'd want me anywhere near our daughter?"

"You're not coping with it very well," said Leena. "I don't think last night was the first time you'd drunk yourself into oblivion. Everybody in the restaurant was concerned for *me* . . . not you. They could see that you'd given up on some essential human qualities. Then you walk in here and faint."

"So what are you proposing?"

"That you have *some* of the experience of the victim," said Leena. "I can't simulate everything. I can't keep you for days in a locked room with little food and in poor or extreme conditions with no sleep. I can't reduce your humanity to the level of livestock and have you brought up to the light, immobilized into a state of total helplessness, and then, possibly the worst thing, have another human being do terrible things to you for hours and days, over which you have no control, not even if you tell the truth. I wouldn't want to. It would reduce me, too."

"So what *do* you do?"

"I can make you feel helpless and humiliated and deliver a certain level of pain," said Leena. "There are psychological benefits."

"It sounds like I have to trust you."

"That's not a common link between torturer and victim, as I'm sure you'll appreciate, but that's part of it."

"And what do *you* get out of it?"

Silence apart from the drip of water. They looked at each other for some moments.

"There's not a minute of every day that I don't think about what happened in the accident," she said. "I went through a red light. I wasn't thinking straight. My head was so full of what my father had done, killing himself, that I was in a state of distraction almost all the time. I was a careful woman driver, not a crazy kid, and my brain suddenly didn't understand the difference between red and green anymore."

"You're punishing your father."

"It's the only way I can keep going," she said. "Otherwise I have nothing. All the money, all the comfort, all the male interest in me, all the possibilities that life has to offer are meaningless."

He stripped. She fastened his wrists and ankles into the four corners of a metal frame lying on the floor. They were silent and complicit. She stepped away from him, reached for a remote that hung from the ceiling, and pressed one of the buttons. One end of the steel frame started rising within some metal runners until it was vertical and Schafer hung spread-eagled within it. The pain in his shoulder joints was immediately excruciating. It was a technique he knew bore results.

Leena pressed another button on the remote, and the metal frame revolved through 180 degrees, so that Schafer was upside down and facing away from her. His hips felt as if they were about to dislocate. Leena selected a two-meter length of rattan cane and swiped the cold air, backward and forward.

FOLEY HAD GIVEN the Turk the all clear once he'd heard that both Leena and Schafer were in the lower apartment and they'd lost sound contact. Arslan entered the elevator codes and went up to the top floor wearing a pair of latex gloves. He had a 9mm Glock 19 with a titanium suppressor, which he did not intend to use. In his pocket he had a twisted leather garrote.

The elevator doors opened onto the apartment. He went through the master bedroom to the en suite bathroom and put together a cocktail of Leena's medications in one of her pill canisters. He picked up a bottle of scotch from the drinks tray and tucked it under his arm. He strode through the art gallery, down the stairs and into the apartment below. He walked silently on treadless sneakers, took out his Glock, and opened the door. The soundproofing of the room meant that he'd heard nothing of what was going on inside. He was momentarily stunned by the sight before him.

"That was the rattan cane," said Leena, slightly breathless. "This is a sjambok. It's made out of rolled rhinoceros hide. You'll notice the difference."

Nothing from Schafer, just gasping. Blood ran from the open welts across his back, buttocks, and hamstrings. It ran in tickling trickles down his body and over his face and forehead and dripped onto the concrete.

"Put that down," said Arslan from the door, the Glock in his outstretched hand.

Leena spun around, her face livid from effort.

"What are you doing in here?" she said, like a teacher whose space had been invaded by a pupil. "Is he something to do with you, Roland?"

"Drop the whip and come to me," said the Turk.

This was better than he could possibly have imagined. His mind opened up to possibilities for a clean finish. It could be a sex session gone tragically wrong.

"He needs this," said Leena.

"He might," conceded Arslan.

"One stroke," she said, and before Arslan could protest she laid the sjambok across Schafer's back. It landed with a dull smack and was accompanied by a stunned silence followed by a gagging scream. Arslan slammed the door shut. Leena threw the whip to the ground.

"Let him down from there," said Arslan.

Leena used the remote to turn Schafer upright and let him down. As his back made contact with the concrete an exquisite agony concentrated itself in Schafer's body. He gritted his teeth.

"Release his feet," he said. "You got handcuffs?"

Leena pointed to the wall behind with its assortment of cuffs and shackles. Arslan threw her a set.

"Cuff his hands behind his back. Leave him on his front."

Arslan looked around while Leena worked on Schafer. He put the bottle of scotch on the table, swung a pulley and rope into position over the two of them, moved the stool underneath. He took out the leather garrote and told her to connect it to the rope.

She knew her work, used a metal caliper to make sure the join wouldn't slip, looped it over Schafer's head. Arslan pulled on the rope. Schafer's head came up and he scrabbled to his knees.

"Sit on the stool," said Arslan.

Schafer sat facing away from him, hands behind his back. His chest expanded slowly and shallowly, as if each breath was agony. Arslan told Leena to tie the rope off to a ring in the floor. He motioned Leena with his Glock toward the table, took the pills out of his pocket.

"You're going to drink these down," said Arslan. "It's either that or . . . violence. I'm easy either way."

The one thing Leena knew from her endless replaying of the car accident was that, while she could stand pain, she could not bear impact. She knew the consequences of impact, and just the idea of it induced a profound sense of dread in her. She looked at the pillbox, contemplated it for some long seconds. She opened the canister and poured out a handful.

Arslan unscrewed the top from the scotch.

"These," she said, holding up a round white pill, "are to make me go to sleep. One is normally enough for an adult to sleep a full night. If I take three of them I might get four hours."

She took six and swallowed them with the scotch.

"These," she said, holding up a half-red, half-gray capsule, "are antidepressants. The red part is the 'anti' and the gray part the 'depressant.' They're supposed to make me happy, but all they do is turn dark black to overcast gray."

She swallowed another handful; the whiskey seeped out of the corners of her mouth.

"Now these are the babies," she said, holding up a rounded blue lozenge. "I take these *all* the time. They really work. Oxy-Contin 160 mg. Active ingredient oxycodone. Known in America as Hillbilly Heroin. These wrap you in cotton wool and tuck you away from life in a little drawer. They cure all known hurt except . . . the pain of loss."

She socked back eight, poured whiskey after them. She took another assorted handful and worked her way through those. She became unintelligible, her legs went, and Arslan lowered her to the floor, where her eyes rolled back and she passed out.

The Turk went to the pulley rope, yanked it tight so that Schafer came to his feet. He pulled tighter and got him up onto the stool and then on tiptoe. The blood thumped in Schafer's carotids. His calf muscles strained and cracked. He felt himself tottering. His mind had achieved great clarity since he'd been returned to upright. The extraordinary pain from the beating he'd sustained had contributed to this. He began to understand something of the nature of religious flagellation. The greater the awareness of his mortal sack through extreme vulnerability, the more he seemed able to concentrate on what was pure and untouchable. He'd never been a believer in God. He'd had no time for the soul or any of that spiritual claptrap. He'd stopped going to church as soon as he was out of his parents' orbit. But now he found himself on the edge of a revelation. The possibility of it excited him.

A man of Middle Eastern appearance came before him. He couldn't imagine how he must look to this foreigner. His face craquelured with blood, like Christ bleeding from his crown of thorns, but then the man was probably a Muslim, what would he know? There was nothing readable in his black, shining eyes.

"You know what I'm here for," said the Turk. "You can make this short or long and drawn out."

"Go fuck yourself," said Schafer.

The Turk disappeared, and Schafer felt the rope tremble, and then his feet lost contact with the stool. He struggled to get back to it as the garrote cut into his neck. Darkness crowded his vision. And just as things started to rush away, he crashed to his knees. The world came back up to him. His vision cleared. The rope tugged him back up until he was once again standing on the stool. Arslan walked into frame with a jar of reddish powder.

"This is a mixture of chili and salt," he said. "Don't make me do this to you, Schafer."

Schafer licked his lips, a terrible dryness in his mouth. He had so little to lose that he decided he might as well see what it was that lay beyond the limit of his endurance.

"Go fuck yourself," he said hoarsely.

The powder tickled as it cascaded down the backs of his legs. Then a burning sensation started and grew until he was convinced that a blowtorch was involved. He swayed on the stool. His body no longer seemed to be his, or was it that the pain was no longer at an endurable level? A strange notion occurred to him: Was this the nature of purgatorial fire? And in that instant, when he thought that he'd ceased to be corporeal but had not yet become nothing, he felt himself suffused with a clean light and an overwhelming sense of gratitude for something that had been conferred on him. And with that thrilling in his chest, he shouted out and leaped from the stool, kicking it away.

The Turk watched, shaking his head. He waited until Schafer's legs stopped kicking. He crossed the floor to where Leena lay, rolled up her boilersuit, and removed her prosthetic leg. He left the light on, shut the door. Minutes later he left the building.

IT WAS A fifteen-minute walk in subzero temperatures to the Bar Hefner on Beim Schlump. Arslan walked past the red leather-topped bar stools and found Foley in a corner with Spokes opposite him in comfortable armchairs. The room was warm and glowed with an amber luminescence, as if viewed through a glass of whiskey.

Foley offered Arslan a seat and a drink. He refused both.

"I'm not staying," he said. "I've got a flight to Istanbul. I'm just delivering this."

He handed Spokes the prosthetic leg. Spokes smuggled it rapidly to the floor by the table.

"What's that about?" said Foley coldly.

"The last thing he shouted out before he died was that what you wanted was in her leg," said Arslan, then hesitated, looking up into his head. "At least that's what I *think* he said."

The Turk shrugged, turned, and left the bar.

FORTY-EIGHT HOURS later, as instructed in Rush's phone call, a British journalist from the *Guardian* newspaper arrived in Hamburg on the 20:30 flight from Heathrow. He took a cab to the Water Tower Hotel in the Sternschanzenpark. He'd made sure that he was going to be given room 1015 when he'd made his reservation. Once there he dropped his bags and immediately lifted the painting from the wall. He stripped out the plastic bag and put it in the bottom of his case without looking at the contents. He opened the curtain and saw the blue block letters in the blackness of the freezing night.

FLEISCH GROSSMARKT

THE COURIER

Dan Fesperman

IN THIS BONEYARD of Nazi memory where I make my living, we daily come across everything from death lists to the trifling queries of petty bureaucrats. Our place of business is known simply as the Federal Records Center, and it is housed on the first floor of an old torpedo factory down by a rotting wharf on the Potomac.

I am told that elsewhere in this cavernous building there is a Smithsonian trove of dinosaur bones and an archive of German propaganda films. But on our floor there is only paper, box after box of captured documents, with swastikas poking like shark fins from gray oceans of text. The more papers we move, the dustier it gets, and by late afternoon of each day the air is thick with motes of decomposing history. Sunbeams angling through the high windows shimmer like the gilded rays of a pharaonic tomb.

Seeing as how the war ended thirteen years ago, you might figure we'd have this mess sorted out by now. But, as I've discovered lately, lots of things about the war aren't so easily categorized, much less set aside.

My name is Bill Tobin, and it is my job to decide which papers get tossed, declassified, or locked away. The government hired me because I am fluent in German and know how to keep a secret. I've worked here for a year, and up to now the contents have been pretty much what I expected—memos from various Nazi ministries, asking one nagging question after another: Have Herr Muller's new ration coupons arrived? Must we initial every page of every armaments contract? How many Poles should we execute this Saturday?

What I didn't expect to find—here or anywhere—was the name of Lieutenant Seymour Parker, a navigator from the 306th Bomb Group, U.S. Army Air Force. Yet there it was just the other day on the bent tab of a brown folder, our latest retrieval from a mishmash we have begun calling the Total Confusion File, mostly because we never know which ministry letterhead will turn up next.

At first, seeing Parker's name was a pleasant surprise, like having an old pal visit from out of the blue. After reading what was inside, I was wishing he hadn't dropped by.

It's been fourteen years since we handed Parker over to the Germans in the spring of 1944, along with three other American flyboys. It was part of a prisoner exchange. The Germans had agreed to ship our boys home via occupied France. We gladly would have done it ourselves, of course, but at the time I was working for the OSS in Switzerland, a neutral country surrounded by Axis armies. To put it bluntly, we had no way out, and neither did the U.S. airmen who regularly parachuted into Swiss meadows and pastures after their bombers got shot up over Germany.

So we escorted Parker and the others up to the French border at Basel and then watched as a haughty SS officer in black ushered them onto a train bound for Paris. From there they would make their way to Spain, to be turned over to American custody for the voyage home.

I had helped Parker pack for the trip. His duffel was filled with cartons of cigarettes, and his head was stuffed with secrets.

The former were for handing out to Germans along the way. As for the latter, well, that was more complicated.

It was the last time I saw him, and from then on our crew in Bern rarely mentioned his name, because surely everything had gone according to plan. Kevin Butchart had volunteered as much a year later, on the same afternoon the radio broke in with the happy news that Hitler had blown out his brains in Berlin. Someone else—I think it was Wesley Flagg—happened to ask if anyone knew what had ever become of Parker.

"Didn't you hear?" Butchart said. "He's back home in Kansas. Down on the farm with Dorothy and Toto, and didn't even have to click his heels. Whole thing went off without a hitch."

Since then, I had thought of Parker only once—last summer, while watching my son play Little League baseball on a leisurely Saturday. It was a key moment in the game. The best player on his team, one of those natural athletes who you can tell right away has a college scholarship in his future, was rounding third as the opponent's shortstop threw home. Runner, ball, and catcher arrived at the plate simultaneously, and there was a jarring collision.

The catcher, a pudgy kid with glasses who had been flinching on every swing, took the impact square in the gut and went facedown in the dirt. As he righted himself and pulled off his mask you could see the conflict of emotions on his face—a rising storm of tears that might burst loose at any moment, yet also a fierce determination to tough it out without a whimper.

To everyone's surprise he held aloft the ball, which had never left his mitt. The umpire called the runner out. The catcher then nodded for play to resume even as tears rolled down his dusty cheeks.

Something about the kid brought Parker to mind. He, too, had that contradictory bearing—flinching in one moment, stoic in the next—and for the remainder of the afternoon I was weighted by an inexplicable gloom. I wrote it off as yet another flashback, one of those anxious moments in which you realize yet again that the war still hasn't left you behind. Then I mixed a crystal pitcher of gimlets for my wife and me, and by the following morning I'd forgotten all about it.

Not long afterward, I was offered my current job at the Records Center. The pay wasn't great, but it sounded a hell of a lot more interesting than signing invoices at my father-in-law's shoe factory in Wilmington, Delaware. So we packed up and moved to a rented town house in Alexandria, Virginia.

When I came across Parker's file, I was standing in one of those golden beams of late sunlight as I pulled the last batch of documents from Box #214. My plan was to knock off early and take my son to the movies. Then I began to read, and within a few paragraphs I was transported back to the afternoon in early 1944 when I first met Parker aboard a Swiss passenger train.

Switzerland was the strangest of places then. Hemmed in by the Axis, its studious neutrality had turned it into an island of intrigue. On the surface it was Europe's eye of the storm, an orderly refuge from gunfire and ruin, a place where weary émigrés could catch their breath and tend their wounds. Bankers still moved money. Industrialists kept cutting deals.

But playing out beneath this facade was a gentleman's war of espionage among the snoops of all nations, and at times it seemed as if everyone was involved—émigrés, bankers, washed-up aristocrats, deal-hunting factory barons, and, of course, the Swiss themselves, who were trying to curry favor with the Americans even as they sweet-talked Hitler into not sending in tanks from the north. Everyone had information to offer—some of it dubious, some of it spectacular—and, as I discovered first-hand, the competing intelligence agencies were all too happy to vie for them by every means at their disposal.

On the day in late March that I met Parker, I was accompanied by the aforementioned Kevin Butchart. We were lurching down the aisle of a swaying train car, bound for Adelboden from Zurich via Bern.

The view out the windows was of an alpine meadow—cows and early spring wildflowers—but our attention was focused on the passengers. Several freshly arrived American airmen were on board, looking tired and dispirited. They had dropped from the skies after their B-17 had limped into Swiss airspace, following a bombing run over Bavaria. Butchart and I had come to scout them out as they made their way to an internment camp. We were hoping to find just the right one for use in an upcoming operation.

We knew we had to tread lightly. Even though the country was filled with spies, espionage was illegal. Swiss gumshoes regularly kept an eye on us, and we would be recruiting an operative right beneath their noses.

The flyboys had to mind their manners as well. The Swiss had already interned more than five hundred up in Adelboden, a resort town in the Alps, where they played Ping-Pong, read paperbacks, hiked around the town, and ate cheese three meals a day. The restless ones who tried to make their way back to the war by escaping into occupied France risked detention at a harsh little camp called Wauwilermoos. It was run by a supposedly neutral little martinet who would have done Hitler proud. Strange people, the Swiss.

I tugged at Butchart's sleeve.

"How 'bout him?"

I pointed at a stout fellow in a leather flight jacket who was munching on a chocolate bar from his escape kit.

"No way," Butchart answered. "Look how worn the jacket is. He's been at it for ages. And stop pointing. I saw your minder in the next car back."

I glanced behind me for the bearded Swiss gumshoe whom I called Alp Uncle, mostly because I didn't know his real name. Nowhere to be seen, thank goodness.

Butchart herded me along.

"Keep moving. We've only got an hour."

He was pushy that way, one of those short, muscular fellows whose aggressive movements can quickly get on your nerves. But as an employee of the U.S. legation's military attaché, this was his show, so I nodded and kept moving.

When Butchart wanted to engage you in conversation he came at you like a boxer, cutting and weaving, as if looking for an opening. Any suggestion that his point of view was flawed prompted an immediate counterpunch. He jabbed at your weak spots until your opinions were on the mat. I had learned not to pick these fights unless I could deck him with the first sentence, or unless we were in the presence of a superior officer, when he tended to pull his punches. For the moment I was inclined to defer to his judgment.

He tugged at my sleeve.

"There's our boy. Next compartment on the right. Skinny guy with red hair. See him?"

About then the train lurched into a long descending curve, wheels squealing, and there was a sudden improvement in the scenery out to the right. A tall blonde milkmaid with braided hair was carrying buckets toward a barn. Wolf whistles and applause erupted in the railcar. One of the flyboys slid open a window and yelled, "Hey, good lookin'!"

Then he was shouted down.

"Close the fucking window!"

"It's freezing in here. You outta your mind?"

"But it was Heidi!" the offending airman protested. "Only she's all grown up!"

Heidi, indeed. My own experience with local women had already provided ample proof that the natives were friendly, even though in this neck of the woods most of them spoke German. But it could be dangerous to let the hospitality fool you.

"Any sign of Alp Uncle?" Butchart asked.

I turned, scanning the car.

"Still out of sight."

Lately our minders seemed to be losing interest. We first noticed it after the German defeat at Stalingrad. The worse things went for the Wehrmacht, the more lenient the Swiss got with the Allies.

I eased closer to our target, but Butchart grabbed my sleeve.

"Never mind. Scratch him."

"Why?"

"Scar, back of his neck. Saw it when he turned to look at Heidi."

"So?"

"So it was probably a major wound, but he went back up anyway. Not our man. We're looking for Clark Kent, not Superman."

Butchart and I had been chosen for this assignment because we knew exactly what these fellows had been through. We, too, had come to Switzerland on crippled bombers that couldn't make it back to England.

I am not ashamed to admit that for me it was a welcome development. It had occurred the previous fall during my seventeenth mission. Seventeen doesn't sound like much until you've tried your first one—a terrifying ride through flak bursts and the raking fire of Messerschmitts and Focke-Wulfs. As a starboard waist gunner in a B-17, it was my job to shoot down these tormentors, a strategy roughly as effective as pumping a Flit gun at a sky full of locusts. If you're lucky you get one or two. The rest eat their fill.

On my sixth run I was sprayed by the entrails of the port gunner when a 20-millimeter shell exploded in his midsection. On the eighth my gun jammed, and I spent the next two hours watching helplessly as bandits blew holes in the skin of our plane. On the fourteenth we ditched in the Channel but were rescued from rafts. Three of our crewmen drowned. After each trip it took me hours to warm up, and all too soon the mission day routine became unbearable: Rise at two a.m. for the briefing. Swallow a queasy breakfast. Inhale gas fumes and the sweet scent of pasture grass while you loaded up in the dark. Then eight hours or more in cramped quarters, freezing most of the way, while people tried to kill you from every angle. After a while the throb of the engines was the only thing you could still feel in your hands and feet. Staticky voices shouted their panic and pain in your headset. Out the gun port you saw carnage everywhere—your colleagues' bombers smoking and then spiraling, spewing black dots as crewmen ejected. That could be me, I always thought, falling toward a field in Germany.

Until finally one day it was me. Three of our four engines were out, and Harmon, our pilot, was nursing us south toward the Swiss border. When he gave the order to bail, we weren't yet sure we had made it. The rest of us jumped while Harmon fought the controls. Fighters were still in the neighborhood, so I didn't pull the rip cord until I was below a thousand feet. Even then, as soon as the canopy opened I heard a Messerschmitt buzzing toward me from behind. I turned awkwardly in my harness and waited for the flash of guns. None came. The plane roared by, close enough for the prop wash to rock my chute. Only then did I notice the large white cross on its side—the Swiss air force, welcoming us with their German planes.

That left me feeling pretty good until I watched our plane hit the ground in a ball of flame and black smoke. Someone else said Harmon jumped just before impact, but his chute never opened.

Swiss soldiers rounded us up. They boarded us overnight at a nearby school, and the next morning they put us on a train for Adelboden, where we were supposed to be billeted in an old hotel. But that's when I lucked out. The man who would soon be my new boss came across me napping in a rear compartment. Apparently what caught his eye was a dog-eared copy of Arthur Koestler's *Darkness at Noon* splayed across my chest. I awoke when I felt someone picking it up, and looked into the blue eyes of an older gentleman with a pipe between his teeth. The pockets of his overcoat were stuffed with newspapers. He took a seat opposite me and began speaking American English.

"Any good?" he said, holding up the book.

"Not bad."

"I'm Allen Dulles, from the American legation."

We chatted long enough for him to find out I was fluent in German and had spent two years in graduate school. He then surprised me by suggesting I come to work for him. I was flattered, but I needn't have been. I learned later that Dulles had made it into Switzerland only hours before the country's last open border was closed, cutting him off from reinforcements.

That meant he had to be creative about finding new employees. Stranded American bankers and socialites were already on his payroll, so it was hardly surprising he would take an interest in me once a bunch of American airmen literally began dropping to him from the skies. I told him I liked the idea, and he said he would see what he could do. Two weeks later I was summoned to his office in Bern.

Only then did I learn I would be working for the OSS. It was the closest thing we had to a CIA, but I had never heard of it. I decided it must be a little out of the ordinary when the job application included an "Agent's Checklist" that asked me for a countersign "by which agent may identify himself to collaborators." They also gave me a code name, an ID number for use in all official correspondence, and a desk in a windowless office in an old brick town house on Dufourstrasse.

Most of my duties involved translation, but I suppose that officially I was a spy, unless there is some other name you'd give a job in which the boss sends memos on tradecraft and insists that you call him 110, or Burns, or whatever the hell you wanted as long as you never used his real name. That first meeting on the train was the only time I felt comfortable calling him Mr. Dulles.

So there I was, then, with Butchart on the train, trying to recruit someone else the same way that Dulles had recruited me, except we were seeking an altogether different sort of prospect.

"What about him?" I said, pointing even though Butchart had asked me not to.

"Where?"

"Last compartment on the left, by the window. The guy with glasses."

The fellow in question looked like one of the younger crewmen, but it was his wariness that caught my eye. While most of the others wore a weary look of relief, this one still had his guard up. There was also a softness to his features, and a little boy wonderment as he stared out the window. You could tell he had never seen mountains like these.

"He's got potential," Butchart said. "Navigator, I'll bet."

"How you figure?"

"The glasses. Must have a special talent or they'd have never let him in the air corps, and they're always short on navigators. Keep an eye on him while I check the next car."

I did just that. A few seconds later Butchart returned, shaking his head.

"I'm liking your navigator more and more."

"Want me to take him aside?"

"Wait 'til we're almost into the station. In the meantime I'll let his CO know. I'll also grab the Swiss officer in charge and start greasing the skids."

"What will you tell him?"

"Same thing Colonel Gill told them when he hired me. That

I'm from the military attaché and we're short on staff and look-ing for volunteers."

By now you may be thinking this isn't exactly the most glam-orous spy mission you've ever heard of, but it definitely beat what I had been doing up to then. Dulles had confined me to office duty, and I was going stir-crazy. It wasn't so much that I craved excitement as that I needed distraction. At least twice a week I was still dreaming about being back in the bomber—the bed rocking as if shaken by a flak burst, a high-altitude chill creeping beneath the sheets. I'd wake up exhausted, hands numb, as if I'd just returned from an all-night mission. Frankly, I was worried about going 'round the bend if something didn't come along soon to occupy my mind.

Butchart had heard I was eager for action, and he had sug-gested I meet his boss, Colonel Gill, who kept track of intelli-gence matters for the military attaché. He said they might have a special job for me.

I told him to give it a try, and it must have worked, because the next evening Dulles summoned me to his place on Herren-gasse. I went after dark, which was the drill for just about every-body who went to his house. He had the ground-floor apartment in a grand old building that dated back to medieval times. It was in the heart of all those arcaded streets in the old part of Bern. Gumshoes kept an eye on his front door, so visitors like me entered through the back, after approaching uphill through terraced gardens overlooking the river Aare.

It was always a treat visiting Dulles. He had a maid, a French cook, some mighty fine port, and plenty of logs for the fire. He also had a couple of mistresses, a Boston debutante married to a Swiss banker and an Italian countess who was the daughter of the conductor Toscanini. Dulles was probably the only warrior in the European Theater of Operations who suffered from gout.

Not that he looked much like a Lothario. He was very much

the old-school gentleman, all tweeds and pipe smoke, with an understated grace that immediately put you at ease. He was a hell of a good listener—which is probably what the ladies liked—and on any topic he zeroed in right away on the stuff that mattered. Glancing into his lively blue eyes when his mind was fully engaged was like peering into the works of some gleaming piece of sophisticated machinery, an information mill that never stopped running. Those newspapers in his pockets were no mere props. He devoured all knowledge within reach and chewed it over even as he engaged you in small talk about, say, the virtues of your university, or the quirks of some mutual acquaintance. Try to slip some half-baked thought past his field of vision and he'd seize upon it like a zealous customs inspector, and you'd end up wishing you had kept prattling on about your alma mater.

When the maid showed me in, there was a fire on the hearth. Dulles was knocking at the logs with a poker.

"Help yourself," he said, gesturing to a decanter of port on a side table.

Someone had left a bowler hat next to it, and I figured there must be another guest waiting elsewhere in the house. Dulles confirmed this suspicion when he dispensed with the usual pleasantries and got right down to business.

"I hear your services are in demand by Colonel Gill."

"Yes, sir. A little something to get me out of the office."

Dulles smiled and nodded.

"I know you're restless, but I do plan to get you out on the beat before long. Still, maybe this will offer some useful practice. Stretch your legs a bit. So you have my blessing if you're so inclined, even if they do think of themselves as our competition. That's not my view, mind you, but some of those Pentagon fellows seem to have a chip on their shoulders as far as we're concerned. So mind your step, Bill. And don't let them try anything fast and loose with you."

"Any reason to think they might?"

"Not really, other than Gill himself. He's bucking for promotion, which always makes a man a little dangerous. Sometimes in a good way, I'll allow, but you never know."

"Yes, sir."

"And Bill."

"Yes?"

"Even if you say yes, if the first step is squishy, don't feel as if you have to take the second one. Don't let pride shame you into doing something foolish. Perfectly fine by me if you bow out. Just don't tell them I said so."

Early the next morning, Butchart ushered me into Gill's office. Gill had set up shop in the back of a legation town house on Dufourstrasse, with a view onto a lush narrow garden. He stood behind a big varnished desk, a tall, trim fellow going gray at the temples. He offered a big handshake and spoke in a smoky baritone, which made for a powerful first impression. The starched uniform and all the ribbons didn't hurt, either.

Butchart stayed in the room after introductions, which was a little annoying although I wasn't about to say so. Gill referred to him by name instead of rank. Maybe that was his way of signaling that the meeting was off the books.

"Kevin here tells me you're a little unhappy over in Allen's shop. All cloak and no dagger, I hear."

"Maybe I'm just impatient."

"A man is entitled to impatience when there's a war on. It's no time to be sitting behind a typewriter. Not that I can promise you much dagger, either, I'm afraid. But at least you'll be out in the field."

"Yes, sir. Sergeant Bu . . . uh, Kevin said you had an assignment in mind?"

"I do. You'd be working it together. Are you familiar with the prisoner exchange that occurred a few weeks ago, those six American airmen we sent up into France?"

"Yes, sir. Did something go wrong?"

"Quite the opposite. Worked like a charm. All six are currently back in the States awaiting reassignment. Apparently the Germans were happy to get their six men back as well. From all accounts they're amenable to doing it again. But were you aware that your boss, Mr. Dulles, arranged the whole show?"

I wasn't, and it must have shown in my face.

"I didn't think so. Well, he did. And he was quite clever about it. Secretive, too. Even my bosses didn't know what he was up to until a few days ago, and that didn't go down so well in Washington. When some civilian wants to put their soldiers at risk, they prefer to be told in advance. Of course, now that it has turned out so well, they're wisely keeping complaints to a minimum. And, frankly, it has opened up an opportunity for a similar effort by us. Which is where you and Kevin come in."

"So it was some sort of operation?"

"Oh, yes. Unbeknownst to us, two of the airmen were functioning as OSS couriers. Apparently Dulles had gathered a lot of information on German troop movements up along the Atlantic Wall. He figured it was too hot to send out by wireless, even by code, so he drilled it into these two fellows instead. Strict memorization. Gave the lessons himself."

In those days it was no secret to anyone that the invasion of France was coming soon, and that's why information on German troop strength along the French coast was at a premium.

"Sounds like a smart idea," I said.

"It was. The only problem is that he left the job half-finished."

"How so?"

"Well, think of it for a minute. In the intelligence business, the only thing better than passing along a lot of good information is convincing the enemy that you actually have a lot of bad information. That way, they're more likely to miscalculate when they try to guess where you're going to come ashore."

"So you'd like to load up a couple of prisoners, too, except with a lot of bad information?"

"Exactly. One is all you need, in my opinion. Then, of course, you find some way to make the Germans suspicious enough to haul in your fellow for questioning. Of course, that means you have to choose just the right man for the job. One who will tell them what they want to hear, but in a convincing enough fashion."

"A good enough liar, you mean."

"Exactly. And what do you suppose would be the best way to make our fellow a good enough liar?"

"Training?"

"Only if you have months or even years at your disposal. We don't have that luxury. We've only got weeks, if that. So I've come up with an alternative. Send in a novice. Just don't tell him he's carrying bad information. That way, he believes in the material enough to make it convincing."

"If he talks."

"Exactly. Which is why you have to pick just the right fellow. Not a hero, or someone who will keep his secret to the bitter end. Someone a little more, well, malleable. A weaker vessel, if you will."

"Someone who will break under pressure?"

"And preferably not too much pressure. Which is why Kevin and you are perfect for the job. You've experienced firsthand what these airmen go through, and you know their state of mind when they arrive. More to the point, you've seen firsthand the ones who can't cut it, the ones who break under pressure."

Like me, I almost said. I could have told him all about my latest nightmare, but I doubt he would have understood.

"So what do you think?" he asked. He seemed quite pleased with himself.

I thought the idea was dubious, and I recalled Dulles's advice.

Maybe it was time for me to bail. Or maybe Dulles had offered an easy escape merely to test me. Bow out now, and he might keep me deskbound for the rest of the war. You never knew for sure what was going on in a mind like his.

So, despite my reservations, I decided to say yes. But first I had some questions.

"How will we make sure the Germans pick him up?"

"I'm afraid that aspect of the operation is above your pay grade, Bill."

It rankled, but it was the right thing to say, even though Dulles would have just winked and said nothing at all. But Colonel Gill, as I would soon discover, could never pass up an opportunity to impress you, even when he should have kept his mouth shut. And just as I was about to reply, he began elaborating on his statement in a way that obviously was intended to show the genius of his grand design.

"Surely a smart fellow like you shouldn't have too much trouble figuring out how we'll do it," he said. "Let's face it, the Germans are all over town. You can't even have a drink at the Bellevue without bumping into half the local Gestapo. So maybe we will have to arrange for a few well-placed leaks. A slipup here and there. Just enough to let them know that our man might be of interest to them as he makes his way through their territory. That's the beauty of it, you see? No need to run too tight of a ship in the run-up to zero hour. The only real need for precision is in picking the right man for the job."

"But then what?"

"What do you mean?"

"Well, let's say they take our man in for questioning. Pressure him. He talks, tells them everything, just like we want. Then what? Is he still exchanged as a prisoner?"

"Oh, we'll make it all work out, one way or another. If worse comes to worst, he'll end up back where he started, as a captive."

"Except in German hands, not Swiss."

"Your concern is admirable, Bill. But have you been over to Wauwilermoos lately? Pretty brutal, I'm told. I'm sure there are some German stalags that would be an improvement over that rat hole. It's wartime, Bill. Besides, anyone who volunteers will know the risks. If he were the hard type, the type to fight to the bitter end, then I'd say okay, you have a point. But this is the beauty of our operation. With the right man, the right temperament, the risk is minimal. So it really is all up to you. Or to you and Kevin, of course."

Translation: Failure would be on our heads, and mostly on mine. By recruiting an OSS man, Gill had arranged for a fall guy who could be laid at the feet of Dulles, his rival. If it succeeded, he could claim he knew better how to use OSS personnel.

I said yes anyway. I can be stubborn that way, especially when I sense that an opportunity, no matter how chancy, might be the only one to come along. And a few days later there I was, entering a train compartment to talk to the young man who we had decided was our hottest prospect.

"MORNING, LIEUTENANT. I'M from the American legation in Bern and I have some questions for you. The first thing I need to know is your name."

The young airman looked suitably intimidated and clutched his escape kit to his chest. But he answered without first asking for my name, which I took as a good sign. Easily cowed by authority, I surmised, even though he carried a decent rank of his own.

"Lieutenant Seymour Parker. Emporia, Kansas."

"Navigator, right?"

"How'd you know?"

"I know a lot of things. Come with me, please. We've got some more questions for you."

"Are you an officer?"

"Like I said, I'm with the legation."

"But the Swiss officers said . . . "

"They've been notified. So has your CO. Let's go."

He looked around at his seatmates, who shrugged. I got the impression they hadn't known one another long, or else they would have risen to his defense.

Parker rose awkwardly. A long flight in a Fortress stiffened you up, especially when followed by an uneasy night of sleep on a Swiss cot in an empty schoolhouse. He followed me meekly up the aisle to where Butchart was waiting, just as the train was pulling into Adelboden. We had arranged for the legation to send down a car and driver, which seemed to impress him. Butchart and I sat on either side of him on the backseat of a big Ford.

If I had been in Parker's shoes, I would have been asking a million questions. He tried one or two, then stopped altogether when Butchart told him brusquely to shut up. If we had been Germans posing as Americans we could have hijacked him every bit as easily. Butchart looked over at me and nodded, as if he was thinking the same thing.

The roads were clear of snow, and we made it to Bern in about an hour. We said little along the way, letting the pressure build, and when we reached the city we took him to an empty back room in one of the legation offices. Seeing the American flag out front and hearing other people speaking English seemed to put him at ease. We shut the door and settled Parker into a stiff-backed chair. The first thing Butchart asked was how many missions he'd flown.

"This, uh, this was my first."

Perfect, and we both knew it. Enough to get a taste of terror without growing accustomed to it.

"Some of your crewmates looked pretty experienced," I said.

"They are. I was a replacement."

"So what happened to you guys up there?" Butchart asked. "You fuck up the charts or something, get everybody lost?"

Parker reddened, and for the first time defiance crept into his voice.

"No, it wasn't like that at all. We were in the middle of the formation and took some hits. Didn't even reach the target. We came out below Regensburg with only two engines, and one of those was smoking. Lieutenant Braden, he's our pilot, asked me to plot a course toward Lake Constance."

"Well, you did that part okay, I guess."

Butchart then eased up a bit by asking a few personal questions. He companionably pulled up a chair next to Parker's and started nodding sympathetically as the kid answered. I say "kid," but Parker was twenty, the son of a wheat farmer. He was a third-year engineering student at the University of Kansas, which explained how he had qualified for navigator training.

As he spoke it became clear that he was a man of simple, innocent tastes. He liked to read, didn't smoke, preferred soda over beer, and didn't have a serious girlfriend. Up to the time of his arrival in England he seemed to have believed that his home-town of Emporia was the center of the universe, and his college town of Lawrence was a veritable Athens. The most important bit of intelligence to come out of this part of our chat was that he had spent the previous summer as a lifeguard at a local pool.

"A lifeguard, huh?" Butchart sounded worried. "You volunteered?"

"Sure."

"And went through all the training?"

"Well . . ."

"Well what?"

"I was kinda filling in. All the regulars had enlisted, so there really wasn't time for me to take the courses."

"Sorta like with your bombing mission?"

"I guess."

Parker went meek and quiet again, as if we'd just exposed him as a fraud.

"Can I ask you guys something?"

"Sure," Butchart said.

"What's this all about? I mean, I know you mentioned something about a job. But what kind of job?"

"A onetime deal. A mission, provided you qualify. You'd be sent home on a prisoner exchange. But you'd have to memorize some information for us to pass along to the generals once you got back to the States. Facts and figures, maybe a lot of them."

"I'm good at that."

"I'll bet. And in return you'd get a free trip home. Not bad, huh?"

He smiled at that, then frowned, as if realizing it sounded too good to be true.

"But why me? There are plenty of other guys who've earned it more."

"Do you always look a gift horse in the mouth? Did you turn down the lifeguard job?"

"No, but . . ."

"But what?"

"I dunno. Something seems kinda funny about the whole thing."

I tried to put him at ease.

"Look, you're a navigator, which means you probably have a head for numbers and memorization. So there you go. You said it yourself, you'd be good at it."

He nodded, but didn't say anything more.

Butchart spent the next few minutes going over the preparation that would be required. He also described the likely route home—up through occupied France in the company of German escorts from the SS. Parker's eyes got a little wide during that part, and Butchart nodded at me in approval.

"So let's say you get caught, Parker. Let's say that halfway through this nice little train ride to Paris, one of those Krauts gets suspicious and takes you off at the next stop for a little questioning. What do you do then?"

"You mean if I'm captured?"

"No, dumb ass. You're already captured. That's why you're part of an exchange. But let's say they decide to check you out, grill you a little. What you gonna tell 'em?"

"Name, rank, and serial number?"

"Yeah, sure. But what else?"

"Well, nothing, I hope."

Butchart got in his face like a drill sergeant.

"You *hope*?"

"Okay, I *know*. Or know I'll try."

"C'mon, Parker, you can level with us. You really think you could handle some Gestapo thug getting all over you? What would you tell him?"

"I like to think I wouldn't say a damn thing."

"You mean like if they try this?"

Butchart slid a knife from his belt. Then he grabbed Parker by a shank of hair and pulled back his head. Before the kid even realized what was happening, Butchart had put the flat of the blade against the white of Parker's neck—steel on skin, as if he were about to peel him like a piece of fruit.

Parker swallowed hard, his Adam's apple rising and falling. For a moment I thought he was going to cry.

"Whadda you doin'?"

"Checkin' you out."

Butchart yanked Parker's head lower while holding the blade steady. Sweat beaded at Parker's temples, and his eyes bulged. When he next spoke his voice was an octave higher.

"I'm not the enemy, okay?"

"Oh, yeah? How do we know that for sure?"

Another tug on his hair, this time eliciting a sharp squeal of pain.

"You coulda been a plant, put on that train to fool us. Or to infiltrate all our other boys and steal their secrets. Air routes, evasion tendencies, stuff about the new bombsight. How come nobody in your compartment acted like they knew you?"

"I'm new!" he said shrilly. "Nobody talks to replacements!"

Butchart abruptly released him and put away the knife. Parker sat up and tried to collect himself, but it was no good. His skin was pale gooseflesh, and he was swallowing so fast that his throat was working like a piston. He touched the spot where Butchart had held the blade. There were still red marks from Butchart's knuckles. A little cruel, no doubt, but I guess it was necessary.

Butchart turned toward me and nodded, and I knew without a word that it was his confirmation signal.

"I'll tell Colonel Gill," he said, rising from his chair.

"You mean I'm out?"

It wasn't clear if Parker was relieved or disappointed, which for us only enhanced his suitability.

"No," I said, avoiding his eyes. "You're in. You passed with flying colors."

"You'll start your training tomorrow," Butchart said. "Tobin here will go over the timetable."

We had two weeks to bring him up to speed on all the garbage information Colonel Gill wanted drilled into his head. Figuring that his taskmaster needed to be just as committed to the "facts" as his clueless student, the colonel assigned a sergeant from his staff named Wesley Flagg to handle the learning sessions.

Flagg was the perfect choice—pleasant, good-hearted, and as sincere as they come. Flagg's earnestness drove Butchart crazy, enough that he assigned me to keep tabs on the lessons. But as far as Colonel Gill was concerned, Flagg's greatest attribute was that he never questioned orders. Even if Flagg were to suspect that the information was flawed, there was virtually no chance he would have raised a fuss. He would simply assume that his superiors knew best.

Parker was a fast learner. Every time I asked Flagg for an update, he gushed about his pupil's ability to handle a heavy workload. But for all his boasting I sensed an unspoken uneasiness about Parker's fitness for the job. Flagg dared to bring it up only once, asking, "Are you sure Colonel Gill has signed off on this guy? I mean, Parker's great with the material, but, well . . ."

"Well what? He's the colonel's top choice."

"Nothing, then."

He never brought it up again.

The night before the exchange was to take place, Butchart asked me to take Parker his consignment of cigarettes. All four of the airmen were getting several cartons to help them spread goodwill along the way. They also might need to bribe some petty bureaucrat, even though the SS would be their official escorts.

Parker was billeted at a small hotel in the center of Bern. Conveniently—as far as we were concerned—it was just down the block from an apartment rented by a pair of Gestapo officers. Presumably they had passed him in the streets by now. He still wore his uniform from time to time, and they would have wondered right away what he was up to.

OSS operatives who worked for Dulles were taught that when meeting contacts it was best to disguise their comings and goings and to rendezvous on neutral ground. In Parker's case I was instructed not to bother, even though it put a knot in my stomach simply to walk into the hotel's small lobby and ask for him by name. A man was seated in the lobby on a couch. I didn't know his name or nationality, and I didn't ask.

Parker was restless, as anyone might have been on the eve of such an undertaking. But somehow he was not quite the same as the fellow I remembered from a few weeks earlier. Was my imagination playing tricks on me, or had he lost some of his callowness as he settled into his new role?

He finished packing in almost no time, so I asked if I could treat him to a beer.

"No, thanks," he said. "I probably won't be able to sleep much either way, so I might as well try to do it with a clear head. But there is one favor you can do me."

"Sure."

"Tell me, is there something funny about this operation? Something that, well, maybe no one has mentioned?"

I made it a point to look him straight in the eye, as much for myself as for him.

"There are always aspects of operations that aren't disclosed to the operatives. It's for their own protection."

"That's all you're allowed to say?"

As he asked it, his face was like that of the catcher in my son's Little League game—vulnerable yet determined, timid yet willing to go forward, come what may. For a moment I was tempted to tell him everything.

But I didn't, if only because the advice I had just imparted was true. It *was* in his best interests not to know. For one thing, the truth would have devastated him. For another, the Germans would have read his intentions immediately. And while it's one thing to have the enemy catch you functioning as a secret courier, it's quite another to be caught operating as an agent of deception. Setting Parker up for that fate would have been tantamount to marching him before a firing squad.

So I tried offering an oblique word of advice, hoping that when the right time came he would recall my words and put them to good use.

"Look, if for some unforeseen reason push does come to shove, just keep in mind that it's *you* who will be out there taking the blows, not us. So go with your own instincts."

It only seemed to puzzle him. Finally, he smiled.

"Maybe I should take you up on that beer, after all."

"Good enough."

He drank three, as it turned out, the first time in his life he had downed more than one at a sitting, and it showed in his wobble as I escorted him back to the room. He turned out his light just as I was leaving.

The actual exchange at the border was almost anticlimactic.

Oh, the SS man showed up, all right, just as he had for the previous swap engineered by Dulles. I suppose he was appropriately sinister with his swagger stick and stiff Prussian walk, and certainly for the way he snapped his heels and offered a crisp Nazi salute along with the obligatory "Heil Hitler."

It definitely got Parker's attention, but I don't recall it striking much fear into me. Or maybe I've rewritten the scene in my memory, having watched countless Hollywood versions that have turned the officer's dark gestures into costumed parody, complete with cheesy accent. I suppose I've always wanted to regard him as a harmless stereotype, not some genuine menace who still had a war to fight and enemies to kill.

Whatever the case, Parker offered me a wan smile over his shoulder as he lined up with his three fellow airmen and stepped aboard the train. They were all a bit nervous, but to a man they were also excited about the prospect of returning home.

I got back to Bern late that night. A taxi dropped me at the legation so I could report that all had gone well. But Butchart and Colonel Gill weren't there, and neither had left word on where to reach them. Only Flagg was waiting, eager to hear how his pupil had fared.

He smiled after I described the scene at the train station.

"I'll admit that for a while I had my doubts," he said. "But you know, by the end I was feeling pretty good about it. Parker's the type who can fool you. Hidden reserves and all that."

"You really think so?"

"Oh, yes. And he was such a fast learner with the material that I even had time to teach him a few escape and evade tactics. Just in case."

"Good thinking," I said weakly.

We said good night, and I walked across the lonely bridge to my apartment. I was exhausted and it was well past midnight, but I don't remember getting a moment of sleep.

Two days later a French rail worker, one of our contacts with the maquis, reported through the usual channels that Parker had been removed from the train at the third stop, well before Paris. No one in our shop said much about it, especially when there was no further word in the following days.

Soon enough I was busy with new assignments. If Dulles had been testing me through Colonel Gill, then I must have passed, because he began making good right away on his promise to get me out and about.

The extra distractions were welcome, and within a few weeks I was no longer dreaming of Messerschmitts and butchered comrades, although Parker's guileless face did swim before me from time to time. Then came the day when Hitler shot himself. Flagg popped his question, Butchart supplied the reassuring answer, and from then on I had no more dreams of Parker. I was content to let him reside in my memory as a quirky sidelight of the war years. At least, I was until coming across his folder at the Records Center.

It was a thin file, with only four typewritten pages inside. But what really caught my attention was the Gestapo markings across the sleeve. As I steeled myself to read it in the sunlight of 1958, it occurred to me that soon there would be little need for fellows like Parker. Only months earlier, Sputnik had fallen to earth after its successful voyage. Bigger and better replacements were already on the launchpad, and, if you believed the newspapers, the chatter in intelligence circles was that half the work of spies would soon be obsolete. Both sides would soon be able simply to look down at enemy positions from high in the sky. But in 1944 we had people like Parker, good soldiers who did as they were told, even when they were told very little.

By the second paragraph I learned that Parker had been considered a probable spy almost from the moment he had boarded the train. By the fourth paragraph I learned they had grilled him for twelve hours, off and on. The details were scanty—they always were in these reports when the Gestapo was pulling out all the stops—but I was familiar with enough eyewitness accounts of their usual tactics to fill in the blanks: Force them to stand for hours on end. Let them pee in their pants while they waited. Beat them, perhaps, and, if that didn't work, beat them harder, or threaten them with a firing squad.

Spy was the word the report kept using, over and over. Twelve hours of this, yet Parker, the veteran of only a single combat mission over Germany, held out. Flagg's judgment proved correct. He had hidden reserves. In fact, he had done us all one better. Lieutenant Parker had tried to escape.

It happened early on the following morning, the report said, right after the sentry left the room for a smoke. The officer in charge okayed the break because the subject had been at his lowest ebb. And at this point in the report, perhaps to cover his ass, the officer allowed himself the luxury of a detailed description of the subject's physical state: one eye swollen shut, bruises about the face and chest, shins bleeding, apparent exhaustion due to sleep deprivation. Yet no sooner had the sentry made himself scarce than Parker had somehow managed to overcome the interrogating officer and throw open the door.

He made it about twenty yards before the gunshots caught him. He then survived another two hours before dying of his wounds. The reporting officer seemed resigned to the idea of being reprimanded for his lapse in judgment, which had led to the loss of a potentially valuable prisoner before any useful information had been extracted.

By then my hands were cold, my feet as well. I sighed deeply, shut the folder, and looked up at the clock. It was an hour past our usual closing time, and my assistant was eyeing me curiously from his desk. He was anxious to leave. What I needed was a stiff drink, although this time a pitcher of gimlets wasn't going to be enough. But first I had one more bit of business here to take care of.

I carried the folder to a table next to my assistant's desk. For a moment I hovered over the burn box. As I prepared to drop in the report for destruction, I like to believe that I was not guided chiefly by an instinct of self-preservation. I was thinking as well of Parker's parents, perhaps still on their farm near Emporia. Having a son of my own now, I wondered what it would be like to hear that your only child had died while protecting secrets that he wasn't supposed to protect, that he had failed in his mission by being too brave and too strong.

But I couldn't bring myself to let go of the folder.

"Sir?" my assistant asked. "Is something wrong?"

"This one belongs with the OSS stuff."

"Classified?"

I paused, still hovering.

"No. In fact, I'd like it to get some circulation. You go on. I'll prepare the translation and a distribution list and have it ready for you to send out copies in the morning."

He was gone within seconds, and I settled back at my desk with the folder still in hand. The list came immediately to mind. Colonel Gill and Butchart, wherever they might be, would receive copies. Dulles, too, down at his big desk in the director's office of the agency we now called the CIA. Or perhaps each of them already knew, and always had. In that case, they needed to know that others had also found out.

But what about Parker's parents? I would spare them the gory details, of course, but they at least deserved the gist of the story, beginning with that first meeting aboard the train. The most important part, however, would be the summation, and I already had one in mind: Your son didn't tell the Germans a word. Not one. In fact, he did exactly as we asked, even if not at all as we had planned. The ball never left his mitt.

HEDGED IN

Stella Rimington

RON HADDOCK USUALLY knew what he wanted to do. Just now, he wanted to put a bullet through the rear tires of the ancient Bentley convertible sitting on the drive in front of his living room window. But he couldn't, any more than he could grind his teeth. He couldn't grind his teeth because he'd got the chewing gum habit during his years as an armed policeman, standing out in the rain guarding embassies or waiting for criminals to make their next move, and he was chewing now to keep calm. And he couldn't shoot up the Bentley's tires because the car belonged to his next-door neighbor, and it had every right to be there. The drive that led from Haddock's gate to his front door didn't belong to him, due to some ridiculous property rights that went back to the time of William the Conqueror. The bastard next door actually had the right to park his car there, which made Haddock angry.

Everything about his next-door neighbor made Haddock angry. It made him angry that the bastard had planted a hedge of conifers fifteen feet high between his house and Haddock's bungalow, a hedge that took all Haddock's light at front and back and incidentally blocked the best track out into the fields when Haddock wanted to go rabbit-shooting.

Perhaps his neighbor shouldn't have made him quite so

angry, because after all, the man was away on business more than a third of the time. But that made him angry, too, because Haddock didn't like people who came and went; it was shifty and unreliable. Criminals, the lot of them, deserved to be shot. The bastard had even woken him up one day in the early morning to get him to unjam his garden gate to let the Bentley in. And he wouldn't sell the drive. When Haddock had approached him about that, he'd said he needed the space for his second car. His number-one car was an Audi that he kept outside his own house, invisible behind the conifers. Evidently he liked to have a second exit when he needed it. Something very fishy about that, in Haddock's opinion.

Where was Phyllis? Haddock asked himself, looking at his watch. It was past noon, and she was supposed to be back from the gym by now to get his lunch. That was the arrangement between them. Three times a week she went to the gym, came back, and made lunch. Then it was his turn—down for the afternoon to the gun club.

With guns, any kind of gun, Haddock was an artist, because he really loved them. Guns were straight. They did as you told them and didn't argue. They were facts, powerful facts, things you could hold, things you could fondle without any comeback, with no complications. He specialized in veteran guns, Lee-Enfields, Webleys, Mausers, Colts. None of that modern arty-farty Russian stuff, or modern anything for that matter. Except for just one gun, his pride and joy, his Barrett sniper rifle, the one gun he really possessed because no one knew he had it. His unlicensed gun, the gun he could only ever use outside, at night, with its wonderful night sight, and then not often. Not just unlicensed—it had never been registered in England at all, because Haddock had picked it out of the hold of a small boat that was running guns to the IRA when he had been on antiterror duty, all of fifteen years ago. Yes, he'd taken a risk, a big one. He'd have been out of the force the day they found out that he'd retained any criminal property, never mind an unlicensed, unregistered firearm.

Haddock grinned to himself. He'd outsmarted his own people and got away with it. Then he stopped grinning. After all, they *had* thrown him out. Thrown him out of Armed Response, anyway, and that to him was out of everything. So he had retired, about five years ago, married Phyllis, and started chicken farming. She'd been some kind of policewoman herself, but she had inherited money and was prepared to settle down. The chicken farming hadn't worked out, so they'd moved here, living mostly on Phyllis's capital and pension in a down-market bungalow in rural Norfolk.

His dismissal from Armed Response had been a bad time— all other people's fault, of course. He'd been at an anti–Iraq War demonstration, part of an Armed Response team. They'd been sitting quietly on the edges of the action, just waiting for something to happen, never thinking they'd be needed. Then this bloke had come along—well, he was being shoved along by about a dozen of the demonstrators, waving their placards and yelling their slogans, with him in front. He was carrying what was obviously a gun, wrapped in brown paper. He waved it at some of the uniformed guys, threatening them. Had he heard Haddock's challenge? Of course he had, they all had, but the Enquiry didn't think it had been properly made. The Enquiry— he snorted to himself—a gang of snooty bastards who'd never seen police action in the raw, never faced a screaming crowd, thought it was all as easy as policing a church garden party. Well, Haddock had shot him, and when they'd ripped off the brown paper, it had turned out to be a wooden chair leg he'd been carrying. Served the idiot right for trying to deceive the police. What had the fool thought he was doing, brandishing an offensive weapon that looked like a gun? How many people had he been going to hit over the head with it?

Haddock looked in the fridge for a can of beer that he wasn't supposed to have before Phyllis got back, and, as he did so, a noise outside the window caused him to turn around and look out. The door of the Bentley was open and there was Mr. Next-Door leaning in, fiddling with the passenger light. Haddock hadn't even known he was at home, and now there he was, off again. He'd already opened the drive gate. Haddock watched him climb into the car. The car rolled slowly down the drive, turned left at the road, and drove away. And he didn't get out to shut the gate. The bastard never did.

Haddock watched him go. How much did he know about the man? Only that he came and went more than was good for him. Foreign sort of name, Lukas, spelled with a "k." There were immigrants all over the place nowadays. He was an average-looking sort of guy, medium build, rather sharp-faced, nothing noticeable, one of those people you could describe in twenty seconds or else it took you half an hour. He wasn't British—not English anyway. Maybe he was Welsh. Unreliable people, the Welsh. Haddock had known a Pole with a German accent who had turned out to be a Welshman from Caernarvon.

Whatever way you looked at it, he wasn't a local, not a Norfolk man. He was some kind of a radio buff, too. He had every kind of gadget in there; you could see some of them from the bridle track that went past his place. Aerials on the chimney. They didn't fit with a thought that Haddock had often had, that he might be one of those secret womanizers, covering up his antics with girls behind a conifer hedge. If he was burying bodies in the garden, Haddock wouldn't be able to see him at it.

A sudden thought struck Haddock. Given that the bloke was certainly dodgy, probably a criminal, did he carry a gun? It was something that had been part of his life's business to recognize, something that could cost you your life if you got it wrong. It was axiomatic with him to run the rule over any stranger, even one in a top hat at a wedding. He hadn't noticed any of the usual slight bulges or the absence of them, for that matter. But that in itself was interesting; maybe the bloke did carry, but made it his business to conceal the fact. That made him a professional. There were ways of moving, ways of not standing still, that kept even an expert guessing. Haddock knew them all, but he still didn't know whether the guy carried a gun, and that was starting to worry him.

He heard the side door opening. That would be Phyllis. It was Phyllis, still in her tracksuit and trainers, with her clothes in a duffel bag over her shoulder. Haddock forced a smile, wrenching his mind away from his neighbor and the fact that he was hungry, and she'd want to have a shower before she did anything about lunch. Why was she so late? His sessions at the gun club were only three hours, and he was in line for losing half an hour already. But it didn't do to shout at Phyllis. She had her ways of getting back.

"Something kept you, darling?"

She clicked her tongue. One of her irritating habits. "Did you remember to empty the kitchen bin? Something's smelling," she said.

"I forgot. Sorry."

"Well, do it now. I'll be down when I've powdered my nose."

It was true that her face was red and her nose looked as though it needed powdering. And for that matter her hair looked as though she'd been pulled through a bush backward.

"Tough routine at the gym today?"

She gave him a glance and disappeared around the corner and down the corridor to the bathroom.

He stored it away in his mind, where it collided with an identical thought that had been lying there since Monday, her last gym session. Same sequence. Just after Lukas had gone out, Phyllis appeared, twenty-five minutes late, looking as though she'd been through the mangle.

Phyllis. Cool, cool Phyllis. Twenty years younger than himself. Not yet forty. Maybe it was best not to say too much, just try to take it easy. Damage limitation, that was the mode with Phyllis. One thing that never went down well with her was curiosity. Any kind of inquiry about what she had been doing or who she'd seen, and she took offense.

He could hear Phyllis in the bathroom now, and it came to him in a flood that he was jealous—dead, mad jealous, angry jealous. Of course it was rubbish; of course Phyllis had been at the gym; of course she wasn't having it off with that Czecho-Hungarian sod who lived next door. But what if she was? By God, if he found she had been, he'd flog her with his police belt, studs and all. Come to think of it, he'd always wanted to do that. He'd flog her to death, and then go out and kill the bastard and then turn the gun on himself. He stopped, suddenly, almost choking, breathing fast, eyes watering, and tried to get a grip on himself.

"Something the matter, dear?"

Cool, ironic Phyllis. He said nothing.

"Well, I mean, you look such an idiot standing there panting with that smelly plastic bag in your hand. Look, give it to me. I'll put it in the bin. Lunch is in that carrier bag. I got it from Marks and Spencer. Your favorite chocolate pudding. Two for one offer today."

"I don't want lunch. I'm going for a walk."

"Relax, Ron, and just sit down. You look as if you've seen a ghost. They don't come in daylight, you know."

He sat down, ate his lunch, and thought. The gun club was off. While Phyllis had her afternoon nap, he was going to look around next door. Now that it occurred to him, he was amazed that he had never thought to do it before.

The bedroom door closed. He looked at his watch. Half past two. He slipped his mobile into his pocket.

"Bye, darling."

"Bye. Have a good time. Don't shoot anybody you shouldn't."

He made a face at the bedroom door and set off down the drive. Police training kicked in. There was no question of making a frontal approach. At the end of the drive, he turned to the right. Forty yards up the road, he vaulted a gate, walked across the field up to the corner of the forest plantation, and turned right toward the hay barn that now lay between him and the two properties. There was no need for concealment—Phyllis couldn't see him from the bedroom and Lukas was out—but he was still glad of the sunken lane that connected the barn to his objective. Leaning against the barn, he took out his mobile and dialed a number.

"Gemini Health Club."

"Is Mrs. Haddock there? I had been expecting to meet her for lunch."

"Who's speaking?"

"My name's Ron Morley. A friend."

"Sorry, Mr. Morley. I can't help. Mrs. Haddock didn't come in this morning. Can we give her a message if she does come in?"

Haddock depressed the call button and slipped the mobile into his pocket. He was thinking clearly now. If not the Czecho bastard, then someone else. Her story had better be good.

He walked down the hill. It was early May. The apple trees were covered with blossoms; the countryside looked beautiful, but Haddock didn't notice it; he didn't do beauty. He reached the bridle path past Lukas's place.

This house was much older than Haddock's bungalow. It was originally a farmhouse, maybe a couple of hundred years old, but small, not more than five rooms. All the land had once belonged to the farm, but at some point a piece had been sold off for the bungalow, hence the problem of the ownership of the drive. The farm outhouses and barns were still standing around the yard, cleaned up now, but you could faintly smell cows and hay. No sign of life.

Haddock walked across the yard and gently tried the house

door. Locked. The lower windows were closed, but one on the top floor was open a bit. He needed a ladder. He walked across to the bigger of two outbuildings and pushed the door. A scurry, then silence. A rat. The place was an empty double-story barn. He climbed the wooden ladder that led to the top floor. There was a range of openings in the front wall flush with the floor, windows once perhaps, that looked directly across to the house. At the back of the barn, a door with a wooden beam above it gave onto the bridle path, presumably once used to hoist in hay from a piled cart. He opened the door and looked out onto the path, then closed it again. He walked back to the front and, squatting down, peered across at the house through one of the openings.

Then he saw the girl. She was standing inside the partly opened door of a one-story stable fronting the yard at a right angle to his barn. It occurred to him that she must have watched his arrival and didn't mind being seen—at any rate, not by him. She now walked out into the yard and, looking up at him, said, "Interesting place."

She was good-looking, except that she was a little too slim for his taste and her blue-gray eyes too noticing for beauty. He wondered if she was a lesbian. He climbed down the ladder and walked out into the yard.

"Looking around?" she asked.

"Yes. I'm considering buying the place."

"You local?"

"Kind of."

Suddenly he noticed something he might have seen before, but for interruptions. A woman's sandal was lying at the edge of the yard just by the barn wall. A flip-flop he'd last seen on Phyllis's foot when she'd left for the gym this morning. No wonder she'd been wearing trainers when she came home. She must have dropped it, or someone had pulled it off. He wrenched his eyes from it and tried to concentrate on the girl.

"You looking around as well?"

"Not really," she said, looking carefully at him, as if to gauge his reaction. "I live here."

"You *live* here? Are you Lukas's wife?"

"Not exactly."

This was getting complicated.

"He's gone."

"Yes. I'm going, too."

"When's he coming back?"

"Not my business."

"What exactly is your business?"

"If you don't mind my saying so, Mr.—?"

"Pearson."

"Right, Mr. Pearson. This is getting a bit personal. Let's leave it there."

She was wearing a parka. She zipped it up.

"Good afternoon, Mr. Pearson. Best of luck with your reconnaissance."

She walked out of the yard and, a moment later, he heard a car start farther up the bridle path and drive off.

A little breeze swirled last autumn's leaves. He'd seen enough, too much. He felt sick, ready to vomit. But he knew what he was going to do, come what may.

He went home, scarcely knowing which way his steps took him. He lifted the latch of his garden gate, passed the flattened turf where the Bentley convertible had stood, put his key in the lock, walked along the corridor, and kicked open the bedroom door. He tore the bedclothes off Phyllis, grabbed her by the hair, and started hitting her. He slapped her with his palm, then hit her with the back of his hand, then punched her with his fist, so her head jerked back. Then he paused, gathering his strength, and she kneed him hard in the groin, so he fell off the bed onto the floor, where she kicked him hard in the ribs.

"You bugger!" she said. "You absolute bugger!"

And that was all. He watched her while she piled some

clothes and jewelry into a suitcase. Then, deliberately, slowly, she tidied her hair, applied some makeup, and walked out of the bedroom, pausing only to say, "I'll be back for the rest. And the house."

He heard the car leave.

He got slowly up, sat down again, and went over every action, every word, in the last four hours. His intention was fixed; he only wanted to be sure that he could do what he intended and stand a reasonable chance of getting away with it. One thing he knew—cold, furious as his wife might be, she would never offer evidence against him. Her own pride would stop her. As for the girl in the yard, she had lied when she'd said she lived in the place. He had never heard her or seen her, and she didn't know him. What she had been doing there he could not imagine, but one thing was sure: she wasn't police. Maybe she was just a rather intrusive sightseer.

The main question was, when would the bastard come back? He walked up the corridor, positioned a stepladder under the trapdoor in the ceiling, and drew down a long parcel. Calmly, he unwrapped it and laid the parts on the kitchen table, first drawing the curtains. He inspected and cleaned each one with a rag, fitted them carefully together, then slipped the complete gun into an old golf bag. He put the bag and its contents back into the loft, stroking it lovingly. His gun.

As he finished, he heard the noise of the Bentley, moving quite slowly up the drive. That was odd; when Lukas took the Bentley he was usually away for several days at a time. Other times, he used the Audi. Where had that been during his afternoon's visit? Must have been in the stable, he decided. So the girl would have seen it. "So what?" he said aloud.

Tonight, then? No, not tonight. He was too done up, like a man without sleep for a fortnight, or maybe like a man whose wife has left him for good without a sausage in the refrigerator. He went to bed.

Next morning, Haddock got up, showered, breakfasted, and, taking his binoculars, followed a route identical to that of the previous afternoon, but he stopped in the shadow of the plantation. He sat on the ground, his back against a tree, warm sun on his left shoulder, and scrutinized the countryside inch by inch, pausing again and again on the two houses. Lukas was certainly there; at one point he emerged and walked into the stable, coming out with some piece of apparatus. Was that what the girl had been looking at? No one else seemed to be there and, above all, there was no sign of Phyllis. In fact, there was nothing moving in the whole of lazy Norfolk but a line of slowly turning wind turbines and the occasional vehicle on the road that passed his property.

Haddock went home, taking care to avoid observation. There was still plenty to do. He put on dark, loose clothing and soft-soled boots, first removing all labels. In a small rucksack he packed spare shoes, trousers, a pullover, and a T-shirt. He added a pencil torch, not to be used save in extremis. He readjusted his watch by the radio and sat down. At nine o'clock, he got the golf bag out of the loft, and at exactly a quarter past nine, he turned off all the lights.

Then he stood for a moment in the bedroom, asking himself whether he really wanted to go through with it. He didn't, but he would. The chase, the hunt, immemorial passion had got to him. He had failed everything in life, his job, his business, his marriage, and now he was going to win. He knew himself to be the master of every technique needed for the job he intended to do.

Besides, he hated the bastard with a real, profound hatred. Lukas, the foreigner, the man who had destroyed his life, taken his wife, stolen his possession. Lukas was a robber. He, Haddock, was a cop.

He checked his watch and left the house by the side door, taking exactly the same route as before. The moon was rising, but it was pitch black in the plantation where he left his spare bundle and the empty golf bag. He pulled a balaclava over his face and adjusted the eyeholes. Then he set off down the track, planting his soles squarely on the surface to minimize noise. Not that it was exactly quiet on this May evening, with rabbits scurrying, bats squeaking, and the noise of an owl in the dark trees overlooking Lukas's place.

Once in the yard, he was safe in the moon's shadow by the barn. As he had expected, there was a light in the curtained ground-floor window of the house; the upper floor was unlit, curtains open. He'd be unlucky if he got no chance of a shot, and at that range, Haddock needed only one.

There was just one bad moment. The bridle track behind the barn was very little used by traffic. But now, just as he crouched in the barn's shadow inside the yard, he heard a car moving quite slowly down it. He saw nothing but a passing gleam—almost as though it were unlit—and to his relief, it passed on, tires lightly crunching the ground, and out of earshot.

Haddock remained motionless for a minute, listening, and then slipped into the barn and up the wooden ladder. He laid down his gun carefully, flat on the timbers where he could see it by the refracted light of the moon. Then he moved to the back of the barn and carefully opened the upper door over the road, fixing it by its bar against the wall. He might need it for a line of retreat. For a moment, he peered into the silent wall of trees opposite, two arm lengths away, and finally moved back to the unglazed window. He squatted, picked up the gun, and then lay on his stomach, his favorite position for accuracy, and trained the gun roughly in the direction of the unlighted window across the yard, which he calculated to be the bedroom.

As he lay there, a nasty thought came to him. When he had done what he intended, what should he do with the gun? He could leave it, but all his instincts were against that. Equally, to hide it anywhere in the neighborhood might indicate that whoever had used it was not far away. Should he take it with him and put it back in the loft? But there would be one hell of a hunt when they found Lukas missing half his head, with a bullet embedded in the opposite wall.

He was pondering this, when he had a shock so terrible that for an instant his heart seemed to circulate above his body and then plunge straight down into his stomach.

"Hello."

The voice was half-familiar, almost mocking. There was no body attached so far as he could see in the dim light. He heard a sort of moan. It was all the air escaping from his lungs.

"Do keep quiet," the voice said. "We didn't reckon on you joining the party. You'd better hand over that nasty thing you've brought with you. It looks dangerous." He tried to speak but couldn't. It was the girl, the girl he had seen that morning.

A deft hand reached out and picked up the gun from the floor and put it behind where she was crouching, clearly visible now, about three feet away. She leaned forward, so he could see her.

"My name is Liz," she whispered. "Liz Carlyle. And you are going to be very quiet, Mr. Haddock. Quieter than you have been so far. Quiet as a mouse, please. Just lie there and watch."

My God. She knew his name. He'd better do what she said. He lay there and watched, trembling slightly with shock.

In the window opposite, a light came on. A figure moved to the curtains, stretched, drew them. The guy was lucky, Haddock reflected. If he'd had the gun, he'd have shot him. Half his mind had come back, but not the half that would have told him he was pretty lucky himself.

It was a signal. Immediately all hell let loose. Beyond the conifer hedge on the other side of the house, a blinding light shone—from his own garden, Haddock realized. The yard below seemed suddenly full of figures. Two men in black, who seemed to have no faces, smashed open the farmhouse door. No problem in recognizing armed policemen. Haddock knew exactly what was going to happen. The two men reappeared half-carrying a struggling figure. They bundled him around the hedge out of Haddock's view, and a car started up and drove off, accelerating.

Every light in the house was on now, plus a light from a generator that had appeared miraculously in the yard. The house was being ransacked from cellar to attic.

Haddock sighed. It seemed the only thing to do. "Who are you?" he asked the girl who was still in the barn.

"Government service."

"You mean MI5?"

"It's you who are going to do the explaining, Mr. Haddock."

A torch shone.

"Where did you get this gun?"

"I had it."

"So I'd thought. You were armed police yourself, weren't you? Is that standard issue?"

"No."

"Well, would you believe?"

Truculence came back to Haddock and washed over him in a warm, familiar wave. He grabbed some of it, like a drowning man grabs water. "Why should I answer your questions? You aren't police. Anyway, you seem to know a lot already. How do you know my name?"

"I know your wife."

"You know my wife?" It didn't make sense.

"And that's the reason we could just be able to deal with this unofficially. You haven't actually done anything, after all. Or we could hand you over. There are plenty of your old pals milling around. Please yourself."

"How do you know Phyllis?"

"Well, she's on our payroll, for one thing. Part-time. She retired when she married you. Or rather, she didn't. Come on down the ladder, and maybe I'll explain."

They were standing now on the cobblestones of the yard. His legs felt so shaky, he nearly fell down.

"Right, then," said the girl. "We have been watching this man for quite some time—on and off, of course. That's where Phyllis came in. That's why you live in your present house. I suppose Phyllis didn't explain that. Know what a 'sleeper' is?"

"Someone that sleeps around?"

"You aren't that dumb, Mr. Haddock. A sleeper is a spy, an intelligence agent, who does nothing till he gets his instructions. Then he acts as required. As sleepers go, Lukas was pretty active. He'd had his instructions and he was carrying them out. Our technique if we find a sleeper is to watch and wait. We learn a lot that way, so long as we are satisfied they aren't dangerous, of course. We may even feed them information, to keep their bosses happy. But we have to keep close to them—it doesn't do to lose sight. So that's how Phyllis got her part-time job. She watched and reported. She was around here with me this morning."

"I know she was here. I found her flip-flop."

"Did you? She must be getting out of practice."

"I thought she was having it off with Lukas."

"You do have rather a habit of jumping to conclusions, don't you, Mr. Haddock? We did think of bringing you into it all. But we decided it might be too much for you—and you do have rather a complicated past."

Haddock rubbed the back of his neck, then spat his chewing gum onto the floor and ground his teeth. He didn't like this girl. She was making him feel stupid, and he suspected she was laughing at him. He'd quite like to hit her but he didn't dare. Nothing else came into his head for a bit. Then he said, "Phyllis. Is she all right?"

"She's fine. You have work to do with her, Mr. Haddock, if the opportunity comes your way. In your own interests, I'd give her a miss for quite some time."

"You mean, I don't call her, she calls me?"

"Yes and no."

"Oh, hell. Can I go now?"

"Yes and no. Don't call us. We'll call you."

He went. They found him in the morning in the plantation. He was fast asleep with his head on his golf bag, snoring.

YOU KNOW WHAT'S GOING ON

Olen Steinhauer

PAUL

WHAT TROUBLED HIM most was that he was afraid to die. Paul believed, though he had no evidence of it, that other spies did not suffer from this. But evidence holds little sway over belief, and so it was for him.

He thought of Sam. The last time they'd spoken had been in Geneva, in the international lounge before Sam's flight back here to Kenya. Years before, they had trained together, and while Paul had done better than Sam on the written tests, it was on the course that Sam had shown himself superior. Later, when he heard rumors that Sam was plagued by suicidal tendencies, he understood. Those unafraid of death usually were better on the course.

But the visit was a surprise. After Rome, the only way he'd expected to hear from Sam was via a disciplinary cable or at the head of a Langley tribunal. But Sam's unexpected invitation to the Aéroport International de Genève had included no threats or reprimands.

"You're just following," Sam told him in the airport. "You're the money, a banker; I'm the deal maker. I'll use my Wallis papers—remember that. You won't have to say a thing, and they'll want to keep you well so you can take care of the transfer. It's a walk in the park." When Paul, wondering if any operation in Africa could legitimately be called a walk in the park, didn't answer, Sam raised his right index finger and added, "Besides, I'll be right there beside you. Nothing works without this fingerprint."

The target was Aslim Taslam, a six-month-old Somali splinter group formed after an ideological dispute within Al-Shabaab. Over the last month Aslim Taslam had begun an intense drive to raise cash and extend its contacts in preparation for some large-scale action—details unknown. "We're going to nip them in the bud," was the way Sam put it.

Sam had come across them in Rome, just after things had gone to hell—perhaps *because* things had gone to hell. Aslim Taslam was in Italy to establish an alliance with Ansar al-Islam, the very group that he, Paul, Lorenzo, Saïd, and Natalia had been performing surveillance on.

Now, their cover was information. Sam—energetic, perpetual-motion-machine Sam—had contacted Aslim Taslam's Italian envoy with an offer of two million euros for information on the Somali pirates who had been plaguing the Gulf of Aden shipping lanes. Which was why he'd called this rushed meeting in the airport. In three days—on Thursday—Paul would show up in Nairobi as a bank employee. He would carry a small black briefcase, empty. His contact at the hotel would have an identical case containing the special computer. "Once we make the transfer, you board the plane back to Geneva. Simple."

But everything sounded simple from Sam's lips. Rome had sounded simple, too.

"You're still pissed off, aren't you?"

Sam shook his head but avoided Paul's eyes, peering past him at the pretty cashier they'd bought the coffee from. He'd just returned from a working vacation in Kenya, a cross-country race that had left a permanent burn on his cheeks. "It's a damned shame, but these things do happen. I've gotten over it, and you should, too. Keep your head in this job."

"But you can't let it go," Paul said, because he could feel the truth of this. Only three weeks had passed since Rome. "Lorenzo and Saïd—they're dead because of me. It's not a small thing. You deserve to hate me."

Sam's smile was tight-lipped. "Consider this a chance to redeem yourself."

It was a tempting thing to be offered a way to wash such dirt off the surface of his soul. "I'm still surprised."

"We're not all cut out for this kind of work, Paul. You never were. But with those losses I've got no choice but to use you. I can't send Natalia down there—a woman wouldn't do. Don't worry. I'll be right there with you."

That was the first and last time Sam had let it be known that he could see Paul's secret soul. After Rome, the evidence of Paul's cowardice had become too glaring for even an old classmate to ignore. Drinking tall caffe lattes in the too-cold terminal, they had smiled at each other the way they had been trained to smile, and Paul had decided that, even if his old friend didn't feel the same way, he certainly hated Sam.

This radical shift in emotions wasn't new. Paul had always been repelled by those who saw him for what he was. In high school, a girlfriend had told him that he was the most desperate person she'd ever known. He would do anything to keep breathing. She'd said this after sex, when they both lay half-naked on her parents' couch, and in her adolescent logic she'd meant it as a compliment. To her, it meant that he was more alive than anyone she'd known. It was why she loved him. Yet once she had said it, Paul's love—authentic and all-encompassing—had begun to fade.

In a way, Paul felt more affection for the two very dark strangers questioning him now than he did for Sam, because they didn't know him at all. It was twisted, but that was just the way it was.

"Listen to this guy," said the lanky one in the T-shirt and blue jacket, who had introduced himself as Nabil. He spoke as if he'd learned English from Hollywood, which was probably what he'd done. He was speaking to his friend. "He wants us to believe he doesn't even know Sam Wallis."

"I do not believe it," the friend—one of the two men who'd abducted him at gunpoint—said glumly. His English was closer to the formal yet quaintly awkward English of the rest of Kenya, though neither man was Kenyan.

"I might believe it if I was an idiot," Nabil said. "But I'm not."

Though they were probably still within the Nairobi city limits, both these men, as well as the gunman in the hall, were Somali. He suspected that simply being outside their wild fortress of a country, stuck in a largely Christian nation, made these jihadis nervous. From his low wooden chair, Paul raised his head to meet their gazes, then lowered his eyes again because there was no point. The windowless room was hot, a wet hot, and he found himself dreaming of Swiss air-conditioning. He said, "I work for Banque Salève. I don't know Mr. Wallis personally, but I came here at his request. Where is Mr. Wallis?"

"He wants to know where Sam is," said the unnamed one.

"Hmm," Nabil hummed.

Paul had followed Sam to Nairobi that very morning. It was on the long taxi ride down Mombasa Road that he'd received the call from Geneva station that Sam had gone missing. Yesterday, a Kenyan witness had spotted him in the neighborhood of Mathare with his Aslim Taslam contact. A van pulled up beside them, and some men wrestled Sam inside and roared off, leaving the contact behind. That hadn't helped his upset stomach, nor had the black Mercedes following him from the airport all the way to the hotel.

There were rumors that Aslim Taslam, in an effort to collect money as quickly as possible, had entered the black-market organ trade. Occasional victims appeared with slices in their lower backs or opened chest cavities, missing vital parts.

But not even in his secret soul did Paul fear this. He could live with fewer hands, with half his kidneys or one less lung. He would never wander willingly into that world of pain, but he didn't fear it with the intensity that he feared the actual end point.

For most people it was the reverse: They feared pain but not death. Paul could not understand this. When a film ends, the viewer can replay it in his head for the rest of his life. But each person is the sole witness to his own life, and when that witness dies, no memory of the viewing remains. Death works backward; it eats up the past, so that even that sweat-stained couch on which he'd stopped loving his girlfriend would cease to exist.

Paul said, "I'm not going to pretend I'm not scared. You've locked that door, and I saw the gun the man outside is wearing. I can only tell you what I know. I work for Banque Salève, and Mr. Wallis asked me to fly here to perform an account transfer."

The unnamed one, who had earlier used his fists on Paul's back, spoke quickly in Arabic, and Nabil said, "All right, then. Let's do the transfer."

"I'll need Mr. Wallis's authorization. Where is he?"

"I don't think you need Sam."

"You don't understand," Paul said patiently. "The transfer is done with a computer. It's in my hotel room. It has a fingerprint scanner, and we calibrated it to Mr. Wallis's index finger."

"Which hand?"

"Excuse me?"

"The left or the right index finger?"

"The right."

Nabil pursed his lips. He had a young, pretty face made barely masculine by a short beard that reached up to his cheekbones. Paul imagined that he would have had to work particularly hard to be taken seriously in an industry full of battle-scarred compatriots. He wondered if, in a final need to prove himself, Nabil would someday end up driving a car full of explosives through a roadblock, or sitting in the pilot's chair of a passenger airplane, praising his god and then holding his breath. Men like Nabil were careless about the only important thing. They were as foolish as Sam.

THERE HAD BEEN a Kenyan contact waiting in his stuffy hotel room. Benjamin Muoki, from the National Security Intelligence Service, was sitting on Paul's bed when he entered, sucking on a brown cigarette that streamed heavily from both ends. After they had exchanged introductory codes, Benjamin said, "This is what happens when you run an operation without proper help."

"Sam got your help, didn't he?"

"This isn't help. I'm giving you a machine, that's all. This is what happens when your people are not completely open with us."

"I don't think we're the only ones keeping secrets," Paul said as he began to unpack his clothes.

"Is that what Washington tells you?"

"Washington doesn't have to tell us anything."

"We get no points for giving you a president?"

"If another Kenyan tells me that I'm going to have a fit."

Benjamin sucked on his cigarette and stared at the floor, where a heavy black briefcase lay. His color was lighter than that of most of his countrymen, his nose long, and Paul found himself wondering about the man's parentage.

"That's the computer?"

Benjamin nodded. "You know the codes?"

Paul tapped his temple. "Right here. As long as the machine works, it should be a cinch. You've tested it?"

The question seemed to make the Kenyan uncomfortable. "Don't worry, it works." He lifted the case onto the bed and opened it up to reveal an inlaid keyboard and screen. "Turn it on here and press this to connect to the bank. Type in the codes, and there you are."

"Where's the fingerprint scanner?"

"The what?"

"For Sam's authorization."

"You'll have to ask him."

Paul wasn't sure if that was supposed to be a joke. "Does it really connect to the bank?"

"How should I know? I'm just the courier." Benjamin closed the briefcase and set it on the floor again. He squinted as if the light were too strong, though the blinds were down. "They picked up Sam yesterday. They suspect him, and so they suspect you. They will be after you."

"They already are," Paul told him. "They followed me from the airport."

That seemed to surprise the Kenyan. "You are very cold about this."

Paul slipped a shirt onto a wooden hotel hanger. "Am I?"

"Were I you, I would be planning my escape from Africa."

Paul didn't bother mentioning that he was here to clean his soul, or that the idea of running had already occurred to him a hundred times; instead, he said, "Leaving's not as easy as it sounds."

"All you must do is ask."

Paul reached for another shirt, waiting for more.

"Listen to me," said Benjamin. "I keep secrets, and so do you. But no matter what Washington tells you or Nairobi tells me, we are in this together. Your friend Sam, he's been captured. He was stupid; he should have asked for my help. There's no need for you to follow in his footsteps. If you show up dead, missing your liver or your heart, then that is a tragedy. The operation is already blown. If you stay, you will die."

Benjamin Muoki made plenty of sense. More than Sam, who placed abstract principles above life itself. Only a man with such a twisted value system could have been able to forgive Paul his failure in Rome. So he agreed. Benjamin whispered a prayer of thanks for Paul's sudden wisdom. They settled on an eight-o'clock extraction, and Benjamin insisted that Paul remain in the hotel until then.

Paul didn't contact Geneva, or Sam's case officer in Rome. They would either agree to eighty-sixing the operation, or they wouldn't, and in that case, he didn't want to be forced to refuse a direct order. There were far better places to die when the time came. Places with air-conditioning. He repacked his bag, left it beside the briefcase computer, and went down to the ground-floor bar. It was there, during his third gin and tonic, that they arrived.

He hadn't been able to see the faces that had followed him from the airport, but he knew that these were the same men. Tall, hard-looking, pitch black. They asked him to come quietly, pressing into his back so that he could feel their small pistols. He began to do as they asked, but then remembered the simple equation Benjamin had drawn for him: *If you stay, you will die.*

He swung his arms above his head. They wanted quiet, so he screamed. Hysterically. "I'm being kidnapped! Help!" The bartender froze in the midst of cleaning glasses. Two Chinese businessmen stopped their conversation and stared. The other few customers, all Kenyans, ducked instinctively even before they saw the guns his kidnappers began to wave around as they shouted in Arabic and pulled him out onto the street, into the waiting Mercedes.

They were infuriated by Paul's lack of cooperation. While one drove, the other pushed him down in the backseat and kept punching his kidneys to keep him still. It made Paul think that, if nothing else, they had no plans to take that organ. But all hierarchies are riddled with fools and bad communication, and there was no reason to think that later, in the operating room, the Aslim Taslam surgeon wouldn't recoil at the sight of his bruised and bloody kidneys.

IT WAS COOLER when Nabil finally returned. No one had turned off the blaring white ceiling light during the hours he'd been gone, but Paul suspected it was night. Nabil looked pleased with himself. He said, "You can do what you came here to do."

"And then I can leave?"

"Of course."

"Then let's get to it."

Nabil tugged a black hood from his pants pocket. "We'll take a trip first."

During his long wait, Paul had begun to believe that things were going too easily for him. Though he was still sore from his rough abduction, once he'd arrived in that bare room, no one had laid a finger on him. They had talked tough and hadn't offered him anything to eat or drink, but other than his hunger he was feeling fine.

Nabil walked him hooded through corridors, down a narrow staircase, and outside into the backseat of a car. An unknown voice asked him to lie on his side. He did so. They drove for a long time, taking many turns, and Paul believed they were turning back on themselves in order to confuse his sense of direction. If so, they were successful. Before they finally stopped, they drove up a steep incline noisy with gravel they later crunched over as Nabil walked him into a building.

When the hood was removed, Paul stood facing three men in a long, wood-paneled room that seemed built solely to hold the long dining table that filled it. Two small, barred windows looked out on darkness and the bases of palm trees; this room was half in the earth. Two of them he recognized from the kidnapping; they smoked in the corner, and the one who had earlier helped Nabil with the interrogation even gave him a nod of recognition. The third one, a heavy man, wore a business suit. His name, Paul knew, was Daniel Kwambai.

Sam was the one with the long Kenyan background, not Paul, and so before leaving Switzerland Paul had browsed the Kenya files for background. Daniel Kwambai, the one Kenyan in the room, was a former National Security Intelligence Service officer who, after a falling-out with the Kibaki administration, was suspected to have allied himself with the Somali jihadis just over the border. The reason was simple: money. He was a gambling addict with expensive tastes that he couldn't give up even after washing out of political life. Here, then, was the evidence. Whatever good that did him.

Kwambai held out a hand. "Mr. Fisher, thank you for coming."

Unsure, Paul took it, and Kwambai's shake was so brief that he got the feeling the man was afraid to hold his hand too long. Then he noticed that the computer briefcase wasn't anywhere in the room; there was only a crystal ashtray on the far end of the table, which the kidnappers used. Paul said, "Well, I didn't have much choice. Can we get this over with?"

"First, some questions," said Kwambai. He waved at a chair. "Please."

Paul sat at the head of the table. Behind him, Nabil had withdrawn to the door; the kidnappers remained in their corner, smoking. Daniel Kwambai sat a couple chairs down and wove his fingers together, as if in prayer. He said, "We would like to know some more about Mr. Matheson, the man you know as Wallis. You see, we discovered that he was working for the Central Intelligence Agency. He wanted to purchase something from us, and we think that by this transaction he was going to try and destroy us."

"By giving you two million euros?"

"Yes, it seems unbelievable. But there it is. Nabil here fears trackers."

Paul shook his head. "It's my bank's computer, and it hasn't been out of my sight."

"Except when you left it in your room and went to the hotel bar."

"Well, yes. Except for then."

Kwambai smiled sadly. "Nabil puts his faith in trackers and things he can hold in his hands. I put my faith in the ephemeral. Data, information. No, I don't think there's a tracker on your computer. I think the act of transferring the money is part of the plan."

Uncomfortably, Paul realized that Daniel Kwambai was nearly there. As Sam had explained it, the virtual euros sent to their account were flagged, leaving traces in each account they touched. As Aslim Taslam moved the money among accounts, it left a trail. Tracking it to a final account was unimportant, because within that data flag was a time bomb, a virus that would in two weeks clear the entire contents of that final account, then backtrack, emptying whatever accounts it had passed through. The more accounts it moved through, the more damage it caused.

In the Geneva airport, Sam had said, "I know, I don't understand it either, but it works. Langley tested it out last month on some shell accounts—wiped the fuckers out."

Now, on the outskirts of Nairobi, Paul said, "I wouldn't call myself an expert in these matters—I've only been at the bank two months—but I don't see how that could be done. If the money moves through enough accounts, tracking it becomes impossible." He shook his head convincingly, because that part was the truth—even having Sam explain it to him had made it no easier to understand. "I don't think it could be done."

Kwambai considered that. He rapped his knuckles on the table before standing up. "Yes, I don't see it either. But something else has ruined our transaction. Which is a shame."

"Is it?"

"For you, yes."

The man's tone was all too final. "What about the transfer? I just need Mr. Wallis's—Matheson's—fingerprint."

Behind him, Nabil moved, and Paul heard a thump on the tabletop. A hand. A roughly chopped hand, the severed end black with old, stiff blood. Paul's stomach went bad again.

"As you see," said Kwambai, "we were prepared to do the transfer. But there's one problem. Your computer. It's not in your hotel room."

That cut through his sickness. He stared at the politician, mouth dry. "It has to be."

"Your suitcase, yes, full of clothes—you hadn't even unpacked. But no magical computer."

Despite the old fear slipping up through his guts, Paul went through possibilities. Benjamin had taken it. He had either secured it because he didn't think it would be needed, or he had stolen it for his own reasons.

The hotel staff—but what use would they have for it?

Or Daniel Kwambai was lying. They had the case somewhere and were sweating him. That, or . . .

Or they had found the case, then checked it for one of Nabil's trackers. And found one. Sam had sworn that there would be none, because they were too easy to detect. But . . . Lorenzo and Saïd. Perhaps this was some act of posthumous revenge. Perhaps Sam had cared about life after all.

"I don't believe you," Paul said, because it was the only role left to him. He heard the door behind him open and glanced back full of nerves. Nabil was leaving; the hand was gone. "Where's he going?"

"I'm going, too," said Kwambai. "It hurts me, it really does. Know that." He spoke with the fluid false compassion of a politician.

"Wait!" Paul said as Kwambai began to walk away. The kidnappers, still in their corner, looked up at his outburst. "Tell me what's going on."

Kwambai paused in mid-step. "You know what's going on."

"But, why?"

"Because we all do the best we can do, and this is the best thing for us to do."

The undertow pulled at his feet; the fear in his intestines felt like concrete. Everything seemed to be slowing down, even his desperate reply: "But you don't understand! I don't *work* for the bank. I never did! I work with Sam. I'm CIA, too!"

Kwambai tilted his head and licked his lips, interested. "Sam said you were, but we weren't sure we believed him."

"Sam said what?" Paul blurted, confused. What was going on?

"Thank you for clearing it up," said Kwambai.

"And?"

Kwambai's hand settled on his shoulder. It was heavy and damp. He patted a few times. "And I must go."

"But the money's real," Paul told him. "It's *real*. And I know the codes."

"But there's no computer. The codes are useless."

"Someone has it. As soon as you find it, I can use the codes."

Kwambai stepped back, frowning. He wasn't a man used to doubt. "But who has the computer?"

"Benjamin Muoki. From the NSIS. He's got to have it."

"Benjamin?" Kwambai grinned. "Well, well. Benjamin."

"You go get it. Or I'll get it myself. Then I—"

"Tell me the codes."

"They're," Paul began, then stopped. "I'll type them in."

"We can't risk you typing some emergency signal. Tell me the codes now," said Kwambai. "Please."

Paul looked up at his fleshy face. "If I told you, I'd need some assurance that I'd be safe."

Kwambai blinked at him then, and suddenly began to laugh. It was a deep, room-filling laugh. "Of course, of course." He shook his head. "You didn't think we were going to kill you?"

Paul tried to remember the man's words. No, he hadn't said that Paul was going to die. He'd never said that. Just hint, nuance. Threat. He exhaled loudly, then, closing his eyes, recited the key combination to connect to the bank, the ten-digit number that accessed the accounts section, and then the holding account number.

"There's nothing else?" asked Kwambai, a smile still on his face.

"No. That's all."

"Good." Again, the politician patted his shoulder. "You've been very cooperative. Aslim Taslam will be sure to let your family know."

And he was gone. The logic of that last sentence didn't arrange itself in his head until Daniel Kwambai was closing the door behind himself and the two men were putting out their cigarettes in the crystal ashtray.

Paul began to say more things, but no one was listening. He couldn't see the men's expressions as they approached; fresh tears made details impossible to make out. He remembered Sam saying, *We're not all cut out for this kind of work. You never were.* Then, as the two men neared—one had already taken out his pistol—he realized they hadn't tied him down. He was just sitting there, waiting for death. They hadn't tied him down!

He stood, knocking the chair over, feeling a burst of hope that remained even as he felt the hammer of the first bullet in his chest. He stumbled, tripping backward over the chair. The breath went out of him; he couldn't get it back. His wet arms floundered on the floor as he tried to find a handhold, and even when the two men appeared, looking down on him, his wet hands didn't stop trying to hold on to something, anything. They kept slipping. The two men spoke briefly to their god.

"Don't," Paul managed, thinking of a damp couch and a beautiful girl who could see his secret soul. Then they all disappeared—the couch, the girl, the soul—as if they had never been.

NABIL

THE IMAM REMINDED him of those unnaturally serene Afghans who first taught him the Truth behind the truth. The hairs of his long beard were thick, black wires that paled to white as they traveled down his robe. Around his lips they were stained yellow by hours spent around the communal water pipe.

His Arabic was fattened by his Kurdish accent, but his grammar was beautifully precise. It almost seemed out of place in this tenement building on the outskirts of Rome. "You have brought your offerings to me, young Nabil, and for this I thank the Prophet (praise be upon him). Though few in number, your people seem to me to be a worthy addition to our holy fight. It is not your heart we question here, but your abilities."

Nabil, sitting cross-legged on the rug before him, kept his head low. "We are gathering weapons, Imam. We have communications abilities and the support of three major tribes in Puntland."

"That is good," said the old man. "But what I refer to is the ability of the mind." He smiled and tapped his weathered skull. "How does one discern truth from deception? How does one know the right path from the wrong, or the easy, one? Even the heart softened with love for Allah must be like stone when facing the infidels. The eyes must be clear."

Nabil wanted to have an answer ready but didn't. He was a fisherman's son. He had no special qualifications beyond the fact that he loved his faith and had learned to speak English like a native. So he waited.

After a moment of silence, the Imam said, "Young Nabil knows when to hold his tongue, which is not only a virtue but a sign of wisdom." He looked at the other men in the room, the young Kurds who now lived as his Roman bodyguards. By this look he seemed to be requesting their input, but they gave none. "And I believe you came to us via our mutual friend, Mr. Daniel Kwambai?"

"We've known him for some time. He is sometimes of use."

"Yes," the Imam said, pausing significantly. "But do not confuse use with friendship."

"We endeavor to know the difference, Imam."

"Those who can help are welcome, but those whose help takes too much from us, those should be dealt with harshly."

Again Nabil nodded but could find no words.

The Imam leaned back and patted his knees. "Let us agree first of all that one does not give one's hand without first knowing the other hand intimately. So it shall be here. We will come to you, young Nabil. You may or may not recognize us—that is of no concern. You should act as you believe correct. That is all we ask. Once we have observed your sense of right, we will come to our decision. Does that strike you as satisfactory?"

"It strikes me as a blessing, Imam," Nabil said, though his chest tightened. How much longer would this go on? He'd brought the money Ansar al-Islam had demanded, had given them a layout of the entire organization, and had even let them keep one of his men. Yet here he was, still feeling very much like the darkest man in the room.

"You are very patient for a man of your age," the Imam told him, as if he could read his thoughts. "This does not go unnoticed." He folded his hands together in his lap. "There is something you can do for us today, in fact. Something that would move things along more quickly."

"However I may be of service," said Nabil.

A smile. A nod. "Downstairs, in the basement of this very building, are two men. They became our guests only yesterday. Through questioning we have learned that they work for the

Americans. One is an Italian, while the other is more despicable because he is not even European. He is Moroccan. A foul, homosexual Moroccan, in fact. What they attempted to do to Ansar al-Islam is not important; it is only important that they failed. I would consider it a great kindness if you would kill them for us."

One of the guards, sensing his cue, stepped forward. He held a long cardboard box, the kind used for long-stemmed flowers, and opened it on the floor in front of Nabil. Inside was a rather beautiful sword.

FOUR DAYS LATER, on Sunday, after he'd finished his Dhuhr prayer and was packing to return to the continent he understood, where when you left you could say exactly what you had accomplished, the American knocked on his hotel room door. He found a light-haired but dark-eyed man in the spy hole who said, "Signore Nabil Abdullah Bahdoon?"

"Sì?"

The man peered up and down the corridor, then lowered his voice and spoke in English. "My name is Sam Wallis. I'm here with a business offer. May I come in?"

Though his impulse was to send the man away, he remembered, *We will come to you, young Nabil,* and opened the door.

Once inside, Sam Wallis was surprisingly—perhaps even refreshingly—straightforward. He wanted information on the pirates. He represented some companies interested in securing their shipping lanes through the Gulf of Aden. "I don't know what your rank is," Sam told him, "but I'll lay odds that the money I can give you will move you upward."

"Upward?"

"In your organization."

Nabil frowned. "What do you think my organization is?"

"Does it matter?" Sam said, flopping his hands in an expression of nonchalance. "There's always some position above our heads that we'd prefer to fill."

"You think like an American."

"I think like a human being."

Despite his pretty face, Nabil was a man of broad experience. He'd trained for three months in the mountains of Afghanistan, then spent a harrowing six months in Iraq on the front lines; then, once his worth was proven, he helped plan pinpoint strikes. Despite what Paul Fisher would later think, Nabil had not had to prove himself to his fellow fighters for years, and it was because of this respect that he would never find himself driving a truck or a speedboat laden with high explosives. He was too valuable to be wasted like that.

It was why he had been chosen to be Aslim Taslam's envoy to Ansar al-Islam's Roman cell. His comrades knew that he would think through each detail and come to the correct conclusions.

So when Sam Wallis offered a half million euros for intelligence on the pirates—a sum that Aslim Taslam needed desperately to further its plans—he did not answer immediately. He stepped back from the immediate situation and tried to see it from the outside.

You may or may not recognize us—that is of no concern. You should act as you believe correct.

Could this relaxed American be a messenger—witting or unwitting—from the Imam? Might this be the initial stage of the test? He pulled the blinds in the room, turned on the overhead lamp, and examined the American's dark eyes. Refusing money from an infidel was a morally unambiguous way of dealing with the situation. But perhaps too simple for the Imam. Too simple to assist the jihad.

If the money was real, then it could buy weapons. Using the infidels' technology and finances against them was a historically proven method of jihad. As for the information on the pirates, it could easily be manufactured, though there was no love lost between Aslim Taslam and those drunken thugs of the high seas.

"If you're serious," Nabil told him, "come to Africa and we'll discuss it further. Mogadishu."

Sam Wallis shook his head. "I'm not going anywhere near Mogadishu. I'm paid well, but not that well. Next week I'll be in Kenya for the Kajiado Cross-Country Rally. Can we meet in Nairobi?"

NABIL WAS CAREFUL not to keep this a secret. He was thinking in layers now. If he kept the American a secret from his comrades, it would look to Ansar al-Islam's observers—who he had to assume were everywhere—that he was either planning to keep the American's money himself or hiding him because he was going to sell real information. Neither of these were true, and in a small house east of Botiala he sat with his five most trusted men and talked them through it.

All five of these tall, dark men were from his village, and in another world they would have remained fishermen like their fathers. But in this world the fish started to disappear from the gulf, their sleek bodies absorbed by the big trawlers from Yemen and Saudi Arabia and Egypt. They watched as the other young fishermen, many of them friends, learned that taking to the seas with speedboats and weapons, full of liquor and marijuana, could bring in more money than fishing ever had. They blew their money on satellite televisions and four-by-fours they sped up and down the coastline, sometimes running over children on the way. Nabil and his friends watched, remembering what the visitors from Afghanistan had taught them.

There were no fish left, and piracy was despicable to them. But there was a third way. A better way.

When he told them of the American, they pulled back visibly, so he took them through his line of reasoning. While the pirates were not their friends, giving them up was not an option. So they would fabricate the information. Transit routes, bank accounts, hierarchies. "And if it looks as if the American is going to cheat us, we will kill him."

"But what of the Imam?" asked Ghedi, looking for unambiguously good news.

That he suspected the American had been sent by the Imam was too much for them to absorb, so he only said, "He wants to teach us patience."

He returned to Kenya by one of the softer land routes, and on Saturday, before the start of the cross-country rally, he entered Sam Wallis's InterContinental room with a look of pain on his face. "I'm sorry, I cannot risk it. It's an impressive amount of money, but in my region of Somalia if you become an enemy of the pirates, your life is no longer worth anything."

Sam settled on the end of his bed and considered the problem. "It's one reason I came to you, you know. Your group separated from Al-Shabaab because of their cooperation with the pirates. I thought you'd have the balls to stand up to them."

"You think you know a lot about me, Mr. Wallis."

"My employers think they do."

"We may not like the pirates, but we still have to live in their country."

"You needn't stay in Somalia."

"It's our home."

Clearly, this argument carried no weight with the American, but he accepted it as the logic of primitive peoples. "I shouldn't tell you this," he said after some thought, "but my bosses say I can go up to two million euros. So I'll do that. The offer is now two million."

It was as Nabil had suspected. No opening offer is a final one, and now he had quadrupled Aslim Taslam's income. "How will you pay it?"

"Account transfer. I can get one of the bank employees to come to Nairobi to take care of it."

"We would prefer diamonds."

"We'd all prefer diamonds, but I'm limited by what my employers are willing to do."

"How quickly can it be prepared?"

Sam considered this. "The race ends next Sunday, then I'll go to Switzerland to set everything up. I can be back the following Wednesday. I'd guess that the banker could make it by Thursday. Will that work?"

BEFORE RETURNING HOME, Nabil set up a meeting with Daniel Kwambai, the man who had originally connected him to Ansar al-Islam. For the appropriate fees, Kwambai had been useful to Aslim Taslam, as well as to Al-Shabaab before Nabil and his comrades left.

They had met face-to-face a few times before, but this was Nabil's first visit to one of Kwambai's houses, a four-bedroom in the low hills north of the Karura Forest. In the comfort of his own house, fat Kwambai chain-smoked and sipped whiskey as if it were water. His house was full of representational art that made a mockery of Creation. It was an unnerving place to be.

While he gave Kwambai the layout of the situation, he was careful to avoid actual names, which didn't trouble the politician. "You'll need a secure place for a transaction," Kwambai told him. "And the money—you can't just send it directly to your account. I'll have to move it around some."

"Through your accounts?"

Kwambai shrugged, pulling at his fat lower lip. "I do have some accounts already set up. They've served the purpose before. I can put them at your disposal."

Nabil had the feeling that Kwambai had been waiting for him, the accounts ready. He reminded himself that Kwambai was a politician, and as such had been thinking in layers since childhood. He was a man to watch carefully.

Kwambai was also nearly bankrupt. With his fall from political grace he'd lost the bribes that had kept his lifestyle and three large houses in operation. Debt was a wonderful motivator. "I suppose you'll ask for a commission," Nabil said.

"What's this attitude?" Kwambai said, waving his empty glass. "I've helped your people for a long time now. Of course I'll need some money—there are bank charges, after all—but without my help you'd have nothing. Remember that."

Nabil acceded that this was true enough. "How about this place?" he asked, looking around at all the decadence.

"What?"

"This house, for the transfer. I see there's a basement. We can bring the banker here blindfolded and take him away likewise."

Kwambai seemed troubled by the idea, which Nabil had expected. Though he had an attic apartment over in Ngara West he could use initially, he wanted to give the politician a reason beyond money to keep security tight.

"We would of course pay you for the trouble," Nabil insisted.

He returned to Somalia and filled in his comrades on the developments. He asked Ghedi and Dalmar to come back with him for the final stage, and after a week, as they settled on their path back through the border, Kwambai called in a panic. "It's off, Nabil. We're not doing this."

"Explain yourself."

"Sam Wallis? One of my friends in the NSIS knows him. It's the work name of Sam Matheson. Of the CIA."

The question posed itself again: Was this a test? It didn't look like one, but the Imam, he knew, plotted in the labyrinthine way he interpreted the Koran. His reach was long, and his thoughts were deep. Might he have knowingly sent an American agent to perform the examination?

But this was what happened when you began thinking in layers: It was addictive. There was always another layer to be discovered, another truth to be found. He said, "I never told you his name."

"Don't be petty, Nabil. You should be pleased I caught this early."

With a smoothness that surprised even himself, Nabil said, "I was already aware of this."

Stunned silence. "You were?"

"Of course. It wasn't important for you to know."

"Not important? Are you mad? Of course it's important! I'm not bringing a CIA agent into my house."

"He's not going anywhere near your house," Nabil said, not knowing if this was true or not. "Only the banker."

It seemed to calm him some. "But still. This isn't what I was expecting."

"If that's how you feel, Mr. Kwambai, then we can double your fee."

Silence again, but there was nothing stunned about it. It was the silence of mental calculations.

"That's my offer," Nabil said, feeling very sure of himself, more sure than he had in a long time. "If you're not interested, I'll take my business elsewhere. We'll know not to approach you again."

"Let's not be rash," said Kwambai.

ON WEDNESDAY HE again found Sam Matheson in his room at the InterContinental. There were heavy rings beneath his eyes, sunburn across his forehead and cheeks, and Nabil wondered if the cross-country race had taken a serious toll on him. He'd verified that a man named Sam Wallis had registered, and that his car had come in eleventh among thirty-eight participants. According to the records, he'd originally signed on with a partner, one Saïd Mourit, but Mourit had been dropped before the race began.

He gave no sign that he knew Matheson's real name, only suggested that they continue their conversation in the street.

"Too claustrophobic?" asked Sam.

"Exactly."

In the nearby city market, they walked on packed earth

among the crowds and vendors hiding under umbrellas. Nabil quietly said, "Mr. Matheson, I know who you work for."

To his credit, the American didn't slow his step. Above, the blazing sun made his sunburn look all the worse. A nonchalant grin remained plastered to his face, and he shrugged. "Who do I work for?"

"The CIA."

"My assumption was that if I'd told you, you wouldn't have accepted the deal."

"You were right."

Beside a table piled high with overpriced fabrics, he turned to face Nabil. He was a few inches shorter, but the confidence in his movements made him seem taller than he was. "The offer's the same, Nabil. Those pirates are a public menace. They're screwing with business. We're getting pressured from all sides to get any kind of intel we can."

"Even from people like us?"

Sam waved that off. "Your group's new. No one knows about you. In a few years, maybe we'll pay the pirates for intel on you. It all depends on what our masters ask for."

"This is something we have in common," Nabil said as he gazed at the intelligence agent who had suddenly opened himself up in a way that he would never have done. It was almost suicidal. What he'd expected was a denial, and then a quick withdrawal. Perhaps even this had been calculated by Rome.

Or perhaps, he thought suddenly, Ansar al-Islam had nothing to do with this, and it was precisely how the American presented it. The CIA just wanted some information.

It was time to make a decision.

"And this man from the bank who's coming tomorrow?" he asked. "What is he?"

The smile faded from the American's lips before returning. It was a momentary lapse—less than a second—but Nabil didn't forget it. Sam said, "His name's Paul Fisher. Yes, he's an agent, too. But the money is real. After he's finished the transfer you can do what you like to him."

"You want us to kill your colleague?"

"I didn't say that," Sam corrected. "It's up to you. Consider it a gift. If you like, you can claim responsibility, and he'll be your first public execution."

"A videotaped beheading. Is that what you imagine?"

"It's not like you haven't done it before."

That was unexpected. "Have I?"

Sam Matheson licked his lips—nervousness . . . or appetite? "As I say, it's up to you."

It was only then that Nabil knew what to do. This man, whether or not he was from the CIA, had been sent by the Imam. Like the blinding sunlight pouring down on them, the realization fell upon him, and he knew. He was to kill a man named Paul Fisher. That was the Imam's desire. Why? Matheson was little help on this; perhaps he didn't know.

"He's become a liability. We don't need him anymore."

Nabil turned toward Koinange Street, began walking, and reached into his pocket. He took out a pair of mirrored sunglasses and slipped them on, signaling Ghedi and Dalmar. "It's a remarkable gift. First, money, and then one of your own. I just wonder why the CIA would give him to us. It's not as if you couldn't get rid of him yourself."

"Despite what people say, the CIA prefers not to kill its own employees."

"You're very wicked, Sam."

Sam Matheson didn't answer. He seemed to consider the statement as they reached the street, and the van drew up, its large door sliding open. Ghedi and Dalmar jumped out and grabbed Matheson by the biceps and flung him inside. Nabil watched the door close again and the van jerk forward and swerve away. He watched it disappear into the afternoon traffic.

As he walked back to his car, he rummaged through his

pocket and came up with a pack of Winstons. He lit one and inhaled deeply. It was the first one he'd had in three days; he was doing well.

When you're being watched, all your actions, however small, take on a presence of their own—each has its own significance and its own variety of interpretations. You light a cigarette, and that might mean that you're nervous, you're relaxed, you've been co-opted by Western forms of decadence, or that you're desperately stopping time in order to invent your next lie.

He had to stop thinking this way. If Ansar al-Islam was watching, the only important detail was the taking of Sam Matheson. They would know that Aslim Taslam left hesitation to those with less faith.

NABIL TOOK SAM Matheson's dry, surprisingly heavy hand from the table and dropped it back into the crumpled plastic bag, then slipped the bag into the pocket of his jacket as Kwambai fed Paul Fisher the lie: "Your suitcase, yes, full of clothes—you hadn't even unpacked. But no magical computer."

Nabil disagreed with this tactic, but Kwambai had been living with the doublespeak of politics for too long. He no longer knew how to be straight, and now he'd gone over the deep end. Yesterday's evidence had been irrefutable. Nabil had returned from the market, having stopped at a mosque along the way to offer his Asr prayer. After Sam Matheson, he'd felt the need for some community. He'd driven up the hill to find Ghedi in the driveway, looking distraught. "He killed him," Ghedi said. "Kwambai killed the American."

Kwambai explained himself as they stood over Sam Matheson's corpse in the basement. "He saw me. Your men brought him through the living room without a hood and he *saw* me. I couldn't let him live."

Kwambai had put two bullets in Sam's chest and one through his neck; sticky blood covered the floor, and the flies had already begun to swarm. Standing over him, the politician began to tremble all over. It was probably the first man he'd ever killed with his own hand. Kwambai said, "His fingerprints. He said we'll need them for the computer."

"Why did he say that?"

"He thought it would save his life."

"So you had a conversation first?"

The politician seemed to have run out of words, so Nabil asked Ghedi and Dalmar to remove the American's hands while he took Kwambai outside and they looked for a spot to bury him among the low, dry trees in his backyard. Together, they dug a deep hole. Nabil stopped once, asked where east was, and kneeled in the dirt to offer his Maghrib prayer, while Kwambai ran into the house for more drink. By the time they finished, it was dark. All four men carried the body to the hole, and then Ghedi and Dalmar were given the unenviable task of cleaning the basement room.

Over those later hours, as they filled the hole and stumbled back to the house, Kwambai's drunkenness faded and was replaced by a strange giddiness. He talked about the act he'd committed, the feel of the pistol, the kick of the bullet as it left the chamber, the American's stunned eyes that slowly lost their sheen. He described these things as a man describes his first time with a woman, with the pleasure of a wonderful thing newly discovered.

The old politician had become a murderer, and he had enjoyed it.

Afterward, the dynamic changed. Kwambai wanted nothing more than to be at the forefront of their operation. He quit mentioning money, only asked endless questions and offered suggestions for improvement, and when they brought in Paul Fisher, he was waiting in the basement to stare directly into his eyes. He no longer cared who saw him, because he wanted to kill this one, too. Nabil had lost control of the operation.

And now Kwambai was twisting the interrogation with his

doublespeak and lies. The computer was sitting upstairs on the long oak table, awaiting the codes and the fingerprint. All he had to do was ask Fisher to type in the code, and they would all be two million euros richer. But Kwambai wanted to stretch this out, wanted to torture the American, and Nabil had no interest in watching it.

So when Paul Fisher said, "I don't believe you," Nabil gave a quick but crucial signal to Dalmar and Ghedi, walked out, and climbed the stairs to the living room.

During the weeks since that bloody basement in Rome, he'd grown so tired of it all. He wondered when the light would begin to shine. People were not dying for the jihad; they were dying for the preparation for the jihad. For the bank accounts and the arms and the escapes from capture. One spent so much time dealing with the moment that the original dream, the one that made him cast away his fishing nets, seemed more distant than ever. How long could this go on?

Even the Imam had asked him afterward if he still had the heart for the fight. For fighting, yes, always. But when you descend into a tenement basement in Rome and find two bruised, broken men tied up, facing a camera on a tripod, and then use a beautiful ceremonial sword to remove their heads, there is no battle rush, no visible battle won. Just a flooded floor, your body soaked in blood and sweat, and the ache in your arms from hacking with a blade better suited to adorning a wall.

Daniel Kwambai's woody house was full of European furniture mixed with Kenyan folk kitsch. It was as uncomfortable as Kwambai himself. Nabil settled at the long table beneath an iron chandelier and opened the briefcase, running his fingers lightly over the keyboard and the flat screen, the things that offered entrance to a Swiss bank's deepest secrets.

It was all still so strange to him. For a fisherman's son, none of this could ever feel comfortable. The computer. The narrow, Vespa-buzzing streets of Rome and the cacophony of Nairobi's taxi horns. The wily, now quite mad, political animal that was Daniel Kwambai. He felt more comfortable with those drunk ex-fishermen the world called pirates.

He heard Kwambai climbing the steps slowly as the muted gunshots filled the house. The fat man paused, looked back, then continued. By the time he reached the end of the table Ghedi and Dalmar had finished. It could happen so quickly.

"I thought they would wait," Kwambai said.

"I told them to do it as soon as you'd left the room. He'd been tortured enough."

"Torture?" Kwambai shook his head. "Perhaps you would have given him all the facts up front, Nabil? We now know that Benjamin Muoki is working with them, but that's all we're going to get because you don't want the poor American feeling distraught."

Nabil shrugged.

"And what if the codes are fake?"

"I've considered that," Nabil said, because he had. If they lost two million euros, then so be it. He wasn't going to give this monster another happy murder.

Kwambai turned the computer around, closer to himself, and sat down. "Well, it's reckless, and with this much money you can't afford to be reckless. You know what's going on here; you have to *think*. That's what Rome expects of you. It's what I expect of you."

It was remarkable, really, how Kwambai was acting as if Aslim Taslam were his own fiefdom. But the politician was wrong. Nabil had been thinking for weeks. He'd been noting Kwambai's own reckless moves and raising each one to the light to see it better, pairing them up randomly to find connections. But only now, hearing his command to *think*, did a single thread of logic form to connect all the disparate clues. It was so perfectly simple that his hands became warm from embarrassment. He'd been thinking in the wrong direction.

Do not confuse use with friendship.

"The hand?" said Kwambai. A pause. "What is it, Nabil?"

Nabil blinked but still couldn't see the old man well. He rooted around his jacket pocket and came up with the hand. He dropped it on the table.

Those who can help are welcome, but those whose help takes too much from us, those should be dealt with harshly.

He heard the crackle of plastic as Kwambai took it out. "This had better work," he heard the Kenyan say. "This thing is foul. You smell it?"

"Disgusting," Nabil muttered as Kwambai powered up the computer.

"Where the hell am I supposed to scan the fingerprint?"

"Perhaps the Americans lied to you, Daniel."

An awkward pause. "Perhaps."

From downstairs came the sound of Ghedi and Dalmar grunting, moving Paul Fisher's body around. Bodies everywhere. Yet here Nabil was, planning on one more, as soon as the money had been transferred.

SAM

"THEY'RE INSIDE," NATALIA chirped through the radio in his ear.

Sam leaned toward the apartment's high window, careful not to touch the tripod and shotgun mike, and gazed across Via del Corso at the mosque, the sound of car horns and buzzing Vespas rising through the heat to him. Ticklish sweat rolled down his back. From her position at an outdoor café, Natalia had a clear view of the entrance, while Sam could see only the upper window to the room where Saïd and Lorenzo would be taken once they'd introduced themselves to the Imam.

It was a tricky operation, enough so that a week ago, sweating in his temporary Repubblica apartment near the station, he'd suggested that Saïd leave town. The Moroccan had gotten up on his elbow, the light playing over his long olive body, and stared, a flash of anger in his thick brows. "You think I can't do this?"

"Of course you can."

"I've built up all the contacts. It's taken months. You know that."

"I know. I'm just . . ."

"We shouldn't have gotten involved."

It was true, perhaps. But by now Sam couldn't quite imagine what life would look like without Saïd in it. "Too late," he said, watching his lover's fleshy lips. "You want me to hide what I'm feeling?"

The Moroccan smiled. "It's what we do. We should be good at it." Seeing that the joke hadn't played well, Saïd kissed him and said officiously, "Plenty of time, young man. We're still on for the rally?"

"Absolutely."

"You and me under the Kenyan stars again. We'll have plenty of time to figure out our future."

Which, Sam noted with satisfaction, was the first time Saïd had used that blessed word, *future*.

So he'd gone over the operation a hundred times more, adjusting details here and there and even bringing in an extra agent to provide coverage inside. Paul Fisher, from Geneva.

"Paul," he said from his window perch. "You're there?"

"Sì," came the whisper.

"Everything's smooth. Just keep doing what you're doing."

Though they'd known each other in the academy, it was a surprise to see Paul again. He was the most visibly nervous agent he'd ever dealt with. Sam even called Geneva to make sure that this was a man he could depend on. "Fisher's top-notch for his age," was the reply, which told him nothing.

While briefing Paul in his apartment, though, Sam had discovered a small P-83, a Polish gun, in Paul's jacket. "Where'd this come from?"

"A Milanese I know."

"Why?"

Paul shrugged. "I like backup."

"Not on this job," he said and put the gun in his desk drawer. "I'm not having you get them killed."

Paul had been sitting at the foot of the bed where Sam had last made love to Saïd. He hated this fidgety man touching those sheets. Paul said, "I wasn't planning on using it."

"Then you don't need to carry it."

Paul nodded unsurely.

While it had taken weeks to set up and could go wrong easily, the operation itself was simple. Lorenzo and Saïd were to visit the mosque and sit down with the Imam in his study to discuss a Camorra arms shipment they had intercepted and wished to sell to like-minded people. From his post across the street, Sam would record the conversation. Natalia would watch the street for activity or reinforcements. Paul was to wait in the prayer hall to help facilitate any emergency escape.

It took them a while to reach the Imam's study. A body search would be de rigueur, as would an electronics sweep. In the far window, a light came on. A young man in a white skullcap pulled the thin curtains shut. Sam held one side of the headphones to his free ear, checked the levels against some language, perhaps Kurdish, being spoken in the room, and began to record.

A total of seventeen minutes passed before their arrival in the Imam's chamber. During that time Sam talked briefly with Natalia and listened to Paul mouthing the late-afternoon Asr prayer with the congregation. Then a door opened in the room, and the Imam greeted Saïd and Lorenzo in Arabic. For the benefit of Lorenzo, they switched to Italian. The proposal was on.

In his other ear, Paul whispered, "There's some activity."

"Problem?"

"Three guys breaking off prayer. Talking."

"It's nothing."

"They're going to the stairs."

"How do they look?"

"Not happy."

Sam felt the old tension rising in his chest. The conversation with the Imam was going well. They had moved on to the makes of the weapons.

Paul said, "They're gone."

"Stay there," Sam ordered.

"*Shit.*"

"What?"

"Another one. He's looking at me."

"Because you're not praying. Now pray."

"That's not it."

"Ignore him and pray."

Silence, just the throb of voices speaking to their god.

"Natalia?"

"All clear."

In his right ear, the Imam mentioned a price. As planned, Lorenzo was trying to raise it. A knock on the Imam's door stopped him. Someone came in. Arabic was spoken. Sam's grasp of the language was sketchy, but he knew enough to understand that they were discussing a suspicious worshipper in the prayer hall. According to the visitor, it was clear from the bulge in his pocket that he was carrying a pistol.

"You fucker," Sam said. "You brought your gun."

No reply.

"Stand up and walk out of there before you get them killed."

No reply.

"You better be walking."

No reply, just the sound of movement, a grunt, and then a single gunshot that thumped into Sam's eardrum. A pause, then

Paul's wavering voice through the whine of his damaged left ear: *"Shit."* On the right, the Imam's room had gone silent. Lorenzo said, "What was that?" Movement.

Saïd: "What're you doing?"

The Imam, in Arabic: "Get them out."

More movement. Struggling.

Natalia: "Paul's out. He's running. Should I chase?"

A door in the Imam's quarters slammed shut.

"Sam? What do I do?"

IT WASN'T UNTIL Thursday afternoon, two days later and a couple hours after he'd gotten the news, that he tracked Paul Fisher to a bar near the Colosseum, hunched in the back with a nearly empty bottle of red wine. Sam waited near the front, observing the shivering wreck of a man who was too drunk to see him. Behind Sam, two Italian men slapped on a poker machine, shouting at it, and he reconsidered the one thing he'd felt sure he would do once he found Paul Fisher.

Though both had made a game of hiding their true feelings, he and Saïd had known from the start, when they were going about their various embassy duties in Nairobi, that they had found something unprecedented. Both had a broad enough sexual history—Sam in the Bay Area meat markets, where you could be as open as you were moved to be, Saïd in the underground discos of Casablanca—but from their second night together they'd opened up more than they had with anyone else before. Perhaps, Saïd had suggested, they were like this because they knew that Sam was leaving for Rome in a month. Perhaps. But six months later, in Rome, Sam's phone rang. Saïd had wrangled a transfer and convinced his superiors that he should offer help to the Americans.

"This is a bed of liars," Saïd liked to say during their secret liaisons in what they started to call their Roman summer. But then he used that fantastical word, *future*, and Sam pounced on him with joyous descriptions of the Castro. Saïd was entranced, though he offered a countersuggestion: Rio de Janeiro.

"Too hot," Sam told him.

"Northern California is too cold."

Now, listening to the angry Italians and *blip-bleep* of the poker machine, Sam wondered what would have happened. Might they have bought a place in some high-rise along the Rio beaches? Or had their optimism been a symptom of the Roman summer, and in the end things would have gone the way of all his previous relationships—nowhere? There was no way to know. Not anymore.

Because of this drunk man in the corner.

Kill Paul Fisher? Sam wasn't that kind of agent—he'd never actually committed murder, and until now he'd never wanted to. Yet as he approached the table he thought how easy it would be, how satisfying. Revenge, sure, but he began to think that Paul Fisher's death would be something good for the environment, the subtraction of an unwholesome element from the surface of the planet.

Terrified—that was how Paul looked when he finally recognized him. Drunk and terrified. Sam sat down and said, "We heard from the carabinieri. Two bodies, minus their heads, were found in the Malagrotta landfill."

Paul's wet mouth worked the air for nearly half a minute. "Do they know?"

"Yes, it's them. They'll turn up the heads eventually."

"Jesus." His forehead sank to the dirty table, and he muttered something indecipherable into his lap.

"Tell me what happened," said Sam.

Paul raised his head, confused, as if the answer were obvious. "I *panicked*."

"Where'd you get the gun?"

"I always have a spare."

"This one?" Sam said as he reached into his jacket and took

out the Beretta Natalia had given him. He placed it on the table in front of himself so that no one behind them could see it.

"*Jesus,*" Paul repeated. "Are you going to use that?"

"You dropped it when you ran off. Natalia found it."

"Right . . ."

"Take it back and get rid of it."

Paul hesitated, then reached out, knocking the wine bottle into a totter. He yanked the pistol into his stomach and held it under the table.

"I unloaded it," Sam told him, "so don't bother trying to shoot yourself."

The sweat on Paul's forehead collected and drained down his temple. "What's going to happen?"

"To you?"

"Sure. But all of it. The operation."

"The operation's dead, Paul. I haven't decided about you yet."

"I should get back to Geneva."

"Yeah. You should probably do that," Sam said, and stood. No, he wasn't going to kill Paul Fisher. At least not here, not now.

He left the bar and took a taxi to the Porta Pinciana and walked down narrow Via Sardegna past storefronts and cafés to the embassy. As he unloaded his change and keys and phone for the doormen, Randall Kirscher came marching up the corridor. "Where the hell have you been, Sam?" Though there was panic in his case officer's voice, nothing was explained as they took the stairs up to his third-floor office. Inside, two unknown men, one wearing rubber gloves, stood around a cardboard box lined with plastic that folded out of the top. Though he knew better, Sam stepped forward and looked inside.

"Sent with a fucking *courier* service," muttered Randall.

Sam's feet, his stomach, and then his eyes grew warm and bloated. Though the men in the room continued talking, all he could hear was the hum in his left ear, the residue of complete failure.

*   *   *

NO ONE SAW him for three days. Randall Kirscher was inundated by calls demanding Sam's whereabouts—in particular from the Italians, who wanted an explanation for shots fired in a mosque. But he knew nothing. All he knew was that, after seeing Saïd's severed head on Thursday, Sam had walked out of the embassy, leaving even his keys and cell phone with the embassy guards.

The next day the video appeared on the Internet, routed through various servers around the globe. Lorenzo and Saïd on their knees. Behind them hung a black sheet with a bit of white Arabic, and then a hooded man with a ceremonial sword. And so on. Kirscher didn't bother watching the entire thing, only asked Langley to please have their analysts do their magic on it. In reply, they asked for the report Sam hadn't filed. He told them it was on its way.

On Saturday, two days after his disappearance, Kirscher sent two men over to Sant'Onofrio, where Sam's debit card had been used on two cash machines to take out about a thousand dollars' worth of euros. They, however, found no sign of him.

Then on Monday morning, as if the entire embassy hadn't been on alert to find him, he appeared at the gate a little after eight-thirty, dressed in an immaculate suit, and politely asked the guards if they still had the cell phone and keys he'd forgotten last week. Randall called him up to his office and waited for an explanation. All Sam gave him at first were oblique references to "groundwork" he'd been doing on a deal to provide inside intelligence on Somali pirates.

"What?" Randall demanded, hardly believing this.

"I got in touch with one of my Ansar sources. A member of Aslim Taslam was in town, and I approached him about selling us intel. I wasn't about to blow my cover by contacting the embassy before we'd met."

"What was your cover?"

"Representing some businesses."

"Sounds like the Company to me."

Sam didn't seem to get the joke. "I talked with him yesterday. He's loaded with information."

"How'd you verify this?"

Sam blinked in reply.

"And how much did you offer him?"

"A half mil. Euros."

Randall began to laugh. He wasn't being cruel; he just couldn't control himself. "Five hundred grand for a *storyteller*?"

Sam finally settled into a chair and wiped at his nose. What followed was so quiet that Randall had to lean close to hear: "He's the one who cut their heads off."

The clouds parted, and Randall could see it all now. "Absolutely not, Sam. You're taking a vacation."

"His name is Nabil Abdullah Bahdoon. Somali. Not a foot soldier, but one of the heads of Aslim Taslam. They're desperate for cash, and we can use it against him."

"Against them."

Sam frowned.

"Them, not him. We're not into vengeance here. We're not Mossad."

"Then think of it this way," said Sam. "We have a chance to decapitate the group before it gains momentum."

"Decapitate?"

Sam shrugged.

Randall stifled a sigh. "Step back. Once again from the top."

"A bomb," Sam said without hesitation. "In the bank computer. Nabil will want to be on hand to witness the transfer."

"Here in Rome?"

Sam hesitated. "Not settled. Probably not here."

"Somalia?"

"Maybe."

"You're going to take a bomb through customs?"

"I can have it made locally. I have the contacts."

Randall considered the loose outline, flicking over details one after the other. Then he ran into a wall. "Wait a minute. How does this bomb go off?"

"With the transfer code."

"So who's going to perform the transfer?"

Sam coughed into his hand. "Me."

"Again?"

"I'll type in the code."

"You're going to commit suicide."

Sam didn't answer.

"May I ask why?"

"It's personal."

"Personal?" Randall said, shouting despite himself. "I really should advise you to see the counselor."

"You probably should."

Silence followed, and Randall found a pen on his desk to twirl. "It's ridiculous, Sam, and you know it. I know you're upset about what happened to Lorenzo and Saïd, but it wasn't your fault. Hell, it probably wasn't even that idiot Paul Fisher's fault. It just happened, and I'm not going to lose one of our best agents over this. You can see that, can't you?"

Sam's face gave no sign either way.

"Post-traumatic stress disorder. That's what's going on here, you know. It's a sickness."

Sam blinked slowly at him.

"I won't insist on the therapist—not *yet*—but I am insisting on the vacation. Aren't you supposed to go car racing next week?"

"Cross-country rally."

"Good. Write up a report on the fiasco and then take three weeks."

Sam was already on his feet, nodding.

"Keep safe," Randall told him, "and do consider the therapist. Voluntarily. I'll not lose you."

But Sam was already out the door.

*   *   *

THERE HAD BEEN an unexpected storm along the south side of snowcapped Mount Kenya that morning, and so by noon he was soaked with mud, and by late afternoon it had dried to a crust, turning his clothes into a lizard skin of hard scales. But he went on. His empty passenger seat set him apart from most of the Europeans and Americans taking part in the rally, and when asked, he told them his partner had dropped out because of business obligations, an excuse they all understood.

At the end of each day, they drank together in tents set up by their Kenyan hosts. The Italians were loud, the French condescending, the Brits sneering, the Americans annoyingly boisterous. A hive of multinational caricatures bound together by speed and beer, business and tall tales about women they'd had. These things were, he reflected, the lifeblood of Western masculinity.

It was Friday, two days before the end of the race, when through his exhausted eyes and muddy goggles he saw Benjamin Muoki standing among the T-shirted organizers wearing a suit, one hand on his hip, and no expression on his face. In his other hand was a bottle of Tusker lager. Sam pulled up amid the other drivers' shouts and hoots, flipped up his goggles, and nodded at Benjamin, who took the cue and wandered away from the camp. Sam checked his time, rinsed off, and changed into shorts, a blue cotton button-up, and leather sandals from his waterproof bag. By then, Benjamin was a silhouette against a backdrop of fading mountains. Sam had to run to catch up with him.

"Here," Benjamin said, holding out his beer. "You need it more than I do."

They shared the bottle in silence, walking slowly, until Benjamin remembered and said, "You're nearly the last one in."

"The rain does it to me."

"I'll pray for clear skies."

"The sun is even worse."

Having known each other for three years, the men used the

exchange of pass phrases not to recognize each other, but to signal if one or the other was compromised. "But really," said Benjamin, "are you driving well?"

"I'm surviving."

"It's a difficult course."

They paused and looked back at the bustling activity of the
camp. Lights flickered on to hold back the encroaching dark. A
dusty wind came at them, raising little tornadoes, then died
down. "Did you receive the instructions?" Sam asked.

"I'm here, aren't I?"

"I mean the rest of it."

"Yes."

"And?"

"What would you like me to say? That I think it's dangerous?
I've said that about too many of your plans to keep on with it."

"But do you see any obvious flaws?"

"Just that you'll end up dead."

Sam didn't answer; he was too tired to lie convincingly.

Benjamin looked into his face. "A life for a life? It's a lot to pay."

"More than one life, we hope."

"We," Benjamin said quietly. "I had a talk with your fat
attaché. I don't think he knows the first thing about this."

Sam felt his expression betraying too much. "You told him?"

"No, Sam. I felt around some. I'm good at that."

"Good."

"It's not on the books, is it?"

"It's above his clearance," Sam lied, but it was an easy lie.
"The computer finished?"

"By Monday."

"I'll be back next Wednesday."

"So I'll give it to you then."

"Not me. You'll give it to someone else."

A light seemed to go on in Benjamin's always-astute eyes.
"Someone even more foolish than you?"

"I'll let you know. You'll give it to him, but you won't say a thing about it. You're a good enough liar for that, aren't you?"

Benjamin's expression faltered. "This is a very stupid man?"

"A nervous man. Just give him the case. He knows what to do with it."

"He knows he'll die?"

"You're full of questions, Benjamin. We're paying you well enough, aren't we?"

"You have always paid well, Sam."

ON MONDAY, AS he sat across from Paul Fisher in the Aéroport International de Genève, he wondered why he was pushing it so far. Was he pushing it *too* far? He hadn't seen Paul since that bar in Rome, and now that they were face-to-face again the prospect of killing him here, now, seemed much more inviting. Easier. More wholesome.

But he'd begun to fall in love with the balance of his plan. One bomb would take out not only the man indirectly responsible for Saïd's gruesome murder, but also the man who had worked the blade through the muscles and bone. Now it was just a matter of persuasion. So after the invention of the technology that would wash bank accounts clean, he assured Paul that he wouldn't be alone—Sam would be there, right by his side, to authorize the transfer with his index finger. That seemed to calm him. Then he told Paul what they both knew, that he wasn't cut out for this kind of work and never had been. "Consider this a chance to redeem yourself," Sam said, and it felt as if, through lies, he had cut to a deeper truth than he ever could have come upon honestly.

His love of the plan kept him moving forward even when, on Wednesday, Saïd's murderer told him his real name and the name of his employer. Sam had put too much work into the plan to let it fall apart now, so he improvised. He absorbed this discovery into his tale, and even encouraged Nabil to murder Paul. He admitted the issue was personal. It was reckless, yes, but his sense of the rightness and beauty of his plan had made him delirious.

Yet it was too late. He realized his mistake only when they plucked him off the street and drove him out of town to that finely appointed house. Even then, however, he clung to hope. They still wanted the money, and if necessary he would type in the code himself. He would prefer if Paul were beside him to accept the blast as well, but he would make do with what was possible.

What he never expected was the politician sitting with a scotch in the living room, the fat one with the round eyes that stared in horror as he was dragged in. Their eyes met, but neither said a thing. Surprise kept them both mute. His captors dragged him to the basement and locked the door, and Sam settled at the table, thinking through the implications of Daniel Kwambai working with Aslim Taslam.

As if he'd read Sam's mind, some ten minutes later Kwambai opened the door and stepped inside wearing a wrinkled linen jacket stretched on one side by something heavy in the pocket. He closed the door and stared at Sam. "What are you *doing* here?" came his falsetto whisper.

"You're playing both sides, Daniel. Aren't you?"

Kwambai shook his head and took a seat across from him. "Don't judge me, Sam. You're not in a position."

"We don't pay you enough?"

"No one pays enough. You know that. But maybe after this money you're bringing I'll be able to quit playing any sides at all. If the money's legitimate. Is it?"

"Sure it is. Is the information going to be legitimate?"

"They don't tell me much, but no, I don't think so."

Sam feigned disappointment. "You going to help me get out of here, then?"

"Not before the money's transferred."

"And then?"

Kwambai didn't answer. He seemed to be thinking of something, while Sam was thinking about the bulge in Kwambai's pocket.

"Well?"

"I'm considering a lot of things," said Kwambai. "For instance, how you would stand up to Nabil's interrogation."

"No better or worse than most men, probably."

"And I'm wondering what you'd say."

"About you?" Sam shook his head. "I don't think you have to worry about that. If he doesn't follow that line of questioning, there'll be no reason to answer."

A sad smile crossed Kwambai's face. "And if he just asks for a reason to end the pain?"

Sam knew what he was getting at, but things had become confused enough by this point that he couldn't be sure how he wanted to answer. The obvious thing to say was that he'd protect Kwambai's relationship with the Company to his dying breath, but no one would believe that, least of all him. The truth was that he recognized that sad look on the politician's face. It was the same expression Kwambai had given just before accepting that initial deal, a year ago, to make contact with the Somali extremists who'd been doing business in Kenya. The look signified that, while he could hardly admit it to himself, Kwambai had already made up his mind.

So he repeated the lie he had used to encourage the coward Paul Fisher: "You still need me. For the transfer." He raised his hands and tickled the air with his fingers. "My prints."

But nothing changed in Kwambai's face.

"Take it out, then," said Sam.

"What?"

"The gun. Take it out and do what you have to do. I personally don't think you can. Not here in your own house. Not with your own hands. And how would you explain it to Nabil? He wants me. Like you, he wants the money. He—" Sam stopped himself because he recognized that he was rambling. Panic was starting to overcome him.

Dutifully, though, Kwambai removed a revolver from his pocket and placed it on the table, pointing it at Sam much the way Sam had pointed the Beretta at Paul Fisher. Unlike the Beretta, this was an old gun, a World War II model Colt .45. Kwambai's eyes were red around the edges. "I like you, Sam. I really do."

"But not that much."

"No," Kwambai said as he lifted the pistol and shot three times before he could think through what he was doing.

BENJAMIN

BENJAMIN HAD LIVED most of his life making snap decisions and only afterward deciding whether or not they'd been correct. Intuition had been his primary guide. Even the occasional services he performed for the Americans and the Brits had begun that way. So all afternoon, as he tracked down a friend who would be willing to drive Paul Fisher to the border, he had wrestled with it, weighing Fisher's life against the comforts of his family. If the Americans cut him off, George would probably not get to football camp this year; Elinah's confirmation party would be more modest than planned; and Murugi, his long-suffering yet intractable wife, would start questioning the shift in the monthly budget. Was one stranger's life worth it?

It wasn't until the trip back to the hotel in his friend's Toyota pickup that he really convinced himself that he'd done right. We're all employed by someone, he told himself philosophically, but in the end it's self-employment that motivates us. The sentence charmed him, provoking a mysterious, proud smile on his lips, and that only made it more disappointing when he arrived at the hotel and learned that it had all been for nothing.

His first clue was Chief Japhet Obure in the lobby, talking

with the hotel manager and the bartender. The local police chief rolled his eyes at the sight of Benjamin. "Kidnapped American, and then you appear, Ben. Why am I not surprised?"

"You know me, Japhi. I can smell scandal a mile away."

Benjamin's disappointment was breathtakingly vast, bigger than he would have imagined. He hadn't known Paul Fisher. Had he liked him? Not really. He had liked Sam, but not the feeble man who affected coldness to overcome an obvious cowardice. And it wasn't as if Paul Fisher had been an innocent; none of the connected Americans who wandered into his country were. But his disappearance hurt just the same.

"Looks like he hadn't even unpacked," Japhet said once they were both in his room.

Benjamin, by the door, watched the chief touch the wrinkled bedspread and the dusty bedside table. But what the chief didn't notice was the empty space, just beside the luggage stand, where the briefcase had been. As Japhet opened closets and drawers, Benjamin watched over his shoulder, but the all-important case wasn't there. Why hadn't Benjamin taken it with him when he'd left?

He knew the answer, but it was so banal as to be embarrassing. He, like anyone, didn't want to run around town carrying a bomb.

Once everything had been brushed for prints, a long line of witnesses interviewed, and darkness had fallen, Chief Obure invited him out for a drink. Benjamin called Murugi and told her he'd be late. "Because of the kidnapped American?" It was already making the news.

By nine he and Japhet were sitting at a sidewalk café, drinking cold bottles of Tusker and eyeing a trio of twelve-year-old boys across the road sucking on plastic bags of glue.

"Breaks my heart to see that," said Japhet.

"Then you should be dead sixty times over by now," Benjamin answered as his cell phone rang a monotone sound. Simultaneously, Japhet's played a recent disco hit.

A house northeast of the city, not so far from the United Nations compound in Runda Estate, had been demolished by an explosion. Benjamin knew the house, and back when Daniel Kwambai had still been in the government's favor he'd even visited it. Still, the fact that the bomb had ended up in one of Kwambai's houses was a surprise.

"Time for a field trip," Japhet said when they'd both hung up.

It took them forty minutes to reach Runda Estate and head farther north, where they followed the tower of smoke down to the inferno on the hill. The firefighters had left to collect more water, and Pili, one of Benjamin's assistants, was standing in the long front yard, staring at the flames. He was soaked through with sweat.

"The explosion came from inside. That's what the fire chief says."

"What else would they expect?" asked Japhet.

Since his boss didn't reply, Pili said, "Car bomb."

"Right, right."

Both Pili and Japhet watched as Benjamin approached the burning house on his own. He stopped where the temperature rose dramatically, then began to perspire visibly, his shirt blackening down the center and spreading outward.

From behind, he heard Japhet's voice: "What're you thinking, Ben?"

"Just that it's beautiful," he answered, because that was true. Flames did not sit still. They buckled and wove and snapped and rose so that you could never hold their true form. Perhaps they had no true form. Wood popped and something deep inside the inferno exploded.

"Do you know what's going on here, Ben?"

The wailing fire truck was returning, full of water. Farther out, headlights moved down the long road toward them. That would be absolutely everyone—government representatives, religious leaders, the Americans, the United Nations, the press.

He took Japhet's arm and walked him toward his car. "Come on. I'll buy you a drink wherever you like."

"A rare and wonderful offer," Japhet said. "You steal something?"

"I've earned every cent I have," he answered, twirling keys around his finger. "I just feel like forgetting."

"This?"

"If I forget it, maybe it'll just go away," Benjamin said, smiling pleasantly as he got in and started the car. In no time at all, they had passed the incoming traffic and made it over the hills and back into the city. It was as if the burning house had never been. Despite the sweltering heat, Benjamin had even stopped sweating.